Adam began whistling to himself as he turned toward the kitchen, then stopped mid-stride as the doorbell rang.

Libby frowned over her shoulder in the direction of the door. "Who could that be at this time of night?" She pushed back her chair, making ready to rise.

"Stay put," Adam said shortly. "I'll get it."

Anyone he encountered on the other side of the paneled door would be unexpected, for they were anticipating no guests. But he was nothing short of stunned when he unlocked the door and opened it to confront the figure beyond.

It was Edwinna Rutledge, all silvery blonde and wrapped in mink, and she smiled exquisitely into his handsome face as she picked up her small overnight case and glided past him into the room . . .

# CHASING RAINBOWS

## ESTHER SAGER

**CORGI BOOKS**
A DIVISION OF TRANSWORLD PUBLISHERS LTD

CHASING RAINBOWS
A CORGI BOOK 0 552 11981 4

First publication in Great Britain

PRINTING HISTORY

Corgi edition published 1982

*Conditions of sale*

This book is set in 9½ pt. Times Roman.

Corgi Books are published by Transworld Publishers Ltd., Century House,
61–63 Uxbridge Road, Ealing, London, W5 5SA

Printed and bound in Great Britain by
Cox & Wyman Ltd, Reading

To Gilbert

# PROLOGUE

## 1960

There is no excellent beauty
that hath not some strangeness
in proportion.

*Francis Bacon*

The screen door clapped shut with that peculiar noise screen doors make: a rickety, uneven sound, but with a certain finality, leaving no doubt that some aperture has been sealed. It is a sound memories are made of, conjuring up with it, years later, the feel of the dead of summer and its blistering heat sweeping across the back of the shoulders, the recollection of irresponsible afternoons, golden-green grass seared brown at the edges from the sun, bright yellow and red flowers, the odor of ground gone dusty from too little rain.

For Libby Rutledge, who was ten years old, the sound on that golden, hot July day had no significance other than the fact that she had once again let the door of the big country kitchen slam on her way out; she always left that way—hurriedly, in shorts and sneakers and unmatched blouse, with outdoor things on her mind and no time to be bothered with seeing to such trivial matters as the proper closing of a door, despite the fact that propriety was a thing to master in this family. She crossed the gray wooden porch that ran the length of the house and stepped down onto the gravel drive, her sneakers crunching the odd-shaped chunks of rock until she hit the grass, where the shoes made no noise. She broke into a skip across the lawn toward Edwinna, who was engaged in maneuvering a croquet ball through a wire wicket with a mallet painted red on each end.

'Bet you can't,' Libby taunted good-naturedly as Winna sent the ball in the direction of the miniature archway.

'Bet I can,' Winna countered with the hauteur already natural to her at eleven. She watched with eyes narrowed in concentration as the ball bumped along the ground, straight on the mark, a sure bet to pass through until it maddeningly lost momentum just short of the wicket and stopped a hair's breadth from the threshold.

'What'd I tell you!' Libby crowed gleefully, her young face lit up in satisfaction. 'My turn.'

Winna frowned, eyeing the croquet ball crossly. 'It's not! We're not playing for real. I'm just practicing.'

'Come on, Winna. Let's play! My turn.'

'Well, you can't use my mallet and ball.' She moved over to the ball and took aim again. 'Go get your own.'

'Where are they?'

'Where d'ya think!' Winna said testily, her eyes fixed on her target. She swung back her mallet and whacked the ball soundly so that it shot through the wicket and bounced along the grass, crossing the gravel lane that led up to the stables. Finally it rolled out of sight under the high boxwood hedges on the far side.

Libby ran back across the yard toward the house, hopping over wickets, and up onto the wide-planked porch again, where, in a corner niche, there was a closet door. It was an old door on an old house, slightly crooked on its hinges, with white paint flaking off and no lock. Like the rest of the house it was soundly constructed but no longer square at the corners or fresh at the seams, and it needed repainting. The rambling, double-verandaed house would get painted eventually, maybe even soon, although it required more urgent maintenance than the simple cosmetic of new paint. And when blue-bloods like the Rutledges saw their finances dissipate over the generations until finally they were no better off than anyone else of the average middle class, it was no longer certain that the once prestigious, still impressive farmhouse could be kept up to snuff.

But Libby Rutledge didn't care about or even understand such things and wasn't thinking of the sorry state of the door when she pulled it open. To her young, optimistic mind, it was nothing more than a familiar door on a comfortable, familiar house that she loved as though it were a member of the family, and she rummaged impatiently inside the closet for a mallet and ball. She selected blue, although she would have preferred the red ones Winna had taken; she pushed the door closed with her sneakered foot before scampering happily back off the porch to join Winna once more down on the lawn.

'I'm going first,' Winna announced.

'No, let's draw. That's fair,' Libby objected, her expression serious.

Winna's eyes opened a little wider. 'I'm going first!'

'Come on, Winna. Be fair.'

Winna's patrician little face, which had the makings of exquisite beauty, went petulant, and she eyed Libby pensively

—auburn-haired, green-eyed, different-as-night-from-day-Libby —then screwed her mouth all the way down. 'Then go first, brat. Doesn't matter how bad I feel about it.' She turned away.

Libby looked at Winna's profile, her face dropping. 'I'm not a brat. I'm fair. Mom and Dad said always to be fair. Come on, Winna!'

Winna seemed small and vulnerable in her despondency. 'Mom and Dad don't care how bad I feel, either. No one does. No one cares.' There was a wistful sigh.

Libby laid down her mallet then and went to her sister. 'I do,' she said sincerely, her eyes saucer-wide in entreaty.

'No, you don't.'

'Honest I do,' she repeated, hurting for Winna's hurt, and she reached out her small hand in compassion. She always felt awful when Winna said things like that. It wasn't true that no one cared, but even if it had been true of everyone else, it wouldn't be true of Libby, ever. Libby would always protect and love and share, because that's the way it was supposed to be between sisters, and besides, it was what she just naturally wanted. Anyway, maybe it *was* all her fault that Winna felt so sad sometimes; Libby wasn't sure. She never meant to steal the show, did not realize that everyone would pay more attention to her, an open-hearted, outgoing child who knew how to ask for affection and get it, while Winna shyly hovered in the background, left out. That hurt Libby, too, and guiltily she tried to make up for the injustice of it all. One more time she rushed to reassure Winna. 'I do, Winna. And Mom and Dad love you too.'

'No one cares!' Winna was nearly wailing.

'I do, Winna. Please, Winna. I do,' Libby begged.

'Then show me.' Eyes still downcast, Winna stole a calculating look at Libby. It was always so easy with dumb Libby, sweet Libby; she always passed the test. No one ever bothered to show Winna they cared about her, and she used to cry about it sometimes—though she'd never tell anyone that—but she'd found out how to make them show her. And it worked. And reaped a double reward: she could get things she wanted, too.

Libby's smooth brow was knit in perplexity. 'How come I have to show you? I just said so.'

Winna's face looked earnestly pleading. 'Because then I'll know for sure. I'll know you really care about me if you'll let me go first.'

'Okay,' Libby said brightly. She didn't really care, anyway; it wasn't in her nature to squabble.

Winna was all silvery smiles again, like her silvery-blond hair and silvery-blue eyes that sparkled in the sunlight. Libby had passed, A-plus, and Winna was the winner. Now she felt better. And had the first turn. 'C'mon. Let's go!' she said then, laughing with Libby, and they played out the game.

'Let's play again.' Libby said eagerly when they were through.

'Nope. It's too hot,' Winna answered and dropped her mallet indifferently to the ground. She walked over to the two slate steps that cut through the narrow rock garden, brushed the dirt from the stones, and plopped down. Libby joined her, sticking her slender legs out in front of her, beside Winna's.

'Mom said we're eating early tonight,' Libby advised absently.

'How come?' Winna had pulled up a tuft of grass and was separating the blades.

'Company.'

Winna glanced over interestedly. 'Who is it?'

'Can't remember.' Libby flexed her toes, then studied the hole in one sneaker.

'Mr. and Mrs. Warren?'

'I don't know. I told you, I forgot who she said.'

Winna grimaced. 'I hope not. I hate them. I hate Tommy. He's so icky.'

Libby smiled conspiratorially. 'Yeah, I know. Mom said the next time he throws up on her chair, she's gonna scream!' She giggled. She wanted to see that lovely, gentle, dark-haired Jocelyn Rutledge raising her soft-spoken voice into a banshee yell. 'I hope she does. That'd be funny! Then maybe they'd make him stay upstairs.'

'Yeah, but he did it up there once, too. Remember?' Winna said with a snicker. She glanced down at her white shorts and neat blue top and picked off an inchworm.

'Yeah, on the rug,' Libby said, sharing the snicker, then frowned. 'How come Mom got so upset anyhow? It's just an old rug, full o' holes.'

'Dummo, it's an Oriental!' Winna said with tremendous exasperation.

Libby just looked at her, not really understanding. Winna knew about those things, indoor things, chairs and rugs and tall cupboards and stuff; she guessed she probably would next year, when she was eleven. 'What's that mean?' she asked.

Winna's expression was matter of fact. 'It means you can't get it all icked up. It's good stuff. If you're gonna be a girl, a lady, you've got to know about those things. And clothes.'

'Oh,' Libby said absently. She wasn't really listening any more, for she had spied a colorful butterfly and was entranced with watching its delicate flight across the tops of the orange and red flowers in the walled garden. It was so fascinating, all that color, yellow and black and red on the gossamer wings, chalky, that rubbed off on the fingers when you touched it. Winna might know about the rug and other fancy things, but Libby knew outdoor things, because she watched, and studied, and made up little stories about ants marching up and down the mounds of their hideaway, and noticed the shades of the grass and fields, how they looked in the sun, how they glistened after a rain, what it all looked like from atop the pinto pony that she galloped up and down the hilly terrain of their property, pretending she was a runaway Indian princess. She was an observer, a sensual person who responded to what was around her—the feel of the ground under her feet, the nuances of the wind—and she had a fascination with the things of nature. She couldn't understand how they came to be, really, how anyone—even God—could have thought up all those things. It was astounding that He knew enough to make trees and mountains and water, and He even knew somehow what they were all supposed to look like! It amazed her mind, thrilled her senses, and she supposed that maybe next year she'd understand all that, too.

'What're you looking at?' Winna asked, noting Libby's preoccupation.

Libby smiled openly. 'That butterfly.'

'Oh.'

'It's neat, huh Winna?' she said, her green eyes bright with interest.

'It's dumb,' Winna said cuttingly, then glanced again at Libby, who hadn't reacted. 'You're always off on a cloud, watching something, something dumb!' she said and was finally rewarded.

Libby was too young to hide the hurt expression. 'What's dumb about butterflies?'

'They just are, that's all,' Winna said superciliously, tossing her silvery head.

Libby made a stab then at juvenile nonchalance, though it was unnatural for her. She had had to study Winna's expression frequently to be able to imitate it properly, and had even practiced a couple of times in front of the mirror. 'And rugs aren't dumb?' she countered and fashioned her face into the 'look.'

Winna laughed in honest merriment at that, a sweet sound that tinkled like bells and floated gently into the breeze, and at that moment she looked just like her father, Trevor Rutledge, the tall, handsome, tow-headed man who loved his well-bred girls and pretty wife and gently impoverished existence on the inherited gentleman's farm with the aristocratic single-mindedness of his class.

'Yeah, rugs are dumb too,' Winna said, 'but I think they're important. You can pay attention to dumb things as long as they're important. You gotta know the difference,' she explained good-naturedly and smiled in sudden warmth at her younger sister.

Libby considered asking how one went about learning the difference, but she didn't because she wasn't that interested in the conversation, and besides, she was hungry. 'Nettie made a chocolate cake. Want some?' she asked.

Winna was interested. 'How d'ya know?'

'I saw it,' Libby divulged.

'Yeah, let's! It's too hot out here, anyhow. Race ya!' Winna challenged happily as she scrambled up, and like two pellets shot out of an airgun, they covered the short distance back to the big white house shaded by overgrown oaks and maples.

Cocktail hour with the Warrens was exquisitely dull. Libby and Winna fidgeted, and Tommy shot rubber bands at the two proper little girls sitting across from him on the screened-in back porch that was often used for company. Dinner was worse, a long drawn-out affair; good conversation, meticulous table manners, and no youthful interruptions were requirements in the formal Duncan Phyfe dining room. Libby thought she'd shrivel up from boredom and sat slumped in her chair, staring around with a glazed expression at the solid brass candelabra and the Currier & Ives prints on the walls, until finally Tommy spilled his milk all over the starched white linen tablecloth that still had the cleaner's creases in it. She waited in breathless anticipation for her mother's promised scream, but none came, and after watching deflatedly as her mother graciously mopped up the mess with her lace-edged napkin, she cast a glance at her father and caught his eye, and nearly giggled at his expression; it suggested he might like to pick up the unattractive Tommy by the collar of his shirt and hoist him out the dining room window. As always, they shared a look, then simultaneously dropped their eyes. From across the table, Winna watched the exclusive exchange, her narrow face suddenly going somber, and when Tommy was banished some moments later to an upstairs bedroom pragmatically denuded beforehand of all Bokhara heirlooms, she abruptly squared her small shoulders and began picking at her peas.

It was another half hour before Libby and Winna were excused to do as they pleased. They were models of decorum in their gingham dresses as they climbed the stairs, but once out of sight they exploded into a dash to their bedroom at the far end of the hall. It was traditionally decorated, frilly with white curtains and dust-ruffled coverlets on the twin poster beds, and all about were scattered horse and rider statuettes, odd memorabilia, and school books. These overflowed into a second room, which had a door leading out onto the second-floor veranda.

'Boy, I thought he was gonna get it this time!' Libby crowed smugly as she stripped off the required dress and squirmed into pants and shirt.

Winna was subdued, chewing on her slender bottom lip as she pondered over her change of clothes. 'Hmmm.'

'Mom never even peeped,' Libby went on disappointedly.

'Hmmm.' Winna selected the green outfit finally, and stepped into it indifferently.

Libby had forgotten Tommy by then and flopped down on the bed like a rag doll, her eyes speculative. 'What d'ya wanna do?'

Winna had gone into the second room and was leaning up against the door frame that led out to the porch; it was her post, a thinking place, and in the twilight she looked out pensively through the screen, past the big oak tree whose limbs hung down low over the porch, and over to the half-obscured roof of the old servants' building, vacant now. She didn't answer the question.

'What's the matter?' Libby had gotten up and stood in the bedroom doorway, frowning at Winna's motionless back.

'Nothing.'

'Something is. You're sure a glumface.' Libby stared at her for a moment longer, then went over and flopped down again, this time on the narrow daybed in the second room.

Winna didn't turn, but remained looking out the door, her face a mirror of unhappiness. 'Mr. Warren doesn't like me.'

Libby was musing about something, her eyes glued to the ceiling. 'How come?' she asked absently.

This time there was no denial, no quick reassurance, only simple interest from the uncomplicated Libby, who was too full of daydreams at the moment to be fully involved in the conversation. Winna's slight frame seemed to diminish into frailty with her dejection, and she focused her stare at the tree, making out the outline of a bird's nest attached at the V of two branches. She wondered if there were eggs in it. 'I don't know why,' she said.

Libby looked over then. 'C'mon, let's think of something to do,' she pressed. She'd like to go chipmunk hunting, or tadpole trapping, or play sardines—except there were only two of them —or go to the carnival in town, where they could ride on the merry-go-round. Now that was a thought; she loved the colors of a carnival, the ferris wheel all lit up, the pink cotton candy, the bright double-striping of the tents where the nickel throw was. But there was company downstairs and that meant no dice, and besides, they'd just have to take Tommy along.

'There's a nest up there,' Winna remarked, slight interest wriggling into her self-absorption.

It was a magic word, and Libby was up off the bed like a jack-in-the-box, crowding next to Winna at the screen door, peering upward. 'Yeah!' she breathed.

Winna eyed her moodily from two inches away: Libby's face was an oval, rounder than hers and not so chiseled—an open face. Right now she was entranced with the nest, and the wheels of her little mind were churning up some little story about Mamma and Papa Bird, Winna had no doubt, because she always did that. And Mr. Warren thought she was cute. Everyone thought so; she did, too. She looked back at the nest. 'Wanna see inside?'

'Can't. Not allowed to play on the porch,' Libby answered matter-of-factly, still staring at the round structure of sticks and dead grass.

Winna shifted to the other foot. 'It's not playing. It's *going*. It's going out to get the nest. Bet there are eggs in it. Blue ones, maybe.' It suggested a thought, and she transferred her gaze to the railing that circled the porch; they could get those eggs, then stand at the railing, hold them out in mid-air, and let go. She could already hear the splat when they landed on the stretch of foundation that she always tripped on because it stuck up too high out of the ground. It was a long way down; that made the spot a good bomb site. 'C'mon. Let's get them!'

Libby frowned slightly, looking at her then. 'How come?'

'We can make egg soup on the stone slab,' Winna said offhandedly.

Libby was appalled and opened her eyes wide. 'There are baby birds in there!'

Winna frowned in exasperation. 'No there aren't! It's just slime. It's not baby birds till later. Don't you know anything? Come on, Libby!'

Libby wasn't convinced, and kept frowning at Winna's face, so close to hers.

'It'll be fun,' Winna pressed, her entire expression lighting up with infectious anticipation. 'Okay. We won't drop them off. But we could look at them!'

'Yeah, but we're not allowed on the porch,' Libby reminded again. 'Mom said so. And anyhow, you can't reach it. You're too short. So am I. You'd have to stand on the railing.' She watched Winna's face drop immediately, and it had the usual effect. 'Okay, I'll hold your legs.'

Winna's expression went helpless then. 'No, you go. I'm scared.'

'Well . . .'

'Go, Libby,' she pressed earnestly.

Libby looked down at her shoe. 'Let's do something else.'

Suddenly the bird's nest became vitally important to Winna, necessary to her happiness, symbolic of restitution for all the evening's imagined slights, which she had barely voiced to Libby. She needed it. Her lovely child's face grew despairing, and she sobbed raggedly. 'If you really loved me, you'd go get it!'

Libby was torn between good sense and the misery on Winna's face; Winna really wanted the thing, and she was so easily frightened, so desperate to know that the sister she loved dearly, as sisters do, loved her just as much. And it was true that no one had said more than two words to Winna all night. Besides, if she didn't go, what would Winna do next? 'Okay,' Libby relented.

Winna smiled radiantly. It'd only take a minute to boost Libby up, and then they'd have the thing to play with. 'Hurry, before someone comes up!' she chirped and followed Libby out onto the porch.

Libby glanced once over the railing, then straight up. Don't look down, don't look down, she sing-songed silently and put a hand on Winna's shoulder as she stepped with one, then the other foot onto the railing. Her heart was pounding so hard she could feel it jumping in her chest, and she wanted to get down, but this was for Winna, who deserved to be happy and was more afraid than she was. She reached up, grabbing an unsteady hold of the branch and worked at the nest, dislodging it finally. Winna looked on with anticipation from her post back inside the screen door, eyeing the nest as it came down with Libby's hand, and she waited gleefully to see Libby's expression when she turned around and saw that her balancing beam had sneaked away; they'd giggle over the trick later.

'Winna, here. Take this,' Libby said in a nervous rush as she twisted her torso to hand Winna the nest, then balance on her sister's shoulder as she hopped down. The hand she threw out met the nothingness of thin air.

Winna watched with eyes wide in amazement as Libby flung the nest away and began to teeter, her arms thrown out and flailing, her young face wrenched with terror as she fought to regain her balance. She caught it, then held it, moving carefully into a tense crouch as she slowly turned away from the precipice and toward the porch. She inched around, balanced precariously on the balls of her feet, the blood pounding in her ears as she concentrated. She was there finally, full into position to spring down onto the porch, when suddenly her sneaker slipped. It thrust her wildly upright again, and she wobbled as she clawed at the air, once, twice, finally leaping desperately for the safety of the porch.

She didn't make it.

The momentum of her spring sent her in the wrong direction, and the world spun around her as she went backward over the railing, head first in an awkward dive toward the ground. 'Winna!' Her sister heard the terrified scream, quickly lost to the wind, then seconds later the sharp crack of bone slamming against granite foundation. Cautiously, Winna went out through the screen door onto the porch. At the railing, she gazed down wonderingly at the inert body below, its slender arms and legs dressed in blue denim shorts and a tan shirt motionlessly askew, the shiny auburn hair spilling out over the treacherous foundation, the tender face turned sideways, eyes closed. She stood there for a moment, thoroughly surprised; it hadn't occurred to her Libby might really fall. She turned away finally, retrieving the nest, which had landed on the porch after all, and then strolled on back into the house, staring at the thing in fascination. There were blue eggs inside, one of them cracked and oozing. She put it down on the bureau, then went over to the bed to sit down thoughtfully and swing her legs. She sat there for awhile, chewing her bottom lip as she contemplated what she was going to do with the eggs, then sighed.

She guessed she'd better get up and go on downstairs first, though, to tell everyone that Libby hadn't made it to eleven after all.

# PART I

## Twenty years later

All are needed by each one,
Nothing is fair or good alone.

*Ralph Waldo Emerson*

# Chapter 1

The Hunt Club dining room had the look of late afternoon: too bright, but clean and fresh as the low sun glared in through the banks of multi-paned windows and sent shafts of vivid yellow light piercing across the rug. It was elegant, like the rest of the club, though casually opulent in the manner of the Washington area's horsey set; there was the required blood-red carpeting, brass chandeliers, softly lit racing scenes along the walls, red and white brick hearths at either end of the room. It was a distinctive room, partly because of its decor, but mostly because of the impressive banks of floor-to-ceiling windows—walls really—though which the rolling Virginia countryside became an intrinsic part of the room, and gave it an open, spacious air. The vacant tables scattered throughout were crisply reset with red eyelet linen tablecloths, stiff white napkins, crystal, and silverware. At the moment the tables had only one occupant, an aristocratic-looking man sitting at his usual place by the window, smoking a cigarette, his gaze turned uninterestedly toward the hunt course off in the distance. His attitude was not that of a lonely man, but one of a man intentionally alone. An introspective man closed off from the world around him.

Despite the bright sunshine, the lights in the large dining hall would have to be turned up in another hour or so, the man figured, for it was nearing five o'clock. He knew that, he'd checked his watch on purpose. He didn't want to be there then, for the room would close off from the outside and take on the atmosphere of a darkened country inn, elegant, yes, but confining and too dim, lit only by the carriage lanterns over the hearths and the hooded candles on the tables; he preferred the natural light, its buoyancy, and anyway, he was in no mood just now for being pressed into polite conversation with all too familiar guests who would soon be filtering in for dinner in Cartier's finest and the Halston, St. Laurent, or Gucci conception of high fashion in evening wear for the current year. He didn't object to them; he was just tired of looking at it all, and after a moment, he stubbed out his cigarette and stood up, pulling a bill from his wallet and dropping it onto the table. It was not an extravagant tip; it was simply more than necessary.

The waiter, who knew him well, waved briefly from his position against the wall on the far side of the room, and Adam Bainbridge returned the gesture absently as he threaded his way up to the double doors at the front. He stopped for a moment when he reached them, replacing his wallet in the inner pocket of his black wool riding coat, then pushed on through, stepping out into the brisk fresh air. The grounds around the modern building were alive with human activity even though it was getting late; other riders, guests headed for the parlor rooms, men with cigars and women with children all milled around. Adam was unmotivated to move off in any particular direction, so he stood where he was, momentarily absorbed in thought. He could have headed toward the low brick building across the way, which contained the gaming room, bar, and lounge, but he did not. He had no taste at the moment for the lewd and boisterous conversations inevitably going on inside, and it seemed an unexplainable lack of interest; after all, he had been part of those conversations all his adult life, had contributed his share of time to gambling and drinking. Yet those pastimes seemed to have gone stale, and if he took to delving for reasons why his well-heeled existence should suddenly seem so banal, he could come up with none. Perhaps it was his age, he thought derisively, and considered the fact that he had just passed another decade.

He moved off finally, in an attitude of irresolution, and walked in the direction of the private stables, his bootheels thudding along one of the maze of macadamed roadways that crisscrossed the grounds of the club. They stretched this way and that, out toward the elaborate hunt course, over to the four outdoor instruction rings, on past the public livery barns to the bridle paths beyond. It was a tremendous operation, this Hunt Club, with facilities for members and non-members alike, although the latter had no access to the special facilities—the masculine gaming rooms, the bar, lounge, or parlors, the modern, brick private stables with over-size boxstalls, the expensively appointed dining hall. No, he thought, those things are only for those of us who would pay for the privilege of being overcharged, who would pledge allegiance, with the cost of membership, to the outward display of our social status. He made an attempt to thrust away his unreasonable bad humor but failed and kept on walking.

His figure was a familiar one to those he passed, many because they knew him well, others because it was a distinctive figure and easily remembered; he was fit, tall, and forty sat well on him, whether he himself thought so or not. It sharpened the angular lines of his face, silvered the edges of his sideburns, feathered the corners of his deep blue eyes with character, and over all, gave him the look of worldly nonchalance; he didn't particularly aspire to masculine comeliness, but he had it in excess, by the fine cut of his features, by the suggestion of waviness in his glossy black hair left indifferently too long, by the virility that was natural to him and was expressed in every movement and attitude. He continued along the roadway, slowing his pace abruptly when he came in line with the public riding enclosures; with no conscious purpose of going to the stable, he had allowed his attention to be snagged by an unknown man and woman standing in the center of the riding ring, an unattractive horse loitering nearby, the reins of his bridle slack and held lightly in the hand of the elderly man. He didn't know why, really, but Adam changed direction and strolled over to the fence.

He watched as the man ineptly slipped the reins over the animal's head and steadied him, then moved toward the woman who stood facing the saddle, her hands running lightly along the edge of it. The man was speaking, the woman smiling tentatively, and after a missed try or two, she fitted her foot into the cradle of the man's hand, allowing him to boost her with difficulty into the saddle. She shifted nervously, settling herself, and Adam smiled involuntarily as he noted the urgency with which she grabbed at the horse's mane.

Another of life's desperate, he thought cynically and wasn't certain why he found the thought so amusing. She was somewhere in her late twenties, he decided. Obviously no rider, she seemed stupidly out of place as she clutched the pommel of the saddle with one hand, the horse's mane with the other, and Adam speculated further on her motives for being there at all. "One of life's desperate" had sprung immediately to mind; it was his own particular turn of phrase, descriptive of one who has just passed some crucial point in life and suddenly understands the concept of mortality, and how quickly time slips away. Time, that is, in which to capture those daydreams and 'somedays' that have been put aside, since there is always tomorrow. He shook his head wryly, allowing the unkind assessment to continue unchecked. The man was leading the horse now, slowly, walking out in front of it as he talked over his shoulder to the woman, reassuring her, Adam supposed.

Yes, he was definitely right, he decided after watching another few minutes. Here was a woman of undetermined age, not young but not yet middle-aged, out to capture a 'someday' before time ran out; he was sure she'd always wanted to learn to ride. She seemed laughable to him as she timorously set out to capture that goal after muscles were too old to adapt easily or correctly, bones were too brittle to mend properly from the assaults they would inevitably sustain, and experience had taught too much to allow her the freedom from fear she would need if she were ever to progress from being a simple appendage on a horse's back to becoming the accomplished horsewoman she no doubt aspired to be. And the sunglasses, my dear? he inquired silently. To block out the glare of the sun that, at this hour, was no longer a problem, or to disguise yourself, to hide from eyes that might recognize you struggling at this hapless venture? He shook his head again. You're a cynical bastard, Adam Bainbridge, he thought with disgust and pushed himself away from the fence, to continue on his way.

At the stable, he located Morgan in his stall, working unconcernedly at a pile of hay in one corner. He watched the big bay horse from the far side of the stall door, starting a moment later when a man came up beside him.

' 'day, Mr. Bainbridge,' the stableman remarked. 'You ridin' this afternoon?'

'I suppose so, Ted.'

'I'll tack 'im up.'

'Thanks.'

Adam moved away, going over to lean against the wall. He drew out his cigarettes and lit one, remaining there, cigarette smoke curling up around his handsome face as he stared out across the stableyard to the hunt course beyond, moved for some reason to speculate on the man that Adam Bainbridge had become. There had been a time when he would have tacked up his own mount, either here or back at the Bainbridge stables, from pure enthusiasm for the anticipated ride, and a time when he would have felt more charitable toward the lady caught in the act of being foolishly human. And it was not even so long ago, that time. Not in reality, although in his present mood it seemed light years away.

His horse was brought to him, and he swung up into the saddle easily, prodding Morgan off through the stableyard. The grounds were immaculately kept, but he paid them no attention. Two cars passed slowly, avoiding the rider, and he moved off onto the shoulder of the road until he reached the bridle paths, selecting one and guiding his horse down onto the wide dirt pathway. There were other riders up ahead, in pairs and threesomes, but he did not join them; he simply rode on alone and had begun to slip back into his uncomfortable introspection when he heard a voice hailing him and the sound of galloping hooves approaching from behind.

'Adam!'

He looked over his shoulder as the woman slowed her horse and fell into step beside him. She was a gorgeous creature with golden hair, adept at handling her mount, and like a great many women, very well acquainted with Adam Bainbridge.

'Didn't you hear me?' she asked, slightly out of breath; the breathlessness suited her, gave a soft edge to her lilting voice.

Adam felt no stir of response to her glowing smile, and his own barely touched the corners of his mouth. 'No.'

'I called to you as you were leaving the stableyard.'

'Well, I didn't hear you.'

He had looked away, offering his rugged profile; she studied it, stung by his seeming indifference. 'Adam, you seem so far away,' she ventured and flipped a lock of long hair behind her back. It fell softly against her shoulder blade, as she wanted it to.

'Sorry.'

She continued to steal glances at him as they ambled along, but his expression was unreadable. His shoulders under the expensively cut riding coat were broad, well-muscled she knew, like all of him, and as always, she felt the familiar stab of excitement; he was a man for women, and though he was closed away from her now, he wasn't always. She recalled the last time they had shared a bed; the memory moved through her like electricity. 'You look as though you're a thousand miles away,' she said after the strain of his silence became too much, and she tried laughing. 'I . . .'

'Genevieve, cut it. I'm not in the mood for chatty conversation right now. If that's what you want, I suggest you go find yourself someone else to prattle to.'

He hadn't meant to be quite so unpleasant to her; the words had just come out that way. Genevieve reacted violently, not only because of the remark, but because of his recent inattention. 'Well, pardon me! The great Adam Bainbridge doesn't wish to be disturbed. Well, that's fine with me. I'm more than happy to leave you to your own unpleasant company. But just remember one thing. When you're in need of someone to warm your bedsheets, don't come knocking on my door. I won't be there. Go find yourself someone else, some little simp who just might be willing to fawn all over your lousy performance!' She jerked her horse around and cantered away.

The ugly little remark seemed fitting to his mood, and he was even slightly amused by it; so like a woman to be venomous in retaliation, though he supposed he didn't really blame her. However, the slur on his virility was wasted on him. At the moment he did not care. She would have been disappointed to know that her dart had completely missed its mark, or rather, had failed to leave so much as a scratch. He was as tired of expensive, clinging women as he was of everything else, and he realized suddenly that that was the gist of this man Adam Bainbridge, forty. He no longer gave a damn.

The woman was back the next week, and as he had done before, Adam strolled over to the fence when he caught sight of her and leaned on the top railing to watch. The same man was with her, an elderly gentleman with silver hair fuzzing the dome of his head and round bifocals askew on the bridge of his nose; there was a kindly look about him as he patiently led the indifferent horse back and forth at the far side of the ring, while the woman clutched the reins, as if hanging on for dear life. Adam's mood had improved only slightly over that of the week before, and he placed one booted toe on the bottom rail of the fence as he took further stock of the woman.

She was slightly built, probably not especially tall, and was dressed in an outfit of jeans, blouse, and shiny new black boots. Observing the boots, he wondered why she had not sprung for the entire outfit, as every green rider inevitably did. He silently congratulated her on having at least that much good sense. The boots could be worn again; the expensive coat and jodhpurs would have had to be put away, relegated to some closet to molder away once she recognized the futility of her endeavor, although perhaps even their cost could have been glossed over with the rationalization that at least the venture had been tried. Her face was not readily distinguishable; he was too far away, and the sunglasses obscured a large part of it, but it appeared pleasant enough, with a good shape to it, and her hair was a dark auburn color, pulled back into a pony tail by a bright yellow scarf. He was standing motionless, absorbed in his appraisal, when Matt Jameson, manager of the Hunt Club and a good friend of Adam, came up beside him and leaned with both forearms on the rail.

'Hello,' he said.

Adam looked over and nodded.

'Haven't seen you around a lot lately,' Matt went on, his leathery face stretched into a smile. 'Business keeping you occupied?'

'As much as always,' Adam said obliquely. The Bainbridge companies were common knowledge, the vast spread of them over diversified industries, and most people who knew that Adam Bainbridge sat as chairman of the board for many of them found that a heady thought. He let the misconception stand; it was irrelevant to him what they thought, as irrelevant as his association with those damn companies his father shoved down his throat. But the fact was, his recent absences from his usual haunts had nothing whatever to do with any professional life. He had none, really, and the thought made him reach for his cigarettes, but instead he drew out a small penknife and picked up a stick from the ground. He began working it with the knife, his forearms still resting on top of the railing.

Matt did light a cigarette, dropping his match to the ground. 'You look preoccupied.'

'Hmm,' Adam murmured and continued to shape the stick. An old stableman had introduced him to whittling when he was a young boy; he had never given it up.

'I was watching Morgan taking fences last week. He's a bit out of shape, and so are you,' Matt said with characteristic bluntness.

Adam glanced at him then and smiled wryly. 'A comment on my inattention?'

'None of my business,' Matt replied matter-of-factly. 'But if you're planning on steeplechasing him, you've got your work cut out for you.'

'Maybe I'm not.'

Matt was surprised; Adam was an inveterate horseman. He made no comment and looked out toward the man and woman in the riding ring, after a time glancing back at Adam, who had fashioned the stick into a letter opener, pointed on one end, bulbous on the other; he was really quite good. 'I hear Christian dropped a bundle the other night.'

Adam let out a short laugh. 'So what else is new?'

'Nothing, but these are supposed to be friendly games. He's out for blood.'

'He ought to be. He's got to bankroll his habit,' Adam

26

remarked, his brow knit in concentration as he surveyed his handiwork critically. He turned the now smooth stick over in his hand before flipping the knife closed and putting it away. The letter opener went in his pocket, too; he always kept these things, if only to toss them in a drawer of his bureau. It was an inconsequential pastime, after all, though a more elaborate letter opener carved out of teak did lie on top of his desk at home, useful.

Matt shook his head. 'You Bainbridges make me laugh. As if you didn't have your own private mint hidden away somewhere.'

'Yeah, we're a laughable crowd,' Adam said with a half smile that held no humor. He straightened. 'But even the Bainbridge investments can't keep up with Christian unleashed.'

'Didn't think you gave a damn.'

'I don't. Except that I don't want him messing up my own comfortable way of living. That would be unfortunate.' It was a flip remark.

Matt looked at him thoughtfully; Adam was not usually so derisive. 'You know, you surprise me. I thought you'd made peace with your lot in life a long time ago. Hit a nerve?' he added, as Adam's expression grew dark. He could ask that; they had been friends for a long time.

Adam, however, was not in the mood for confessions. 'Drop it,' he said.

'No problem,' Matt said easily. 'It's just that you've got that grim look of a man with a lot on his mind.'

'Maybe I'll tell you about it sometime,' Adam said, his gaze going off into the distance; his eyes were veiled.

Matt accepted the dodge and turned his attention, along with Adam's, to the man and woman in the ring. But unlike Adam, Matt knew that these two had been coming to the stable steadily now for two weeks, and he himself had chosen her mount carefully; it was important. The man and woman never stayed more than half an hour or so, paying the exorbitant fee for the full hour's ride even though they never used the full time, and apparently their session was over now. The man was leading the horse in their direction, to the nearby gate, and was speaking over his shoulder to the rider who, even from this distance, looked drained from the exercise.

They were approaching at a slow walk and had almost reached the open gate when it happened. A terrier with a shrill bark appeared out of nowhere and slithered under the fence, rushing the horse and rider. The animal was instantly transformed into panicked horseflesh and threw up its head, wild-eyed. The elderly man, obviously inexperienced with horses, made an attempt to grab at the bridle but missed, and the horse reared slightly, adroitly unseating his rider. It was not a dramatic fall; the woman merely slid off to one side and landed with a thud on the ground.

Some part of the old Adam wished he wouldn't smile, but he did; after all, it had been such an inglorious dismounting. He had taken too many falls himself not to have a horseman's attitude toward them: if you were going to be thrown, let it be with propulsion, so that you were flung far and wide to land with a sound crack on the ground. Otherwise, it was not really worthwhile. There was no excuse for such an inept slippage from the saddle; even a novice should have been able to compensate, provided she possessed a modicum of natural balance. He had been right, he thought with a sigh; the woman was hopeless.

The elderly man was fussing over her, helping her up while she brushed the dust from her clothing. She appeared shaken but in control, and Adam watched as Matt hurried through the gate to them, taking charge of the horse. They came out together, horse in tow, the woman on the arm of her companion, glasses once more in place, and they stopped not far from where Adam still stood at the fence.

'You're certain you're all right?' Matt was asking worriedly.

'I'm fine,' the young woman said, touching the scarf at the nape of her neck briefly.

Matt glanced at Adam then. 'I'd like you to meet one of the club's more illustrious members.' He motioned with his head for Adam to join them.

He did, pushing himself away from the fence, resigned to meeting this woman with the unattainable daydreams. Matt made the appropriate introductions. 'This is Adam Bainbridge. Adam, Sebastian Vickery.'

'A pleasure,' the man called Sebastian said as they shook hands.

Adam nodded, smiling, then turned his attention to the woman; up close, she had turned out to be quite attractive with her fair complexion and shining hair. 'And the lady?' he inquired, forestalling Matt's introduction. He didn't know why he was feeling so perverse. Because of his disenchantment with the world in general? Because he thought this woman and her daydreams foolish? Because she was smiling prettily in his direction, as every woman invariably did; a pretty smile for a pretty man? Whatever it was, it moved him to slip into his most charming manner and speak in a tone exactly opposite to it. 'I hope you're not hurt after your tremendous fall,' he said with exaggeration.

The woman's easy smile didn't fade, but grew warmer. 'No, I'm fine. And it was hardly a tremendous fall,' she answered in a quiet, engaging way. 'Any fool can be handily catapulted off a horse. It takes a real master to simply slither off to one side and plop onto the ground.'

Matt hid his smile of wry amusement as he watched some of the complacency drain out of Adam's expression; after all, he had deserved it. The slam had been uncalled for, and the woman had neutralized its effect with her simple remarks. Like turning into a skid. Matt decided it was time for an introduction. 'Adam, I'd like you to meet Elizabeth Rutledge. Elizabeth, Adam Bainbridge.'

'Please. Call me Libby,' she corrected and held out her hand. Adam took it, surprised by the firmness of its grip; it didn't fit his assessment. He studied the expressive face with a new interest.

'Well, you seem to be getting the hang of things,' Matt observed then.

'A bit,' she laughed. 'As long as no one shifts direction too suddenly.'

'Just give it enough time.'

'Of course,' she returned, then smiled down at the ground for a moment before looking back toward her companion. 'Sebastian? Ready to go?'

'Yes, m'love. Ready when you are.'

'Matt, we'll see you tomorrow. And thank you. Adam, it was nice to meet you,' she said, extending her hand again in farewell.

During the course of their brief conversation, he had shifted his weight onto the other foot, moving off slightly to the left of where he had been standing. He accepted the hand she offered, slowly, almost unconsciously, though not for any reason of rudeness or perversity; that was all gone. Rather, he was simply unable to react more quickly. He was staring at her, gently clasping the slender hand held out a little too far to the right of him, and though being thunderstruck was not an emotion familiar to so worldly a man as Adam Bainbridge, he was thunderstruck then, for he had just come to the shocking realization that Libby Rutledge was blind.

# Chapter 2

'Sebastian. Make another turn, will you?' Libby said, momentarily loosening her grip on the horse's mane to test her balance; it wasn't perfect by a long shot, but improving. The late sun was bright, picking up the rich red highlights in her hair, and she smiled in genuine satisfaction. The nectar of success, or even near success: it was like an intoxicant. It wasn't until Sebastian had brought them into the turn itself that she finally felt the need to grab hold again, but she wasn't discouraged; she would master it eventually.

Sebastian, meanwhile, was fussing with a bit of grime spotting his neat blazer, whose buttons strained across his generous paunch. It wasn't a pudginess of age, as he often told himself, but of character; Sebastian Vickery was a gourmet. He glanced at the speck, flicking at it with his fingers, and wrinkled his button nose, sending his glasses off kilter again. He righted them with the tip of one finger. 'Filthy, this,' he mumbled, 'should've worn m' overcoat.'

'What is it, Sebastian?' Libby asked, her face dimpled in a smile. Sebastian's mumble was not so low as he thought; besides, her hearing was more acute than most people's. 'What did you say?'

'Nothing, pet!' he tossed over his shoulder in a kindly voice, forcing a hearty laugh, and he tugged once on the reins in his hands. Never in a thousand years would he have let on to her that he found this entire endeavor distasteful, that he loathed the very sight of horses or anything even remotely connected with dirt, sweat, and manure. No matter that it was a bright, clear day, or that the riding enclosure was spaciously square and open, and afforded a panoramic view of the tree-lined roads wending through the club grounds, the paddocks and pastures, the tall gray barns and sweeps of rolling meadows off in the distance. He simply didn't care for the whole thing, but would never have said so; it was far too important to Libby, and he cared far too much for her. 'Nothing! Simply talking to old Dobbin here!' he added.

'That was good, Sebastian, that turn. I'm doing better. I can let go now on the straightaway. You're a magician!' She complimented him purposely. She was fully aware of how he felt and hated forcing him into an activity he loathed; however, the riding was so important to her that there was no other choice. After all, one didn't go about asking willy-nilly for the extraordinary except from those who would willingly offer it, and for whom she was confident she could one day reciprocate the favor. And at the moment, that meant only Sebastian Vickery, her confidant, friend, and self-appointed mother hen, a patient, kindly man who would trudge back and forth across the length of a dirty riding ring day after day in the late afternoon sun, all for the sake of Libby's need.

'Magician,' he was mumbling again, 'if I were a magician, I'd blink m'self right out o' this horse sty. Foul place . . . oop!' he said and side-stepped, creasing his brow again. 'A gift from above,' he quipped and tried to chuckle at his pun. 'How're ya doing, girl?' he called back loudly.

Libby waved her affirmative response, knowing that he was looking at her; the direction of his voice told her that. What she did not know was that Adam Bainbridge, astride his bay horse, Morgan, was also watching her from the far side of the white fence by the road. Several times in the past few weeks she had known he'd been there; Sebastian had told her, though he'd made no great thing of it. There was none to be made; they hardly knew each other, had met only the one time, two weeks before. She'd forgiven him the mild rudeness of that day; everyone had such days, as she knew probably better than most, and she'd put it down to one of his. And anyway, he'd left a good impression that inspired tolerance, or rather, an interesting impression; a person's voice and presence told her a great deal, and his had a certain quality about them. But she didn't know him well enough to identify that quality precisely. She might like to, but, of course, that was up to him.

But though Libby was unaware of Adam that day, Adam was acutely aware of her, as he had been ever since Matt's introduction two weeks before. It had made him a regular fixture at the club, at least in the late afternoons, when he could be found, any day, watching as a dandified little man in a blue wool blazer and gray pants led a blind woman around and around on a horse. Had he been asked, he would have called it coincidence that he was always in the vicinity of the ring when they arrived. He could not even explain to himself why it was he was so intrigued. She was attractive, yes, with her oval face and auburn hair; in fact, she was unusually so, when one became familiar with her expressions, had the opportunity to watch them, as he had. And it was an oddity, of course, a blind woman attempting to learn how to ride. But that was only a partial explanation of his interest in Libby Rutledge; there was some sort of indefinable compulsion to it. A need to contemplate the quiet courage the woman exemplified, a courage out of the realm of his experience, perhaps? He didn't know, and shifted in the saddle.

Sebastian was blowing his nose into a starched linen handkerchief. 'Have you had it, Sebastian?' Libby inquired kindly. He had hay fever, or dust fever, or perhaps more rightly, horse fever, Libby thought wryly and suppressed a smile.

'No, no! Simply caught a bit of fluff up m'nose. Let us carry on!'

'Well, I've had it myself. What do you say we quit for today?' It took every bit of her concentration, this relearning of old skills and adjusting them to new circumstances, and that in turn took all her energy.

'Whatever, pet,' he said gratefully.

As usual Matt Jameson was there to take the horse; he made a point of being there, and on that day Adam dismounted and joined him at the gate. 'You know something, little lady?' Matt said as they approached. 'You're gonna make it yet!'

'What you mean to say is that I don't wobble so dangerously any more.' Libby laughed.

'No, there's a little more to it than that. Here, come on, I'll help you down.' He touched her leg to indicate he was reaching up.

'No, wait. I'd like to try it myself.' She waved him away.

Before anyone could protest, she had slung one leg over, her hands grasping the pommel and cantle of the saddle, and she slipped her other foot out of the stirrup and hopped to the ground. She landed beautifully, squarely on both feet; Adam brought back the hands he had unconsciously reached out to catch her.

'Very nice,' Matt complimented with a grin, and his remark might have been a commentary on her powers to bewitch; even rough-cut, leathery Matt Jameson, a man who seemed weathered beyond his forty-five years, had been moved by her, had found somewhere deep inside him a compassion that was not often used. That vulnerably courageous look about her had dredged it up, and instinct told him the encouragement was important.

'Indeed, indeed,' Sebastian agreed, 'the lass is a sprite, a nimble, airy . . .'

'Sebastian,' Libby admonished with a brief laugh and tilt of her head. 'Don't overdo it.' The small commotion was making her uncomfortable; it always did. We all do what we have to, with some success every now and then, and let's let it go at that, she wanted to say, but didn't. She reached out unobtrusively then in search of Sebastian's arm, and it was Adam who took her hand gently to guide her over. She started visibly, accustomed to having people speak before touching her.

'Who . . . ?'

'Over here,' Adam said, acutely uncomfortable that he'd startled her.

'Oh! Adam. I didn't know you were here.'

Nor had he identified himself, and he wondered to his further discomfort how she had known it was he. His voice, he supposed; yes, she would be more inclined to recognize voice patterns and remember them. Which led him to wonder if his was particularly distinctive. 'Yes, I am.'

She was standing close to him and could detect the faint aroma of his aftershave; she liked the musky scent. It mingled with the dusty smell of the riding ring, the pungence of fresh hay, live horseflesh, saddle leather, yet stood out from it all. 'You've been riding?' she asked.

'Yes.' It took a moment to respond, and a brief, wry expression passed across his face as he looked at her; yes, he had been, if that's what you called going from the stable to here. He suddenly made the decision to take Morgan out over the fences. 'You're through for the day?'

His voice from above her really did have a nice quality to it: resonant, very masculine, she thought. She was putting together pieces of him and liked what she saw in her mind's eye. 'Yes. It takes awhile to get the stamina up to snuff,' she said and smiled in a genuine way that kept Adam's eyes on her. After a brief hesitation, she looked to her left. 'Sebastian, it's time, don't you think?'

'I think,' he agreed.

They made their farewells, and with Sebastian's arm, Libby moved out of the field of Adam's presence; there seemed to her a distinct difference between it and simply the fresh air around her. She heard him speak briefly to Matt Jameson, then stride off in the direction of his horse, she assumed; she heard the faint nicker and the snap of bridle leathers. Yes, he did seem a very interesting man, this Adam Bainbridge. She hoped she would see him again.

Winna's letter was waiting in the mail when they got home. Eagerly, Libby settled herself so Sebastian could read it to her. She put her purse in the proper place, on the table by the front door of her apartment, and took a seat against the cushions of the deep blue living room couch. Sebastian warned her than the letter was short—the usual six lines or so—but she didn't care; it had finally come. She smiled openly as she listened to Sebastian speak Winna's words:

> Hon,
>     Staying in Rome at the moment. Had a rotten air trip from Paris, but then I've never liked flying, so don't pay attention to me. The traffic is terrifying! But Libby, it's such a beautiful city. The colors! I'll cable an address.
>
>                                           Love to you,
>                                                 Winna

Well, not a lot of information, but it was some version of Winna's voice nonetheless; she missed it. It had been four years since she'd last heard it. Except, of course, for the overseas phone call last March, a combined birthday and Christmas present, too early for one, too late for the other, but it had been better than nothing at all, as six lines of greeting were better than none at all. A breezy greeting, like Winna herself. 'Rome, huh?' she commented idly, then glanced in Sebastian's direction. 'We should go there someday, Sebastian. You and I. In your little four-speed car with the lurching clutch. It is the clutch, not the driver, right?' she teased with a wide smile. That was for him an intentional jest, to ward off his reaction to the letter; she hoped it would help.

It didn't. Sebastian had laid the buff-colored sheet of expensive writing paper down, face up, with the crease in the middle balancing on the top of Libby's Queen Anne dropleaf, and he was staring at the handwriting, his mouth pursed. Every other person in the world wrote in script he thought; Winna's handwriting was closer to calligraphy—huge stylized letters that swept dramatically across the heavy vellum paper that cost a fortune to air mail. Lovely, flat letters that Libby had no way of reading. 'She should've sent a tape,' he said as he got up from the couch opposite hers, one with a multicolor chinoiserie pattern that complemented the solid blue. He went to the kichen, where he was as comfortable as he was in his own, down the hall; he had spent a lot of time in it, 'helping', always to the tune of Libby's laughing, exasperated objections. She was as self-sufficient as they came. 'Tea, pet?'

Libby was preoccupied. 'No thanks. Sebastian. And she hates tapes. Microphones. You know that.'

He put the water on to boil, then came to stand in the space joining kitchen and living room; the kitchen was not really a separate room, but seemed so because of the counter that set it apart. He would have smiled affectionately at the picture of her relaxing in this apartment she had worked so hard to make comfortable and useful for herself, if the letter hadn't come; as it was, he frowned. 'One doesn't write ordinary letters to you. One sends tapes. In this day and age of technology, one sends tapes. She has a recorder. Or she can put her mind to the mastery of braille.'

It was an old conflict, as old as Sebastian's association with her, some ten years now. 'Sebastian, I've told you so many times. She hates the microphone. She simply can't talk into it. It makes her nervous. I wish you'd accept that.'

'I don't.' It was said without the absentminded edge that sometimes tinged his statements. 'She should be able to, for you.'

Libby wanted to scream at that. The 'shoulds' of the world —there was no such thing. There was only 'is' and 'are'. Reality: her whole life was lived on that premise. And the reality of Winna and a tape recorder was that she couldn't use it; there was no other motive, despite what Sebastian wanted to think. 'Well, she can't,' she said shortly and hated the tone of voice. Winna and Sebastian in the same conversation, however, always induced it, and she hated that, too. 'Let's please not discuss it. It's been a long enough day already,' she said in her firm, quiet voice.

The tea kettle was shrilling, and Sebastian returned to the kitchen. Libby joined him, finding his arm so she could reach up and kiss him lightly on the cheek. His return smile was paternal, though shadowed. 'Then we won't talk about it, pet, not any more, but she should've sent a tape,' he got in one more time.

Libby sighed. 'Fix your tea, Sebastian. It just so happens, I've made something that'll go nicely with it. For you.' She moved over to the other counter, and although her words were light, she was frowning; she wouldn't let him have the last word. Not about Winna. 'And the letters are just fine. Forget it. Besides, I'll always have you to read them to me, huh?' she remarked and turned to smile over her shoulder.

'Yes, you'll always have me to read them. You'll always have me to be here.' But he wouldn't forget the letters; he wouldn't forget any of it.

Adam pulled his car into the gravel drive and headed in the direction of the house. It was mid-April, nearly three weeks after an unusual blind woman had happened into his life, and many of the trees were beginning to bud. The drive wound to the right past a thatch of birch trees, and as he rounded it, the monstrosity of a Tudor-style estate rose up before him. He pulled all the way around the immense circular drive and parked his car near the door.

It was nearly twilight; for as long as possible he'd put off leaving his apartment in the exclusive Washington suburb of McLean and had only begun to think of making the drive into the surrounding Virginia countryside when the clock on the mantle had struck five thirty, demanding he make his departure if he were going to be on time. Promptness was an obsession with his family; if he wanted to be spared his mother's clipped reproach and the drone of his father's oratory on the virtues of punctuality, he knew he had to be on his way. He had grabbed up a light raincoat on his way to the door and had turned, before flipping off the lights, to cast a last look around the apartment. It was a thing he did whenever he left for the Bainbridge estate; it was as if he could absorb the atmosphere in his own habitat and take it with him, the feel of the quiet tree-lined residential streets outside, of the sleek look inside; gleaming glass and chrome furnishings, the stylish green suede couch, the modern paintings hanging on the walls. The memory buffered the assault on his senses of the tomblike ancestral home he was headed for, seemed to neutralize the cloying feeling of the nearly priceless heirlooms moldering away inside: Louis XV ormolu desks, silk-upholstered bergéres, collections of Ming china and Aubusson rugs faded even paler with age. In contrast, the fresh, wide-open look of his own apartment appealed to his sense of simplicity. And perhaps represented some small salute to rebellion.

He stepped from the Jaguar and strode up to the heavy paneled door, banging the large brass knocker sharply as he waited for it to open. When it did, he stepped inside past the butler and was about to greet him when he heard his mother's heels tapping briskly across the gray slate floor as she came to greet him, the sound echoing hollowly through the cavernous hallway. 'You're late, Adam,' Augustine Bainbridge observed, leaning up to kiss him dispassionately on the cheek; she was dressed in mauve, as always.

'Only slightly,' he said and returned the required caress.

'It disrupts everything. It's nearly seven, and we're eating in half an hour. There'll be hardly any time to talk. Come along, your father's waiting in the library.'

The trick here was to keep some semblance of equanimity as long as possible; Adam's comment was inaudible, and he followed as she led the way toward a doorway at the far side of the immense hall. He detested these family dinners; they were such stilted, difficult affairs, like everything to do with the Bainbridges. He had accepted the telephoned invitation with resignation, however, for an uncomfortable amount of time had elapsed since his last visit, and, besides, there were things he needed to talk to his father about.

They entered the paneled library, which was walled on two sides with leather-bound books. His father sat in a Georgian wingback chair near a tremendous fireplace. 'I know,' Adam said, his expression mild as he crossed the richly patterned rug. 'I'm late. How are you, Father?' he inquired, reaching down to shake hands for a moment.

'I'm fine,' Julian Bainbridge said and motioned for his older son to sit down. His thin frame seemed lost in the great chair, his once robust size diminished now by age and failing health. His wizened face contained ice-blue eyes as sharp as ever, however, and they took in Adam's appearance thoughtfully. As always, Adam was casually but expensively well dressed: a tan cashmere sports coat, white shirt open at the muscular neck, crisply tailored slacks. 'You look well,' Julian Bainbridge said finally.

'I am.'

'Good. Manning!' He raised a heavily veined hand at the butler, who hovered in the doorway. 'Bring a bourbon and water,' he instructed, then glanced at Adam. 'It is still bourbon, isn't it?'

'Yes.'

Julian nodded back at the butler, watching him disappear before turning back to Adam. 'Where were you?'

Adam raised his eyebrows. 'What do you mean?'

'You admitted you were late.'

Adam's mild expression dissolved into conscious composure,

and he massaged his forehead slightly, looking up when his hand dropped. 'I had several things to do,' he lied.

'You and Christian,' his father remarked in a tone holding a sigh. 'Always too busy to be on time. What if . . . ?'

'Skip it,' Adam said tightly. 'I'm here. And anyway, where is Christian? I thought I was going to have to endure the pleasure of his company too.'

'He's away,' Augustine answered and lifted her sherry glass to her thin lips. She had been a beautiful woman once, with regal bearing and sharp, good features. It was she who had transmitted the extraordinary good looks that characterized her two sons. But her own looks had faded now, a victim of inattention and the ravages of pessimism. 'Seeing a woman. And from an excellent family, I'm thankful to say.' She smiled faintly. 'He tells us she's lovely.'

Adam accepted the glass the butler offered before disappearing again, then said dryly, 'It would naturally be a woman. Or a poker game.'

'His spending is unconscionable,' Julian remarked, frowning.

'I want to talk to you about that. He's put a proposition to me and asked that I discuss it with you.'

'After dinner,' Julian dismissed, pursing his small mouth. 'Christian's propositions never sit well on an empty stomach.' It didn't strike him as odd that Christian hadn't taken up his idea with him directly, despite the fact that they shared the same house. Adam was the elder son; it was right that he should be the conduit for all financial matters. It had been the way of Julian's own generation, and he had passed the custom down. 'Let's talk now about you. Are you involved with anyone?'

It was such a predictable sequence: a diatribe on his tardiness, a short harangue against Christian's reckless spending, with a remark now and then about Adam's own extravagance, and then the focus on his marital prospects. Adam wondered for the hundredth time why he didn't just go ahead and marry someone to save himself the trouble of these interrogations. He shifted in the uncomfortable armchair and drained his glass. 'I'm as involved as I always am,' he answered indifferently.

'Adam, you've just turned forty,' Augustine observed, her lips pursed together in disapproval.

'Thanks for reminding me.' Adam said dryly and stood up. 'I'm going to make another. Be back in a minute.' He left the room, returning some moments later with his glass refilled.

Julian was sitting with his thin legs crossed, an indulgent smile settled on his face. He picked up the conversation where it had left off, as if Adam had not abruptly interrupted it for a matter of minutes. 'Forty isn't so old for a man to be unmarried,' he allowed with a paternal air that didn't quite fit. 'I was about that when I finally married you, Augustine,' he reminded, then looked at Adam. 'But it's time to be thinking about it. Adam, you've sown your wild oats long enough. There are other considerations.'

Ah, yes. And now the considerations. Adam clinked the ice around in his glass, staring moodily into it awhile before finally looking at his father. 'Considerations? Like the fact that I will eventually be too old to father a son?' he inquired mildly and took a long drink, watching his father over the rim. 'That would be unfortunate, wouldn't it? For there to be no one to carry on the precious Bainbridge name?'

'Adam, you're being rude,' Augustine admonished.

'Sorry.'

'That's exactly right,' Julian responded, unperturbed. 'There've been many generations of Bainbridges. There will be many more. I've got my doubts that Christian will ever amount to anything. As a matter of fact, I know he won't. But you're different. Someday it'll all be yours. You're the elder son, and it must be done properly.'

'Of course,' Adam said with marked derision, his eyes narrowing. He could no longer play out the charade, no longer disguise how distasteful he found all of this. Or was it just that he'd never quite realized the depths of his disgust before? Whatever was eating away at him, he couldn't fight the rising tide of acerbity. 'God forbid the Bainbridges should disappear off the face of the earth. What a blow to humanity. Of course, you realize that I could sire all girls,' he tossed in and was rewarded by a hardening of his father's expression.

'That was an unnecessary remark.'

'This entire conversation is unnecessary!' he exploded then.

'As it should be,' Julian put in smoothly, a mild light in his eye. 'You know where your responsibilities lie. I shouldn't have to tell you. Adam, Adam,' he placated then, smiling his old man's tired smile, his white hair silvery in the lamplight. 'There are any number of women around. Pick one.'

'And shall I get her pedigree first?' he demanded. 'What would you like? Oh, blue blood, of course. Any preference as to color of hair and eyes? Shape of legs? Turn of figure? Oh, of course not. That's my worry. Just so she's got the proper breeding for the perpetuation of the line, right? Well, I warn you, I can make no guarantee as to the quality of character in my offspring. They just might be unfortunate enough to inherit something from me,' he said acidly and stood up, pacing moodily over to the fireplace.

Julian didn't react. He didn't understand his son particularly well, but he was used to him; the outbursts weren't uncommon, though they usually weren't quite so vituperative. 'I would assume you'd know what's suitable,' he said calmly.

Adam wheeled around, his hands thrust in his trouser pockets, drawing back his jacket, and his face was hard with anger. 'Suitable? Someone perfect in every way, right? Goddamn, you people make me sick!'

'Adam!' Augustine gasped.

'Let him be,' Julian directed and stood up. 'See to dinner, Augustine.' He watched his wife stand up and walk briskly from the room without a backward glance at either of them. 'Now,' he said, turning to face Adam, who was massaging his forehead again. 'What's wrong?'

Adam looked up. 'Oh, please. Don't go all fatherly concern on me. It's a little late, and it doesn't really suit you,' he said almost wearily now and looked down at the glass in his hand.

'Adam, we don't understand each other, I know that. You don't agree with me a lot of the time. I realize you have your reasons for not wanting to be pushed into a marriage that might be strictly for convenience, and perhaps I can understand that better than you think,' he said with a rare honesty as he glanced toward the door through which his wife had passed. 'However, our status in life demands certain things. I had thought you were conscious of that. I thought I'd made you conscious of it. What is this attitude? What's pushing at you?'

Confidences weren't something he shared with his father. 'Nothing's pushing at me. I'm just tired.'

'Of what?'

The perfect question: of what? Everything. 'I lead a hectic life, you know,' he said dryly. 'It wears a man down.' He tried to smile then; it was time to lay down their swords. But Julian wasn't ready.

'I want to know what your remark meant,' he said, peering hard at his son.

'Which one?' Adam asked wearily.

'The one that implied you find being a Bainbridge somehow objectionable, find us objectionable. You've certainly benefited handsomely from being born into this family. From what I and the generations before me strove to preserve for you,' he said cuttingly.

40

Adam laughed sharply. 'Thank you so much. I'm sure I've profited by it.'

Julian shook his head. 'You seem to have some sort of personal problem at the moment that has you going at yourself and us, and that you don't care to discuss. You're a grown man, so you'll have to work it out for yourself. But don't try to lay whatever disaffection you may be feeling for yourself at the feet of the Bainbridge name,' he said sharply, with unusual insight. 'You've been free to do as you want, and if you're not satisfied with something at the moment, then that's your problem. Now we'll forget this conversation for the time being, but just keep in mind that time's passing. There are things you have to do.'

He was finished and turned to leave the room. Adam watched him go, his eyes veiled, then drained his glass before following him to the dining room. It had started more poorly than usual, this evening he had wanted no part of in the first place, and he was certain it would only get worse.

# Chapter 3

Libby was securing the stirrup iron at the top of the leather strap, beneath the flap, when Adam said hello. She wasn't startled this time, for he no longer made the mistakes he had early on; he had touched her arm before speaking, then offered his name in a way that gave her equal footing. 'Pretty soon you'll be knocking them out over fences,' he said.

She returned the smile she heard in his voice, and gave the strap a brief tug. 'Hi, Adam. Someday, maybe,' she replied lightly; they'd become casual friends over the past weeks, and their paths seemed to cross nearly every day.

'And with Sebastian out in front, as always, coattails flying out behind him,' the little man said with a sigh. He stood in his usual position, at the horse's head. It was another clear spring day, but that didn't improve Sebastian's outlook on his immediate surroundings.

Libby laughed at the picture he conjured up in her mind. 'We'd take the purse, Sebastian. No doubt about it!' She brushed a lock of hair away from her face.

Adam was still smiling. 'I'd like to see that. It would only take a little familiarization with the hunt course, and you'd have it made.' He hesitated a moment, looking down into Libby's face. She was still smiling, her head tilted to one side, and he drew out a cigarette, lit it, then slipped the gold lighter back in the pocket of his tan riding breeches. 'Which leads me to the point, Libby,' he went on, 'that it's about time you got acquainted with more than just the riding ring hereabouts. I've decided the restaurant would be the perfect place to start. May I take you to lunch?'

It was succinctly and accurately put, the invitation, for it had been decided on consciously and carefully in the week following the dinner with his family. It was time he got to know her better, time to put an end to this lingering fascination that had made him rearrange his life over the past weeks to coincide with her late afternoon visits to the stable. The other women in his life still came and went as usual; she hadn't affected that. But she had affected him in other ways, colored his whole frame of mind, exerted some sort of indefinable hold on his attention that kept drawing him back, and he needed to break that hold. The luncheon would accomplish that, and then he'd be free to go his own way.

Libby was hesitating, a pensive look on her face. She would like to have lunch with him, but acceptance required some forethought, and she hadn't had time for that. She didn't want to put him off, yet her circumstances required that she not rush into these things without examining them a bit. Besides, the timing was a problem; that alone would put an end to the question of whether to accept. 'Thank you, but that's really difficult for me. You see, I'm not free until early afternoon.' She smiled regretfully, straightening her glasses with a light touch of one finger.

'Then how about a late lunch? Tomorrow?' he pressed.

'Well . . .'

Sebastian stepped in. 'That's an excellent idea. My dear, you need a respite from all this singleminded activity, not to mention one from the company of an old man like me. And my allergies need a respite, too,' he added without thinking, then caught himself. 'Not that I object, of course! No, no. Don't mind a bit!'

'Then it's agreed. Tomorrow,' Adam said, taking advantage of Sebastian's unexpected assistance.

Libby laughed; she couldn't fight them both. And she did really want to go. 'All right. That would be lovely.'

'I'll pick you up.'

'No,' she said flatly. 'I'll meet you here. I'll arrange for a taxi.'

Adam began to object. 'Libby . . .'

'Adam, I do it all the time.' Her voice was quiet but authoritative. 'Please. I'm perfectly able to get about. Two o'clock? Would that be all right?'

Adam looked at her pensively for a moment, then relented; there was no other choice. 'Two o'clock. That would be fine.'

Libby arrived exactly on time the next day, wearing a simple russet-colored shirtwaist dress. It was a hue tailor-made for her auburn hair and fair complexion, the dress itself the careful selection of the devoted buyer of her favorite store; the dress was perfect for the lines of her figure—extraordinarily good lines,

Adam noted, and frankly female, that began as a shapely leg appearing initially from the taxi, then became a slim, mature body that stepped gracefully from the car with no need of his assistance. She wore no jewelry except a fine gold chain circling her slender neck; he didn't know it was an heirloom of her mother's, worn for sentiment's sake, but only that the lack of glitter—a glitter characteristic of the women he knew—was appropriate. She needed no embellishments of any kind; they would have detracted from her own natural loveliness.

She had traded the dark glasses for lighter ones that were less conspicuous, and he noticed them immediately, for they allowed him his first glimpse of her eyes. They seemed quite arresting, perhaps her best feature, almond in shape with a color he couldn't discern through the lenses without making a point of it. He paid the cab driver, then turned to Libby and gave her his arm; they began to walk toward the front of the Hunt Club restaurant.

'Adam, you needn't be quite so terrified I'm going to crash into something,' she told him frankly after they'd gone some distance. She smiled up at him unself-consciously, very aware of his usual aftershave, and the fine texture of the fabric of his suit. It was soft—cashmere, she thought.

'Was I so obvious?' He was smiling wryly, chagrined.

'Only to me,' she said and laughed. 'Please, we can walk right along. God, how I hate creepers! Simply lend me your arm. I can follow your motion, and warn me when something's coming. Tell me about steps, right or left turns, but on the straightaway, let's not dawdle along!'

He threw back his head and laughed; she was marvelous. 'Forgive me. I'm new at this sort of thing, but I promise. No more duck walk.' He cast her an appreciative glance, then headed on up the walkway.

They entered the restaurant, and he waved away the maitre d', escorting her to his usual table near the window, and drawing out a chair for her. It wasn't accomplished with his usual savoir faire, however; she had her own methods, needing, as in all things, to touch and feel, and he nearly bungled the entire thing for her with his gallantry, all but causing her to sit down in mid air. She rescued the situation with an adroitness born of long experience; he, for the first time in years, suffered the hot flush of embarrassment. It took him a moment to recover, but when he had, he sat down opposite her.

'Adam, next time you just rest my hand on the back of the chair. I'll do the rest,' she said gently and smiled.

44

'Right.' He hurried on past his discomfort. 'Would you like a drink?'

'Yes. Wine would be nice. Chablis.'

While he signaled for the waiter, she listened to the strains of the soft music coming from discreet speakers in the ceiling; she recognized Chopin. It set a nice mood, rather romantic, as it mingled with the quiet hum of conversation going on around them, the gentle clatter of silverware and china being removed from a table somewhere nearby, the sound of Adam himself, across the table, as he spoke quietly to the waiter and shifted slightly in his chair; it was leather, like her own, she could tell by the soft creak. This was her world now, since that day twenty years ago, a world of sounds and scents and movements and intuitions; she had made it work for her, turning disadvantage to advantage whenever she could, and had only a few more hurdles that she knew of to go over. There might be more, of course; life was like that, but one took them as they came. When the waiter left she smiled in Adam's direction and clasped her hands on the table in front of her. 'So, tell me about you, Adam Bainbridge.'

He was lighting a cigarette and looked up past his hand held in mid-air. 'That's my line,' he said with a brief laugh, slightly taken aback.

'No, it's mine,' she countered with assurance, and heard him flick the lighter closed. He was watching her steadily, noting that she had unclasped her hands and was passing them unobtrusively across the table in front of her, the touch of her fingers as light as a feather. He responded finally.

'Times have changed. I seem not to have noticed until now.'

'Possibly,' she allowed, then went on to explain herself with no coquettishness. 'You have the advantage, you know. You know at least some basics about me. What I look like, for example. All I know about you is that you're one of the more "illustrious" members of this club, as I recall Matt having once introduced you. Doesn't that afford me first crack?' It was said with a lilt, to lighten the thrust of her initial statement.

'Of course,' he said and studied her for a moment. 'What would you like to know?'

'Oh, who you are, where you come from, what you do.'

He laughed. 'After that lead in, I thought you were going to ask me what I look like.'

Her smile parted her lips slightly. She might be missing a faculty, but she was a woman; she could play the game, too. 'And what would you have told me?'

'That I'm short, fat, and terribly unattractive.'

45

She laughed quietly, and he signaled for the waiter to set down their glasses. She heard the man's movements and waited until he had gone before answering. 'That's not true.'

He raised his eyebrows. 'How do you know it's not?'

'Well, you're not short. I know that for several reasons. The level of your voice, for instance. It's quite far above me. The fact that your arm is set higher than mine. And also, when I convinced you I wasn't going to trip over thin air and you picked up your normal pace, I was almost sorry I'd told you to walk naturally. Short men don't have such long strides.'

'Very neat detective work,' he said glibly.

She didn't smile this time. 'Don't be fatuous, Adam. It's the way I have to live,' she said quietly and without rancor.

He covered his renewed discomfiture with a long drink of whiskey. He had ordered it straight; he knew now why that was. Setting his glass down, he looked directly at her. 'And the rest? Fat and terribly unattractive?' His voice held a trace of annoyance.

Highly sensitive to nuances of tone and mood, she tilted her head. 'I'm sorry. I really shouldn't have said that, but it was honest. Be forewarned. I take some getting used to.'

He relaxed back in his chair, smiling ruefully. 'My fault. A right-handed swordsman never can parry a left-handed lunge without some practice. I'm a quick learner, though.' He was rewarded with her genuine laughter, and glanced briefly at the stream of diners filtering in and out of the doors; there was a steady flow, but the room was not crowded.

'All right. So tell me now all about you,' she repeated.

'Oh, no! We're not through yet. You still haven't finished with "fat and terribly unattractive." ' Why was he pursuing it so hard?

She accepted his lead. 'Well, now, there you've got me, almost. I can only guess at not fat. You seem too fit when you walk. Don't forget, I have senses rather more developed than you might suspect. You get a very good idea of motion when walking close to someone. And as for the other, well . . .' She felt off balance for the first time as she spread her hands; oddly enough, Adam was gratified to note it.

'Okay. You're off the hook. Not fat is correct, and as for the other, well . . .' he said, repeating her hesitation. 'That remains to be seen,' he finished with an enigmatic smile.

'Good. Now start your narrative.' Her cheeks dimpled as she smiled encouragement.

'Where?'

'Anywhere.'

'All right. Let's try born, bred, and raised here in Virginia.'

'Ah? So was I,' she commented.

'Where?' he asked interestedly, sipping his whiskey. He saw that she was making a movement toward her wine glass.

'Not my turn,' she demurred pleasantly as she continued the unobtrusive search for her glass.

'Here,' Adam said abruptly, reaching to hand her the glass, and in his haste, he knocked over the salt shaker. The expensive, cut-glass container tinkled against the table as it fell but didn't break. 'Oh, hell,' he said under his breath, righting it again. He was not only acting like a schoolboy, but feeling like one, too. What had happened to Adam Bainbridge, man about town?

Libby sighed. So it was going to begin, after all. She had hoped neither of them would have to go through it; dreamer, she thought. 'Adam . . .'

'No, no!' he said testily, raising his hand. 'It's all right. A minor accident, that's all.' He was uncertain toward whom his irritation was directed. Her? That was unfair. Himself? Positively.

Libby took a breath. 'Now look, Adam. Stop trying so hard, and we'll both feel a lot better. I should've said this before, but I didn't, stupidly. I come prepackaged with a set of instructions, and it'll only take a moment to go through them.' She smiled warmly, getting into the proper frame of mind.

'We've gone over "What To Do When You Take Libby Out For A Walk." Now let's run through "What To Do When You Take Libby Out To Lunch." I handle my own little bit of territory here in front of me. Whether or not you noticed, I've already located everything and am perfectly at ease with it. When something new is given to me, I get its bearings. If I can't, I'll ask. You might remark to the waiter to be certain, when he puts down my plate, that whatever I have to cut up is directly in front of me. It's such a nuisance to send peas flying all over my lap! But that's about all there is to it. You go on about your business, I'll go on about mine. If I have a problem, I'll speak up. If not, consider the situation under control. End of lecture.' She stopped, holding all emotion in abeyance; it was a crucial moment.

He said nothing for a long time, his face a study in conflicting emotions. The lunch had been planned to dispel the notion that she was any different from any other woman he'd ever known, except for a small matter of sightlessness that seemed almost inconsequential on the surface by the way she handled herself.

47

He was merely entertaining an acquaintance who didn't affect him any differently than all the other women he had known. Except that she had so far managed to embarrass, amuse, and surprise him, and now this. He was touched more deeply than he'd ever have suspected he could be. How long had it taken her to work up that lilting précis calculated to define boundaries and set others at ease, both at the same time? Years of overturned salt shakers? And how God-awful to know you required instructions at all. He rapidly ticked off a mental list of activities, wondering how many more sets of instructions there were. And where was the one entitled, "How To Set Libby Free"? He knew it didn't exist.

She listened with composure to his silence. So, she had been right; he was going to retreat now that he was beginning to grasp the scope of what being with her entailed. Well, she was prepared for it; it had happened before. 'You're very quiet,' she observed and picked up her napkin, folding it over once.

'Yes, I know,' he said quietly. 'It's because you're very remarkable.'

That was unexpected, but she could field it. 'No, I'm not. I simply do what I have to.' An alarming suspicion struck her suddenly; his voice had not been unnerved, as she had expected. Which meant one of two things: acceptance, or . . . 'Oh God, Adam! I've made you feel sorry for me. No!' she said almost angrily, her lips pressed together, and she made a movement to rise. 'I'm leaving!'

It was a practiced movement and came nowhere near to jarring the table, but Adam reached over and grasped her wrist, partly to steady her, but more to force her back down. 'Stop it! Sit down! I have no intention of letting you leave at the moment, and besides, I don't relish the thought of being responsible for the cost of your flouncing out of this room!'

Astounded, Libby sat back down slowly, then burst out laughing. Adam did too, for the humor of his unthinking remark, and for Libby's genuine amusement. She continued to laugh as she expanded the suggestion to a picture in her mind. Finally, she got herself under control and put both hands palm down on the table. 'How refreshing you are! How positively marvelous that you can so blithely take a shot like that at something as conceivably pathetic as a blind woman!' Bless you, Adam Bainbridge, she added to herself.

'My dear Libby,' he said with a wry smile, 'you're anything but pathetic, and though I'd like to be able to take full credit for being the one—at long last!—to restore some measure of equilibrium to this so-far disastrous lunch, I confess I made the remark without thinking.'

'All the better,' she said gaily. 'And you'd better not find me pathetic, because I'm not, and would you please be so kind as to read to me from the menu? I'm famished!'

He did, with pleasure and ease, and supplied the waiter with their order. Friendly acquaintances came and went, stopping by their table to speak, and when they were alone again, Libby picked up her wine glass and smiled easily. 'You haven't finished telling me about yourself, you know.'

He looked at her in some exasperation. 'You've got to realize it's not so easy to simply blurt out facts about yourself. I've been meaning to work up a short resumé, but I just haven't had the time,' he remarked, covering an unaccustomed self-consciousness.

She pursed her lips, lightly touching the gold chain around her neck. 'Okay, I'll give you a lead in. Why are you one of the more illustrious members of this club?'

'You don't mince words, do you?' he asked with a brief laugh.

'I can't afford to,' she said in her straightforward way. 'Everyone else has the benefit of what they can see to make deductions. I can't do that. If I were to sit around here in my own little world waiting for someone to offer information I might happen to be interested in, I'd be here till doomsday, still none the wiser.'

He chuckled to himself, then took another drink of his whiskey before answering, again evasively. 'I'm illustrious because the Bainbridges are illustrious,' he said shortly.

'Oh really?' She ignored the derisive tone and tilted her head interestedly. 'Why?'

'They just are.'

'That's no answer.'

'Libby, what do you want me to say?' he asked, frowning in unaccustomed frustration. Why did this woman make him so uncomfortable? Because circumstances, and she herself, demanded that she be dealt with in a perfectly straightforward manner? Because none of the accepted rules of male-female interplay and its coquettish verbal dancing applied? He didn't care to admit how hard it was to drop the banter. 'All right then. We're illustrious because we have money to burn and do so in a way that would turn most people's stomachs. Will that do for an answer?' he said harshly.

She smiled to herself; he did really sound so uncomfortable.

49

Most people were when forced to speak the outright truth, even she, though she'd learned to overcome the discomfort to a great degree. Head on was the way of her world; it pretty well had to be. 'If it's true, yes,' she said simply.

'All right. It's true,' he said moodily.

'Good. We're progressing.'

'Now you're being fatuous,' he accused, eyeing her with momentary disapproval.

She laughed. 'You're right. Apology submitted.'

'And accepted.'

'Go on. What do you do?'

'Not a damn thing.' He lit another cigarette.

'Adam!' Her mild laugh was tinged with remonstrance.

'It's true,' he said with an easy smile that lifted one corner of his mouth, deepening the hollow of his cheek. He decided that banter wasn't entirely out of place after all. 'I don't need to do a damn thing. I'm loaded. I just told you that.'

She pursed her lips, more aware than he that some things between a man and woman transcended barriers of all kinds. She tilted her head. 'You're being facetious.'

'Not really. I play at working sometimes. Check the annual reports of some of the Bainbridge companies. You'll find my name there. At the head of the list. Chairman of the Board,' he said off-handedly. He glanced at the waiter clearing the table next to them, then turned back to look at Libby. Her face was alert, receptive to this recital of his, some thoughtful emotion reflected in the slight smile on her lips.

In fact, she was wondering why he was so derisive. 'What's wrong with that?' she said.

'Because those are absolutely meaningless positions,' he admitted. 'They require that I show up at a prescribed conference room on a prescribed day and take my prescribed place at the head of a long table where I have the pleasure of sitting for three or more hours listening to some stupidly enthusiastic executive popping off about profit and loss figures and drawing intricate formulae that I don't particularly understand and couldn't care less about on a blackboard that squeaks and travels around the room as he writes. And while I sit there holding up the others by my esteemed presence at this ridiculous meeting, I hope no one will notice that I'm doodling on the pad of paper in front of me, bored to tears. You know,' he said then, his blue eyes turning thoughtful, 'I've often suspected those damn meetings of being responsible for the fat loss figures that keep cropping up. After all, there's always a brand new spanking fresh pad of yellow legal paper sitting in front of each place, with a new number two pencil sharpened to a lethal point right beside it. Every damn time. It must cost a bloody fortune! And that's not to mention the salary of the poor dolt of a secretary who probably showed up early and collects overtime just so she can sharpen all those pencils and hunt down all those pads, those obscenely unused pads.'

Libby was laughing. 'You make it sound so funny.'

'It is funny. Pathetically so,' he said, his expression darkening.

'That's all you've ever done?' she went on interestedly, resting her elbow on the table, cradling her chin in her hand.

'No, I took a crack at running one of those companies, once,' he said quietly, his eyes veiled. 'Years ago.' And so, another startling admission for Libby Rutledge. This was a subject he seldom discussed.

Something in his tone made her straighten and finger her water glass. 'You didn't like it?'

He rested one forearm on the edge of the table and leaned forward slightly. 'I hated it,' he said truthfully. 'The climate of four closed-in walls didn't agree with me. Nor did I particularly agree with the climate of the business,' he added, trying for a tone of indifference. Why the hell was he telling her all this, anyway? 'The red numbers had their finest hour under my leadership.' He sat back abruptly and picked up his whiskey glass, downing the rest of it. He knew far more than he cared to admit about those complicated formulae on the blackboard, how they worked, or more correctly, how they didn't work, how a man trapped where he didn't belong couldn't juggle them enough to right them again; it had been an interminable four years, painful for everyone involved. 'So, I cut everyone's losses and went on my irresponsible way,' he said, sitting back up in his chair. 'I only took up those vainglorious posts when Father got too old for it all. Or too bored. He never told me which,' he added flippantly. 'But it was a foregone conclusion, anyway. Only a Bainbridge heads up a Bainbridge company. Anything else is unheard of.'

Libby let it ride; after all, they weren't here to trade their darkest secrets. 'And after you left the company . . . ?' she prompted.

'I went from pillar to post,' he said impatiently, wanting to be done with the conversation. 'Traveling a lot, dabbling in this and that. Doing not a damn thing, really. I told you that. Believe it.'

Libby looked down toward her hands; she hadn't meant to

make him uncomfortable. 'You have brothers and sisters?' she asked abruptly.

Adam's laugh was distinctly unpleasant. 'A brother. And you think I'm an unconscionable waster? Wait until you meet Christian!'

'I don't think you're an unconscionable waster,' she said softly, raising her head.

'Thank you, but you have no way of knowing that.'

'You're right,' she said simply and smiled.

For a fleeting moment, he came close to wishing he were someone else. He caught himself, however; he was too old for that sort of wistfulness. The waiter spared him the necessity of making a further comment by appearing with their food.

They ate in relative silence, Adam watching her unobtrusively. She was very sure and methodical, with her silverware arranged in an orderly fashion, her fork selected and used, then replaced in exactly the same spot on the plate while she unhurriedly located her water glass and sipped from it. Except for her very careful movements, however, she seemed no different from any other diner in the restaurant. Their plates were cleared away finally, coffee was brought, and Libby was quietly sipping hers, listening to the sound of Adam's spoon in his cup, when he spoke. 'All right, Miss Elizabeth Rutledge,' he said lightly, 'it's your turn.'

She smiled. 'Where should I start?'

He grinned. 'See? It's not so easy, is it?'

'No, it's not.'

'You said you were raised in Virginia. Where?'

It was one of her favorite subjects, and she smiled. 'In the Valley.'

'Ah, yes. It's beautiful countryside,' he said, then stopped abruptly. 'Libby, I . . .' he began awkwardly.

Libby knew exactly what had happened; it always did to people who weren't used to talking to her, who thought that every word must be qualified, and many words stricken from use. She hurried to reassure him, dismissing his imagined faux pas with a wave of her hand. 'That's okay. And you're exactly right. We were smack in the middle of it, at the foot of a small mountain. We had a lot of property, fields and pastures, a portion of the mountainside. You know, I always thought that the spring was the most beautiful there, the most exciting time,' she said eagerly; she could remember it so well. 'Everything just . . . burst forth! The trees, the fields, everything so miraculously green and spectacular. We had a field that ran up toward the mountain—it was a foothill, really, and you could stand up there at the top and see for miles. You'd think you were looking out over a patchwork quilt, all different shades of green and yellow, with spots of bright color for houses and barns. And those wonderful old dairy barn silos sticking up here and there. Ah! There can't be anywhere like it in the world!'

Adam hadn't realized he was holding his breath until he expelled it when she had finished; he hadn't been prepared for the recital. 'You . . . weren't always . . .' he tried, again awkwardly.

'Blind?' She supplied the word for him because she knew it was a difficult one for most people at first and sometimes forever. 'Go ahead and say it, Adam. It's all right. And no, I wasn't always blind.'

He didn't know how to continue; he seemed not to know how to do anything with this woman. Libby sensed his confusion and went on; besides, she wanted to avoid other questions that she didn't intend to answer at this time. 'I was ten. It was an accident. Unfortunate, but it happened,' she said matter-of-factly. She knew how to set the tone; it had always been up to her, and she had learned how beautifully. 'But some things can never be taken away, you know, and I have all these memories. I was always a watcher. I noticed things, a lot of things, which is good. It gives me a real treasure trove of things to see behind my eyes,' she added with an open smile. 'So, anyway, that's where we lived. It was a nice big old house, rambling, everything kind of threadbare. By the time we—Winna and I—came along, the Rutledge money had kind of disappeared into nothingness, and all that remained was the house and property. It was a little hard to keep up. Winna used to call it genteel poverty,' she laughed. 'I suppose she was right. But it didn't matter to me. I loved it, and I was broken-hearted when it was sold.'

'Why was it sold?' he ventured.

She knew by his tone he was still dissecting every word, and though she didn't want to discomfit him, she couldn't help the infinitesimal hesitation; this was another painful subject. 'Mom and Dad died,' she said softly.

'I'm sorry.' She seemed young to him, right then, with a new kind of vulnerability about her. Her face was turned toward the table, her lips pressed lightly together. 'When did it happen?'

'Four years ago. It was a boating accident.' Accidents seem to be rampant in her family, she thought and felt depression tug at her. She raised her chin a bit.

'I'm sorry,' he said again. 'Were you close to them?'

53

Confrontation, as always, was the best remedy; she held on to that thought as she spoke slowly. 'Very. They were . . . well, they were wonderful people. Frankly, I wouldn't be where I am now without them, Mother particularly. She was just designed to be a mother,' she added with a jagged little laugh and fingered the necklace unconsciously. 'And it was because of her that I can be so independent.' It was said with genuine pride, both in herself and in the woman who had been her stanchion, her friend. 'You see, I was never treated as if I were particularly different. Never pampered, or waited on, thank God! That's disastrous. Sometimes it might even have seemed as if they were being a little callous about their lack of protection, but they weren't. Not at all. It's the way to do it, and nowadays, in this age of technology, there are so very many things available to help you get along when you're blind, to help you readjust, if you know about them. Well, they saw to it that we knew about it all, and so here I am. I went to certain schools for a time, but only for a time. Most of it was accomplished at home. After that, I went to school with everyone else, just doing my own thing a little differently. Yes, they were unique people, Trevor and Jocelyn Rutledge.'

'And your sister . . . Winna is her name?' He wanted to know everything about this woman who spoke so openly, so calmly about a life he couldn't imagine.

Libby was smiling warmly again. 'Yes, Winna. Edwinna is her proper name. Oh, Winna was marvelous. She did everything she could think of. It was important to her.'

'You're close to her, too, aren't you?' he asked, quietly. She had spoken so eagerly; he couldn't help but ask the question.

'Yes. We always were. Oh, of course, now that we're adults, our lives have taken very different paths,' she allowed. 'Winna likes to travel. She's been in Europe for quite awhile now. There was some money with the sale of the farm, and it makes me happy that there was enough so she could do what she wanted. I don't hear from her as often as I'd like, but then you'd have to know Winna!' she laughed. Yes, breezy, busy, fun-loving Winna, who hardly had time in her hectic life to write; Libby hoped she'd indeed cable an address, so she could send her a tape. But you could never tell with Winna. And even if she sent one, she could never be sure Winna hadn't moved on before her tape arrived at what had become an old address. Libby rested her chin on the hand propped on the table, momentarily lost in thought.

Adam was staring thoughtfully into his empty coffee cup, and he absently reached over for the pot and refilled both his and hers. It had been done without a word, but she said 'Thank you,' making him smile wryly and decide to ask the question roaming around in his head. 'You mentioned you weren't usually free until early afternoon. Do you get out a lot, I mean besides coming here and insisting that Sebastian get his patent leather shoes all dusty?' He hated the supidity of the way he had phrased his question.

'Does he?' Libby asked incredulously.

'Does he what?'

'Wear patent leather shoes!' she laughed.

Adam's own laugh was tinged with relief; he was making an ass of himself, but she didn't seem to mind. 'Yes.'

Libby was frowning heavily, fussing with the subject in her mind. 'Why in the world would he do that?' she asked, more of herself than him. She loved Sebastian dearly, but sometimes he was really too much. 'I must speak to him about it,' she murmured.

'Libby, it doesn't matter. It was an asinine thing to say. But while we're on the subject, where in the world did you come up with Sebastian anyway?' He didn't mind this time that he sounded rude; the man was a real character.

Libby almost giggled. 'I know, isn't he a card? But he's a love. He practically adopted me, quite a few years ago. He's a retired English professor—a widower—and he lives several doors down from my apartment. Somehow he just decided to take me under his wing, especially after Mom and Dad were gone. They knew him, of course, because, well, it's just been years that Sebastian's been in my life. And listen, if you think *you've* had a hard time coping with my routines,' she added with a characteristic bluntness, 'you should've seen Sebastian! He's all thumbs and left feet anyway, and what with always rushing around to help me when I didn't need it a bit, I think over the years I've replaced one entire set of glasses and most of my plates. One Christmas, he gave me a full set of unbreakable china. "For when I come to dine," he told me in dead seriousness.' She laughed again, savoring the private memory.

As Adam watched, his own face lit into an involuntary smile; hers was so infectious. One elbow was propped on the table, the opposite hand resting on his hip, drawing back his jacket as he listened, and he was about to prompt her to go on when she did anyway.

'It's not that I'm laughing at him, only *about* him, because he's one of a kind,' she said. 'But he's so devoted and sincere, and by now he's like family. He does things for me that I can't do for myself. I mean, no matter how self-sufficient you work at making yourself, there are still a certain number of things beyond your reach.'

'And so you live alone,' he said wonderingly. It wasn't a question, simply a statement.

'Of course.'

And stay home alone a lot when there's no one to come get you out? Is that why you're not free until early afternoon, when Sebastian can come to get you? And have you come to grips with that one, as you seem to have with everything else? he wanted to ask. 'Does he spend a lot of time with you?' was what he said.

'Well . . . only in the evenings sometimes. And of course, he comes with me here, after I get home from work,' she said casually.

'Work?' Adam was flabbergasted and even blinked once.

Libby sighed silently at herself; she really ought to stop dropping the remark like that. Satisfactions needed to be gotten where they could, of course, but she was getting a little old for the game. She had no desire to bait Adam further, though, and didn't leave the statement dangling this time. 'I'm a teacher,' she said in clarification.

'A teacher,' Adam echoed, nodding unconsciously in bemused acknowledgment. He was surprised, yet he should've expected something like that by now. Of course she would be. This woman would be totally blind, and live alone, and go out to work and be a teacher. And want, against all odds, to learn how to ride. 'Who do you teach?' he managed to ask.

'Blind children.' She made a movement of dismissal then with her head; enough was enough. 'Come on, let's talk about other things.'

'One more question,' he interrupted quickly. 'Why do you want to learn to ride? You don't need to prove anything more.'

She raised her eyebrows. 'I'm not proving anything. I already know how to ride. I just need to learn how to ride blind.'

He was startled, but pressed her. 'Why?'

She hesitated noticeably for the first time; discussion of Libby Rutledge seldom included forays into the psychology of her motives or disclosures of her innermost thoughts and needs, and certainly not the first time around. However, right now, with Adam Bainbridge, her self-imposed restrictions didn't seem to want to hold. At length she answered. 'Because I need it. I need what it can give me. Desperately, you could say,' she said slowly, the depths of her emotion betrayed by the unnatural tightness around her mouth.

He was still watching her steadily. 'And what is that?'

'Freedom from the chains of darkness.'

That single sentence stayed with Adam for a long time, long after Libby's departure in the taxicab, long after his drive to nowhere and his restless dinner at some out-of-the-way eatery, until late in the evening when he returned home to his apartment to shed jacket, tie, and shoes and stood at the undraped bank of sliding glass doors in stocking feet, collar pulled open, cuffs rolled back, stared unseeingly out into the ink of the night on the other side. It was a sentence eloquently revealing, and it haunted him, for no real reason at all and for all the reasons in the world.

The chains of darkness. How unyielding they must be, and yet she wore them beautifully, with grace and a quiet acceptance. She had worried that he would pity her, but she wasn't one to inspire it. He didn't know this woman, really, but he'd watched her for weeks, at first from across a dirt riding ring, then from across a luncheon table, and the face she turned toward the world around her wasn't one trembling with valiant bravado. It was confident, calm, untainted with the disease of self-pity. A vulnerability was evident there, yes, but not of the nature that would have led him, or anyone, to suspect she still had this one more hurdle to negotiate. Only the sentence had done that. And he was truly awed by the goal she had set herself; in her place, he would never have dreamed of such freedom, he thought, nor possessed the fortitude to seek it out. But she might even attain it; the courage to try was written in her face, too.

After a time he walked over to a well-stocked bar cleverly arranged within the confines of a tall, traditional secretary the designer had thrown into the décor for contrast, and mixed a drink, more bourbon than water and no ice. His handsome face was pensive as he lifted the glass to his lips and stared down at his desk top; the teak letter opener lay there, along with assorted personal notes to himself, an ink pen with no top, a canceled stamp, and a small, leather-bound copy of *Kon Tiki*, well worn. He transferred the same moody gaze to the room around him, a beautiful room really, expensively furnished, rich with color: deep olive green on the long double-sectioned suede couch, wine-red in opposing armchairs, neutral whey-colored carpeting, chrome, glass, brass, silk wallpaper in a discreet Oriental motif of birds and bamboo blossoms. The room of a man with every advantage, every opportunity, an open-ended bankbook, fine taste. An odd feeling came over him, the same one that had been with him for weeks, since that day he'd been confronted with a blind woman who had the audacity to think she could learn how to ride.

'What's the matter. Adam old man? Feeling suddenly outclassed?' he said aloud with a dark bitterness in his eyes.

A blind woman who lived alone, and taught school, and rode horses. An unimpaired man who'd been born to privilege, and foundered companies, and drank too much. What a hell of a lousy commentary on life.

# Chapter 4

Libby listened to Sebastian pouring out their tea. The living room of her apartment in Fairfax was shadowy with the onset of dusk, and lit at the moment only by two matching orange ginger jar lamps on the Pembroke tables nearest the fireplace. Libby was curled up in the corner of the couch, her head resting on one hand. After a time, she heard the smart sound of a magazine slapping against the shag carpeted floor. 'What, Sebastian?' She smiled even as she asked the question; she could guess what was on his mind.

'Nothing, pet,' he said mildly, separating the flattened beetle from the magazine with a napkin. 'Simply removing an uninvited guest,' he said predictably and glanced at her. She was in jeans and a red checked blouse, her long hair loosened from its ponytail and spilling around her slim shoulders. The picture of a lovely, refined young woman, he thought and glanced toward the sliding glass doors, toying with the thought of moving them out onto the terrace. It was Libby's favorite spot, that narrow, third-story enclosure; it overlooked the common grounds of the apartment complex, and she liked to sit there where she could listen to the strains of the children playing below, feel the light breeze ruffle her hair, and smell the fragrance of the billowing maple trees out toward the busy road. The evening was chilly, however, and he rejected the idea. Turning back, he handed her a cup, then watched briefly as she checked the level of the liquid with one fingertip and relaxed back against the cushion. He did the same then and sighed in contentment. 'Ah, the subtle pleasures of an early evening tea!'

Libby looked over sympathetically. 'Tired, Sebastian?'

'The bones are weary, m'love, but the mind is as fresh as clear spring water,' he answered loftily and smiled warmly at her.

Libby was used to his ways and could feel the warmth of his smile on her. 'You're such a dear.'

His eyebrows knit together. 'So I am, but pray tell, for what this time?'

'For taking me out there to the club day after day when you know as well as I do how much you detest horses and everything about them.'

He frowned dismissively. 'Oh, you exaggerate . . .'

'Not even a little bit. I know, Sebastian,' she told him, then smiled affectionately. 'And I love you all the more for making the effort.'

' 'Tis no effort, pet.'

She laughed, her head falling back slightly. 'It's a monumental trial!' she said, then remembered something. 'Sebastian, are you wearing patent leather shoes?' Her brow above the light-colored glasses was creased.

Taken aback, he glanced down, contemplating the film of dust covering the shiny black surfaces. 'A very astute deduction. How'd you know?'

'So you are! Sebastian, no one wears good shoes to a riding ring! Don't be silly. Wear something more practical!'

'Patent leather is practical,' he objected. 'And just how, lassy, did you come to see my patent leather shoes?'

She smiled mysteriously for a moment, then relented. 'Adam told me at lunch the other day.' She picked up the crewel pillow beside her and began plumping it.

'Ah!' he said, relieved. 'I thought perhaps you'd divined the material by a mere whiff of their scent. I wouldn't put it past you,' he jested, then grew thoughtful. 'Our Adam has been missing these past few days,' he observed.

Libby was quiet as she kept looking toward the pillow, her finger absently tracing the pattern of raised needlework; it was her own handiwork, painstakingly done years before with the aid of her mother's patient teaching. 'Yes,' she said after a moment.

Sebastian studied her, noting the slight tightening of her lips, the composed expression: like many, he might have taken her for younger than her thirty years had he not known better, and were it not for the nearly imperceptible lines around her mouth that became more evident upon closer inspection. Age lines. Laugh lines. Lines of too much experience. His eyes went gentle. 'The luncheon,' he said quietly. 'It wasn't successful?'

She looked toward him dispassionately. 'What's successful, Sebastian?'

'Did you enjoy yourselves?' he asked carefully.

Libby didn't answer immediately; instead, she slid forward on the couch and placed her cup on the coffee table, picking up the spoon to toy with it. 'I can only speak for myself.'

'And?'

'Yes, I enjoyed it.'

Sebastian hated these conversations; however, he'd been dealing with Libby and her handicap for a long time. He wished away the slight tension in her jaw and asked, as he had to, 'You think he didn't?'

She didn't look up. 'I don't really know.'

'There were difficulties?'

She sighed with frustration then and looked toward him. 'Sebastian, there are always difficulties! Don't you know that by now?' she demanded crossly, then bit her bottom lip. 'Sorry,' she said immediately.

He too moved forward on the seat cushion and began dusting the tabletop with a napkin, his expression disapproving. 'Don't speak to me in that tone of voice, as if you're the one at fault! You're perfectly adept at social situations, and I'll hear none of it.'

Libby sighed and brushed back a stray lock of hair. 'Sebastian, my social adeptness doesn't run to being able to alleviate acute embarrassment. No one likes being caught in the act of being ineffectual. Nor do they like finding out that being kind to the reality of me is rather more complicated than it might have seemed.'

Sebastian was unmoved. 'It's not your problem. If the man hasn't the grace to . . .'

'Don't, Sebastian.'

He raised his eyebrows. 'Don't?'

'Let it go.' She sat back again, almost wearily.

'Is this Adam Bainbridge so important?'

She remained quiet again for a time, then answered finally, 'I don't know.'

'Well, he's just been busy,' he rationalized, glancing at her briefly. 'There are things for the man to do. After all, he's not like us, with nothing better to do with our time than while it away in the luxury of the Hunt Club riding ring!' he said facetiously.

Libby took a small breath and looked toward him, forcing a light expression. 'Yes, you're probably right. He's busy,' she agreed without conviction. 'And as for having nothing better to do than idle away time, you may not, professor, but I do, and I've got to get myself organized for tomorrow's workday.

61

Besides, I'm tired. Mind?' She tilted her head, smiling apologetically.

He understood. 'No no! Of course I don't mind. Go on, I'll clean up.'

'No, Sebastian. You don't have to . . .'

'Rightly so,' he concurred. 'But I want to. Go tend to things. I'll secure the fort on my way out,' he insisted and rose with her. She looked as though she were about to protest again, then gave in as he gently guided her around the table, his hands on the backs of her shoulders. 'Go!'

'Thanks.' She hesitated briefly at the edge of the hallway, then disappeared into it, listening, as she went, to the sound of him clearing away their dishes.

In the bedroom she could still hear the muffled strains of his housekeeping. She crossed to the windows and drew the draperies; it was too early, actually, but this was part of the routine. She lived by routine, lest she forget things eyesight would've reminded her of, and the draperies had become part of the routine when she'd added the automatic flipping on of light switches to her habits; it saved disconcerted guests who found themselves sheathed in her familiar darkness from inquiring in embarrassment about the lights. She straightened the fabric of the hangings, then moved over to the mahogany dressing table that had been hers as a child and sat down.

She had meant to address herself to the removal of the scant makeup a cosmetician had patiently taught her to apply, but instead sat pensively, her hands resting on the tabletop. They were graceful hands, with long slender fingers, and after a time they began to move unconsciously across the objects resting there, finding and fingering the small collection of cut-glass perfume bottles grouped in one corner. She knew they were blue and green and red; they'd belonged to her mother, and Winna hadn't wanted them when the contents of the old farmhouse had been broken up four years before. Actually, Winna hadn't wanted any of it; too hard on her emotions, Libby thought gently. She was still the same shy, vulnerable Winna despite her outgoing adult veneer; Libby knew that's all it was, a facade, and that her seeming indifference to the things in the old house had actually been a mask for the hurt of suddenly having to put her childhood so visibly behind her. Libby understood; she'd felt the same way, only, as always, she'd been able to handle it better emotionally, had needed some of the keepsakes for her memories and hadn't had the difficulty Winna did in taking them. Unbeknownst to Winna, she'd put some things in a box for her, too, and stored them in a closet in the spare bedroom; she knew Winna would want them someday, and when that time came, Libby would have them for her. It made her smile; still the same old Libby: there to protect. They'd probably call it maternalism, at this stage of the game, she thought with a wry smile, and considered how quickly the years had gone by. Difficult years, but good ones, nonetheless, years of loss and gain, heartache and laughter, years she and Winna had passed together, bonded by their sisterhood, by the reciprocal affection Libby cherished, and the adversity they'd shared. Libby's hand moved on, across the metal braille template and carved-handled stylus, the gold necklace, odd makeup containers, a change purse, until finally it arrived at the small child's stuffed toy nodding up against the window sill. She picked it up, brushing it softly against the side of her face.

It was another memento of childhood, its soft caress across her cheek bringing to mind this time her father, who'd given the woolly lion with yarnball body and head to his young daughter when she was eight; he'd been so pleased with her delight, as always, and she'd been ecstatic with his return from the long trip and with the little gift. That had been the way between them, and she remembered the incident vividly, enough so that she'd preserved the small toy as a helpmate in bringing him close again every now and then. The fuzzy head she knew to be yellow and white drooped sadly now, she could feel, the victim of the passage of time and the wear of repeated handling as Libby sought to remember, and after a time, she put him back in his spot near the window, frowning slightly for the bittersweet melancholy she'd allowed to drift down over her.

'Libby!' Sebastian called. 'I'm on m'way!'

' 'Bye,' she called back and listened as his key shot the bolt on the outer door.

The sound of his voice effectively cleared away the mists of another life and carried her back to the new one, bringing to mind in particular his remarks about Adam Bainbridge. He'd wanted to know, in his unprying concern, whether Adam was important, and she considered the question as she sat there; it tapped at so many doors.

The consequences of her accident had not prevented her from growing to maturity; she'd been robbed only of sight, not of womanly emotions. The need for love, male companionship, intimacy—they were all there, in the proper place. Two men in her adult life had gotten close enough to understand that, briefly. They might not have filled the deeper needs, but they'd let her taste her womanhood, let her learn the feel of a man's hard body lying next to hers, sharing hers, had introduced her to intimacy and the pleasures of lovemaking that she, in her natural capacity for sensuality, could openly enjoy. Thank you, gentlemen, for that at least, she thought dryly. And there had been others, too, over the years, but, like Adam Bainbridge, they had not lasted even the first round. Nearly a week had elapsed since her luncheon with Adam, and she hadn't seen or heard from him at all; to her knowledge, he had not even been to the club. It could hurt, if she let it, the inability of these men to see her as she saw herself: like any other woman, only confronting life on a different plane. But fortunately, unlike so many of the other hurts, it wasn't a constant; it only ached when touched directly, as when an interesting, appealing man flashed in and out of her life. No, Sebastian, she answered silently, it's not Adam that's so important really. It's just the fact of him. 'You remind me of a man caught up in a revolving door,' she told Adam aloud by way of dismissal, then sat for a moment expanding on the picture in her mind, beginning to smile with the wry sort of humor that had been her salvation all along.

She roused herself finally and tended to her business. After three-quarters of an hour, she was redressed and comfortable, her tired body wrapped in a soft chenille dressing gown belted loosely around her waist. Barefoot, she collected a book from the stack of reading material on her bedside table—among them Browning's love poems, an Agatha Christie, yesterday's *Washington Post*—remembered to flip off the light switch, and padded to the living room, depositing the book on a couch as she passed by toward the kitchen. It took a few minutes to pour out a mild drink and return to the sofa, but finally she was settled with her legs stretched along the cushions, and she picked up the book, written, like the others on the night stand, all in a pattern of raised impressions. It was a fairy tale about a little girl who followed a string, and tomorrow she'd be reading it to a dozen young children whose adventures into the land of hope were on the string of Libby's voice.

Adam sat back against the leather captain's chair in the club lounge and tossed his cards on the table. The air in the room was thick with stale tobacco smoke, the atmosphere dim and masculine, and he picked up his whiskey glass, draining the contents. 'Fold,' he said indifferently.

Four ascotted, wealthy businessmen seated around the table glanced at him briefly, then looked back with interest at the cards in their hands. 'I'm in,' Christian Bainbridge assured and played out the hand, pulling his winnings to him when the last cards were turned up.

His tanned face a study in shadows under the low-hanging Tiffany lamp, Adam ran a hand through his hair and picked up the glass again to stare into its emptiness as if it held far more interest than anything around him. The stakes were proportionate to the wallets at the table, and after a moment Christian flipped several chips in his direction.

'What's that for?' Adam asked, glancing up.

'Repayment of debts.' Christian's tone was very much like everything else about him: smooth, manicured, artificial.

Adam studied him briefly, one eyebrow slightly arched, then gathered up the chips wordlessly and dropped them in front of him. A waiter passed, and he signaled, holding up his empty glass in comment.

'You in?' Christian asked as he began reshuffling.

'No. Deal me out.'

Christian's smile was rakish. 'Suit yourself. You're losing anyway.' He expertly cut and flipped the cards back into one deck, pulling briefly at the turtleneck collar at his neck, then glanced again at Adam and said, 'I ran into Genny the other day. She was inquiring about you. Said she hadn't seen you in awhile. On the outs?'

Adam looked over with detachment. 'Meaning?'

'I thought you had a thing for the lady.'

Adam accepted the drink from the waiter, briefly smiling his thanks. He turned back to Christian and eyed him over the top of the glass. 'You thought wrong.'

Christian's smile was casual. 'So you won't mind if I give her a call?'

'I don't give a damn what you do, or her either.'

Christian raised thin eyebrows, leaning back to run a hand through his blue-black hair. Except for his dark hair, he looked very unlike his brother; he was slightly built, his eyes were brown, and his features, although handsome, had little of Adam's virile strength. 'What's with you, anyway?' he asked, frowning mildly. He didn't particularly care; they stayed clear of each other unless accidentally thrown together. But he was prompted to ask the question because Adam seemed more out of sorts than usual. And he was drinking heavily. A light dawned suddenly, and Christian smiled slowly. 'Ah! Had another discussion, didn't you? I hear you were down for dinner while I was gone.'

Adam was in no mood to fence. 'It's none of your business what I did or didn't do when I was there. And show a little less disdain. If it weren't for me, they'd have tossed you out on your ear a long time ago.'

'Not on your life,' Christian laughed pleasantly. 'What would they do without me, the dutiful, loving son who stays at home? They're lucky they see you once a year. Better look out, they just might write you out of the will.' He picked up his own drink and watched Adam with a crooked grin.

Adam let out a short laugh. 'You'd like that, wouldn't you? Well, forget it. I may be no prize, but at least I wouldn't wipe the precious Bainbridge fortune off the face of the earth in one poker game.'

'You're an unpleasant bastard.'

'Yep,' Adam said mildly and upended his glass.

Christian began to deal again, flipping the cards in place with a precision born of long experience. He kept his eyes on his hands, his tone casual as he asked, 'You talk to Father about the money?' He seemed indifferent to the interested looks their conversation was inspiring around the table.

Adam set down his glass. 'I told you, it's none of your business, but since you're trying so unsuccessfully to hide your avarice, yes. I talked to him. And I told him to keep your dole just as it's always been. And I was kind enough not to mention the loans I made to you. Keep that in mind. I'll expect the favor returned sometime.'

'Favor? Jesus, how do you expect me to . . . ?' Christian began with a frown, his polish chipping away slightly.

'Live on your modest allowance?' Adam finished with a wry half smile that held no humor. 'That's your problem. It'd only keep the people in China fat and happy for the next two decades.'

Christian was now uncomfortably conscious of the interested looks, the speculative glances at his winnings. 'Forget it,' he mumbled.

'I intend to,' Adam returned easily. Actually, if he didn't dislike Christian's basic personality so much, he might have felt slightly sorry for him at the moment. He wore the look of an unstaked gambler suddenly found out. And Adam had indeed talked to his father about Christian's request for a larger stipend; although there was little love lost between the brothers, he felt some responsibility to protect the family from Christian's extravagance. His own life style had always been one of optimum comfort, but it didn't have the same quality of intemperance—except in some respects, he thought moodily as he glanced at the near-empty whiskey glass; it suddenly seemed so ugly, and so useless, the shallow glass ringed at the bottom by a small puddle of amber liquid. And as irrelevant as everything else I've ever done, he thought with strange bitterness.

'Ante up,' was called, and Adam absently watched the game progress, his attention drifting between it and the luxuriant red leather-cushioned bar across the room. It was crowded with drinkers, some on stools, some leaning up against the edge, and the wave of a female hand caught his eye. He nodded to it, then dropped his eyes; that affair had been even briefer than the one with Genevieve. He thought about her for a moment, the golden Genevieve with the golden hair and golden body, molded to please a man, her every gesture and attitude calculated to excite —and nearly as shallow as that puddle in the bottom of the glass. Poor Genevieve in her designer clothes and Gucci shoes, the sad, sorry, jilted woman who had struck out so poisonously at the man she'd once claimed to love. He remembered the remark; she'd aimed where no arrow could pierce. He might not have done much, he thought, but he'd done the women, and he derisively raised his empty glass in salute to his single claim to distinction.

'Another, Mr. Bainbridge?' the waiter inquired mildly.

Adam started and had the grace to glance up almost sheepishly. 'No, thank you. I think I've emptied my quota of liquor bottles for one night.' He looked around at his companions; the poker hand had been played out, and the conversation was familiar: old men talking about young women. Their jibes and leers seemed particularly distasteful at the moment, and he began to have thoughts of leaving.

'Yeah, and how about that broad with the old man?' one roué was remarking just as Adam began to push back his chair. 'The one perched up on Matt's glue factory reject? Gives you a real laugh, doesn't it?'

'Who?' someone asked.

'The redhead,' another supplied. 'Auburn, I think they like to call it. They come all the time, the two of them. Pay a fortune so she can ride up and down along the fence. Huh! She can barely sit the nag!' There was a chorus of laughter.

'Someone said she was blind,' another man remarked.

'Blind?' the voices echoed.

Christian laughed laconically and cut the deck again. 'Jesus, why doesn't the poor broad get wise?'

The table literally shook and a glass fell over as Adam's fist slammed down onto it, and the group of men stared at him in stunned silence. He was on his feet, towering over the table, his clenched fist remaining where it had hit, and his blue eyes were like ice as they made a slow circuit of the startled faces and finally came to rest on Christian. 'You should be so wise, you stupid bastard, and then maybe you wouldn't sound like such a jackass every time you open your mouth,' he spat and kicked back his chair, striding around it and across the room toward the door.

'What's with him?' someone inquired, twisting around to watch Adam's exit.

'He's drunk,' Christian said dismissively, and began to deal the cards.

A loud bell rang stridently out in the corridor, signaling the end of class, and twelve voices raised in anxious chatter pierced the relative quiet of the small schoolroom.

'Just a minute!' Libby objected into the confusion of scuffling feet and the buzz of voices. She momentarily stilled the noise. 'Tomorrow we're going to finish our reading, and then we'll talk about the whole story, so if you haven't understood something so far, think about it tonight and get your questions in order, okay?' She smiled inquiringly out toward the row of metal school desks.

'Yes, Miss Rutledge,' the twelve dutiful voices chorused.

'All right. Now wait for Mrs. Coolidge.'

The sighted aide had entered by that time, along with a man who stepped off to the side of the doorway to watch in silence. 'I'm here, Miss Rutledge,' the aide said to Libby.

Libby glanced briefly in her direction. 'Good. Okay, everyone. Stand up and take the hand of the person next to you. Got it? Jennifer, do you have Mrs. Coolidge's hand?' A small voice piped up affirmatively, and the aide took her cue.

'All lined up and ready to go,' she said.

'Good. Class dismissed, and I'll see you all tomorrow. Jeff, don't let me hear later that you were teasing anyone at recess,' she warned good-naturedly.

'No, ma'am,' the boy answered on his way by.

'Have fun,' she said then and listened to the sounds of twelve small pairs of feet filing out of the room.

She remained seated after the children had gone, clearing the top of her large teacher's desk at the front of the room. It was a modern schoolroom, much like any other except for its uncommon teaching aides; it was clean, fresh, and windowed along both one interior and one exterior wall. Libby worked rapidly, anxious to get on with the afternoon; there'd be the pleasant congregation of her colleagues in the teachers' lounge until the taxi came to pick her up, the quiet time at home spent in unwinding from her day's activities, then the workout at the club, if Sebastian were willing. Which he would be, of course; he knew that this grasping for the remembered elation of being on horseback overrode everything else at the moment. She stopped what she was doing and thought about it again, the fingers of one hand absently toying with the lapel of her chartreuse dress. It could be done, she knew it could; it was only a matter of relearning balance, of firming up her seat in the saddle again, adjusting to the feel of the motion, and then she'd have it: the freedom, if only for a matter of an hour. It was a heady thought, and she only regretted having voiced it so blithely to Adam Bainbridge. It wasn't her habit to confide that sort of thing to others; this was her world, as she'd accepted it, with only this last adjustment to make, and she didn't know what had prompted her to let that man see into it. Well, it was of no consequence, anyway; she'd never see him again. She stacked her materials together and leaned down to take hold of her briefcase, then sat bolt upright again when a masculine voice broke into the silence.

'Libby?' Adam said.

She recognized the deep voice instantly, but made no show of it. She listened as his footsteps approached, then finally responded with detachment when she felt him standing by her desk. 'Yes?'

He watched her quietly for a moment, looking at the thick hair falling loosely around her shoulders, at the glasses resting on her fine cheekbones, the unreadable expression on her face. 'It's Adam.'

She busied herself again with putting her teaching materials into the briefcase. 'Hello, Adam.'

He found himself at a momentary loss for words, then shook off the discomfiture, smiling down at her. 'You're a marvelous teacher.'

She raised her eyebrows. 'Oh? How do you know that? In fact, how did you find out I work here in the first place?' She went on with her task, very businesslike, her hands brushing him off by their refusal to be still.

'Matt told me. And as to your first question, I was watching you from the other side of the glass.'

'I see,' she said, her mouth tightening slightly. Yes, you're good at that, she thought. Watching. Keeping your distance. I shouldn't blame you so much, but I do. She didn't verbalize those thoughts but spoke frankly nevertheless. 'Do you find my incapacities so fascinating? If so, then you've come to the right place. Now you've got twelve of us—no, excuse me, thirteen —to ogle at.'

He let out a breath, thrusting his hands in the pockets of his suit trousers. 'I deserve that, I know,' he said quietly.

She had too much experience with rejection to be thrown very far off balance by his acceptance of her rebuke, but she did stop what she was doing long enough to look momentarily toward the sound of his voice, her expression pensive. She didn't speak, however, and when she returned to what she'd been doing, Adam stilled the motion of her hands by placing one of his on her arm; she drew it away immediately.

He looked at her calmly. 'I know I should've called you.'

'It wasn't necessary.'

'Don't be so matter of fact. It doesn't fit the situation.'

She laughed more harshly than she wanted to. 'Fit the situation? My dear Adam, fitting does not apply to my situations. They can't be categorized, so there are no rules. They just are what they are. And kindly don't burden us both with a painful apology. I've grown accustomed to their absence,' she said with a deep frown and despised him for causing her to make that admission. Dammit, he didn't matter; her life was a good one. She needn't be so acutely aware of its present incompleteness simply because he was there; other men would come along, she knew, then sighed suddenly. Enough time hadn't gone by, that was all. Another week or so, and it wouldn't have mattered one way or the other about Adam Bainbridge. If only he'd waited, so that the process of helping him justify his withdrawal didn't have to be such a trial. 'Forget it, Adam,' she said angrily.

'No, I won't. I want to talk to you.' He sat down on the edge of the desk, watching her intently.

'There isn't anything to say.'

'There's a lot to say, and I'd like to say it over dinner.'

She looked toward him briefly in disbelief, then frowned. 'No,' she said flatly.

'I deserve that, too, but I don't intend to accept it.'

'You have no choice.' Her attitude was authoritative, unrelenting.

He studied her thoughtfully for a moment. As he'd already learned, artful maneuvering would get him nowhere with this woman; he opted finally for her own approach. 'I know you think I was put off by our luncheon, by the fact that you're blind. You're right. It shook me up, but not in the way you think.'

She was listening; she'd finished inserting her teaching materials into the briefcase and snapped the locks, setting it on the floor before swinging her legs around so she could stand up beside the desk. She didn't look once in his direction, but she was listening. That was why she didn't move away. 'How do you know what I think?'

He smiled wryly at that, his blue eyes light as they moved briefly down her slim figure standing not far from him; she looked particularly good in green, and in a dress that was softly molded to the lines of her body. 'Because I know what I would've thought, what anyone would reasonably think. And because of the chilly reception I'm getting right now. You may be a bit unusual in some respects, but you're a woman, and you've got that marvelous capacity of making me feel like the bigger boor for having the temerity to ask you out to dinner after the way I've handled things. You don't need the gift of sight to make me understand exactly how many degrees of heel you think I am for simply dropping out of your life like that.'

She bit back the unwanted smile, looking toward him. 'And just how many degrees do you think that is?'

'Somewhere very far on the minus side, whatever it is,' he parried, beginning to smile more widely as he watched the edges of her mouth quiver.

She sat back down, slowly, and looked toward him with studied interest. 'Why were you shaken by our luncheon?' she asked bluntly.

'Have dinner with me, and I'll tell you.'

'You can tell me now.'

'I could, but I don't want to. It's not the sort of thing that goes well with such an academic atmosphere. It requires someplace a little more comfortable, a little more forgiving.'

Of course. She'd been right all along, she realized, and her expression went cold again. 'Why? To make what you've got to say that much more palatable? No, Adam, I don't think so . . .'

Suddenly he became angry at both of them. At himself for his constant inability to deal with her. At her for the barriers she'd erected. She'd managed to disconcert him more than any other person ever had, had brought him face to face with things about himself he wasn't sure he wanted to own up to, and here she was not even giving him a chance to explain.

71

'Dammit, Libby! Has your handicap made you so insensitive to the failings of others? Have you forgotten that we're all human and unfortunately act that way a lot of the time? I . . .'

'Don't you dare preach to me!' She stood up and faced him rigidly, her body tensed in anger. 'No, I'm not insensitive to the failings of others. And God knows they're rampant around me! No, it's just that I've been the object of all those weaknesses too many times. I'm afraid my own need for self-preservation overrides my need to help everyone else cope with their own inadequacies. I'm sorry you found my "handicap" so difficult to deal with. I forgive you. There, that should help a bit,' she said coldly. 'Now, excuse me. I have things to do.'

She picked up her purse and reached inside, withdrawing the collapsible cane. She deftly stretched it out to its full length, put her purse over her shoulder, then reached down and picked up her briefcase. Adam quickly rose and stepped in front of her, putting both hands on her arms. 'I'm sorry. I had no right to say that.'

'No, you didn't. Goodbye, Adam.'

'There's nothing I can say?' His eyes searched her face, looking for some sign of capitulation.

There was none. 'Nothing,' she confirmed, moving away, and he watched her walk to the door, her cane sweeping across the floor in front of her, searching for unexpected obstacles.

'Not even that I find you the most remarkable woman I've ever met and that what I can't deal with is that I don't come anywhere near to measuring up to you as a person?' His face was shadowed, tense.

She stopped in the doorway but didn't turn around when she answered. 'That's a stupid thing to say.'

He looked at her motionless back. 'It was a compliment. And painfully true.'

'In whose eyes?'

'In mine.'

'I'm sorry for you then.'

She still hadn't turned; he studied her for another moment, then answered. 'Thanks a lot, but that's not exactly the kind of emotion I like to inspire in people. Especially you. In the words of a woman I once had lunch with, "Oh God, if I've made you feel sorry for me, I'm leaving." '

Libby's silence was unreadable, stretching Adam's tension nearly to the breaking point before she finally answered. 'I'm sure you can flounce out of a room far more effectively than I can.'

His shoulders relaxed, and relief tugged at one corner of his mouth. 'Where do you want to have dinner?'

'What did you have in mind?'

'A very nice French restaurant I know.'

She wouldn't let him off that easily, and besides, neither of them needed that kind of added tension. She still spoke from over her shoulder. 'No. French restaurants are filled to the brim with divine crystalware for you to demolish. Come to my apartment. You won't have to cope then with my not knowing my way around, and I won't have to cope with your embarrassment. And anyway,' she relented. 'I'm rather a good cook. Shall I give you the address?'

'I already know it.'

Her hesitation was infinitesimal. 'Then come at eight,' she said finally and walked out of the room.

# Chapter 5

Adam stepped into Libby's apartment precisely at eight o'clock and was overwhelmed by the richness of color there. It was unexpected, such bold use of complementary blue and orange, with a tasteful integration of pattern and texture, and he glanced around at the sofas, wing chairs, and double-draped sliding glass doors before looking back finally at Libby with a measure of renewed surprise. She was in flattering blue herself: a patterned hostess gown that flowed around her feet and was belted at the waist with a navy satin sash. She secured the door behind him and turned with hands clasped loosely in front of her. 'Good evening, Mr. Bainbridge,' she said with a light smile.

'Good evening, Miss Rutledge.' He appraised her appreciatively a moment longer, then took her hand and gently rested a bouquet against her fingers. 'I've brought you flowers, in the hope that they might assuage to some degree the bad taste my past indiscretions have left with you.'

She laughed in surprise and brought the flowers to her face. 'Hmmm, how nice. Carnations. What color?'

'White. And blue around the edges.'

'Perfect,' she remarked and turned, going to the kitchen where she unerringly arranged them in a vase. It took a moment, and when she'd set the arrangement on the near countertop, she looked in his direction. 'How's that?'

'Exquisite.' He was smiling as he came over, and he stopped on the far side of the counter.

'Good. What would you like to drink?'

'Bourbon and water, but please. Let me.' He strode around the counter then, joining her in the narrow kitchen.

'No,' she dismissed with a wave of her hand and moved away from him to a corner of the inner counter where she ran her hands lightly over several cut-glass decanters grouped there. She selected one and poured and mixed his drink, turning when she'd

74

finished to hand it to him. She leaned back against the counter, feeling for her own glass nearby as she waited for his comment. 'All right?' She tilted her head, smiling inquiringly.

He was watching her with a quiet half smile. 'Fine. And may I be so gauche as to inquire how you do that?'

'Not at all, and there's nothing especially tricky about it. Every decanter has a different shape and cut-glass design, as you can see.' She turned slightly, gesturing toward the glassware. 'The bourbon is round, the scotch is square, and the rye is shaped like a pear. It's easy. But if for some reason I can't distinguish the shapes, I check the patterns on the glass. One is a bay leaf, one is an emblem, and one is an overall design. And, of course, when all else fails, I smell it.' She grinned, taking a small sip from her glass.

He stood with one hand in his trouser pocket, absently jingling the change there, and shook his head. 'Remarkable.'

She pushed herself away from the counter then. 'No, as I said, it's not. Just practical. Here, let's go in and sit down.' She led the way, going into the living room to settle herself on one end of the couch. He took the opposite corner. 'We'll eat in about an hour, if that's all right,' she said.

'That's fine,' he said absently, his eyes roaming the room again. Most of the wood grain in the furnishings was cherry, uncluttered except for a carefully placed object here and there. A grouping of framed snapshots was arranged on one level of a tall étagère that stood against one wall, along with odd mementos, a thriving fern plant, and various leatherbound books. She was a reader, he noted to himself, then looked at her, mentally correlating the appealing room to the woman; they were in perfect harmony. 'You have a lovely apartment,' he commented.

She smiled and shifted more comfortably against the arm of the couch. 'Thank you. It's taken me a long time to get everything just exactly as I wanted it. I'm very comfortable here now and would hate to have to move and start all over again.' She hoped she could keep the small talk flowing for awhile. Anything of more consequence could come later; at the moment, they needed to regain their footing. It seemed to her he was of the same opinion, when he spoke again.

'Did Sebastian help you set all of this up?' The brief motion of his head encompassed the whole room, and he looked at her curiously over the rim of his glass.

'No, not really. Mother was responsible for a great deal of it. I've been here for a long time, and little by little, I collected everything. Got it all arranged to my liking. At first Sebastian would bring me little gifts, dainty, delicate porcelain things. I finally put them away, before he could break them all.' Her smile was engaging, and it prompted Adam to set his glass down and speak abruptly.

'I meant what I said earlier today, about your being remarkable.' The light tone was gone, and he looked at her steadily.

She wasn't ready for it just yet and brushed involuntarily at her hair. 'Would you like another drink?' she asked quickly.

He was mildly surprised, then glanced at his nearly full glass and laughed. 'I've been accused of drinking too much upon occasion, but I'm not quite hopeless yet. No, not right now, thanks, and besides, don't worry about it. When I do want one, I'll get my own.'

She smiled self-consciously. 'Sorry, and I did mean to tell you that. The first one's always on me. After that, you're on your own.'

'Fine,' he said with some impatience, then stretched his arm along the back of the couch. 'Libby, I want to talk to you seriously. We could go on and on like this, chitchatting, and I'd eventually wind my way around to the subject by some artful verbal two-stepping. I'm quite good at that, in my way,' he added dryly. 'However, it's not the way I want to deal with this, or you, and frankly, I don't think you'd accept it.'

Well put, she thought and shifted again, smoothing her skirt. He was right; it wasn't her way either. No, her habit was to run head on into these things—the direct approach, so that potential wounds were neutralized even before they could be inflicted, or were avoided altogether. So why did Adam Bainbridge, whom she had come close to despising, suddenly make her want to skirt the issue, to play the little game? In the long run, it wasn't easier; she'd found that out. It only delayed the inevitable recognition that the barriers were too high to overcome. 'All right,' she said slowly, setting her own glass down on the table beside her. 'Have your say.' But my God, Libby, she thought. To leave it wide open like that. She usually orchestrated these things.

Now he seemed uncomfortable with her go ahead; his abrupt movement across from her on the couch told her that. 'I apologize for dropping out of sight like that, with the implication that I wanted no part of you.'

Ouch. 'You're forgiven. I told you that before,' she said quietly, looking down toward her hands.

His rugged face lit with a brief smile. 'With no sincerity whatsoever. That's what you thought, isn't it?' he pressed.

She raised her head as she picked up her glass again, sidestepping adroitly. 'What I thought doesn't matter at this point. I'm assuming you're in the process of explaining . . . things, so please. Go on.'

He studied her composed face and tugged briefly at the knot in his tie, half hidden under the light cashmere sweater. It was too late in the year for the layered clothing he wore: sports coat, sweater, white shirt, worsted slacks; he knew that, but it was the look he'd wanted. It suddenly struck him as ironic that his calculated appearance should go so unappreciated, and he smiled briefly at himself. She remained quietly waiting for him to go on, and he noted that her wine glass was empty; it suggested a momentary diversion that he welcomed. 'Your glass is empty. Like some more?' At her nod, he rose and attended to the small matter, refilling his own drink at the same time, then finally sat down and looked directly at her. 'You know, you've got the capacity to make people uncomfortable with themselves.'

'I know that far better than you ever will.'

She'd misunderstood again, and he went on quickly. 'Uncomfortable because of the fact that you've accomplished so much despite the odds against you. Since it appears you don't intend to help me out at all,' he added, 'I guess you'll have to sit by and listen to me hypothesize about your feelings.' He raised his hand in objection when she looked as though she were about to speak, then immediately remembered to vocalize his gesture. 'No. Don't say anything. Let's go ahead and do this my way.' He stopped for a moment, marshaling the words; explaining himself was not something he did often, or with ease. 'I believe you thought I couldn't cope with you, that I, like probably dozens of other people you've run up against, don't have the strength of character to withstand your making me feel like a fool. I know I tried too hard to be helpful and botched it—I sat around dissecting every sentence before I uttered it in fear I'd say something I shouldn't. And I did do those things. And I felt like a fool, you're right. That's hard to take, I admit it. But my character doesn't happen to be that weak, despite what you may think. It didn't put me off. It simply made me feel like a fool, period. I'll get over it. I already have. That is, until the next time I do something stupid, and then I hope we'll both laugh at it, the way we did at least once that I can think of.'

He paused. That had been the easy part; the rest was more complex. He wasn't anxious to elaborate upon his inadequacies, imagined or otherwise, especially to a relative stranger, and more especially when he wasn't certain just what they were. However, he stood ready to waltz with the subject now for the sake of propping this relationship back up on its feet. It was important, and he needed to make her understand.

Libby took the opportunity of his brief silence to acknowledge his supposition. 'Yes, you're right. That's exactly how I thought you were reacting.'

'I know.'

She smiled then. 'And since you were so kind as to be honest with me, I will be, too. I'm glad you don't feel that way.'

'I wasn't being kind. Just honest. I'm glad we've cleared the air.' He lit a cigarette, pocketing the gold lighter as he sat forward slightly, then relaxed again, studying the end of his cigarette for a moment before getting on with it. 'And now, to the reason why I took so long to see you again.'

Libby understood his hesitation; his inference had been patently clear, and she knew that to delve too deeply too quickly was dangerous. It was with her; it would be with him, too. 'Adam, you needn't elaborate, at least not now. You've told me what I . . . needed to hear. I think we ought to let it go for the time being.' She smiled warmly, tilting her head.

He studied her thoughtfully, one eyebrow slightly arched. 'Well, let's just say that I've been absorbed in examining the rather startling contrast between your life and mine. That was about the only thing I was trying to deal with. Not you. Me. And perhaps how I could go about asking you to let me in on the secret of your world and its success.' he tossed in.

The remark took her by surprise, and she laughed involuntarily. 'Now, that's funny! And here I've spent all this time trying to figure out how to have some small success in the other world!'

Her continued laughter brought a smile to his face and relieved all but the most masculine of his emotions as he watched her from across the couch. When they'd first met he'd found her unusually attractive. Now he decided she was really very beautiful, especially when she smiled; it lit up her face, dimpled her cheeks, was more engaging than any smile he'd ever encountered. He looked from her face down to her figure, slim and soft and womanly; it was an effort to draw his eyes away, but he did when her laughter subsided and she sat bolt upright.

'My God, dinner! Adam, is it just me or do you smell something burning?'

He glanced uncertainly over his shoulder toward the kitchen and frowned. 'No, I can't say that I do.'

'Well, I'd better get into the kitchen or else you'll have to spring for a pizza.' She rose, tossing him a teasing smile.

'Need help?'

She was already halfway across the room and waved a hand in his direction. 'I told you once. There's to be none of that sort of thing unless I ask. Now, be like any other man. Relax and let yourself be waited on.'

With a smile of genuine amusement, he watched her go, then did as he was told. Rising, he browsed through the room, and stopped for a long time at the tall unit of shelves, studying the snapshots there. There was an old one: two nice-looking adults, two nice-looking children, age somewhere near five or six. A pretty family, with two little girls as different in appearance as night and day, one auburn-haired—Libby, of course—one with silver-blond hair. Edwinna. He moved on to a more recent shot of Jocelyn and Trevor Rutledge, taken, he suspected, sometime shortly before they'd died, probably on some sort of vacation, for it had the glossy, artificial look of a cruise lounge photo. Next to it was Edwinna again, a full-fledged adult and stunning, her silver hair long and snaking seductively along one shoulder, her almond eyes sultry as they turned half-lidded toward the photographer. He studied it for a long time, moving on finally to the last picture. It was Libby, taken possibly last year, for her face had maturity, and he picked it up, walking with it to where she was setting the table in the dining area adjacent to the kitchen.

'You're awfully quiet,' she remarked, tossing him a smile as she laid out the silverware.

'I'm snooping,' he said lightly. 'I like this picture of you. It looks recent.'

'Oh.' She straightened, looking thoughtfully down toward the table. 'Adam, before I forget. Would you light the candles on the table after a bit?'

He glanced at the silver candlesticks in the center of the white linen tablecloth, then back at her. 'Of course. Who took it?' he pressed.

Libby frowned in puzzlement. 'Took what?'

'The picture.'

'Oh! Sebastian.' She smiled indulgently. 'He's funny, you know. He just hated that there wasn't a recent one of me there. I told him it didn't matter, I'd never know the difference, but he'd have none of it. So he marched me downstairs out onto the lawn and fiddled and fiddled and posed me till I thought I'd scream. Finally, he was ready. I pasted on the smile, then I heard him mumbling.' She was laughing by that time. 'Let me warn you now. Look out when he starts to mumble, because you know something's wrong! Anyway, seems he'd forgotten to take the lens cover off the camera. I could've throttled him! So, we started all over again.' She sighed heavily, remembering the ordeal.

He looked from her to the picture. 'Well, I agree with Sebastian. It should be there.'

She shrugged. 'I suppose. It doesn't really matter to me. I only keep the others there because it's sort of the thing to do. And I've often wondered how that picture turned out anyway.'

He smiled slowly. 'It's good. Very good. It captures your smile.'

She gave it to him then, in person, and it prompted him to ask the question very much on his mind, not that he knew quite how to couch it. 'Libby, how does a . . . how do you go about forming a picture of someone in your mind?'

She sighed. 'Adam, you've got to stop dodging the word. Blind. Please, use it where it's appropriate,' she told him mildly. 'And as to your question, there are a lot of ways. I've already told you it's fairly easy to get a general impression of someone. Well, the rest is mostly imagination, although it can be helped along a bit.' Unlike him, she was unconcerned with the question, as she was with everything else at the moment; his company was very comfortable. She walked back into the kitchen, returning after a moment with several serving dishes, aware that Adam hadn't moved. 'Why do you ask?' she said when he remained silent.

'Pictures, I guess,' he answered with a shrug. 'I was standing there looking at those images. And it made me wonder about the images you have in your mind. Of different people. Of yourself. How do you view yourself?' He looked at her thoughtfully. How unfortunate she couldn't appreciate her own beauty.

She smiled a little. 'Oh, in no particular way,' she said. 'I don't think about it much.' Well, it wasn't a lie, really; just not an absolute truth.

'All right, then. What about other people? I'm interested. How exactly do you go about forming a more detailed opinion of what someone looks like?'

He obviously wasn't going to let it rest. She clasped her hands in front of her then and began to explain. 'Well, I listen. Voices tell you a lot. Height comes with proximity, as I mentioned before. Physique with body movement. I get a general outline of someone, then I conjure up a face for it, with a lot of imagination and sometimes a bit of assistance from the hands. Hands are very useful things when you're blind. If you can feel it, you can see it, you know.'

'Meaning?' he pressed.

'Here. Like this.' They were standing close together, and she reached up, touching first the collar of his shirt and sweater, then moving on up to his face, touching it lightly with both hands, the flat of her fingertips passing across his cheekbones, down to his chin line, one hand remaining there while the other traveled up to his forehead before running lightly down the bridge of his nose, all with whisper softness. It was an experience beyond his imagination to be touched so sensually, as if in loving caress yet without the emotion behind it, and then to be expected to withstand it all stoically, as though every nerve in his body hadn't just been activated. He wasn't entirely successful; he put his hands involuntarily on her waist, gently drawing her closer. She let her hands linger briefly on his face, then abruptly removed them, taking a step backward. 'You have very strong features,' she said, smiling self-consciously.

He didn't move. 'So now you've got a picture of me in your mind.' He wanted to run his hand along her cheek, to touch her the way she'd touched him.

She pressed her lips together before forcing herself to look up toward him composedly. 'Yes.'

'What is it?'

She needed to pass it off and laughed slightly. 'You see yourself in the mirror every day.'

'I want to know how you see me.'

She took the offensive then, smiling away her discomfiture; after all, she might as well be honest. 'I think you must be a very attractive man. Clean-cut features always are. What is your coloring?' She looked at him with studied interest.

The obvious hedge broke the spell, and he laughed. 'Oh no! I asked for your picture.'

'All right,' she relented and began to rattle off a description. 'Straight, narrow nose, angular jaw, clean-shaven, no mustache, although it would probably suit you well, and blue-gray eyes. I give you, let's see, blond hair. You're tall and fit. Well dressed, but really, Adam, it's too warm for a cashmere sweater. Now, how did I do? What color are your eyes, really?'

He was smiling quietly, his voice lower as he answered. 'I don't intend to say how you did or didn't do. If that's how I look

81

to you, that's how I look. Someday I'll do the same for you,' he added enigmatically.

It renewed the tension between them, and Libby smiled quickly. Turning, she said over her shoulder, 'Better light the candles. Dinner's almost ready.'

He watched her for a moment longer, then became aware of the picture in his hand. He returned it to the shelf, setting it back in its place next to Edwinna's, and had the candles lit by the time she re-entered with dinner. He let her direct the meal, as she wanted, and when she'd served their after-dinner coffee, he settled back in his chair and grinned. 'I hope you noticed that I didn't knock one thing out of place tonight.'

She laughed as she dropped one cube of sugar into her coffee. 'I noticed, but actually, I didn't expect you to.'

'Thank God. I've managed to restore the lady's faith in me,' he said drolly.

She simply smiled and sat quietly as she sipped her coffee. She listened to the sounds of his spoon clinking against the porcelain cup, wondering what he was thinking, and thought perhaps he was watching her, for the quality of his silence was pensive. She was about to say something when he spoke.

'Libby, how were you blinded?'

She'd known it would be asked eventually. It had to be, if they were going to continue getting to know each other. It wasn't information she gave out freely; it had happened so long ago; and any retelling of the incident skirted dangerously close to emotions she guarded closely. But with Adam, it was time. 'It was an accident.'

'What happened?' he pressed gently.

She took a breath, toying with the edge of her saucer, then looked up toward him. 'I fell off a porch and struck my head.' She forced a smile; it was designed to tell him that everything was all right.

'You were ten, you said?'

'Yes.'

He lit a cigarette before going on. 'What were you doing?'

'Trying to get something for Winna. A bird's nest.'

Adam frowned unconsciously at the mental image. Child's play. Two pretty little girls playing on a porch, giggling, catching sight of a bird's nest, fascinated to see inside. One started up after it—the one with more courage, or had it been the luck of the draw? 'Didn't anyone tell you not to play around on porches?' It was asked harshly, in sudden and useless anger at the cruel incident.

She didn't catch his tone, thus had no reason to wonder at his anger. 'Oh, we weren't playing on the porch. You're right. It was forbidden.'

'Then why . . . ?'

Libby sighed again. The telling was still difficult, even after all these years. 'There was a small porch off to the side of our bedroom, a flat, square thing with a railing, close to a big oak. Winna would always stand at the door looking out, daydreaming, I suppose. She did that day and saw the nest. She wanted it.'

He was frowning heavily. 'So why did you get it?'

She recognized the tone this time; she'd heard it too many times from others. From Sebastian, especially. She tried to temper the edge in her voice. 'Adam, you don't understand. Winna was afraid. In order to reach the nest, you had to get right up on the railing. We weren't tall enough otherwise. Winna hated heights, she still does. I . . . she wanted the thing so much. She couldn't have known what would happen. You don't think about things like that when you're a kid.'

Possibly not, he thought. 'She couldn't have caught you when you started to fall?'

Libby pressed her lips together for a moment. 'She wasn't there. She'd gone away. I don't know why,' she said dismissively, then closed her eyes as some private pain she couldn't keep at bay suffused her expression. 'Oh! When I think what it must've been like for her just to watch me disappear over that railing!' And she'd thought about it so many times, what her own horror would've been had the roles been reversed, had she been the one to watch as her sister went head first toward the ground. She closed her eyes more tightly, to try to shut out the image of Winna's young face contorted in the anguish Libby knew she'd suffered. Adam nearly rose to go to her, to lay a hand on her arm to ease the drawn look about her mouth, but he didn't. He simply sat tensely until she went on. 'Of course, it wasn't her fault. It was no one's fault. It just happened. But she took it so hard. It was awhile before she could even go down and tell Mother and Dad what had happened,' she said intently, as if explaining something vitally important. 'And then, after that, she was distraught about it. For years, and I don't think she's ever gotten over it. It worries me sometimes. It's a burden I don't want her to carry around.' She looked down toward her cup, unconsciously moving it in its saucer.

Adam didn't know quite what to say. He was treading on unfamiliar terrain, cautious of speaking of things beyond his personal experience, but he wanted her to know what he felt.

About her. 'If it's a burden to her, I can't believe you haven't lightened it for her. You care so much, don't you?' he said quietly. 'I suspect your blindness hurts you almost more for her than for yourself. You're someone who'd feel that way.'

'How do you know what I'd feel?' she demanded sharply, raising her head in defiance, then bit her lip. This wasn't an argument; she wasn't being pressed to defend anything, or anyone, as she'd so often been in the past. Particularly with Sebastian, who seemed uncharacteristically unable to understand any of it. Sebastian, who read things between lines that weren't even written. No, Adam wasn't arguing with her; he was only trying to empathize. There was no need to explain about Winna, her fears and insecurities. About Winna's guilt, how desperately she needed to know that Libby didn't blame her. And she didn't; she never had. No, there was no need to snap at him as though he didn't understand how important it was to protect Winna from the guilt that could've ruined her life. She gave him a conciliatory smile. 'I'm sorry. I didn't mean to be so short with you. Yes, I hurt for Edwinna. She's not a particularly strong person, and I'd do anything I could to help her. I always have, and I always will, and she feels the same way about me. Not everyone understands things between us sometimes, but it doesn't matter to me. I know what the battles have been, hers and mine.'

'And you've won your battles with more courage and grace than I've ever run up against,' he said, his eyes almost caressing as he watched her face from across the table. 'I don't know Edwinna, but you—you could be all torn up with anger and fear and anguish and all the other emotions there are to feel. But you're not, or at least you don't wear that look. Yours is a face of strength, and courage and character. I don't see any other.' It wasn't idle flattery; he was beyond that with her.

'Thank you for the compliment,' she said, smiling briefly. She thought perhaps someday she'd tell him about the other faces, when the ghosts rose up and needed resettling once more. But not now; it was time to close the discussion. 'I don't know about you, but I'd like some brandy. What do you think?'

He studied her for a long time, unable really to take his eyes from her. She was quite a woman. He understood that the conversation was finished, that it was time to stop delving into what made them both who they were, at least for the moment. 'I think that's an excellent idea, but I'll get it.' She'd already risen, and he stood up quickly, catching her arm lightly as he came around the table. The evening would be over soon, ended on a note of light conversation, he knew, but there was one more issue that needed addressing. It was one of the other things he'd spent days thinking about, that he'd come here tonight to tell her. As he looked down at her face turned expectantly up toward him, he wondered briefly how to approach it. Head on. Isn't that what you'd tell me, Libby? he asked silently and began to smile slowly. He reached for her hands and took both of them in his. 'I said I'll get it,' he said softly. 'And before we drop all conversation of importance, there's one last thing I want to tell you.'

His hands were warm, holding her gently but firmly, and she felt a renewed discomfiture. She wondered if he realized just how magnetic a man he really was. 'What?' she asked and smiled with a breeziness that took effort.

He deliberated a moment longer, then answered. 'You told me there was one thing you wanted more than anything else in the world.'

She tilted her head quizzically.

'You want to learn to ride again, isn't that right?'

It was out of the clear blue, and she wasn't following him. 'Yes . . .'

'Sebastian Vickery is all good intentions, but he's no horseman.'

'Adam . . .' she said, frowning in incomprehension.

He was smiling again, his eyes veiled. 'You told me it was important. That it would give you freedom, didn't you?'

'Yes, but . . .'

He dropped one hand then and touched her lips gently with one fingertip, silencing her. In the quiet of the room, their shadows played on the wall, and he took a step closer. 'Stop interrupting me,' he said, his voice pitched low. 'You want that freedom and need it, and Libby, I'm going to be the one to give it to you.'

## Chapter 6

'. . . and so you see, if she let go of the string, she'd be lost. She'd have no way of getting back,' Libby was explaining the next morning to a classroom of rapt faces. She tugged lightly at the collar of her sleeveless dress, loosening it; even for the late morning, it was unusually warm.

'You mean forever?' a small male voice asked in dismay.

'Brian, tap your bell first,' Libby said mildly, then went on. 'Well, supposedly, yes.'

'Wow!'

Libby smiled to herself and relaxed against the back of her chair. 'You have to remember, it's only a fairy story, that she followed the string for adventure. And she didn't let go of it, so she wasn't lost forever.'

Another bell rang, with a tone slightly different from the one on Brian's desk; it was Libby's method of making for orderly discussion. There would come a time when the children no longer needed it, when they'd leave this special classroom with its special psychology and lessons, and go out into the world of regular schools, where they could raise their hands and be called upon just like anyone else. 'Alice?' Libby looked inquiringly toward the left, absently reaching up to tighten the gold clips pulling back her hair.

'Well . . .' the lispy voice began tentatively. 'But I don't understand why the goblin queen wouldn't take off her shoes!' she complained, and Libby could picture the intense little frown.

'Well, because she had toes! None of the other goblins had toes, and she was very embarrassed.'

'But everyone has toes!' Alice objected in frustration.

Libby smiled again. 'People have toes, the little girl holding onto the string had toes, but the mountain goblins didn't.'

'How come?'

'Because they just didn't,' Libby explained patiently and

picked up her metal template, tapping it absently on her hand. 'The man who wrote the story made up the goblins in his head, and the way he saw them was without toes.'

Alice's brow creased in a deep frown. 'You mean there really aren't little people who live down under the mountain in a cave who don't have toes?'

Libby laughed softly. 'No, honey. It's just a story. It's just make believe.' A third bell interrupted as a small hand tapped at it furiously. 'All right, Timmy, all right. What?'

'How come she followed that string anyway?' he demanded.

'Because she found it one night, running through her room.'

'So?' he went on belligerently.

'So,' Libby said, gearing her tone to his, a technique she'd found long ago to be effective, 'If you found a thread, hardly visible, running through your bedroom one night, don't you think you'd follow it to see where it led?' She looked toward him expectantly, shifting in her chair so she could cross her legs.

'No.' It was said flatly, and the little boy scowled down at his desk.

'I would!' an eager female voice piped up then. 'I would!'

'Yes, you probably would, Bonnie,' Libby remarked dryly. 'You'd like a little adventure, wouldn't you?'

'Yeah!' she breathed.

The bell in the corridor interrupted them, and there was a collective groan of disappointment. The aide entered and saw to the customary routine of dismissal, with one minor alteration. 'Jennifer,' Libby said as the children were rustling to their feet, 'stay for a moment. Mrs. Collidge, I'll bring her out with me.' The other children were arranged in a single file, and when they'd gone, Libby rose and made her way to the desk next to Jennifer's, sitting down to face her with hands clasped on the desktop in front of her. 'You were very quiet today, Jennie.' Libby waited, but the only response was the child's uncomfortable movement in her chair. 'You didn't like the story?' she pressed. She had a special feeling for this child; Jennie's circumstances were so similar to her own: a perfectly normal childhood suddenly, accidentally destroyed, with the child's emotions and experiences too immature for her to know quite how to deal with it all.

Jennie's dark head motioned unintelligibly. 'Mmmm.'

Libby pursed her lips for a moment, then smiled encouragingly. 'It's a good story.'

'It's not real!'

Libby sat back and laughed gently. 'Of course not! That's

what makes it so nice. Anything can happen,' she said optimistically.

Silence.

Libby leaned forward then, reaching out to find and clasp the child's hand. 'Jennie, what's wrong today?' she asked softly.

There was an involuntary sniff, and the small hand turned itself upside down and grasped Libby's tightly. 'I hate it! I hate everything!' she said with despair and began to sob.

Libby listened in silence, waiting for Jennie's crying to subside. When it had, she spoke calmly. 'I know, honey. I did, too.'

'It's not fair!' Jennie withdrew her hand and threw her head down on the desk, her bobbed hair spreading out over her arms.

'Of course it's not fair.' And just how does one explain to a nine-year-old that most everything in life isn't fair? Libby thought with a sigh and felt the child's anger at the world as it traversed the short distance between them. Well, at least she had that; she was going to need her anger to help disinfect the wound.

Jennie raised her head at Libby's quiet acknowledgment. 'It was Melissa's fault,' she accused suddenly.

Libby knew who Melissa was: the neighbor's child who had insisted Jennie go out in the street after the ball. 'That's not fair either, Jennie,' she said.

'But if she hadn't made me, none of it woulda happened.'

'Possibly. But let me ask you something, Jen. Did you ever stop to consider how bad Melissa feels? Don't you think she hates what happened as much as you do? She didn't mean it.'

Jennie sat listlessly in her chair, dejectedly tracing the edge of the desk with one fingertip. 'I s'pose.'

Libby wasn't going to let this go by, and she wondered briefly what made people so different, some so able to forgive—so desperately willing to forgive, as she'd been—others so able to blame. 'Jennie, you must think about it,' she said seriously. 'I know it's difficult, but you mustn't keep all the sorry for yourself. Give a little to Melissa. She needs a lot too, and especially from you. Most especially from you.'

Jennie was quiet, but Libby thought perhaps she'd made some small dent. She searched her mind for something more to say as the silence stretched out, but it was Jennie who finally broke it. 'Does it ever get better?' she asked in a small voice.

Libby smiled compassionately, reaching out to touch Jennie's hand again. 'Yes, it does. Or rather, Jennie, it gets easier. And that's nicer.'

Jennie frowned. 'How?'

How, indeed? 'Well, better means that things change. Easier means that things stay the same, but you learn to live with them. Better doesn't take work. Easier does, and that makes it nicer. You always feel more proud of yourself when you work at something and finally accomplish it. It's called self-satisfaction, and honey, it's important.' She looked toward the young girl fondly.

'Hmmm,' Jennie mumbled, unconvinced.

Oh, I know you don't understand! Libby wanted to cry. I didn't either for a long time, and sometimes I still have trouble. The silence was growing again, and she abruptly changed the tenor of the conversation. 'I'll just bet there's something you haven't thought of,' she said after a moment, her tone suggesting she knew of a nice secret.

'What?' Jennie looked up, curious despite herself.

A smile began playing at the corners of Libby's mouth; this was her specialty, jostling away dejection. 'I'll bet you never thought how nice it is to be able to live on your imagination.'

Jennie straightened a little more; Miss Rutledge always knew interesting things. 'What d'you mean?'

'Well, I simply mean that people like you and me have a lot of memories stored up, lots of things we remember, and we're free to pull them out and look at them any time we want to!' she said gaily. She could feel Jennie's responsiveness and pressed her advantage, adding conspiratorially, 'There's something else, too.'

'What?' Jennie was alert now and leaned forward in anticipation.

'We get to see things any way we want!'

'We do?'

'Well, of course!' Libby laughed. She touched the gold chain at her neck, tracing its path across the slender column of her throat as she looked merrily toward Jennie. 'You can make people look any way you want them to. Fat, thin, short, or tall. You can make a rainy day be sunny, if you want, unless you go out without your umbrella, of course,' she teased and was gratified to hear a giggle. 'Imagination is a wonderful thing. You can do anything you want with it, and we get to use ours all the time.'

Jennie sat up eagerly now. 'I'll bet Mrs. Rumson's fat and ugly!'

Libby raised her eyebrows. 'Who's Mrs. Rumson?'

'She just moved next door. And she's mean.'

Libby tried to keep from smiling, but couldn't; Jennie's tone was so decidedly cross. 'Oh?'

'Yeah! You know what she does? She throws rocks at cats!' she huffed.

'She does!' Libby said, infusing shock into her tone. 'How do you know that?'

'My brother Billy told me, and once she yelled at me, and I wasn't even in her yard! She has an awful voice, an' I just know she's ugly!'

'And fat,' Libby added without hesitation.

'With a real long nose,' Jennie picked up deliciously.

'That's got a wart on the end of it.'

'And huge, glumpy feet without any toes!' Jennie crowed triumphantly, before going off into a spasm of giggling.

Libby was smiling in satisfaction and waited for Jennie's hilarity to subside. When it had, she said, 'See what I mean? Imaginations are great. Now you don't have to let poor old Mrs. Rumson bother you because you've got her number.'

'Yeah, she's a warty old witch!' Jennie snickered, unwilling to give up the new game.

Someday, perhaps soon, Libby thought, she'd have to explain to Jennie that the little pastime had to be tempered with judgment; at the moment, it was harmless and had achieved its purpose. 'Hmmm, but that's enough now about Mrs. Rumson. Feeling better?'

'Uh huh. Miss Rutledge, I think you're wonderful,' Jennie said sincerely.

Libby laughed warmly, giving Jennie's hand a final squeeze. 'Well, thanks. Now, come on, we've got to find Mrs. Coolidge . . .'

'I'm right here. I thought I'd come back and see if you needed any help.' The aide stood in the doorway and glanced briefly toward Adam. She knew he'd been there since she'd dismissed the class earlier, and he leaned now against the wall near a large, raised map of the United States, one hand resting on his hip and drawing back his black riding jacket. He was looking steadily at Libby, a half smile curving his lips.

'Oh, we're fine,' Libby said. 'Except that I think Jennie's ready to go out and play with everyone else and might not be able to wait around for me. Feel like going now, Jennie?'

'Yes, ma'am,' she said happily.

'I'll take her.' The aide collected the young girl, and when they'd gone, Libby shifted in her seat and made a movement to rise.

'I think you're wonderful too,' Adam said in a low voice and pushed himself away from the wall.

Libby sat back down abruptly, putting a hand to her breast. 'Adam! Please, don't do that! You scared the life out of me!'

He knew better, of course, but hadn't been able to resist. 'I'm sorry.' He came over and sat down opposite her on the edge of her teacher's desk. 'Libby, you were a marvel with that child.'

She was still trying to recoup. 'How long have you been here?'

'Since you dismissed the class. Well, slightly before, actually.'

'You have a habit of watching me . . .' It was disconcerting, because she had no way to reciprocate. Because it left her at a disadvantage. Because it was him.

'I like to,' he answered honestly and ran a hand through his hair. 'There's a lot to watch, and I meant what I said. You're a magician with these kids.'

She sighed then. 'I'm not a magician, Adam. I simply know where they're coming from. I've been there, remember?' She looked up toward him, smiling briefly.

He studied her silently for a moment. 'Yes, I remember.'

'And all I did for Jennie was patch her up,' she went on. 'It'll hold for awhile. It usually does, until she gets to thinking about things too much.'

'And when that happens, you'll do some more patchwork, and keep on and on until finally she's on her own two feet. I'll tell you, if I were in her shoes, or any shoes in this classroom, I certainly would hope I had you for my teacher.' He smiled slowly, cocking his head to one side as he watched a mild flush come to her cheeks.

'Thank you. And speaking of teachers,' she said then, needing to change the subject, 'we're still on for this afternoon?'

'I don't always show up at the local schoolyard dressed in my jodhpurs and boots, you know,' he said and stood up, giving her a light smile.

'Well,' she laughed, 'I didn't tell you to come that way. And anyway, I was supposed to be meeting you at the club. Why . . . ?'

He reached for her hand as she rose, directing her over to the desk. 'Don't pull that on me again.'

They stood close together for a moment before she moved around to begin gathering up her things. 'Don't pull what on you again?'

He arched an eyebrow in mild annoyance. 'That "I'll meet you there" routine.'

'Adam, I'm perfectly capable of getting around by myself, you know,' she said, glancing toward him.

'I know, and I'm perfectly capable of coming to get you.' He crossed his arms, watching as she stacked everything neatly together.

She stopped what she was doing then and let out a breath. 'Adam!'

'Adam what?' he asked innocently, a smile tugging at the corners of his mouth; she had such an adamantly independent look on her face, and though he liked it, he wasn't about to let her get away with it.

She said nothing and went back to work, frowning down at the desk. 'Oh, I don't know,' she murmured.

He didn't respond immediately. Let her be agitated for a moment, apparently because of him. It was her turn, anyway, he thought dryly. She was still frowning as she put her things into the briefcase and didn't look up when she spoke again.

'Adam, the fact that I let you . . . I mean, that you're going to help me learn to ride again certainly doesn't obligate you to chauffeur me around. All we have to do is meet at . . .'

'The club,' he picked up, 'where we go about having our half hour's lesson and then, fini! You go your way, and I'll go mine.' He cocked his head, eyeing her narrowly.

'That's exactly right,' she said and smiled calmly. They were on different ground, certainly, since the night before, but this matter of teaching her to ride was completely removed from anything else that might be between them at the moment. It was purely a practical arrangement, and she didn't intend to impose any more than she had to.

He contemplated her composed expression with narrowed eyes. 'Perhaps, like you, I take a little more interest in my students.'

'Adam, there's no need . . .'

He let out an impatient breath. 'Cut it, Libby. I came because I wanted to.' And because it suited the way I intend to go about all this, he thought. 'Now, don't be so damned independent. It damages my male ego.' He said it with a wry smile and waited for her reaction.

It was an involuntary laugh. You're impossible to argue with, she told him silently. 'Well, then, never mind. Far be it from me to go around bruising egos,' she said facetiously, her momentary hesitation gone. She snapped the locks on the briefcase, set it beside the desk, then withdrew her cane and began stretching it out. Adam gently took it out of her hands and put it away.

'You don't need that. You've got me.' He picked up her purse and settled it over her shoulder.

'Adam!'

He brushed the underside of her chin lightly with one finger. 'I thought we'd just established the vulnerability of my ego,' he said easily and picked up her briefcase. 'Now, here. Take my arm.' He held it out, and when she'd finally relented and placed her hand lightly near his elbow, he smiled down at her, resisting the urge to draw her close. 'All set?'

'All set,' she said, giving in to his chivalry, and they walked arm in arm from the room.

Adam was tightening the girth on the saddle. It had taken them just under an hour to stop at Libby's apartment so she could change, then be on their way again through the mid-afternoon stream of traffic to the Hunt Club in its exclusive location on the wooded outskirts of town. They'd arrived earlier than was Libby's usual habit, as Adam had intended, and when he had finished adjusting the sheepskin pad under the girth, he glanced around absently at the familiar riders milling about the stable-yard, nodding pleasantly when one or two waved. Then he looked over his shoulder to check on Libby. She stood where he'd stationed her, at the head of the horse, gently rubbing its muzzle, wisps of her copper hair blowing in the soft breeze. He gave the cinch one final tug and slapped the panel down over the buckle. 'Okay, up you go,' he said and stepped toward her, taking one of her hands in his.

She held it lightly and ran her other hand along the horse's muscular neck toward the withers as she came forward. When she was standing by him, she looked up, mildly perplexed. 'Adam, this is a different horse,' she observed.

'I know.' He said it matter-of-factly and stepped back, positioning her to face the saddle. 'Now, take hold of the pommel, and I'll give you a leg up.' With one hand he guided her booted foot into the stirrup, then gave her a quick boost as she swung into the saddle.

She shifted around, getting her seat. 'You know, Matt thought it was a good idea to stick with the same horse until I got completely confident. This one's so much bigger.' She smiled down toward him, hoping the casual tone disguised her nervousness.

He glanced up, contemplating her composed expression for a

moment. 'I know.' He returned to the horse's head and straightened the reins, then tossed them back over the animal's head.

Libby smiled more widely, trying for unconcern. 'What's his name?' she asked conversationally.

'Morgan.'

'Hmmm, nice. Morgan.' She was struck by a sudden thought. Perhaps they were taking liberties. 'Will Matt object to my riding him?' She pressed her lips together, looking uncertainly in his direction.

'Matt has nothing to say about it.' Adam's tone remained bland as he continued to inspect the horse's tack.

'Oh. Why not?'

'Because it's not his horse. It's mine.' Finally satisfied that everything was in order, he patted Morgan's neck and came to stand facing the saddle, then pulled her foot gently out of the stirrup. 'Hold tight for a minute.'

She wondered at the directive, and frowned slightly, then felt the saddle give. Suddenly, he was in the saddle behind her, his body pressed directly against hers, his powerful arms reaching around her waist as he gathered up the reins. Completely unnerved, she grabbed at Morgan's mane. 'Adam! What're you doing!'

He tightened his arms as he steadied the prancing horse. 'It's okay,' he murmured near her hair.

She could feel his breath warm on the side of her face, smell the musky scent of his aftershave, and though his embrace was secure, it didn't help to keep real terror out of her voice. 'What are you doing!' she repeated and involuntarily clutched at one of his hands; it closed tightly over hers.

The fact of their near intimacy in the saddle might've been lost on her for the moment but it wasn't on him. He held her quietly for a time before answering. 'I'm going to teach you to ride. But first, I'm going to take you for one.'

'I can't,' she said flatly, pressing her lips together.

'Of course you can.' He began placing her hands where he wanted them: one entwined in the mane, the other holding onto the saddle.

'Adam, I can't! Now, let me down. Please let me get down!' she insisted, the corners of her eyes beginning to sting. Damn him.

Adam kept an eye on her tense face, studying it thoughtfully, then after a moment, he spoke calmly. 'Libby, listen to me. You're never going to learn to ride the way you've been going about it. Not really ride. Oh, yes. You'll learn to sit a horse at a dead walk, but is that really what you want? You want freedom? I'll give you freedom, teach you to ride anywhere you want, at any gait. But before you can do that, you've got to know what it's like, how to compensate for it. Blind.' It came out easily, as he'd hoped it would. 'And you can't do that by yourself. Now come on. You're perfectly safe. I won't let go.'

Like it or not, his embrace was having its effect. 'Adam, I can't,' she said more mildly.

'I didn't think "can't" was in Libby Rutledge's vocabulary,' he said with calculation.

'There are lots of words in my vocabulary you haven't heard yet,' she murmured darkly.

He chuckled at that, brushing his cheek along her hair as he threw his head back slightly. 'I can imagine,' he said with feeling.

She was quiet for a long time then, looking down toward her hands. Finally, she raised her head and spoke quietly over her shoulder. 'Adam, I'm afraid,' she said honestly.

It made him shift and pull her more closely against him. 'I know,' he said softly. 'But that's never stopped you before, has it?'

She was silent a moment longer. 'All right. All right, we'll go. But if you kick this horse and make him take off, you'll regret it for the rest of your life, so help me God!' she vowed and braced herself.

He laughed, then carefully nudged Morgan with his boots. The big bay moved forward, visibly making every muscle in Libby's body contract. 'Relax,' he said as they ambled out of the stableyard onto the roadway, and when her taut shoulders had loosened, he leaned closer. 'Better?' Her answer was a brief nod, and he smiled in satisfaction. They were drawing curious looks as they made their way along the shoulder of the road, their bodies moving together in rhythm with the horse's movement, and when they reached the bridle paths, Adam guided Morgan down onto one of the wide dirt pathways.

Libby was smiling by that time in genuine ease. 'Adam, is it very beautiful?'

'Is what very beautiful?' he asked obtusely, rousing from his reverie.

'The landscape. This is some kind of bridle path, I assume. We left the roadway awhile ago.'

'Oh. I've never really thought about it, but yes. I suppose it is.' He glanced around vaguely, then back at her face.

'Tell me about it,' she said softly and relaxed completely, resting her head against his shoulder.

He was lost again for a moment, this time to the feel of her weight settled against him, the fragrance of her unknown perfume mingling with the scent of her hair. Lilacs, he thought; soft and fresh and utterly feminine. Like she was. He roused finally, looking around. Tell her about it? All right. He took note of the white birches lining the pathway, the meadows stretching back from them on either side, of the other riders some distance ahead, one traveling in their direction, a pair approaching side by side from the other. An unremarkable scene really and not difficult to describe, unless, of course, one took into account the subtle shadings of color, the particular blue of the sky that afternoon, the splashes of unexpected red from the riders' coats. And what about the angle of the sun? That was what really gave it all the character of the moment. It was off to their left and waning, tossing great yellow shafts of light down into the break in the awning of trees overhead, painting the ground below vividly light and dark. As if he hadn't understood before, he suddenly realized the shocking scope of Libby's handicap, comprehended fully how far-reaching and crushing a blow had been dealt to her. More than ever, he wanted to express some useless sentiment of sympathy, but he didn't. He wouldn't deal with her in that way. 'All right,' he said with a strange quietness. 'I'll tell you about it, but you'll have to bear with me. I'm not terribly eloquent.' And he began then, finding the exercise wholly foreign but oddly satisfying as he watched her expression grow dreamy, and he was disappointed when, after a time, he finally ran out of things to say.

'You're good at this,' she complimented, turning her head slightly to look up toward his face.

'Don't flatter me, lady. I'm immune.' It was said glibly, to cover a sudden self-consciousness.

'I'm not. I meant it.'

He didn't comment further, but checked to be sure that her hands were still properly placed on the saddle. He regretted the need for it, actually, for it made her stiffen and draw away from him, but he reminded himself he was here to be teaching her something, not merely catering to his own personal inclinations. 'Come on. It's time to pick up the pace. Morgan's got a nice slow gait. You'll hardly feel it at all.' He checked her grip one more time, then moved the horse out, increasing his hold around her waist as Morgan broke into a trot.

It came as a shock to her at first, the new up and down motion she'd once known so well, and she pressed her lips together, getting the feel of the movement. Adam was a consummate rider, and after they'd gone some distance, she barely felt the tightening of his legs as he finally booted Morgan out into a full canter. His gait was like a treasure she'd lost then found again, gentle, deep and rolling, and it came upon her all at once, joyously, that wild, let-loose sensation of ground falling away behind her, the wind in her face, the feeling of freedom she'd so long yearned for but never been able to have. Suddenly, she was whisked away, carried on the wings of the wind and dropped back into another time, another place, onto a field in a valley at the foot of a mountain, and she could see the high hills on both sides of her as she raced across the meadow atop a painted pony. She was a child again, whole again, free as a bird, and she wanted to reach out and take hold of the feeling to clasp it to her forever, never letting it slip away again.

Adam kept Morgan stretched out in an easy lope for a good distance, then finally brought him down, making a smooth transition from canter to walk. When they were again settled into a quiet amble, he smiled slowly in satisfaction and looked around expectantly at Libby's face. It was wet with tears coursing uncontrollably down her cheeks.

'Libby!' he said in consternation and reined Morgan in to a standstill. She couldn't answer and shook her head, dismissing him with a vague wave of her hand. He dismounted abruptly and reached up, touching her lightly on the leg. 'Get down.'

She averted her head, wiping at the tears that were falling more rapidly.

'I said get down,' he repeated sternly, his worried frown deepening. She gave in finally, and he lifted her down to her feet, facing him. 'Libby?' He tried to raise her chin so she'd look at him, but she pulled away. Suddenly, the last threads of her control gave away, and she began to sob violently.

He caught her as she started to slump. Pulling her hands from her face, he yanked off her glasses, threw them to the ground, then drew her against him, tightly closing his arms around her. She clung to him desperately as she cried, her wrenching sobs tearing from her to beat against his chest, and he put his face against her hair, murmuring her name over and over. Never in his life had he felt more helpless than he did then as he held the tormented body in his arms, nor more shaken to discover that sorrow could have such appalling depths. So, it had been a mistake after all, this gallant ride. It had been meant to thrill her; instead, it had crushed her. And as they stood there locked together by her despair, he knew it was not he, Adam Bainbridge, that she clung to but simply another human being whose nearness might prevent her from being swept down completely into the hell of her anguish. He shifted his hold, pressing her face more tightly into his shoulder as he caressed the back of her head, and after nearly a quarter of an hour had passed, her sobs finally subsided into exhaustion. He didn't loosen his embrace immediately, however, for she remained quietly resting against him, drained.

After a moment, he pushed her back slightly and looked with troubled eyes into her face. It was ashen, and stained with tears. 'Libby,' he said gently.

She averted her face, stepping back. 'Where are my glasses?' she asked woodenly.

He wanted to reach out and draw her close again, to say a thousand things, but it was out of the question; she was locked away. He leaned down and retrieved her glasses, watching as she wordlessly replaced them. The chasm between them yawned immense in the growing silence, and he knew it was useless for him to try to bridge it; he'd been the one to create it. It was going to be up to her, and after a moment, he gave her the choice. 'Do you want to go back?' he asked tonelessly.

'Yes,' she said, turning away.

So it was done. He moved past her over to Morgan, who stood untethered, reins hanging slack on his neck as he curiously watched the two of them. Adam took hold of one leather strap and reached out for Libby's arm. 'Here, I'll help you up.'

'Adam,' she began tiredly, drawing away.

'Don't worry about it,' he said in a tight voice. 'You ride. I'll walk.'

It was obviously what she wanted, for she came over then and let him help her back up into the saddle. He slipped the reins over Morgan's head and began leading him back in the direction from which they had come.

It was only a mile or so back to the stable, but their silence made it seem like ten. Adam walked it leadenly; Libby rode it wearily, and when they reached the paddock, he helped her down. 'I'll take you home.'

Libby was looking at the ground and glanced briefly in his direction. 'No, I'll call a cab.'

'Libby . . .'

She frowned. 'Adam, please.'

It was the final stone on the wall separating them, and Adam let out a slow breath. 'All right. I'll make the call. Stay here. I'll be right back.' He was gone only a short time, and when he returned, he touched her briefly on the arm. 'He'll meet us at the front of the building. Here, take my horse,' he said shortly to a nearby stablehand and handed over the reins. 'Come on, let's go,' he said to Libby and put her hand on his arm. It rested there almost absently, so very differently from earlier in the afternoon. She was merely a woman in need of a guiding hand; he was a man kind enough to provide it. They reached the main drive finally, and Adam brought them to a halt at the curb of the walkway leading up to the restaurant. This was where it had all begun; fitting, he thought, that this was where it all should end.

'You don't have to wait,' Libby said tiredly, running her fingers through her hair.

Adam didn't respond immediately, and pain was reflected in his eyes as he kept them on her face. He was absorbing every detail of her features so he could bring them to mind again in the years to come, when this day was no more than a distant memory. He wanted to remember them, for no one in the past had ever had such a dramatic effect on him, nor would anyone in the future. The damage he'd done was irreparable, he knew; she had too much to contend with to be saddled with a man who so clumsily tore open her wounds. He should've gone about things her way: slowly. It was obvious she knew best. But in his need to—what? demonstrate his masculinity?—he'd succeeded only in adding new stress lines to her lovely face. Adam Bainbridge, man for all women, he thought bitterly. You've successfully crushed her one hope for escape. She'll probably never ride again. She'll only have the new fears, new hurts you've so kindly given her to deal with. 'No,' he said finally. 'I'll see you safely into the taxi.'

She didn't answer, and Adam realized that her exhaustion was complete; she could barely stand up. He didn't touch her, however; he knew better than that, and was grateful when the taxicab arrived within a few minutes.

'Okay.' He opened the door, bringing her hand to rest on the edge of the window, and watched as she settled herself in the back seat. It was the final moment, arriving on him like a sledge hammer as he stepped back, ready to close the door. 'I'm sorry.' The words escaped before he could stop them. He'd fought the urge to say that; now he had openly acknowledged the reality of what was happening between them.

She waved briefly—dismissively, he thought—in his direction. He closed the car door and stepped back up on the curb. The taxi driver pulled away, and Adam watched expressionlessly as Libby Rutledge was driven out of his life forever.

## Chapter 7

Matt Jameson strode into the lounge and stopped inside the door, giving his eyes a moment to adjust to the interior light. It was three o'clock and not particularly crowded inside; several couples were scattered at tables around the floor, and a young man in a dusty shirt and riding breeches leaned against the back wall, talking discreetly into a telephone nestled into a lighted alcove. The bartender behind the cushioned bar was cleaning a glass, his linen cloth deftly circling its inner perimeter, and he seemed completely uninterested in the lone man sitting at the end of the bar, staring fixedly at the half empty whiskey glass cupped in both hands out in front of him. Matt contemplated the man for a minute, then crossed the room and took the stool next to him. 'Hi, Brendan. Scotch on the rocks.' he said to the bartender, then turned to Adam, giving him a long, appraising look. 'Spending a lot of time in here, aren't you?'

Adam shifted but didn't look up; instead, he raised his glass, drained it, then signaled to Brendan, clunking the glass back down on the counter in comment.

'How many does that make?' Matt's tone was casual as he drew out a half crushed pack of cigarettes and tossed it on the bar in front of him.

'Who cares?' Adam said and frowned at his hands.

Matt shot him a look, accepted his drink, then watched silently as the tall Irishman refilled Adam's glass with straight Jack Daniels. Adam pulled it over, but didn't pick it up immediately. 'Got problems?' Matt ventured after a moment, watching Adam's somber expression in the mirror across the way. When there was no response, he lit a cigarette and flipped the match into the ashtray. 'You're not going to solve them by falling into a whiskey bottle, you know.'

'For what it's worth, I'm not going to solve them, period.' Adam's eyes were unreadable, and Matt studied him narrowly.

Actually, he was surprised at the frank response; he hadn't thought Adam would say even that much. Matt had watched him now for two days, sitting here at the bar, shrugging off any attempts at friendly conversation while he brooded over the rim of a whiskey glass. Matt had let him alone the first day and even the second; three days, however, was one too many, and anyway, he had a reason now to confront him.

'That sounds pretty final,' he said finally.

Adam smiled without humor. 'You got it.'

Matt picked up a napkin lying nearby, creasing the corner, and glanced over casually. 'Have anything to do with Libby Rutledge?'

Adam looked at him for the first time. Amazingly, his eyes held no glaze from the alcohol, only shadows. 'Why do you ask?'

Matt shrugged. 'Your interest is no secret, at least to me. People don't stand around watching someone day after day without attracting some attention, you know,' he said dryly, then contemplated the napkin for a moment. 'She hasn't been around for a couple of days,' he remarked.

The hollows in Adam's cheeks grew deeper, and he looked back down at the bar. 'I took her riding,' he said tonelessly.

'I know. I saw you. Something happen?'

Adam's laugh was harsh. 'Oh, not much. I only scared the living hell out of her.' His eyes went hard at some private memory, and he picked up his glass and took a long drink.

Matt reached over and put his hand on Adam's arm, forcing the glass back down on the table. 'Don't,' he said sharply.

'Why the hell not?'

Matt studied him again, then abruptly dropped the casual tone. 'She means that much to you?'

Adam looked at him, then at the lighter he'd drawn out of his pocket; it lay heavy in the palm of his hand, solid gold, engraved with his initials in one corner, and he stared at it as though he'd never seen it before. Did she mean that much to him? Only if the extraordinary counted for anything. He thrust the lighter back in his pocket and lit his cigarette with a match. 'She's a hell of a woman.'

Matt smiled briefly. 'I know that. I've watched her, too.'

'You don't know the half of it,' Adam said quietly then. 'You should see her sometime with those kids she teaches, or watch the way she's taken her life in hand and made something out of it. She lives alone, did you know that?' He gave Matt a half smile. 'Good old Sebastian, he only brings her here. You might suspect he does everything for her, but that's not so. It's probably the other way around, actually. Yes, good old Sebastian,' he repeated and stubbed out the cigarette roughly.

Matt did the same and eyed Adam over the rim of his glass. 'Sounds like you might be a bit jealous.'

Adam turned to shoot him an acid look but lost it midway. After a moment, he let out a slow breath. 'Maybe I am. At least he'd have known better than to rush her into something. He wouldn't have scared the living daylights out of her because of his need to . . . ah, what the hell!' He looked away moodily, studying the liquor bottles lined across the shelf behind the bar. After a time, he said in a subdued tone, 'She'll never ride again.' Or get within two feet of me, he thought.

Matt was drumming his fingers on the bar. 'How do you know you scared the living daylights out of her? Have you asked her?'

'I don't have to ask her, dammit!' Adam exploded and looked over at Matt. 'You weren't there. She came unglued, cried her heart out. Jesus, I never knew anyone could hurt like that,' he added with clouded eyes, and miserably ran his fingers through his hair.

'You just said she was scared, not hurt.'

'Look, Matt. Thanks a lot,' Adam said impatiently, 'But I don't feel like going into it. It's too complicated. Suffice it to say I did the lady a tremendous disservice, a lady who's got more courage and grit than you or I'll ever see in a lifetime.'

'Well, if she's got so much courage and grit, what makes you think you've ruined it all for her?'

Adam tried to temper his mounting irritation; he didn't want to talk about it any more. To anyone. 'Because it was something she was trying to overcome,' he said in a clipped voice. 'It was so very important to her, and she was only beginning the battle. You don't understand that, but believe it. And you don't win battles by diving in head first. I didn't understand that. She did. It's as simple as that.'

'You're sure of that, huh?'

'I'm sure of it.' Adam said dully and emptied his glass.

'Okay.' Matt looked at him a last time, shaking his head, then drained his own glass. He laid out two bills on the counter, slid off the stool, and slapped Adam once on the arm before striding back across the room.

Libby was waiting at the door, on Sebastian's arm. Matt had told her ten minutes or so, and she was right on time. 'He's all yours,' he said and briefly let his eyes run down the length of her; she looked lovely in the sleeveless green dress, with her deep auburn hair worn loose. She seemed so vulnerably feminine as she looked up at him with a tentative smile, her eyes hidden by the lenses of her glasses, and he was suddenly conscious of Adam sitting dolefully behind him; Matt supposed he might fall apart, too, over a woman like Libby. They didn't come along very often. Especially not at his and Adam's stage of the game. He thrust the thought away and smiled. 'He's not in such bad shape. At least not from the whiskey. And don't tell him I told you he's been swimmin' around in that glass for two days. He wouldn't like it.'

'No,' Libby said absently and frowned. She had filled Matt in only obliquely, enough so he'd understand how much she needed to find Adam. She had suspected Adam had misread the whole episode, and Matt's comments about his behavior over the past two days only confirmed that. She looked again toward Matt. 'Would you do me one last favor? Would you take me about halfway, get me going in the right direction. Sebastian, would you mind very much if I asked you to wait? I'd like to talk to him alone.'

Sebastian smiled warmly, patting her hand gently, anything to get Libby out of the state she'd been in for days. She hadn't been so distressed since Edwinna's breezy flight to Europe four years before, on the heels of the sale of the farm. He looked at Adam across the room, moodily staring into his glass; well, at least there was sounder basis for her distress this time. 'Of course not, pet,' he said. 'I'll just go on over to one of these tables here. Take your time. They have cream soda here?' he inquired of Matt as an afterthought.

'I don't know. I wouldn't dare ask,' Matt said dryly, then looked at Libby. 'Come on. I'll take you over.'

He led the way, conscious that Adam wasn't going to see them approach; he was still too engrossed in his romance with that damn glass. He brought Libby to a halt directly behind Adam and left her then, patting her gently on the shoulder before heading back across the room. Libby stood uncertainly for a moment, then clasped her hands in front of her. 'Hello, Adam.'

He didn't respond, and Libby sensed that he hadn't turned. She bit her lip, then tried again. 'Please, Adam. Can we talk?'

Still nothing, and the cloak of heaviness she'd been shrugging off settled down over her. She'd been right, then; it had all been too much. She'd tried to explain to Sebastian that no man in his right mind welcomed such an unbridled display of raw emotion, not under any circumstance, but especially not when he'd only been trying to help. Nor would he put himself in a position in which all that anguish might be thrust upon him again. Well, all right; she'd accept that if she had to, but still, she needed to explain. Desperately, she tried the only thing she could think of. 'If you don't talk to me, I'll turn around and flounce out of here. You'll have to pay for everything I break, and believe me, I'll make sure to hit every table.' She held her breath, willing him to say something. Anything.

Somewhere inside Adam a tight spring was abruptly released; her voice hadn't been enough to penetrate but the words were. He turned slowly, looking over his shoulder at the familiar oval face turned toward him uncertainly, and he thought as he stepped down beside her and reached for her hand that there was nothing in all the world so enchanting as Libby Rutledge when she smiled.

They were reseated at a table in a quiet corner of the lounge, Libby with a tall glass of iced tea, Adam with his half-finished whiskey. She shifted nervously in her chair and toyed with a bent straw lying near her hands, then finally looked toward him, forcing a smile. 'I won't keep you long. I simply want to apologize.'

It roused Adam; he'd been unable to take his eyes from her, or even speak since he'd taken her hand over by the bar, but at the unexpected statement, he came to and looked at her perplexed. 'Apologize?'

Libby's tongue touched her lips. 'Yes. I know I should've come here before now, or called you, but I . . .' She faltered and looked down toward the table.

Adam sat forward, trying to read her expression. 'Libby . . .'

She ignored his quiet tone, and went on resolutely. 'I'm so very sorry about what happened, that you had to witness all that. And after you so . . . kindly tried to do me a favor. It was my fault entirely! And I didn't mean to be so rude . . .'

'Wait a minute! Wait a minute!' His frown was deepening, and he picked up his glass.

'Adam, put it down,' she said quietly, motioning with her head toward his hand. 'Matt told me you'd been . . . well you just shouldn't drink so much, that's all. I don't blame you, of course, but it's no good. And this'll only take a moment. After that, you can put it all out of your head . . .'

'How the hell do you do that so well?' He was mildly irritated, as he set down the glass, then smiled ruefully. 'Never mind. It doesn't matter. And just what prompted Matt to be so talkative?' He arched an eyebrow as his annoyance surfaced again.

Libby hastened to vindicate Matt. 'He simply told me where to find you. How else do you think I knew where you were? I would've called . . .'

'I never gave you my number.'

'I know it, though. Well, you are listed in the book,' she added hastily, and took a sip of her tea.

'True,' He smiled briefly, then sobered. 'Libby, look. I don't know what this is all about . . .'

She flinched at his apparent irritation and hurried on. He had other things to do, of course. She wondered briefly what they were, then thrust the curiosity away; it was none of her business what this man did with his time or with whom he spent it. It might have been, under other circumstances, or if she'd been someone else with some other kind of life, but she wasn't. 'That's what I'm trying to tell you,' she said quickly. 'It's difficult to explain, and perhaps you won't be able to understand, but I owe you at least an explanation.'

'Libby,' he tried again in near exasperation.

'No, Adam, please!' She raised her hand. 'I've never been in a position to have to explain myself in this way before, and I'm not quite sure how to do it. But please. Just listen to me. Please.'

He drew a breath to speak again, then stopped. All right. Let her have this say she felt was so important; he'd straighten her out later. 'All right,' he said and propped his elbows on the arms of his chair.

She nodded once. 'I know you think you upset me . . .'

He couldn't help but interrupt. 'Upset you? That's rather an understatement, don't you think? Upset you and scared the hell out of you!'

She looked at him stupidly. 'Scared me?' It took her completely by surprise. She'd turned everything over and over in her mind, agonizing over what he must have thought, and had finally concluded that he must have thought he'd made her unhappy. 'Scared? That never occurred to me,' she mused, momentarily preoccupied with the concept.

It was Adam's turn to be completely at a loss. 'Then . . . what?'

She smiled sympathetically. 'You mean, what possessed me to take on like that, so that you found yourself with a weeping madwoman on your hands?' She tried to smile again, but couldn't. 'I . . . it's . . . Adam . . . Oh! How do I explain this to you?'

He had no idea what she was trying to say, but the fact that he'd misunderstood was patently clear. He reached across the table, closing his hands over hers. 'Libby, just tell me what you feel,' he said softly. 'That's all in the world I want to know.'

She eased her hand away; she couldn't speak objectively with him touching her. She picked up her glass, then set it back down immediately. 'Let me try to backtrack just for a moment. Maybe that'll help me make you understand.' she said slowly. 'You see, I have this theory about first times. I call them that. It means the first time you have to do something after some terrible thing has happened to you. For me, of course, that was being blind.' She paused, looking toward him uncertainly. 'Do you know what I mean?'

He was watching her intently, his fingertips pressed into a pyramid against his chin. 'Yes. Go on.'

'Well, they're really quite dreadful, I think, those new first times. They're like hurdles that you have to find some new way of getting over. That sets up all kinds of emotions. Frustration, anxiety. But also, they dredge up so many old emotions; they remind you of whatever terrible thing has happened to you in the first place, and you've got to relive all that. Or at least I do. But I . . . I've never shared one of those experiences with someone else before. Or rather, I've made sure I haven't been with another person, because I know how I fall apart. You can learn to live with everything after you do it enough times, but that first time! Well, it's just dreadful.' She looked down, tracing the edge of the table.

If only he had known; he'd never have let her go that day until he'd helped her drive away all those old ghosts. 'Libby,' he said gently.

She raised her head abruptly, hurrying on past what seemed like sympathy in his voice. She hadn't come for that, only to explain, to release him. From whatever. 'No, I'm not through,' she said. 'I've taken all the hurdles for the first time now, most of them a long time ago, except for this thing about learning to ride again. And you were perfectly right in what you said about *really* riding again. I didn't realize it until you took me for that ride, and if I'd known, I might not have consented to go with you.' She sat forward earnestly. 'Adam, I never in all the world would have knowingly subjected you to that. You see, I thought I'd gone over the hurdle. After all, I've been riding now for weeks. But as you said, walking sedately around that ring wasn't the way to do it, so that when you showed me again what it was like to really ride, it was the first time over the hurdle. The real first time. I hadn't even been near it before. And I fell apart. I only wish I'd been able to control myself until I was out of your earshot.' She blanched at the memory, turning her face away from him.

'Honey,' he murmured accidentally.

The endearment was confusing, and she went on as if he hadn't spoken. 'Adam, I was so terribly rude to you. First I blow up in your face and then I don't even have the decency to explain. I have no real excuse, not one that's acceptable at any rate. I can only tell you that it's acutely embarrassing for me to make such a scene. I . . . Adam, I'm so sorry. I don't blame you for trying to wash away all remembrance of it, and me.' She swallowed the final word.

He sat forward. 'That's what you think I was doing? Washing you out of my mind?'

'Well, I . . .' She paused. Was she really going to admit to him that she had assumed she might be that important in his life? Come on, Libby. This is the real world. She forced a calm voice. 'Adam, I just meant that I don't blame you for being so put off.'

'Seems to me we've had this conversation once before, or something close to it.' he said softly. 'Only then you did blame me for being put off. And just like that other time it so happens you've got it all wrong.'

She really didn't like the way he could throw her. For days she'd been agonizing over her behavior, unable, in her embarrassment, to approach him until now. And then, when she thought she'd sorted it all out, he'd reacted oppositely to what she might have expected. She looked toward him, at a loss. 'I couldn't have gotten it all wrong, Adam. I was there. I acted, well . . . that was simply no way to accept the favor you were doing me. By falling apart. By being so incredibly rude when you were being so kind.'

'Will you please stop using that word?' Now his annoyance was open. 'I wasn't being "kind". I don't like that word. It has nothing to do with what's between you and me. And, my dear Libby, you do have it all wrong again. I thought I'd ruined it all for you, that you'd never ride again because of me.'

'Ruined it all?' There was complete disbelief in her expression, and then she began to smile slowly. 'Oh, Adam, no! You gave it to me. It was marvelous! I've dreamed of that feeling of being completely . . . free. There's no other word for it. No more walls, no more tabletops, no more of all those things I can't live without. No, Adam,' she said quietly then, 'You didn't ruin it. You made it.'

He reached for her hand, taking it in both of his. 'Libby, I didn't want to hurt you so.'

She didn't draw away. 'Hurt me?'

'By bringing it all back.'

'I thought I explained that to you,' she said softly.

He nearly got up and took her in his arms, but didn't. He would wait until the time was right. 'You did, and I accept and understand it. However, I want you to know that I would never have willingly caused you pain.' Her only answer was a nod, and he reluctantly let go of her hand. 'Libby, there's one last thing I want to say to you, but before I do, do you mind if I get a glass of water or something? The cigarettes help a bit, but I've got to have some kind of glass to wrap my hand around,' he said wryly and watched her blush.

'Go ahead and finish your drink,' she said. 'I just thought . . .'

'You thought right. I drink too much. Brendan!' he called, and his glance was intercepted by Sebastian, sitting some distance away. The sight inspired him. 'Bring me whatever Mr. Vickery over there is drinking.' He gestured toward Sebastian.

Brendan sighed and moved over to the small refrigerator under the counter. Even Adam Bainbridge? he thought sourly.

Libby bit her lip but said nothing. Adam turned back to her and appraised her for a moment before going on. 'Libby, we've got to get off this rollercoaster.' Her expression was uncertain, and he smiled, ruefully. 'You've apparently been agonizing over this thing for days, for your own reasons, and so have I, for mine. It just so happens that those reasons are at opposite ends of the stick. Nor is it the first time that's happened with us. Libby, I . . . what the hell is this?' he asked abruptly, scowling down at his glass.

'Cream soda,' Brendan said shortly and set the can down beside the glass before walking away.

Libby was lost in a paroxysm of laughter, and as he watched her, Adam's frown of disgust bloomed into a grin. 'You mean to tell me Sebastian actually drinks this stuff?'

'I told you, he's one of a kind,' she shrugged when her laughter had subsided.

'From the sublime to the ridiculous,' he murmured, eyeing both glasses for a moment, then pushed everything away. 'Forget it. Libby, what I was trying to say before is simply this. Could we please get this relationship onto some kind of even keel, so that I'm not always at a loss to know what to do, and you're not always imagining all sorts of things that don't happen to be true?'

She'd picked up the straw again and was playing with it. 'Adam, you're not the kind of man who's ever at a loss to know what to do.' The tension that sparked between them was almost suffocating, and she wished suddenly she hadn't said it.

Adam was quiet for a long time. 'You're the damnedest woman I've ever run up against,' he said finally, his gaze moving slowly over her face.

She raised her head. 'And you're the damnedest man I've ever run up against. Who else in this day and time would so gallantly sweep a lady off her feet and take her for a ride? Tell me something, do you ride a white steed?'

The caress in his eyes grew to something more, and he answered in a low voice. 'For you, yes. And now, my sweet Guinevere, I think it's time we depart this place. I've seen enough of these four walls, and besides, Sebastian's getting lonely. Come on.' He rose, stepping over to help her up. She took his arm, holding it tightly as he pressed her hand to him, and when they'd gone perhaps halfway across the room, he stopped abruptly. 'Stay here a minute,' he instructed and left, then returned moments later.

'What was the matter?' she asked, tilting her head.

'I forgot something.' He began to walk again.

'What?'

'A present for Sebastian.'

'What?' she repeated curiously.

He looked down at her for a moment, then began to grin. 'A can of flat cream soda.'

# Chapter 8

The rest of May was warm and full of springtime freshness. Libby and Adam spent time coming to know each other, slowly, not as lovers yet but as romantic friends, for their courting was cautious. It was a tacit understanding, this mutual discretion; the waters ran deep for both of them. For Libby, careful orchestration was a necessity in her life, and she knew that this man had the power to alter that life irrevocably. And for Adam, his time for love had come with Libby, and he would risk none of it by a casual rush into intimacy. It would have been so easy for both of them; all the mystery and sexual magnetism were there. They each had needs and desires that suddenly only the other could fill. But there was more to their relationship than that; they wanted there to be more, and for the sake of having it all, they resisted and waded the waters slowly.

Their separate lives went on as they had before, but they meshed them more and more as the days and weeks went by, sharing quiet candlelit dinners, walks and drives along the Potomac; Adam would lower the top of his silver Jaguar and speed along the highway, watching with satisfaction and some deeper emotion while Libby gloried in the feel of the cool river breeze racing through her hair. There were museums where people were encouraged to touch the objects on display, musicals, even a trip to the zoo. And picnics. It was on those lazy weekend afternoons in the sun that Libby learned to whittle, often with Sebastian looking on as Adam guided her work with his hands over hers; and it was then that Adam learned to write in braille, then tried to read it, all to the strains of Libby's gentle, encouraging laughter. They talked and explored and learned. And above all else, they gave; Adam gave to Libby a whole new vista of sounds and sensations, for he took her everywhere, while Libby gave to Adam a whole new world of quiet unsophistication, caring, and honesty.

And in that month too, Libby learned to ride again; Adam taught her, as he'd promised, though not through any half-hearted efforts at the back of a riding ring or even thrilling adventures out across the countryside. Rather, he worked her seriously, relentlessly on the end of a thirty-foot lunge line for an hour or more every day, an unyielding taskmaster as he endeavored to give back to her what she'd once had and wanted again so desperately. He put her through the paces mercilessly, over and over: walk, trot, canter, around this way, then back again, heels down, toes in. Libby, keep your head up and straighten your back. It was grueling work, demanding; he brooked nothing less than her best effort every time, and she often despaired of the travail. It wouldn't last long, however, that feeling of weary surrender to defeat, for Adam wouldn't let it; he'd recognize her expression of frustration and remove it when he helped her down from the saddle, effectively wiping it away with a gentle word of encouragement and a lingering kiss on the lips. She knew what he was doing and let it work, starting over again with him the next day, and the next, until finally, by early June, he had her out in the fields astride her own mount and competent, his partner in accomplishment.

And so it was that when Adam received the unexpected call home by his father, he made the trip with more than his usual impatience; he resented spending time away from Libby. The butler admitted him to the house, and he strode right in, crossing the hall to come to a standstill in the portal of the living room; his mother was there, talking in a low voice to Christian, who wore an expression of decided strain. Adam didn't attempt to guess the reasons for it, however; he was interested only in finding out what had prompted Julian to call him down on such short notice. 'Mother,' he said in greeting from the doorway, and went in.

Augustine looked up, glancing at the clock on the mantle before moving toward him. 'Adam, you're early.' She gave him the inevitable passionless kiss.

Adam's eyebrow twitched imperceptibly. 'How pleasant for you. Where's Father?'

'In the study. He'll be in after a moment. Of course, he wasn't expecting you for another half hour.'

Adam ignored the accusatory tone, nodded to Christian, then moved over to a window where he stood looking out, his hands thrust in the pockets of his gray silk suit. Christian watched him for a moment, then strolled over, glass in hand. 'Something to drink, old man?'

Adam didn't turn. 'No thanks.'

'That's a first,' Christian murmured caustically and adjusted his ascot. When Adam remained silent, he crossed to a chair and sat down. Augustine disappeared, and after a moment, Christian coughed, 'I had a talk with Father.'

Adam turned then and eyed him with detachment. 'Good for you.'

'You really did a job on me, you know.'

'Oh?'

Christian's smooth voice went edgy. 'Come on, Adam. Don't be so innocent. You know damn well what I'm talking about. Jesus! I couldn't get a loan out of the man if I were Chase Manhattan. How the hell does anyone expect me to live on what he gives me?' he muttered.

'Try,' Adam said shortly. He watched unemotionally as Christian got up abruptly and crossed to the bar to pour out another two jiggers of scotch.

'You sure?' Christian motioned politely with the decanter.

'I'm sure.'

'Not drinking, huh?' He was smiling again; no sense in beating a dead horse, for the time being, anyway. He picked up his glass and strolled back over to Adam.

'Not at the moment. But I might very well start again if I have to stick around here too long. Where the hell is he, anyway?' He glanced in irritation at his watch.

'You on the carpet too?' Christian seemed pleased with the idea and observed Adam's impatient frown. When Adam ignored him, pacing over to the fireplace, Christian's eyes narrowed slightly. Such a calculated thrust was usually guaranteed to get a rise; odd that it hadn't. As odd as the sudden temperance. He lifted an eyebrow and smiled mockingly. 'Well, it appears I'm having the distinct pleasure of contemplating a changed man. No unpleasantness. No booze. I'm impressed.' He jiggled the ice around in his glass, clinking it against the sides.

Adam was leaning with one arm crooked on the mantle. He watched Christian dispassionately, immune to the sword rattling, and his thoughts strayed involuntarily to Libby. He wondered where she was, what she was doing. He'd had to renege on their dinner date and his promise to dazzle her with his mastery of the kitchen. She'd laughed in disbelief at his claims, then quickly kissed him when he protested. He'd done it on purpose; it always brought a sweet apology. And in fact he believed he was a good cook, of some things. Steaks; that's what he'd promised and he'd deliver. He put the private thoughts away and concentrated again on Christian. 'Keep contemplating. You might just learn something.' he said mildly.

Christian raised his eyebrows; unusual indeed, the continued pleasant manner. 'Have anything to do with that blind broad you've been romancing? I hear tell you've been teaching her how to ride, even gallivanting around the countryside with her on your horse. Nice touch, I must say. I never thought of that. I'll have to remember it the next time I'm out to pick up a skirt.' He smiled snidely and raised his glass to his lips.

Adam crossed the room in three strides and jerked the glass away from his mouth, spilling scotch down the front of Christian's immaculate linen shirt. He stood towering over his brother, his blue eyes narrowed and glinting like steel. 'Go to hell, you stupid bastard.'

'Good evening, Adam,' his father said from the doorway and came in, ignoring the tension crackling in the air. Augustine entered briskly behind him, and Adam stepped away from Christian, defusing his temper with effort.

'Good evening, Father.' He shot Christian a last look, then crossed to shake hands. The elderly man reciprocated, laying a hand on his shoulder.

'Sit down,' he said, motioning to the couch, and took the monstrous chair by the fireplace. When Adam was settled opposite him, one leg propped on the other, Julian smiled. 'Your mother tells me you've been here for some time. Good. That's the way it should be. Drink?'

'He's on the wagon.' Christian said and perched on the arm of a chair.

Adam didn't look over and answered for himself. 'No thanks. What was it you wanted to see me about?'

Julian waved a hand. 'Oh, there's time for that. Let's talk about other things first.'

'I don't have time to talk. I have things to do. I only came to . . .'

'Adam, you must stay for dinner,' Augustine interrupted, her lips pursed in disapproval. 'You were invited for dinner.'

'I'll have dinner another time.'

'You must stay for dinner,' she repeated intractably. 'Your place has been set and you've been included in the head count.'

And God forbid my silverware should have to be taken off the table or my head removed from the pot. He checked an involuntary smile at the absurd image the thought conjured up. He'd have to remember it; Libby would be amused. 'All right.'

Julian was studying him thoughtfully. 'Good. Now, how've you been? You look well. Very well, as a matter of fact. Better than I've seen you look for a long time.' His brow creased lightly in concentration as he took in Adam's appearance; it was relaxed.

'Thanks,' Adam said, then cocked his head. 'Father, what did you want?'

Julian gave up the appraisal and sighed. 'Such impatience. Always in a hurry. All right.' He slapped a palm down on the arm of his chair in punctuation. 'Jessup Bigelow is leaving.'

Adam's expression was blank. 'Jessup Bigelow?'

'Head of Bainbridge Manufacturing.'

'I don't know him.' Adam drew out his lighter and lit a cigarette.

'Of course not,' Julian said sharply. 'You haven't once been to a board meeting, or you would.'

Adam let out a small breath. 'Sorry.'

'You have responsibilities.'

'Father, get to the point,' Adam said and made the mistake of looking at Christian. His complacent smile only added to Adam's mounting irritation.

'The point is,' Julian said emphatically, 'he's leaving. Got another position. If you'd been to the meetings, you'd know we did everything we could to keep him on. Even to the point of renegotiating his perks, which were formidable as it was.'

'Look, since you seem to know so much about what's going on, why the hell do you have to keep digging at me about those damn meetings!' He made a movement to rise and go over to the bar, but checked it. He dragged on his cigarette instead, looking at Julian over the curl of white smoke. 'You don't need me there.'

Julian's pupils were like pinpoints. 'If you were living up to your responsibilities, I wouldn't have to know so much. However, since you aren't, someone has to stay on top of things. But!' He held up a commanding hand at Adam's imminent objection. 'That's neither here nor there at this point. It no longer matters. Directly.'

Adam looked at him warily, gauging his father's expression; he didn't like it. 'Oh? Why not?'

'Because you're going to replace Jessup.'

This time he did get up and stood for a long time at the bar, stirring the light highball. When he turned, his eyes were veiled. 'We've been through this before, remember?' He arched an eyebrow coldly. 'With Textiles.'

115

'Yes, I remember. The bad taste is still with me,' Julian returned cuttingly. 'But that was a long time ago.'

'Not long enough.'

'Long enough, Adam. It'll be different this time. It's a plum position. Manufacturing outproduces all the others two to one.'

Adam's laugh was harsh as he approached his father slowly. 'What makes you think it'll be different this time?'

Julian's expression grew dismissive. 'You're older now.'

'So?'

'So, you're old enough to know how to apply yourself.'

The muscles in Adam's jaw were working imperceptibly. 'Applying myself has nothing to do with it. I loathed that job. I thought I'd made that clear before.'

Julian squinted. 'You've got responsibilities. You're the elder son. I haven't been particularly pleased with you much of the time, but I have no other choice.' His tone was biting, and he didn't even bother to glance in Christian's direction. 'Adam, look. I've left you alone up to now, and I've always done for you what I could. It's time what I've done was reciprocated. And it's time, as I've told you before, that you looked toward your position in this family. It's time you did something, Adam.' Every word was underscored, and he watched Adam cross back over to the bar.

He only set the empty glass down, however, and returned to take his place on the couch, holding the upper hand in the conversation with his continued silence. He picked up the cigarette burning in the ashtray and finally looked at Julian, smiling pleasantly. 'You're right.'

Julian eyes him cautiously. 'Right?'

'That it's time I did something.'

'So you'll take it on?'

'I didn't say that.' Adam shifted, studying his cigarette as he rolled it around between his fingers. 'I simply said it was time I did something.'

'Well, there's plenty to do at Manufacturing.'

'I imagine.' Adam's voice was quiet, and he stubbed out the cigarette before flashing a brief smile at his mother.

It was a side to his son that Julian hadn't seen before, this absence of adamant refusal or quick temper. Julian had learned to deal with the other; this new attitude required careful assessment before he tried to combat it. 'You appear to have something already on your mind,' he ventured after a moment.

'No, not particularly.' Adam clasped his hands comfortably behind his head, sliding down on the couch.

'Then why don't you head up Manufacturing?'

'I didn't say I wouldn't.'

'But you didn't say you would.'

Adam's hands touched the wavy hair whispering across the collar of his shirt at the nape of his neck; it needed cutting, he thought idly. 'That's right.'

Julian frowned. 'Adam, I'm in no mood for sparring. A decision has to be made. Manufacturing can't go without a helmsman. Not for long.'

'I'm not sparring,' Adam said honestly. 'Did you actually expect me to make up my mind tonight?'

'I'd hoped so.'

'Well, I'm sorry, but I don't intend to.'

Julian sighed. 'All right. I'll give you a week.'

Adam straightened on the couch and laughed. 'Oh, you will? Thanks, but I'll let you know when I'm ready.'

Julian looked at him steadily for a moment, then conceded defeat. 'It'll be soon?'

'Yes, it'll be soon.'

Christian had withstood his enforced silence as long as he could. He never took part in these conversations; they didn't include him, and his contribution was inevitably some sarcastic closing remark. He stood up now and returned to the bar to fix another drink. 'Yeah, it'll be as soon as he's had a chance to talk things over with his lady love,' he tossed over his shoulder.

Both Julian and Augustine riveted their gaze on Adam. 'You have someone?' Julian inquired interestedly.

The question was always irritating and deserved an irritating answer. 'No, not that I know of. Having something infers ownership. I don't own a woman. That I'm aware of, anyway,' he said mildly.

'Adam, your father wants to know if you're involved,' Augustine snapped.

Christian was watching with amusement, for once rather empathetic with his brother. He himself had been dragged through the routine innumerable times, though not with the same ferocity; Adam, of course, had responsibilities. 'Go on, Adam,' he said, leaning back against the bar, his face lit with a crooked smile, 'tell them how involved you are.'

Adam shot him a dark look, then decided to give up the little game. Three on one were lousy odds, anyway. 'Yes, there's a particular lady I've been seeing,' He relented, stressing the noun.

117

'Good.' Julian had recovered for the moment from his previous defeat and was smiling widely. 'Who is she?'

'Just a lady I know.'

'Adam, what's her name?' Augustine pressed with a frown.

Adam looked at her for a moment, his expression unreadable. 'Elizabeth.'

'Libby,' Christian supplied from across the room. 'Libby Rutledge.'

'She's from a good family?' Augustine might have been inquiring as to the pedigree of one of the Bainbridge brood mares for all the emotion in her voice.

Julian was watching his son closely; it was time for the fireworks to begin again. None came, however, and that prompted him to watch even more thoughtfully. Adam looked over at his mother pleasantly. 'Of course.'

'What are your intentions?' Julian asked then.

Adam eyed him narrowly, though his smile was still easy. 'My intentions are simply to continue to know her. She's quite unusual.'

'Christ, is that ever an understatement!' Christian snickered loudly from across the room.

Julian and Augustine both looked first at Christian, then at Adam. Adam didn't trust himself to give his brother even a glance, and he composedly lit another cigarette. 'What does that mean, Adam?' Julian was watching him sharply again.

'It simply means she's quite a woman,' he said shortly.

Christian dropped the bomb with pleasure. 'Quite a woman and also quite, quite blind.'

Augustine gasped and put a hand to her breast.

'Is it true, Adam?' Julian demanded.

Adam had risen, but rather than striding back over to the bar, he went around to the window and stood looking off into the distance for a long time. Finally, he turned to face his family. 'It's true,' he acknowledged quietly.

'What possessed you to . . . ?' Augustine began, then sat back abruptly.

'Get involved with a blind woman?' Adam finished for her, and he smiled slowly; it was a comfortable smile, softening the hard, angular features of his face. 'Nothing. And I didn't get involved with a blind woman. I got involved with Libby.'

'It's the same thing,' Augustine said unhappily and rested her forehead in her hand. Oh, God, these boys had been the trial of her life; when was it ever going to stop?

Adam was looking at her blandly from across the room. 'No, it's not the same thing at all.'

'You seem quite taken with her.' Julian was leaning back in the wing chair, one eyebrow slightly arched; this new Adam was remarkably interesting.

'I am. She's the most fascinating woman I've ever known.' Adam turned back to the window, watching a jay land on the branch of a large oak tree out on the lawn. He couldn't decide whether he wanted to go on discussing her with them or not; they had no capacity to understand, wouldn't even if they met her, he suspected, yet he needed to wipe that smug expression off Christian's face. He'd have preferred doing it with some solid object, if the truth be told. He made up his mind finally and turned again. 'I hesitate discussing her with any of you,' he said, his eyes darkly serious. 'She's so far above the caliber of anything you, or even I, as a matter of fact, have ever encountered before, but I'll tell you this much. She's taken what could've been a very tragic life and made it into something so admirable it would astound you. She's a teacher. She teaches blind children. Teaches them how to read and . . . well, whatever, but more than that, she teaches them how to be blind effectively. I'm sure that's a concept you couldn't even begin to grasp.' His voice was suddenly angry, for the futility of his attempt to explain.

'Adam gets his kicks by riding her around the club grounds on his mighty steed.' Christian remarked then with an inebriated sneer. He'd begun to sway and bumped up against the bar again.

It was Julian who silenced him before Adam had a chance to. 'Shut up!' he spat in his acid, old man's voice. 'And stop leaning all over the furniture. If you can't stand up, then get out!' Christian's expression went petulant, and he took another long drink. Julian turned back toward Adam. 'What's this about riding?'

'I taught her how to ride again,' he said shortly.

Julian's eyebrows's lifted. 'She rides?'

'Yes, she does. Beautifully.'

'That's impossible,' Augustine declared flatly, arranging the gold bangles on her wrist with studied indifference.

Adam turned on her. 'How the hell would you know! You don't know how to do anything except read a goddamned clock!' He turned roughly back to the window, closing his eyes in an effort to regain some measure of control.

Augustine looked faint, and Julian suppressed a smile. 'That's enough,' he directed. 'Your mother's constitution isn't up to

119

your scathing remarks, and besides, Manning's just indicated dinner is served. Let us be on our way. Christian, go rinse your face in cold water. I don't want you soused at the table.' He looked at his youngest son with heavy disgust as he rose, then at Adam, who'd turned back to face them. 'Bring her around sometime. We'd like to meet her,' he suggested casually.

'Perhaps I will,' Adam said tightly. 'Perhaps I just goddamn will.' He looked at Julian darkly a moment longer, then strode out of the room.

# Chapter 9

Libby slowed her horse at the crest of the hill and then felt the light tug of Adam's hand on her reins as he brought both their horses to a standstill side by side at the top of the rise. Her hair tossed about her shoulders as she relaxed and let her reins go slack; Adam was close by now, the hard calf of his booted leg resting reassuringly against hers, and she turned to him and smiled for a thousand reasons. 'That was marvelous!'

He was watching her proprietarily and grinned. 'I'm glad you thought so. But be forewarned. The next time you're in the mood for a race, I'm not going to let you win by holding Morgan in. I'm only telling you now so it won't be too big a shock when you and Daisybell here get left in the dust.' As if he'd get that far away. Ever.

'You're on, Adam Bainbridge. And quit calling her Daisybell. It hurts her feelings. I'm told she's got a pedigree as long as your arm, and she likes to be called Sheba, if you please.'

Adam laughed, dropping Morgan's reins. 'Right. Let's take a breather. Want to get down?'

'No.' She looked away, lifting her chin to the feel of the open space around her. 'What hill is this?'

'Two over from the bridle path, the higher one. You can see the roof of the stable way off to the right, over your shoulder. It's black, pitched steeply, with, let's see . . .' He narrowed his eyes, studying the distant building, 'Shingles, I think. The sun hits it just off to one side.'

She pictured it, then caught the scent of the meadow. 'The clover's blooming,' she remarked.

'Hmmm.' He said it absently; he was admiring her fine profile, the way her thick hair shone a rich gilt-edged auburn in the summer sun, and he resisted a sudden urge to reach out and run his fingers through it.

'Matt says he's going to graduate me to a chestnut mare. He says she's got nice gaits. Easy.' She looked toward him eagerly.

It broke his reverie, making him frown lightly. 'We'll see. I'll be the one to make that decision when the time comes. I happen to know that particular mare, and she's skittish. I won't have you up on some fool of a horse.'

Her response was an acquiescent smile as she combed her fingers through her hair, straightening it. 'How was dinner last night?' she asked suddenly.

He grimaced. 'Obnoxious, as always.'

'Adam, you're always so cold about them,' she chided.

Her rebuke didn't move him. 'That's the way I feel. They're cold people. It makes for chilly relationships.'

'Have you ever taken a good look at them? Maybe they're not so bad after all. Everyone has at least a few good points, you know.'

'Forget it, Lib.' He smiled humorlessly and lit a cigarette, dragging deeply on it as he put the lighter away. 'I'm sure they'd appreciate your trying, but I've been around a little too long. Believe me, they are what they are. Cold.'

Libby let it slide; she didn't know enough about the Bainbridges to argue any further. 'What did your father want, if I might ask?'

He contemplated her a moment with a half smile; of course she should ask, and of course he'd tell her. 'He wants me to take over one of the companies.'

Libby was quiet for a long time, shifting slightly in the saddle; unconsciously, Adam reached out and briefly laid a steadying hand on her arm. 'You hate that,' she said finally.

'You're right.'

'Are you going to do it?'

'I doubt it.'

'You say that as though you've given it some consideration.' She was turned toward him, every sense leveled on his presence beside her.

His eyes drifted from her to the meadow beyond; it was verdent and shot with the white pompoms of blooming clover, the avenue of birches off in the distance below them swaying gently in the breeze. When he looked back at her, his face was shadowed. 'My dear Elizabeth, it's about time Adam did something with himself, don't you think?'

'Don't say it like that.'

'Like what?'

'You know what I mean. Adam, I hate it when you're so derisive.'

Thank you, he thought and flipped his cigarette into the grass. His voice when he answered was bland. 'Don't let it upset you. It's just a natural attitude.'

'It isn't, and you know it. But, Adam,' she said in sudden earnestness, 'don't do it. Not if you don't want to. There's nothing worse than being trapped into something you hate. What about Christian? Can't he do it?'

He laughed in genuine mirth. 'You know, Libby, I think it's time you were introduced to the Bainbridge clan. Then you'd stop making such ludicrous remarks.' He was glad she'd brought it up; he'd wondered how he was going to broach the subject. Yes, it was time she met them, or rather, time they met her; let them have a look at real quality for a change.

Libby's face wore a reproachful look. 'Adam, that's an unpleasant thing to say.'

'Perhaps. But Libby, my love,' he said, tossing in the endearment offhandedly, 'stop trying to make things in my life the way they were in yours. You were very close to your family. I'm not. I never was and I never will be. And I meant what I said. Would you like to drive down?' He watched her, gauging her reaction.

It was startled. 'Oh. Well . . .' Off balance for a moment, she hedged. 'Think they're ready for me?' she asked lightly.

The easy smile drained from his face. 'Stop it,' he said sharply. 'And I hate it when you say things like that.'

'Adam! I was only joking!'

'Well, it's a lousy joke.' He eyed her disapprovingly for a moment, then relaxed the frown. 'However, in a completely different context, I'm not so sure they are ready for you. It'll give me a great deal of pleasure to watch you outclass them hands down. And you can assess the incomparable Christian for yourself then. I'll try to see to it that he's there. I'd hate like hell for you to be deprived of listening to the drivel that comes out of his mouth every time he opens it.'

The unforgiving acerbity made up her mind, and she raised her chin slightly. 'Yes, I'd like to meet them. And make my own assessments, as you say,' she said pointedly.

Her defiance made him smile; she was always so staunchly fair-minded. After a moment, he went on casually. 'I thought perhaps we'd stay the night. It's not that short a drive. We could go down Saturday, come back Sunday.' He lit another cigarette, watching her closely over the top of his hands as he cupped them briefly around the lighter.

Libby recognized the step toward a more intimate relationship and looked away. She deliberated for a long time over the suggestion, so much that Adam had decided she was going to refuse when finally she turned back to him. 'All right. Yes. That would be nice.'

He dropped the subject then; it had set up an electric tension between them that was for another time and place. 'Good, I'll set it up. And now, ready to ride on, or shall we go back?'

She was grateful for his nonchalance and picked up her reins. 'Well, let's head in the direction of the stable. I've got to get home early. Sebastian and I have a date with the supermarket.'

They turned back, slowly making their way down the hill. They rode on across the meadow in companionable silence, and at the edge of the line of trees, Adam turned them; it was a more private route, following the direction of the bridle path on the far side, and what they both preferred. Libby seemed lost in a world of her own, riding quietly beside Adam with her knee grazing his every now and then. Finally she roused herself, looking over. 'Adam, I've been thinking of something.'

He came to from his own abstraction. 'What?'

'Well, it's about Jennie.' She paused for a moment, biting her lip. 'I'd like to bring her out here. Riding, I mean. She's having such a hard time. We all try, and she tries, too, but she just can't seem to throw off the dejection. I thought if I could show her that there are ways to get some relief from it all, it'd help.'

He considered the suggestion as he watched her. 'She ever ride before?'

'I don't know, but I suspect not.'

'Then it might scare her to death. You have to remember, you had had riding experience. You'd been completely at home on a horse once, as you are now.'

She smiled at the compliment. 'I know. And I can't answer for Jennie, as to whether it would frighten her, but I just thought . . .'

'And how were you proposing to go about all this?' He eyed her narrowly.

'Oh. Well, take her up with me, the way you did. Put her up in front of me.'

That's what he'd suspected. 'No,' he said flatly. 'That's out of the question. I won't have some frantic kid desperate to get off dragging you down out of the saddle.'

'Adam!' Her startled objection was tinged with laughter. 'If we were just in the riding ring, there's not that much that could happen. And you said yourself that I'm fine now. I can hold my own.'

'Libby, I said it's out of the question. I won't allow it.'

She drew a small breath. 'Adam, if I want . . .'

'And just who's in charge here? You or me?' His face was set in stern lines.

'Adam . . .'

'That's right. Me,' he said shortly. 'I haven't spent all this time getting you readjusted and fall-proof just so some kid can come along and break your neck for me.'

There was a quality about his protectiveness that prevented her from getting angry. 'I doubt very seriously I'd break my neck,' she countered mildly.

He reined Morgan over slightly, directing them away from a ditch. 'That's exactly right. You're not going to. I intend to see to that. Now, if you feel that strongly that the child might benefit from it all, then I'll take her up. But not you.'

'Okay.'

He looked at her abruptly, a suspicious smile blooming on his face. 'And that's exactly what you had in mind in the first place, wasn't it?'

She worked at keeping the innocent expression. 'Adam . . .'

'Wasn't it?' he pressed, his smile widening involuntarily.

Her cheeks dimpled then. 'Well, actually, it had crossed my mind. But!' She raised a hand. 'I meant it. I'd take her up, too. And I think I could with no problem.' She looked toward him seriously, her eyebrows lifting.

He merely shook his head, chuckling under his breath. Libby let it drop for the time being, and when they'd almost reached the point of crossover into the bridle path, she spoke up again. 'Adam, what do you think about a riding school for the blind?'

He reined them to a halt; there wasn't much further to go, and he was reluctant to reach the stable. And for the hundredth time, as he let his eyes briefly roam her face before answering, he wanted to remove her glasses. They tested his patience, giving him merely a tantalizing glimpse of those marvelous eyes he wanted to know. 'I haven't ever thought about it,' he said after a moment.

Libby looked toward him with sudden intensity. 'Well, I have, Adam, it could really be something!'

Yes, he supposed it could. 'There are a lot of things to consider, though. As we said about Jennie, I'm not sure everyone would go for it.'

He realized her idea hadn't been a spontaneous one when she went on eagerly. 'Yes, I know. Not everyone goes for anything. But, Adam, think about it for a minute. Think what it could give to those who did want to try. And who stuck with it, whether they'd ever ridden before or not. It could all be set up under very controlled circumstances. I shouldn't have to explain that to you. You've been through it once, with me.'

'Hmmm.'

'Adam, just think, if I'd done this years ago, how far ahead of the game I'd have been,' she said seriously.

He reached over and caressed her under the chin, his eyes softening. 'Libby, you've always been ahead of the game.'

She touched his hand involuntarily as he drew it away. 'Oh, no. You're looking at years of experience with trying to cope. You should know by now it wasn't always easy. I showed that to you once.'

'Yes, you did,' he said quietly; it wasn't a memory he savored.

'Adam, I think it's a workable idea,' she pressed.

'You're probably right.' He leaned back in the saddle, crossing his arms. 'And just tell me. Who's going to do all this? Not you. Not alone, anyway. Matt?' He thought a moment, narrowing his eyes briefly. 'He's a good horseman. He's certainly capable, and just might be willing to give it a try.'

'Well, I'd thought about him, yes.' She became engrossed for a time in fingering a stray thread at the knee of her jodhpurs, then finally spoke without looking up. 'But I . . . what came to mind first was you,' she ventured.

He straightened, genuinely nonplussed. 'Me?'

'Well, yes, Adam.' She looked at him then, tilting her head.

He laughed abruptly; she was dead serious. 'Now, that's a real laugh! Adam Bainbridge, Good Samaritan, teacher of the blind. That ought to elicit a few snickers around the barroom!'

'Adam, I told you I hate it when you sound like that!'

He glanced at her quickly, his sarcastic mood instantly evaporating; he'd made her really angry. Her lips were tightened into a thin line and her chin was thrown up slightly. 'I'm sorry, Lib.' He reached for her hand. 'I didn't mean to squelch your idea like that. It's a good one. I just think you've got the players in the wrong place, that's all,' he said in a conciliatory tone.

She pulled her hand away. 'No I don't, either! You've got this view of yourself that's so out of focus, it's absurd! You've got everything all neatly categorized, haven't you? You, your family, the whole world. Somewhere along the line you decided

126

to be a cynic, and you haven't bothered to try to revise your opinions, any of them, no matter what. You can't take the time to open your eyes, pardon the pun, and see yourself or anyone else as they really are, can you? Well, I suppose that's your problem, but it's stupid. And you're not a stupid man. As for teaching the blind, you did it once, and you could do it again. What's really the matter, Adam? Afraid someone might find out you've got a little sensitivity after all?' She bit her lip. She hadn't meant to be so judgmental and instantly despised the outburst.

He didn't; the diatribe against his self-image was not only eloquently revealing but like a caress, coming from her. He looked down at his hands for a time, then back at her. 'Maybe,' he said quietly.

She was drumming her fingers against the saddle. 'Adam, I'm sorry. I didn't mean to turn on you like that, but honestly! Sometimes you make me so mad. You're entitled to your opinions, of course, but I just don't happen to agree with some of them.' They were moving again; Adam had started them walking, silencing her momentarily as he told her to duck. They crossed through the barrier of trees, and when they were on the other side, Libby said calmly, 'Why is it such a laugh for Adam Bainbridge to teach the blind? You could probably do it better than most people I know. You know exactly . . . oh, never mind!' She looked away abruptly. And just who was she to tell him who he was and what he could do? It was annoyingly pompous, and besides, too many other people in his life had tried to do the same. His father, especially. His silence seemed deafening, and she was about to say something in further apology when he spoke.

'And just what kind of setup did you have in mind?' He'd been watching something off in the distance, and he didn't look at her as he asked the question but lit a cigarette instead.

'I didn't really have one in mind, Adam, I'm sorry I brought it up. Sorry I said what I did.' She looked over at him, trying to smile.

They'd reached the macadam road, and he moved them off onto the shoulder, oblivious to the wave of a hand in a passing car. 'It'd take a lot of work.'

'Adam, it's only an idle thought I had.'

'And a lot of money.'

'Adam!' she said in growing frustration.

He looked at her then, curiously. "And just who are you intending to gear it toward? Children? Adults?'

'Adam . . .'

'You were thinking of the children at the school, weren't you?' His eyes softened momentarily as he watched her expression change.

'Initially, yes.'

'Facilities would have to be built, special horses obtained, transportation provided, a lot of long, hard work on a one-to-one basis with each student. There'd have to be some way to acclimate them beforehand, familiarize them with horses and equipment. It's a tremendous project. And still you couldn't be certain it'd work.'

She shouldn't have broached the subject at all, but especially not to a businessman before she'd worked out some of the details; of course he thought she was being foolish, when she had no ammunition for rebuttal. She blanched under his apparent criticism and tried to end it once and for all. 'Adam . . .' she began firmly.

'I'm lousy with kids.'

It was so unexpected, she was speechless for a moment. She recovered immediately, however, and said with quiet encouragement, 'How do you know?'

He flipped his cigarette away and glanced at the barn looming up ahead of them. 'I'm too impatient.'

'You weren't with me.'

'That's entirely different. You're not a child, and anyway, I had my reasons.'

She raised her eyebrows. 'Oh, really? What were they?'

He recognized the imminent digression and import of the question before she did, but sidestepped adroitly. 'It was so important to you. And you were getting nowhere.'

She helped him get firmly back on the track. 'What does that have to do with your patience?'

They were nearly at the barn; the paddock was alive with other horses, riders, and stablehands, and he pulled Morgan to a standstill. Sheba followed suit, and Adam looked at Libby, studying her face turned accurately in his direction. 'I wanted you to learn.'

'Why?'

'Because you needed it.'

'You don't think there are others with the same need?' The breeze was blowing wisps of her hair about her face, and she brushed them away as she kept her attention focused on Adam.

His gaze had drifted off again to something in the distance.

'You'd have to have more than one instructor. No one could take on more than one or two kids at a time.'

'I suppose that would come in time, and that's, as you say, assuming the idea could work at all.'

'Where were you proposing to get the money for all this?'

That did it; she'd never once meant to imply that she'd brought it up to him because of the money. 'Adam, it was only a thought! I hadn't even gotten past your first question in my mind. Let's drop it, okay?'

'Just where would you figure into all this, while I'm out there toting all these frantic little kids around on my horse?'

She was silent for a very long time, listening to him, trying to understand. 'Does that mean it's something you'd consider doing?' she asked finally.

He looked at her for a moment, then clucked to the horses. 'I told you. I'm lousy with kids,' he said and headed the horses through the gate.

Libby's marketing took an hour and a half, and Sebastian brought the four brown bags into the apartment with the aid of the doorman, setting them on the countertop under the cabinets. He tipped the man, closed the door behind him, and came to stand in the kitchen doorway, watching as Libby distributed the groceries to their proper places. Winna's cable lay open on the edge of the counter, and he looked at it, frowning involuntarily. He hadn't been the one to read it to her, though he'd scanned the contents before they'd left for the shopping center; Adam had done that, when he'd brought her home from the club.

'Damn,' Libby muttered, and Sebastian glanced over quickly. She was on her knees on the kitchen floor, feeling around for the package of steaks.

'Here, pet.' He retrieved it, putting it in her hands as he studied her moody expression. She'd been wearing it ever since she'd come home.

She smiled briefly and stood up. 'Thanks, Sebastian.'

'Doesn't suit me to see those creases in your brow,' he commented after a moment.

She gave him a rueful look and opened the freezer door. 'I know. Makes for age lines, right?'

'You've a bit to go before worrying about that.' He studied her again; he didn't get a chance to do that anymore, now that Adam had come along, although he didn't begrudge their time together. He liked Adam; the man was educated, articulate, well able to handle himself and the world around him. And he obviously cared about Libby, which was the paramount consideration. A brief smile passed across his face as he contemplated his paternal machinations. Well, that was the way he felt about Libby, and was why he was mildly disturbed by her deep preoccupation. 'Tell me, pet. All is going well?'

'Of course. Why do you ask?' She'd finished with the groceries and made her way past him into the living room, where she sat down on the couch.

He joined her. 'Your expression. It's worried. The cable, perhaps?'

She pressed her lips together. Actually, she'd been grateful that Adam had been the one to collect the mail from the box downstairs; it had spared her the aggravation of Sebastian's reaction. And given her a comfortable feeling besides; the telegram from the sister she loved being read by the man she, what? Loved? A shadow passed across her face and she looked off toward the fireplace.

Sebastian was aware of it. 'Yes, the cable is disturbing,' he said and sat back against the cushions.

'There's nothing disturbing about the cable,' she nearly snapped and looked toward him.

'Odd she should get in touch again so soon.' He couldn't help it; he was uneasy.

'Sebastian, she said she'd cable her address, dammit!' She bit her lip; she hadn't meant to curse at him. Not at Sebastian. She was tired, that was all; and she had things on her mind.

He was watching her with his lips pursed. 'Pet, there was no address in the cable.'

Well, all right, so there wasn't. And all right, so it was odd that she'd cabled the friendly message so soon after the other. 'Lib,' it said, 'Was just thinking about you and wanted to drop a line. Have been caught up in all sorts of activity—parties, sailing. I went skiing! You should've been there to see me go head over heels! But the slopes of Austria are divine. Hope you're well. Love to you, Winna.' Libby smiled for a moment as she remembered the words. They stuck in her mind verbatim, for the fact of their being Winna's, but also for the fact of her blindness; it improved memory ten-fold. 'Yes, I know,' she said after a moment to Sebastian. 'I know there's no address, but what does it matter? She's in Austria now, anyway.'

'So? Austria has fallen off the map?'

She didn't want to argue and wouldn't. Why couldn't he be like Adam, who'd simply read the telegram, obviously pleased by Libby's pleasure; he'd kissed her when she'd smiled. On the mouth. It brought back her disquiet, and she gave Sebastian a beseeching smile. 'Sebastian, please. Don't. Okay?'

Sebastian looked at her and sighed. It would do no good, anyway, to try to talk to her, make her understand that there was some motive behind Winna's sudden spate of correspondence; for Winna, two messages constituted a spate. Everything she did was with calculation, as he'd tried to impress upon Libby for years, and he never deluded himself that Winna might be merely regaling Libby with affectionate long-distance chitchat. Affectionate chitchat? He wanted to spit. 'All right. But I'll not let this worried expression go by. It's Adam, then?'

Oh, Sebastian, how can you be so obtuse sometimes and so astute at other times? she thought. She pushed away the discontent about his attitude toward Winna and smiled briefly. 'Yes.'

'Might I pry?'

'It's just a conversation we had today. It was a little . . . oh, I don't know.' She moodily picked up the throw pillow beside her, holding it to her chest.

'An argument?' He frowned. An argument didn't seem plausible; that took two, and only she seemed uncomfortable. Adam had been his usual relaxed self when they'd spoken briefly in the hall.

'No, not really. I just brought up something I've been thinking about. A riding school for the blind.'

'A novel idea,' he remarked.

'Hmmm. I asked Adam what he thought about it.' She looked toward him, flopping the pillow back in its place as she curled her legs beneath her.

'And?'

'Well, I'm not sure. I put it to him that he'd make a good instructor for it.'

Sebastian's eyebrows rose. 'He disagreed?'

Libby brushed her hand across her forehead, letting her fingers run back through her hair. 'I don't know. Well, he did initially, yes, and I lambasted him.' She sighed audibly. 'I shouldn't have done that. I've always hated it when people try to tell me what I think and who I am. I can't believe I was doing it to him. It smacks of pomposity, you know.'

'Pompous? You? I can't conjure up the image!' He laughed warmly, unwrapping a peppermint candy from the dish on the coffee table.

She smiled fondly. 'Thanks, Sebastian, for your undying confidence.'

He took her back on the track. 'It made him angry?'

'No, actually, it didn't seem to. I don't know what it made him. He went on after that about the school, talking about what it would entail. Frankly, he gave more thought to the ins and outs of it than I have.' She pursed her lips, remembering his quick calculations. He had a facile mind, ingenious as it grasped a concept and ran with it.

'So, he's interested?' He popped the peppermint in his mouth, relaxing back again.

'I don't know. I just . . .'

He eyed her thoughtfully. 'It troubles you. Why?'

She took a deep breath and shifted around to face him squarely. 'It troubles me because I wouldn't want him to get involved with it simply because he thinks it would please me. That's no proper motivation. He's already got his father all over him to do something he hates. The last thing he needs is for me to put the same kind of pressure on him.'

'You think he'd do it simply for your sake?'

Libby smiled at that. 'I hadn't realized how presumptuous that sounds.'

Sebastian chose his words carefully. 'You two have become good friends.'

'Hmmm.' She was preoccupied again; the same shadow passed across her face. After a minute she said quietly, 'He's asked me to meet his family.'

'How suggestive.'

'Sebastian!' She looked toward him sternly. 'He proposed it mostly because he and I don't see eye to eye on the subject of what kind of people his family might be. We have a bit of a running argument going, and I guess you could say this visit is a way of settling it. Or something like that.'

Or something like that. He smiled to himself. 'I see.'

She was tracing the edge of the sofa arm, looking down toward her hands. 'We're going to stay the weekend. Saturday and Sunday, that is.'

'Ah. When is this?'

She shrugged. 'Oh, I don't really know. He merely suggested it. I said I'd go.'

'You don't really want to, do you?' His light expression had gone serious.

I want to do a lot of things, Sebastian, she thought. To run, to fly, to hold onto this man who thrills me. Whom I love. Yes, say it to yourself, Libby. Whom I love. And who's known a thousand women in his lifetime. And who's never had to cope with me on so personal a basis before. 'It presents certain problems, traveling with him, that's all.'

Sebastian was unmoved by her tone of qualification. 'Oh? What problems?'

'Just certain problems.'

He frowned, watching as she uncurled her legs and stretched them out on the floor in front of her. 'You've gotten that tone in your voice again, as if you were the problem.'

She looked toward him seriously then. 'Sebastian, let's be realistic. You and I know what it's all about. He's never had to cope with me on a fulltime basis before, in a place where I'm not completely acclimated. That brings certain pressures to bear, pressures he's not been exposed to before. It's not like taking me out for an evening, or for an afternoon. It's one thing to deal with my handicap under controlled circumstances, quite another to do so in unfamiliar surroundings, where I have to cope with so many things he takes for granted. And there are personal things about traveling with him, things I . . . oh, I don't know, Sebastian! I said I'd go, but I don't know.'

'Elizabeth,' he said sternly, but looked at her with the gentlest of eyes. 'How important is this man to you?'

She was looking down toward her hands, clasped around her knees. 'That's not an easy question to answer.'

'Don't hedge with me, missy. Not with me. You seem quite comfortable in his company,' he said with understatement. 'You like to be with him.'

She didn't look up. 'Yes.'

'And he seems quite comfortable in yours, from what I can ascertain.'

'Yes . . .'

He cocked his head slightly as he peered at her lowered face. 'Then give him a chance. And if he's not going to be able to go the whole road, best you find that out now, huh?' She'd looked around slowly, pulling her legs back as she straightened. Sebastian studied her for a moment, then reached over and took her hand. 'Don't close the door before it's even had an opportunity to swing open,' he said quietly.

She was looking toward him, affection written in every line of her face. 'You're right. Thank you, Sebastian. As always, thank you.' She held onto his hand a moment longer, then let it go. 'And for the jewels of wisdom that you always seem to have stuck in your back pocket, you need a reward. Dinner's on me. Steaks, soup, or chicken pot pie. Take your choice, professor, but make it quick. I'm going to light the fire.' She was up in a moment, giving him a merry smile as she went by.

He watched her go with his own smile of warm satisfaction; she deserved such happiness, the kind Adam Bainbridge could give her, if only he would. He stood up then, following her into the kitchen, watching as she went about preparing their dinner to the strains of some tuneless melody she hummed.

And neither of them noticed Winna's telegram as it drifted up off the countertop behind them in the draft of their activity and floated gently toward the floor below.

# Chapter 10

It was two weeks later, when July came blazing in on the
rockettails of dead summer heat, that Adam took Libby down to
the Bainbridge estate; her tour began at the drive, and he talked
her along it, down the lane, across the wooden bridge at the
stream, around the circle to the house. She pictured the ivy-
colored Tudor mansion Adam depicted as they stepped from the
car, its diamond-shaped latticed windows, turrets, stucco faded
to ecru with age, and when they finally stood before the front
door, she was surprised to feel him lift her free hand and rest it
on some metal object out in front of her.

'And then there's this thing on the door.' He shot her a wry
glance out of the corner of his eye; she wore a light summer suit,
beige, with a sleeveless blouse tied at the throat, and she was
looking interestedly in the direction of her hand. He looked back
at the door. 'They call it a door knocker. It's a gargoyle actually,
brass, a nasty-looking thing with a lion's head and the body of a
man. Really grotesque. Makes you think twice about going in.'
He removed Libby's hand and rapped the knocker against the
heavy oak door.

Libby looked up toward him curiously, ignoring his comment.
'Do you always knock?'

'Always.' He nodded briefly to Manning when the door
opened, then stepped inside, walking with Libby into the very
center of the hallway.

'This is an immense room,' she remarked. The hollow echo of
their footsteps on the stone floor hung in the air, deafening
against the stillness around them, she listened for sounds of
other activity but heard none.

Adam was watching her, aware of her sudden tension; her
smile hadn't its usual softness and her shoulders were stiff. He
covered the slender hand resting on his arm with his own. 'Yes,'
he said quietly and went on as if by rote. 'It has a vaulted

cathedral ceiling, the main staircase is off at the back, and there's very little furniture around. Some large tables and an armoire-type thing. It's all paneled in mahogany.'

Manning stepped forward. 'Shall I announce you, sir?'

Adam glanced at him briefly. 'No, thanks. We'll find everyone.' When the man had gone, he looked back at Libby and brushed a finger under her chin. 'Don't be nervous.'

'Oh. Does it show?'

He gazed laughingly at her. 'To me it does. You don't normally cut off the circulation in my arm. Libby,' he said, sobering again, 'It's all right. Now, I imagine everyone's out in the garden. They usually are this time of the year. It'll give us some time to get acclimated. Come on, we're still on tour.' He began walking across the hall toward a wide room, counting off their footsteps as they went.

So he understood, after all; Libby was relieved and at the same time chagrined. She'd spent untold hours deliberating over some innocuous way of making him aware that she required familiarization with positively every aspect of her new environment if she were to get around comfortably on her own, as she'd want to; she couldn't abide simply being an attachment on someone's arm. And she'd blanched at the thought that he'd find the concept initially staggering and ultimately disheartening. Sebastian's wisdom rang in her ears. 'Give him a chance.' Well, she'd hardly even begun to and already he'd laid her misapprehensions to rest.

'Fifteen steps from the center of the hall to here,' Adam was saying. 'It's the living room, by the way. Later, we'll take it from the stairway. I daresay you'll be following that path more often.'

She let out a quiet breath. 'How did you know to do that? Not too many people realize . . .' Looking toward him pensively, she let the words drift off.

'Libby, I'm not completely stupid,' he said calmly. 'I spent a long time contemplating how you might go about finding your way around some place you'd never seen before and came up with the bright idea, if I do say so myself, that you might count the steps. At least initially. I've never seen you do it, but then, I've never seen you accustom yourself to a place you weren't familiar with. How'd I do?'

'Beautifully. You're right. That's what I do sometimes. One way is as good as another, but . . . oh, Adam. I'm so sorry!'

He frowned. 'For what?'

'Oh, never mind,' she murmured and looked off toward the floor.

He didn't pursue it. 'Come on, we've got a lot of ground to cover. We're going into the living room, and believe me, you'll have no difficulty whatsoever getting around in here. The room is chock-a-block with furniture. I'll wind you through it.'

Which he did, then through two drawing rooms, the library, music room, and the enormous dining room. Their repartee was as always: rapid-fire, lighthearted, and of their own brand; it almost seemed they were somewhere else, on their own ground, not burdened by the trappings of his past or her anxieties of the moment. Adam took them upstairs finally, making a circuit of the hallways, though not the myriad of bedrooms, for there were simply too many, and it was when they'd returned to the landing at the top of the front staircase that they encountered Augustine. She stood at the foot of the steps, looking up.

'Manning said you'd arrived, that you'd been here for some time.' One thin eyebrow arched as she studied the couple at the top of the steps.

Adam composed his expression, then descended the stairs. He made the appropriate introductions, his eyes on Libby the whole time. She was smiling warmly and extended her hand. 'Mrs. Bainbridge. I'm so glad to meet you.'

'Hmmm.' Augustine wasn't looking directly at Libby but uncomfortably off to the left of her as she took her hand briefly. She turned to Adam then. 'Your father and brother are out in the garden waiting. That was very rude, Adam, not coming straight out. I'll let you explain yourself.' She turned abruptly and walked briskly across the hall, disappearing into the living room.

Libby was biting her bottom lip. 'I think we should've gone out first,' she said.

The annoyance in Adam's expression faded only slightly as he looked from the living room doorway back to Libby. 'Forget it. You're going to be introduced around on my terms, not theirs. And don't take it personally. That's Mother's natural attitude.'

Libby said nothing, but let him take her through the house out onto a wide veranda, then down several steps to a patio at the edge of the garden. At the sight of them, Christian and Julian rose; Augustine had rejoined them and stood stiffly nearby. Adam brought Libby directly forward. 'Father, I want you to meet Libby. Libby, my father.'

Julian took her hand, appraising her with a sharp eye; she appeared to be perfectly at ease as she smiled openly, her thick auburn hair drawn back at the temples and shining copper in the sunlight. She came barely above Adam's shoulder in heels and had her free hand resting in the jacket pocket of her tailored suit. His eyebrow twitched involuntarily; they made a nice-looking couple, the two of them. As if they belonged together. 'I've been waiting to meet you, Miss Rutledge,' he said at length. 'My son seems to find you inordinately fascinating. Which is a first.'

Cold, Adam had called them. Difficult seemed more apropos. Or was impossible closer to the truth? Libby realized she was wrinkling the sleeve of Adam's suit and loosened her grip. 'It's a pleasure to meet you, Mr. Bainbridge,' she said simply, and smiled.

Christian strolled over and preempted Adam's introduction. 'And I'm Christian,' he said smoothly. He was looking her over curiously; he'd never actually seen her before, this blind woman who rode horses and had captured his brother's interest so unexpectedly. She was damned attractive.

Libby forced a smile one more time and offered her hand. There was a small silence after their exchange, which Adam ended. 'Mother, we'd love some iced tea.' He was watching her with mild amusement; she seemed patently unable to cope as she stood clasping and unclasping her hands. She nodded once, then moved off in search of the butler.

'Sit down,' Julian directed then, moving over to his chair under the canvas umbrella.

Adam smiled indulgently. 'In a moment.' Instead of joining the group, he walked with Libby to the edge of the patio. Withdrawing her hand, he faced her out toward the garden, placing his hands lightly on her shoulders as he stood close behind her. 'You're looking out over the garden,' he said quietly. 'I'll take you through it later, but first let me explain it to you. Envision a quarter of a mile or so straight out before you. That's how far it extends, and a thousand feet or so on each side. It's planted with trimmed boxwoods. They form the design, very geometric, rather like a maze, and inside each small hedgeway are flowers. Every kind you can imagine, and don't ask me to name them, because I can't. But there's every color in the rainbow, and it stretches as far as you can see. The pathways running through it are red brick, and there are small concrete benches sitting about.'

The short recitation had two purposes: to set her at ease again, but more important, to make a point to his family. She was here under his auspices and would receive his primary attention; he'd effectively shut out the Bainbridge influence as he stood dealing with her on their own terms. If she suspected what he was doing, she made no direct comment but fell quickly into their routine as she relaxed. 'Oh, come on, Adam. Name me one flower at least.' She tossed a teasing smile back over her shoulder.

He caught it with an easy grin, then narrowed his eyes out toward the garden. 'Well, let's see. Marigolds, I guess.'

She laughed. 'Marigolds! I would have expected you to name something else. Marigolds, huh?' she repeated thoughtfully.

'And zinnias. I think that's what they are.'

'Yes, they are.' Augustine stood at his elbow, some unrecognizable emotion registered in her eyes as she studied Libby's face angled away from her. 'Also ageratum, alyssum, geraniums, carnations. There's some flox.'

Adam was mildly surprised; she wasn't often so accommodating. 'Thank you, Mother. Sometime you can give me a proper lesson, so that I don't leave Libby in the lurch on her flowers.'

She looked at him, the momentary emotion disappearing from her expression. 'Your tea is here. And I'm sure Libby would like to sit down.' She turned abruptly and went over to sit by her husband.

Libby and Adam joined them then; they sat down together on a wrought-iron bench cushioned with gay print pillows. At once Julian picked up the conversation. 'Well, Adam, I understand you've been here for some time. You should have let us know.' He watched as Adam set down his tall glass of tea and wound Libby's arm through his.

He looked back at Julian pleasantly. 'I was showing Libby around.'

'Oh, and what did you think?' Christian's voice was smooth as he asked the question. He didn't know exactly why he felt the need to annoy her; perhaps it was because she and Adam were sitting there perfectly at ease now, making everyone else uncomfortable.

Libby looked toward him with a light smile. His impression was so different from the one Adam gave off. Milder, smaller. Indistinct. 'It's lovely, from what Adam tells me. I suspect the cupboard in the library is more along the lines of a secretary, however.' She shot Adam a quick smile. He received it blandly, smiling wryly back at her as he pressed her hand; it had been a private exchange, exclusive of everything else around them.

It affected Julian adversely. 'Adam tells us you're a teacher, Libby. That you teach blind children.' His hawklike face was lit with apparent interest as he settled back in his chair and faced her directly.

139

'Yes, that's right.'

'That seems an amazing accomplishment, considering your handicap,' he said.

The easiness drained from Adam's expression, and he stared at his father for a moment. Let him play whatever games he wanted with his sons; under no circumstances was Libby to be his prey. 'You couch your remarks so well,' he said darkly.

Julian looked at him sharply. 'Adam, let the girl speak for herself.'

'Father . . .'

Libby pressed his arm. 'Yes, Adam. Please. Let the girl speak for herself.' Her smile was still in place as she kept her face turned toward Julian. 'Mr. Bainbridge, it's not necessarily a remarkable accomplishment, and considering my handicap, it's rather appropriate, don't you think? I mean, who would better understand what's involved? Would you?' It wasn't said rudely, though that seemed the accepted mode of behavior around here, she thought dryly. However, this was her territory; she didn't accept others treading lightly on it, no matter who they were.

Adam relaxed; it appeared the prey had talons of her own. He watched his father as he picked up his tea and sipped at it.

'No, I don't suppose I would,' Julian conceded. 'What ages are these children?'

Libby smiled in genuine warmth. 'Their ages range, but they're all young. Ten, eleven, some eight or nine.'

'All blind since they were born?'

What had happened to the weather, or the sorry state of the economy, or the tinder box situation in the Middle East for topics of conversation? Adam thought acidly. His expression was openly annoyed as he extracted his arm from Libby's and lit a cigarette. 'Father, I think we can save the searching discussion for another time, don't you?'

'It's the girl's work. I'm interested. I'm always interested in people who work for their living,' Julian shot.

'Like you?' Adam countered.

Julian's smile was cutting. 'Like me. I've carried my responsibilities far past the point where it should have been possible to stop.'

Adam made a movement to rise but sat back again when Libby restrained him with a hand on his arm. She was smiling sweetly in Julian's direction, apparently determined to keep the conversation on track. And pleasant. 'I'd be more than happy to tell you about my work. And none of the children was born blind. Neither was I. I don't know whether Adam has told you that. It makes quite a difference. I teach these particular children because I can empathize. My circumstances are the same, and I teach them the same way I was taught.'

Julian looked at her inquiringly. 'What is the difference between the two?'

Libby tilted her head. 'The two what?'

'Being born blind and . . . not.'

'I'd think that would be obvious.'

'Oh?'

'Yes,' Libby said mildly.

The conversation wasn't proceeding to Julian's liking; it was she who held the bait, he who found himself snapping at it. 'I'm afraid it's not so obvious to me. I have no experience with blind people.' He glanced at Augustine sitting quietly nearby; her expression was inscrutable, completely opposite to Christian's —he was watching with open curiosity.

Libby took a sip of her tea, carefully replacing it on the glass-topped table beside her. 'Since I wasn't always blind, I have memories to fall back on. Memories of things I learned as anyone else would. There's a vast difference between instructing people on how to deal with things they already have some knowledge of and attempting to teach someone who's never seen anything at all,' she said pleasantly.

Julian's eyes were glinting. 'I see. So it's not so bad then, if you weren't born blind.'

Adam wanted to kick himself for bringing her here; he should have realized what Julian would put her through. His own eyes were snapping and he'd opened his mouth to speak angrily when Libby preempted him.

'Mr. Bainbridge,' she said coldly, her chin thrown up. 'I'd never presume to make statements about things I had no knowledge of. It surprises me that a man of your stature wouldn't proceed the same way. And since I suspect that your limited knowledge of sightlessness leaves you poorly equipped to converse on the subject, I feel it best we leave it alone. However, I'd like to point out one thing to you, since you've seen fit to remark upon it. Losing one's sight after having had it is probably one of the most traumatic experiences in this world. No, it's not easier to accept. In some ways, it's harder, though God knows it's a close race all around. We have a greater psychological impact to deal with, since we know what we're missing. Does that make sense to you?' She regretted nothing she'd said, only that this was Adam's father, and that she'd suddenly made it impossible to stay on. She wondered vaguely how Adam would handle telling her it was time to leave.

Julian's thin lips had curved into a smile. 'Yes, it does. And perhaps you're right. We should drop the subject for the moment. Forgive me if I've offended you.'

'I'm not offended, simply disappointed,' slipped out before she could stop it. Good, Libby, you might as well ice the cake, she thought resignedly and turned involuntarily toward Adam, trying to divine his reaction.

It was darkly satisfied, and he had no intention of relieving the momentary tension in the air. Christian finally did. He sat forward in his chair, his tea glass cupped in both hands and lowered between his knees as he looked Libby over appreciatively. 'Well, since Adam's preempted the rest of us by taking you around the house, perhaps I might have the pleasure of escorting you around the grounds? You'll . . .'

'No,' Adam said flatly, his eyes trained on his brother.

Christian frowned lightly. 'Now, old man, that's no attitude . . .'

'No.' Adam's tone was curt; he'd had enough. He looked abruptly over at his mother. 'I think Libby might like to get settled. Where will she be sleeping?'

'In the blue room,' Augustine said tightly.

'Manning's brought up her things?'

'I assume so. I instructed him to.'

'Fine.' He looked at Libby. 'Come on. Let's go.'

Libby set down her glass, making a movement to rise. As she did so, the hem of her skirt caught on a rough spot in the wrought iron, unbalancing her briefly, and it was with a deft movement that Adam kept her from sitting back down abruptly; he caught her under the arm, as if he'd had the intention all along of slipping his arm under hers. There was a murmured exchange of brief partings, and they left then, making their way back through the house. 'That was an impressive departure,' she said sourly as they were ascending the front staircase.

'Don't worry about it.' He wore a preoccupied frown, and when they reached her bedroom he ushered her inside, then turned her gently to face him, his hands on her shoulders. His eyes were shadowed as he looked down into her face. 'Libby, I'm sorry.'

'Sorry?' Gone was the unwilling truculence of before; she was looking up toward him with regret. 'You've nothing to be sorry for. I do. Adam, I didn't mean to be so argumentative, to fight with him the first time we came face to face, but . . .'

'You had every right. The man's a vulture. I should have known what he'd put you through.'

So, she hadn't angered him after all. Her tension relaxed. 'Yes, he does like to toy with people, doesn't he?' She smiled a little.

He wasn't amused. 'That he does, but he's not going to with you.'

She touched his arm. 'Adam, I'm a big girl, remember? And do you honestly think this is the first time I've had to field that kind of response? If you do, then you're terribly naive.'

His own tension dissipated with her easy smile. 'No, I'm not naive, and perhaps it's not the first time. However, I had no intention of bringing you down here just so he could pick your bones clean.'

'Don't worry about it.' She gave him a pert smile. 'And anyway, we've got a bet going, don't we?'

He frowned. 'What bet?'

'That they're not quite as bad as you've made them out to be.'

A grin suffused his face slowly. 'And tell me, which way are you leaning at the moment?'

'Well . . .' She hedged teasingly, then laughed. 'No way. One conversation does not a decision make. I do take a little getting used to, you know. Remember?'

'No, I don't remember,' he said flatly.

They were on level ground again. 'Well, try.'

It was his turn to laugh, and he dropped his hands from her shoulders. 'Ever fair-minded. Libby, you do take the cake! Now come on, let's get you established.' And he put her hand back on his arm and took her around the room then, into the bathroom and back, afterward leaning up against the bureau with his arms crossed as he made her repeat the process by herself.

'How'd I do?' she asked when she'd returned to stand near the four-poster bed. Silently, she was apologizing to him again. It'd been her biggest concern, the business of her personal quarters; he'd handled it as though they'd done it together all their lives.

'Beautifully. You pass.' He watched her for a moment longer, then finally pushed himself upright. 'I thought we'd go riding. Up to it?'

'Of course. I was planning to ask you if we could.' She'd turned toward the bed and tossed him a smile over her shoulder as she began to unzip the suitcase that had been placed on top of it. 'Give me a minute to change. I'll meet you downstairs.'

'No, I'll come get you.'

'Adam!' It was the months-old conflict between them; her

143

independence versus his intractable chivalry. Or something. She turned to give him an exasperated look when suddenly she felt him beside her. He removed her hands from the suitcase, positioned them around his neck, and took her into his arms. And he kissed her then, full on the mouth as always, but with a new demand and with undeniable passion as he pressed her against him, holding her immobile in his strong embrace. She responded to the searching kiss, involuntarily, then with complete consciousness as she tightened her arms and softly massaged the nape of his neck. It made him groan softly as he pulled her closer and molded her body intimately to his while his mouth hungrily sought hers. They stood locked together for minutes, their desire begging for release and threatening to overcome them completely. Finally, he released her.

'I . . .' She stopped; she couldn't really speak or even remember what she'd been about to say.

His breathing was shallow, and he combed his fingers sensuously through her thick hair, as he looked with passion-dark eyes into her face. 'That was to knock that damnable self-sufficiency out of you. I get tired of hearing it.' His voice was husky, caressing. 'Now, change your clothes. I'll be back in ten minutes.' He kissed her again, lingeringly, then turned and left the room. She listened to him go, her pulse still elevated and racing with the electric feel of his hands on her. It'd been a long time coming, their surrender to desire; now it left her dazed, from the intensity of her own reaction, from the overpowering thrill of his demanding virility. She'd never known anything like it, and after a time, she turned back to her suitcase, barely able to bring to mind what she'd been doing with it.

As for Adam, he stood on the far side of the door, waiting for composure to return; he hadn't meant to do that just then, but he hadn't been able to help it. The last threads of his self-control had finally snapped when he watched her making the slow circuit of the bedroom; it had been Libby at her most vulnerable, left alone to negotiate unfamiliar terrain, and Libby at her strongest as she went about doing so with careful determination and a smile on her lips. It'd been too much for him, that desperate independence. And while he loved it for making her who she was, he despised it for keeping him from protecting her—as if he could. Well, he could, in some respects. The last remnants of his uncontainable desire slipped away for the moment as he remembered the earlier exchange with his father, and he turned away from the door finally, striding briskly downstairs and out of the house. His family were still on the patio where he'd left them, and he went directly over to stand towering above Julian. 'I'm going to tell you this once, and that's all.' His voice was steely. 'Don't ever do that to Libby again.'

Julian looked up mildly. 'Sit down. I don't like people standing over me.'

Adam's blue eyes were icy as they bored into Julian. 'Too bad. And I mean it. She's a guest in this house. Save your insinuating and unpleasant remarks for those of us who don't give a damn about what you think.'

Julian spread his hands defensively then. 'I asked the girl a simple question or two.'

'You asked her an insulting question or two. And she's not a girl.'

Julian shook his head, his thin body shrouded in his son's shadow. 'I didn't mean to be insulting. I was merely interested.'

'Like hell you were.' The muscles in Adam's jaw were rigid, and he thrust his hands in his pockets. 'You were doing your damnedest to make her uncomfortable.'

'If that's all it takes, then she's not the woman for you.'

'I'll make that decision,' Adam snapped. 'And I don't intend to stand around here equivocating with you. I'm telling you. Lay off.'

Augustine had risen from her chair nearby. 'Adam, don't argue with your father.'

Adam glanced at her, his eyes narrowed. 'I'm not arguing. I'm advising,' he said shortly, then turned on Christian. 'And you. Keep your hands off.'

Christian had traded his tea for a highball and looked at Adam, feigning a wounded expression. 'I was merely trying to be friendly. God but you're touchy. And tell me, does the lady know you've got such a foul side to you?' His hurt expression slid into a mocking one.

Adam never knew why he started these things; the dialogue was inevitably the same. He drew a breath, then abruptly ran a hand through his hair; it was time to put an end to it all. Decisions that had been tentatively made suddenly gelled, and he looked around slowly at each of them in turn. Augustine was standing stiffly by her chair; Christian had begun to ruminate into his cocktail glass. Julian's expression was unchanged. 'I could take Libby right now and leave,' Adam said finally, his tone grim. 'Frankly, it's what I'd rather do, but there are a few more issues to address around here, and I intend to do that. Not right now, but later. And if I'm touchy,' he said, shooting a narrow glance at Christian, 'it's because you leave me no other choice.

Your patent disregard for Libby's feelings is appalling. Mother, you could've welcomed her into your home graciously, but instead you chose to remark acidly about the fact that we hadn't joined you immediately. You started everyone off on the wrong foot. I'm frankly surprised at your subsequent modest displays of benevolence, but then I really oughtn't to be. I've been around Libby long enough to know she tends to affect people that way.' He studied his mother for a moment, then turned to his brother. 'Christian, I apologize. However, your reputation precedes you, and I want it clearly understood between the two of us that Libby is out of bounds. Period, paragraph. As for you, Father.' He turned back to Julian, his anger surfacing again momentarily. 'I meant what I said. I'll not have you running her through the mill.'

Julian stood up, his eyes hard, though he wasn't entirely displeased. Adam was undeniably impressive as he stood tall and unrelenting before them, his handsome face filled with unforgiving conviction. The way a son of his ought to be. He arched an eyebrow, taking a step toward Adam. 'You do not issue the orders in this house. I do.'

'I issue the orders when it comes to Libby.' Adam locked eyes with him, and it was Julian who dropped his gaze first. Adam felt no sense of victory; he simply intended that he be clearly understood. He watched Julian for a moment longer, then took his hands out of his pockets. 'I assume I've made myself clear. Now, we're going riding. Don't look for us until late afternoon.'

And he turned on his heel and strode back into the house.

# Chapter 11

They rode for several hours. Adam had put Libby up on one of
the more manageable mounts in the Bainbridge stable, although,
she thought to herself when the horse moved out at a prancing
walk, it was all relative, like everything else in the world; she
hadn't sat a horse with so much spirit since she'd been a young
girl. Well, it would be good for her, and in truth, she'd been
flattered that Adam considered her up to the challenge.

It'd been a puzzling afternoon, in some ways; Adam had said
nothing about their passionate encounter in her bedroom, though
she was well aware they'd passed over yet another threshold, in
his eyes as well as her own. He'd been more proprietary than
ever before, more inclined to touch her and to linger when they
reined in their horses and sat taking a quiet breather, at the top of
a rise or in the hollow of a lea where they sought shelter from the
brutal July sun under an umbrella of maple branches. And she'd
discovered she was waiting for the unexpected touch of his hand
on her arm or lightly along the contour of her cheek with an
anticipation bordering on exquisite pain. There was no more
denying him, or more correctly, herself; their impassioned kiss
had touched every fiber of her being.

But while he was attentive when they were quietly resting side
by side during those short respites, he was more than a little
preoccupied as they ranged out over the property. At one point,
she'd actually had to call his name three times before he
responded, and she'd given him a quizzical look, tilting her head
as she spoke again. 'Adam, did you hear me?'

He glanced at her abruptly; he'd been lost to serious thought,
frowning off into the distance until her voice finally penetrated.
He smiled ruefully and reached out to touch her hand lightly.
'Sorry. Had my head in the clouds. What?'

'Hmmm.' She studied his presence beside her, smiling
tentatively. 'Is something wrong?'

'Not a thing.' He smiled again, quietly. He was tempted to tell her then what was on his mind, but didn't. Later would do just as well, when he intended explaining himself to everyone. 'What did you ask me?'

She didn't continue to press him; they'd always had an understanding between them, to talk about things when the time was right. Obviously it wasn't now, and she shook her head. 'Oh, it wasn't important. Just wanted to see if you were paying attention, that's all.' She'd given him a quick grin, and they'd ridden on, returning to the stable shortly after five o'clock, in time to reach the house for the ritual of cocktails in the drawing room.

Libby had been expecting a repeat of the earlier conversation, but there was none. Dinner, which followed promptly at seven thirty, was also pleasant. She was enormously relieved; the last thing she wanted was a duel with any of Adam's family, and though the initial exchange with his father had been unavoidable, she was determined there'd be no more. She'd be sweet and demure, exactly as she knew Julian had expected her to be in the first place. The thought came to her as they assembled in the library for after-dinner coffee, and she stifled a small grin. She'd have to remember to tell Sebastian; he'd be amused at the idea of her as the model of restraint. Adam saw the suggestion of a smile pass across her face as they were seated together on a long couch, and he leaned close as he slid his arm along its back, behind her. 'What's funny?' he asked near her ear.

She smiled mysteriously. 'Nothing,' she whispered back. 'Just a private conversation with myself. On the virtues of propriety.'

He looked at her with an uncomprehending half smile, then abruptly glanced at Julian when he spoke. He sat across from them, in his usual chair by the fireplace. 'Adam, I'll be needing to talk to you alone at some point this evening, once coffee is finished.'

Adam smiled pleasantly, propping one leg over the other. 'Talk to me now.'

Julian eyed him; Adam's armor of equanimity had been invincible all evening, even through Christian's light sparring over the dinner table. 'Libby needn't be bothered,' he said shortly.

Adam glanced once at Libby before looking back at Julian. 'Libby doesn't mind. There's nothing you can't say in front of her.'

'Don't be belligerent.'

Adam laughed. 'I'm not.'

'It's a matter of business.'

A flip remark was on the tip of Adam's tongue, but he checked it. He removed his arm from the back of the couch and lit a cigarette. 'Father, what is it you want to talk about?'

Julian sighed. 'All right. Since you have no intention of being accommodating, we'll talk about it now. I've put a proposition to you. You promised I'd have a quick response, and as yet I've heard no decision from you. I thought I'd made it clear that Manufacturing cannot be damaged by your flights of inconsistency.'

Libby opened her mouth automatically to object, then shut it. Restraint, Libby, she reminded herself. And it's not your battle. She felt Adam shift on the couch beside her, but when he spoke, his voice was friendly. 'I didn't promise you an immediate response. I told you I'd have an answer for you when I was ready.'

'Then let me have it. Now.' Julian's expression was cold.

Adam didn't flinch. 'Perhaps I haven't made up my mind.'

'Ah!' Julian spat in exasperation. 'Games, you only want to play games! When do you intend to act like a man? When do you intend to take on . . ."

'My goddamned responsibilities!' Adam stood up abruptly and paced across the room, turning back to Julian as he tried to get his temper under control. 'Do you know how sick and tired I am of listening to you harp on my responsibilities?'

It was Julian's milieu, and he countered with razor-sharpness. 'As sick as I am of your shirking them.' Libby might not have been there for all he cared; he didn't for a moment think to modify his conversation because of her presence. 'There are things to be done. You will head up Manufacturing,' he ordered.

Adam had regained his composure. He looked Julian up and down, then slipped one hand calmly in his pocket. 'No, I won't. I'm very sorry, Father, but I don't intend to die a slow death trapped inside those four smothering walls. That's final. You might as well save your breath.'

'I see.' Julian narrowed his eyes in contempt. 'You'll continue, then, with your irresponsible ways, squandering your time and money, hopping from bedroom to bedroom?' This time he did look at Libby; he didn't know her well enough, however, to read the expression on her face. He looked back at Adam. 'I won't stand for it.'

'I don't imagine you have much choice.' Libby's voice was clear as a bell, and she was looking directly toward Julian. Such untempered abuse wasn't something she could sit by and stoically listen to, as everyone else seemed able to. Not under any circumstance, but especially not when it was Adam being so unjustly vilified. Let the man throw her out now; she'd welcome it, but not before she'd met him head on.

Adam looked at her sharply. 'Don't fence with him, Libby. It's not worth it, and I won't have you involved.'

She looked in his direction, her chin raised firmly. 'I can't sit here and listen to . . .'

'Then leave the room!' Julian spat. 'I'd hoped to spare you the displeasure of seeing my son at his worst. Or is it your best, Adam?' His voice went smoothly mild. 'On the other hand, you might as well see him as he is.'

'I already have,' Libby said coldly.

'You take up for him easily.'

'You cut him down so easily,' Libby countered immediately. 'And you do it with such pleasure.'

Adam was massaging his forehead and tried to step in. 'Libby . . .'

Julian wasn't finished, and his eyes were glinting as he continued to look at her. 'Who are you to tell me what to do?'

'Who are you to tell him what to do?' Libby demanded.

Christian was watching the exchange with delight. Good for her; she was making the old man really angry. Neither he nor Adam, in all their years' experience, had ever managed to do that quite so effectively. He glanced at Augustine sitting tight-lipped nearby, then looked back at Julian. 'Perhaps she's got a point,' he tossed in.

'Shut up!' Julian spat.

'All of you shut up!' Adam exploded in exasperation. He glared at Julian, then looked at Libby, his expression involuntarily softening. 'Lib . . .'

She turned toward him defensively. 'Adam, I . . .'

'No more,' he said firmly, but he nearly laughed. Such a slight little thing, so capable of taking on the whole world if she thought she was right. His eyes lingered on her a moment, then moved around to the others. 'Now, you'll all listen to me, since I'm the topic of this pleasant conversation.' He was standing in the middle of the room and turned to Augustine. 'Mother, would you like to get your two cents in before the time's up? No? All right.' He turned back to Julian. 'Father, I will not now or ever head up Manufacturing or any other Bainbridge company. I will not sit on the board of any company or have one thing to do with any of them. Is that clear?' He waited a moment, watching

Julian narrowly. 'Good. Since you have no comment, I assume it is. And as for your remarks about my intentions, it's none of your damn business what I intend to do, irresponsible or not. However, since you seem to be so interested,' he said dryly, 'I'll tell you that I do happen to have something in mind, although the plans haven't gotten under way as yet.' He was facing Julian but looked directly at Libby. 'It's going to take a lot of work, but I intend to see to the establishment of a riding school for the blind.'

Libby's head snapped up, and she drew in a sharp breath. Julian looked from one to the other of them, his eyes narrowing. 'What kind of absurd idea . . .' he began, then for once had the grace to amend his comment. 'What possessed you to consider such a thing?' he demanded.

'A lot of things, and I don't intend to stand here and discuss them with you. First of all, you'd have no understanding of the concept. Second, there's a lot of initial work to do, none of which has been started yet. But I will tell you that I think it's about time the Bainbridge money was put toward some useful purpose so that it benefits a few more people than the four rather pathetic ones in this room.' He was talking to Julian but was watching Libby closely; he'd expected some other kind of reaction than this tense silence. His pensive look turned into a frown, and he crossed the room to sit down beside her. 'Libby?'

She looked up again, startled as he put a hand on her arm; his unexpected announcement had completely overshadowed the disquiet of her continued antagonism with his father. Suddenly, all she wanted to do was get away. To think. 'Adam, I think I'll go on up. You have a lot to discuss with your family, and frankly . . . I'm tired.' She looked toward him intently, then rose, turning toward Julian. 'Mr. Bainbridge, I apologize for my outburst, in principle, not in context. Adam, I can make my way.'

He knew that determined expression all too well. And it wasn't the time or place to discuss her reaction, anyway. 'I'll take you up,' he said, rising.

She smiled briefly. 'To the stairs, then. I'm all right after that. Honestly.'

She said a quick good-night around the room, and they left, crossing the hall to come to a standstill at the foot of the staircase. Adam turned her toward him then when they were out of earshot of the others, and his frown returned. 'Libby, what's the matter?'

She pressed her lips together. 'Not now, Adam, I'm tired.

Honestly. And after all that, I'm rather embarrassed for the scene I made. It seems I can do nothing but fight with your father, and I'm sorry, but he's dreadfully unfair. Please make my apologies again.'

He was trying to read her expression but couldn't. 'Never mind that, Libby, I thought . . .'

'Adam,' she pleaded.

He realized it was no use, not for the moment. He let her go finally, watching as she made her way up the staircase, one hand on the wide banister, then disappeared around the landing at the top. He looked after her for a moment, then turned abruptly and strode back into the library.

Libby traversed the length of the hall, the backs of her fingers running lightly along the wall for guidance. She found the blue room with no effort; it was the fifth door on the left, straight ahead. She went in, closing the door firmly behind her, and crossed to the bed, turning to sit down on the mattress and ease backwards in weary relief. She was tired and troubled, and she wished suddenly that Sebastian were somewhere close by. Dear old Sebastian, who could always put things into perspective with his kindly voice and wise words. She lay there for a long time, then finally shimmied all the way up on the mattress and turned on her side, placing her glasses on the small table beside the bed. At length she fell asleep, but it was a fitful rest, filled with angry conversations and distorted images of some version of Adam sleep-walking through a life he lived because of someone else's dreams, and when she awakened finally, it wasn't because her dreams had become so urgent, but because there was a hand softly caressing her cheek, nudging her out of unconsciousness. She sat up abruptly, then fell back when the same hand pushed her down gently.

'Libby, you were dreaming,' Adam said quietly. 'It's only a dream. It's over now.'

'Adam?' Her mind was foggy and she reached up to find his arm.

He put his hand over hers. 'I'm here. It's all right. You were crying,' he told her. He'd come in to find her caught up in some nightmare, tossing and turning on the bed, and had discovered her tears when he'd sat down beside her and gently touched her cheek.

The images returned to Libby, some of them, fuzzy, incoherent, and she shook her head, dissolving them but not the residue of heaviness. 'What time is it?'

'Eleven.'

'Oh. Turn on a light,' she remembered. He reached over and flipped on the small lamp beside the bed. 'Did you just come up?'

He was watching her eyes, no longer hidden by the glasses. They were beautiful, clear, with the loveliest shade of green he'd ever seen. 'Yes, I've been talking to my family. Straightening them out on a few things. I think, finally, we all just might understand one another.'

She brushed a hand tiredly across her face and realized she was without her glasses. She reached for them, but Adam caught her hand. 'No more, Libby,' he said. 'Not with me.'

She brought her hand back slowly; she felt suddenly self-conscious without her glasses, and with Adam sitting on the edge of the bed, effectively blocking her from sitting up and swinging her legs over the side. He was leaning over her, his weight resting on one hand.

'I . . . thank you for waking me. I have to change.'

'I came in here to talk to you and found you all caught up in a nightmare. What is it, Libby? What's troubling you?' He looked at her steadily, with worry in his eyes.

She tried to move again, but he wouldn't let her. She turned her head away. 'Oh, just things.'

'You're not happy about the riding school. Why not?'

She let out a breath and looked back toward him. 'If you'll just let me up . . .' She tried pushing on his arm.

He didn't move. 'No, tell me.'

'Oh, Adam. I know why you're doing it, and it's for the wrong reason.'

He raised his eyebrows in surprise. 'Oh really?'

'You've got to want to. You've got to want to do the thing for yourself.'

'And you think I don't?'

'I think maybe you think it would please me,' she said in a low voice.

'You're awfully sure of yourself, aren't you?' he said with a slow grin and watched her flush. He looked at her for a moment, then added, 'And you should be.'

She bit her lip. 'Adam . . .'

'Libby, do you know that I'm in love with you?'

She attempted to speak, faltered, tried again, then put her fingertips to her lips.

He laughed wryly. 'I see that you don't.'

'Adam . . .' she said softly.

'Well, I am. I think that would naturally make me want to

please you,' he said and dropped down onto his elbow so his weight rested lightly on her.

'Adam,' she said in a rush, before she lost her chance to speak; she knew that moment was dangerously close. 'You asked me what I was dreaming about. Well, it was you. It was you, walking like a dead man through some life that someone had chosen for you. Your father, me, someone else. It was something you were doing because someone else wanted you to, and you hated it.'

He was watching her with a half smile. 'I've already put a stop to doing something I hated. I'm rather interested in the notion of doing something I want to do. For me. I hope you'll go along with it. Since you're rather inextricably involved, I think we should have no problems there.'

'Adam, are you sure?' She looked up at him worriedly, acutely conscious of his breath near her cheek.

He kissed her once, lightly. 'Libby, I love you dearly, with all my heart, as a matter of fact. But believe it or not, I wouldn't take on something I truly didn't want to do, not even for you. I confess I might be tempted, I confess my first contemplation of the idea was because of you, but that's as far as it goes. The fact is, I *want* to do this thing, whether or not it'll work out. For me.'

'That's all that matters then.'

'It's a large part of it, yes, but not all. There are other things, you know.' It was time to end the conversation, far past time, and he leaned down, putting his mouth on hers. She put her fingertips on his lips between them, forcing him away slightly. 'Adam . . .'

He frowned in mild impatience. 'This better be important, Lib.'

She was stalling, and she knew it, but she was suddenly nervous. Intimidated by his well-known worldliness. She wanted this man more than she'd ever wanted anything in her life, but suddenly she also wanted to bolt like a frightened filly. She knew he was waiting, and she said the first thing that came to mind. 'I'm sorry I blew up at your father like that.'

His frown deepened, and he sat up. 'Frankly, you impressed him. Of course, he'd never tell you that, but he told me. He likes people with spirit. And as I said, we cleared up a lot of things.'

Well, so much for that. Libby thought and bit her lip. 'Adam, are you certain you really want to go ahead with the school?'

So, he'd been right; the hedging was unmistakeable now. 'Hmmm.' He sat up straight and took both of her hands in his, pulling her up, completely off the bed.

'Where are we going?' she asked in confusion.

He had her hand and was walking her across the room. 'Over here.'

'Over here where?' She held onto his hand with both of hers, completely at a loss as to what he was doing. Finally, they came to a standstill.

'To the mirror.'

'Why?'

He was watching her with a caressing smile. 'I want you to see someone.'

'Adam . . .'

He stood her squarely in front of the full-length mirror and came around behind her, running his hands with a feather-light touch along the sides of her body as he took her into an embrace and pulled her back against him, letting his chin rest on the top of her head. He was a man who definitely knew women; there'd been only the suggestion of a caress along the sides of her breasts, but it had been enough. Every nerve in her body had come alive. 'Look at that,' he said lightly.

'Adam!' she said and laughed nervously.

He was smiling at her in the mirror and went on conversationally. 'You don't see her, do you? Well then, let me tell you about this woman in the mirror. I told you once I'd do that, remember? This woman, she's exquisitely beautiful, with soft, very thick auburn hair that shines all the time. She should never wear those glasses of hers. They mask the perfection of the bones of her face. And besides, she has the most beautiful eyes in the world, perfectly shaped with very dark lashes. I'd say they were her best feature if she didn't have the figure she does.'

Stupidly, she flushed all the way up to her forehead. 'Adam,' she said again, looking down toward the floor. His hands were clasped loosely around her waist, her own hands resting on his forearms.

His blue eyes held a mixture of laughter and deeper emotion. 'Of course, that's only speculation on my part,' he continued easily, 'but some very astute dressmaker gives it a helping hand. She knows just where and what needs flattering.' He unclasped his hands, softly running them up the sides of her arms and to the nape of her neck, where he combed them slowly through her hair. 'It does induce a lot of daydreaming, which, by the way, I could end very quickly, you know.' He was still watching her reflection as he reached around abruptly and unfastened the top button of her dress, his hand skimming ever so lightly across the line of her breast.

Both of her hands flew up and grabbed his, desperately holding it still.

His smile went gentle. 'That's what I thought,' he said quietly, looking down into her face as he drew her more tightly against him. 'There's one more thing about this woman in the mirror. She's afraid.'

She bit her lip so hard it hurt. 'Yes,' she said in a low voice. He kissed her hair. 'Why?'

She hated the slight trembling that came to her shoulders; he continued to hold her calmly, changing the position of his hand only slightly, gently, over the soft rise of her breast. 'Why?' he pressed, his voice suddenly muffled against the skin of her neck.

'Adam, I'm blind! Do you realize what that means? All that it means? Nothing is simple . . .'

He raised his head and kissed the side of her chin. 'That's not going to do it, honey.'

She took a breath. 'It's forever. There's no changing it.'

'Hmmm,' he murmured and moved his lips down her throat.

'It's something you'll always have to deal with,' she pleaded, throwing her head back so her neck was arched, fully exposed. The movement was completely involuntary, female, a response to his unrelenting caress.

'Hmmm, I know,' he said and gently worked his hand free, loosening another button. He ran the back of one finger slowly along her breastbone, beneath the fabric, letting it move halfway up the rise of soft flesh, then back again. It was an incredibly sensual experience he was giving her as he talked; she couldn't see him, or know where he'd touch her next, or even if he would, and he knew innately how to play it, softly, suggestively, making her catch her breath each time.

'Think about it, Adam!' she managed to say.

One more button went in response, and she had to tell him.

'Adam, I'm not very experienced,' she confessed in a voice barely above a whisper. He said nothing, but continued to kiss her neck, and she wondered if he'd heard her. 'Adam, I said . . .'

'I heard you.' He undid the last button, separating the fabric of her dress with a caressing touch that barely made contact with her skin. He turned her to face him then, his eyes moving down to her arousing half exposure. It was an effort to draw his gaze away, but he did finally, lifting her chin as he looked into her face. 'You don't need experience. I'm going to give you all you'll ever have to have.'

Her hesitation fell away as she felt him run his hands along her bare skin beneath the dress. She reached up, gently taking his face in her hands. 'Adam, I do love you,' she said softly.

'Then show me,' he said with sudden urgency and picked her up, carrying her to the bed. He placed her there, then lay down beside her, taking her demandingly into his arms. By the dim light of the small blue bedside lamp near the four-poster bed, she gave herself up to him then, glorying in the pleasure of his exquisitely gentle lovemaking, and as had happened once before, on another hot July night twenty years before, Libby Rutledge's life started all over again.

# PART II

Love to faults is always blind,
Always is to joy inclin'd,
Lawless, wing'd, and unconfin'd,
And breaks all chains from every mind.

*William Blake*

But jealous souls will not be answer'd so;
They are not ever jealous for the cause.
But jealous for they are jealous; 'tis a monster
Begot upon itself, born on itself.

*William Shakespeare*

## Chapter 12

It was Christmas time, and snowing heavily. The snow clouds that had come in late November were now entrenched, flurrying away the days until the ground lay covered. Out in the countryside, the snow still wore its bridal white, but in the city it had gone grimy from the footfalls of harried shoppers churlishly tamping it down into the pavement. It was the ugliest part of oncoming winter, that ravaged snow, all rutted and stained with automobile exhaust smoke. Ugly, that is, until the strings of blinking colored lights and boughs of holly went up all across the storefronts and street lights; then it became beautiful again, all a part of the magical look of Christmas.

Or at least so Libby thought, for she remembered that look well. It was one of her favorite memories, just as Christmas was her favorite time of the year, reviving memories of her parents, each with a mittened child in tow as they strolled along the snow-covered streets of the city. It had been an annual ritual, that trek into the city, and Libby had never forgotten the awe and delight she'd felt as she looked at the strings of enormous lights and twinkling decorations overhead, listened to the ringing of the red-suited Santas on each busy street corner, thrilled to the anticipation that one of those frilly dolls sitting beneath the storefront Christmas trees might somehow find its way to another tree in another place, its small red tag inscribed with the words, 'Merry Christmas to Libby, Love from Mom and Dad.'

The streets, the decorations, and even she herself were older now, but she could still recapture all those feelings of youthful wonder and sought to every year. It was why she'd dragged Adam and Sebastian out on this cold, blustery night of December first. Arm in arm the three of them strolled that evening, Libby in the center, their woolen scarves wrapped tightly about their necks and blowing as they leaned into the wind and went from block to block, listening to the carols blaring from loudspeakers set high above them. And though she knew it was willingly that the two men set the Christmas scene for her, she knew, too, how grateful they were to bring her home again; as they stood on the woven mat in the hallway outside her apartment door, stamping the snow from their boots, the two men punctuated every footfall with a complaint.

'. . . and the next time you're in the mood for a hike out into the blizzard, my love, kindly let me know in advance. I'll bring my snowshoes.' Adam fitted his key into the lock and opened the door. Glancing down at her with a crooked smile, he ushered her inside. Sebastian moved on past them into the depths of the darkened room and flipped on a light near the chinoiserie couch. His navy wool overcoat was buttoned all the way up, and his knit cap was pulled down around his ears, nearly covering his eyebrows. 'A deathly chill,' he said with feeling and grimaced, pulling his gloves off one finger at a time. 'With the dawn they'll be wheeling me out on a stretcher, nothing more than another regrettable winter statistic.'

As Adam helped her out of her coat, Libby was trying not to laugh and doing a poor job of it. She combed her long hair loose when it was free of the restricting coat, letting it fall along her shoulders and down her back; its color was vivid against the gray wool of her sweater ribbed at the neck and covering a white Oxford cloth shirt, and Adam watched her laughter finally erupt, lighting up her face. She began shaking her head as she left him at the coat closet and crossed the room toward the kitchen. 'You know, you two just kill me. You'd think you were going to drop dead from a little fresh air!' She went on into the narrow room, flipping on lights, and continued to smile as she reached up into the cupboard and began bringing down cups and saucers. Then she moved over to the stove and put the water on to boil.

In the other room, Adam strolled to the couch and sat down. 'That's what it is, huh? Fresh air? I call it pneumonia weather.' His blue eyes were laughing as he propped one leg over the other. 'But for you, my love, there's no weather too harsh for a look at the Christmas bells. And the hustlers on every street corner ringing for the last dollar in your wallet.'

Her indulgent laughter filtered out into the room. 'You're an incurable cynic, Adam Bainbridge. And go on, both of you, say what you will. You can't faze me in the least, because I love it all.' At the inner counter, she dropped two lumps of sugar in a cup; after a moment's deliberation, she dropped in another. Well, it was Sebastian's own problem, the span of his waistline.

She grinned at that, then turned to the opposite counter, where she reached for a cake container. She looked out toward the two men in the room beyond.

'And I want to tell you, Mr. Bainbridge, you're going to see the biggest, most glorious Christmas tree you've ever encountered, right here in my living room!'

'And with the help of one Sebastian Vickery dragging the thing in from the meadows, as always,' Sebastian murmured resignedly, then shot a sudden bright look at Adam.

He fielded it with a dry grin. 'Yes, Sebastian, I imagine I will. And stay awhile, why don't you? Take off your coat.' He gestured good-naturedly toward the man still standing near the coffee table. Adam had loosened the collar of his own checked shirt another button and pulled it away from his muscular neck, and he watched with a trace of amusement as Sebastian methodically complied with his directive.

Under the heavy coat Sebastian wore two securely buttoned sweaters; it took him some time to shed all three garments and hang them neatly in the closet, and when he returned, Libby had joined them and was seated beside Adam, carefully preparing their coffee. He took a place on the opposite couch and watched as Libby passed around the cups then settled back naturally into the crook of Adam's arm. 'Hmmm, nothing like a cup of hot coffee after a walk in the brisk outdoors,' she commented and propped her feet against the drop-leaf table.

Adam was looking at her silently; the faint scent of lilacs drifted up from her throat, so familiar now, so appealing. She was relaxed, obviously at peace with herself, and she closed her eyes after a moment; her dark eyelashes lay softly against the delicate bones of her cheek, no longer hidden by the glasses she'd worn for so many years. At length, he leaned close and spoke softly into her ear. 'Enjoyed that, did you?'

She smiled serenely. 'Hmmm. And I revert, you know —completely back to a child at Christmas. I'm only warning you.' She laughed at that and turned her face toward him, inviting his kiss; he complied, directly on her mouth.

After a time, Sebastian cleared his throat. 'Perhaps it's time I hie m'self home?'

It broke them apart; Libby opened her eyes and gave him a fond smile. 'No, Sebastian, you shouldn't hie yourself home. At least not before you've had a piece of cake. I made it just for you.' She set down her cup and rose, heading off again into the kitchen. Adam's eyes were eloquent as they followed her slender back into the other room, and it was only Sebastian's renewed cough that finally drew his gaze away.

He was fingering the collar of his plain white shirt when Adam looked at him. 'I don't mean to pry, of course,' he said, beaming an apology, 'but I was simply wondering when the two of you intend to make all this permanent.'

Adam reached for his cigarette case, now part of the room's furnishings. He tapped a cigarette on the edge, took a moment to light it, then relaxed against the couch. 'When Libby decides I've had sufficient time in which to make my escape, should I feel the need. She's got this thing, you see, about not pushing me into something I'm going to regret one day.' He smiled briefly. 'I'll humor her along for awhile, if that's what she really wants, but only for a while. If I'd had my way, we'd have been married months ago.'

Sebastian nodded as he brought the porcelain cup down from his lips. 'Yes, the gal is stringently reasonable and fair. Always has been. Always will be.'

Adam's expression went mildly impatient. 'Call it what you like,' he said and was about to remark further when a clatter sounded from the other room, followed by Libby's sharp oath and her reappearance moments later in the kitchen doorway; she stopped there and stood with her hands on her hips.

'Well, Sebastian, you can forget the cake. I just dropped it.'

At her annoyed look, Sebastian frowned worriedly and opened his mouth to voice a hearty dismissal; it was Adam, however, who spoke first. 'Good shot, hon,' he said casually. 'I certainly hope you made it count and hit something really important,' he added, watching her steadily.

His nonchalance had the usual effect; she stood there, caught up in her frustration, a moment longer, then let out an audible breath. Faint chagrin began to displace her cross expression as she relaxed against the doorframe. 'Well, of course. I'm sure I got at least half the cookbooks on the counter,' she improvised.

Sebastian was on his feet, anxious to repair the situation. 'Not to worry. There's plenty in m'own pantry to fill the bill. Leave the mess. We'll see to it later.' Not waiting for anyone's remark, he headed for the door, stopping to pat Libby's cheek paternally. She wasn't in the mood to object to his exaggerated concern or his unnecessary trip down the hall, and merely smiled. When the door had clicked shut behind him, she looked in Adam's direction; he'd shifted forward on the couch and put his cigarette down in the ashtray.

'Come here,' he said, extending his hand. He watched her

push herself away from the doorway, and took her hand as she approached, guiding her down beside him. When they were settled back against the sofa cushions, he slipped his arm across her shoulders. 'Forget it. It's no big deal.'

'I know, I know,' she said, gesturing in mild agitation. 'It's just the frustration sometimes.' She frowned briefly down toward her hands, then sighed. 'Sorry. And I probably ought to go in there now and do something about the mess before Sebastian has a chance to return and get in a dither of helpfulness.' At that, she smiled genuinely. 'He will, you know.'

Adam laughed and swung his arm up over her head as he leaned forward to reach for his cigarette. 'I know. So let him, if that's what he wants.' He sat back, looking at her in abrupt seriousness. 'And while we're alone, there's something I want to talk to you about.' He paused briefly, dragging on his cigarette, then said, 'Mother and Father want us to spend Christmas with them.'

'Oh.' The news was totally unexpected, and she sat up a little straighter.

Adam smiled darkly at her reaction. 'Yes, I know. Shocking, isn't it?'

'Adam, don't say it that way.'

'No, I know. They're making the effort, right?'

'Right,' she said firmly. 'Adam, you do need to see them. You've only been down once in the last five months.'

'And it's been damn pleasant not to have to listen to all their rubbish.'

Libby ignored him; if she agreed, she would only fan the flames of his disaffection. She still harbored the hope that they could all find some basis for compatibility, and in her small ways even worked toward it. Her silence in the face of his derision was one of them. As the silence continued, he elaborated. 'Besides, I don't intend for there to be a repeat of that disastrous time when I took you down in July.'

She smiled impishly. 'Oh, it wasn't such a disaster, you know.'

He caught her inference and grinned briefly. 'No, not all around, you're right.'

She looked up earnestly then, dropping the playful manner. 'But, Adam, nor was it such a disaster in other respects, either. To you, maybe, but not necessarily to me. First times are always difficult. You should know that by now. And you've never given any of us a chance to take the next step. You can't protect me from it, or from anything, forever, you know. Besides,' she added, 'how bad can it be?'

Adam didn't answer and let his gaze drift absently over to the etagère across the room, looking at but not seeing the group of photographs there; another had been added, one of him and Libby sitting together on the couch in his apartment. Libby listened to his silence, then rested her wrist on the arm of the couch. 'Adam, we're all going to have to get along sometime, or at least make the effort.'

He knew that, of course, although he never envisioned his life with Libby as being intricately entwined with that of his family; there were too many things separating them, and that was the way he wanted it. If Libby didn't understand that completely, it was simply because she chose not to; the importance of 'family' was too ingrained in her beliefs. He looked back at her. 'I'm not sure anyone will get along. Ever. Make the effort? Yes. Someday, we'll make the effort. I'm just not sure now is the time.'

Libby nodded. 'All right. I accept that. And anyway, Christmas might be difficult. There's Sebastian. Adam, Sebastian has to be with us.'

He was preoccupied again, studying the smoke curling up from his cigarette. 'Hmmm, of course. I hadn't planned it any other way.'

Libby was aware of his abstraction and tilted her head. 'Adam, you're not saying everything. What's the matter?'

He shot her a look, then grinned ruefully to himself; he'd be in real trouble if she were able to read him with her eyes, too. Of course, she was right; he wasn't being completely frank with her. His initial inclination had been to turn the invitation down flat, no questions asked, for the sake of preserving the sanctity of their first Christmas together. And yet, the invitation did offer a solution to a logistical problem he'd been wrangling with for the last two months, since the time he and Matt Jameson had made a special trip to a special place to purchase that special gift for Libby; it had to be presented in just the proper manner. The backdrop of the Bainbridge estate could provide that, and it was the one reason he was vacillating about rejecting the invitation. 'Nothing's the matter,' he answered finally. 'I was just wondering if maybe we oughtn't give it some consideration after all.'

Libby frowned perplexedly; reversals weren't the norm for Adam Bainbridge, as she'd come to learn very well. 'You make about as much sense as I do most of the time,' she complained facetiously.

It prompted him to eye her, then grin slyly. 'That was a low blow,' he remarked and ducked as a thrown pillow came flying by almost instantly. Quickly extinguishing his cigarette, he reached over and grabbed a second pillow from her hands. In moments he had her securely pinned against the couch, one arm behind her back, the other one caught firmly at the wrist in his strong grip. 'Give in?' he inquired pleasantly.

She was laughing. 'Didn't anyone ever tell you not to pick on people smaller than you?'

'Didn't anyone ever tell you not to start things you can't finish?' he countered mildly and released her. 'You asked for it, as I recall.'

She feigned a look of disdain. 'I was merely retaliating for the slur on my character.'

He laughed and glanced back over his shoulder as he heard the knob at the front door rattle. 'That's Sebastian,' he commented unnecessarily and looked back at her. 'We can think some more about Christmas. Besides,' he said as he rose to head for the door, 'Mother might not be able to handle my giving her too much advance notice.' It was said strictly for Libby's benefit, and as always, he was rewarded by her keen look of exasperation.

Sebastian's offering was carrot cake; among the three of them, they saw to its serving, fresh coffee, and the removal of the ruined cake. Libby took the opportunity later, when she and Sebastian were momentarily alone on the living room couch, to assuage his concern over the earlier incident; he had yet to drop the overly jovial manner. 'Sebastian, you've got to stop getting so upset every time I feel aggravated about myself.'

He finished his cake and set the plate on the coffee table. 'It was merely a miswhack,' he dismissed immediately.

'Exactly,' she said, laughing at his apt description. 'Do as Adam does. Ignore it. There's nothing more deadly to a fit of temper than indifference, you know.'

'I'd hardly deem it indifference on Adam's part, and as for myself, I wasn't the least bit concerned.' At her skeptical look, he gave in. 'All right. And reassurance accepted.'

She nodded in satisfaction and sat back as she heard Adam's footstep at the edge of the tiled kitchen floor. But rather than join them on the couch, he crossed to the cozy dining area and sat down at the gateleg table there. Libby knew immediately what he was doing, of course; she could hear the clink of his china cup as he set it down on the wood surface, then the rustle of papers, the hollow sound of large sheets of drafting paper being unrolled, and the thud of objects being put at the corners to weight them down. He'd be quickly absorbed, as he always was, and she relaxed back in the cleft of the couch arm, her saucer balanced in the palm of one hand as she listened to him get down to work.

Adam and the riding school for her children: her two greatest loves intricately woven together, one a part of the other and all of it a part of her own life now; the sense of fulfillment it brought was nearly beyond description. In the months since that night in July when Adam had announced his intention to start a school, the initial planning and development had gotten under way. Libby would forever be its inspiration, but it was Adam who was its life's breath. He was a natural entrepreneur, as it turned out, and a formidable one when driven by conviction. It was he who conducted the endless planning sessions with architects, consultants, and engineers, he who compromised nothing in his effort to bring their dual dream to fruition. She sometimes accompanied him to the meetings, when they fit into her schedule, but sat back quietly for the most part, listening in admiration as he conducted the discussions; she was sure she'd never have been so effective in coming up with results and possibilities based on the opinions offered by the professionals; it was his forte, this harnessing of ideas and driving them to realities, and she'd often wished, as she sat there listening, that Julian could be witness to it all. She'd never voiced the desire, however, for it was inspired, she suspected, by some version of vindictiveness; nonetheless, it would do Julian good to have a few of his unjust accusations flung back in his face, a loyal inner voice insisted. She stilled it as she heard Adam change drawings at the far side of the room. It had begun as such a simple operation, this idea of hers, but had burgeoned over the months, with each new inspiration, into a unique and complex facility, and the blueprints he was studying that night were the fifth revisions. They included plans for outdoor and indoor instructional rings, a stable to house hand-picked ponies and horses, a clubhouse, auditorium, and bunkhouse, with all the facilities for an overnight or weekend stay. 'A bunch of dudes, you're all going to be,' Libby had told the children affectionately and laughed into their clamor of excitement. She smiled at the recollection, then looked over interestedly when she heard Adam toss his pencil down on the table in front of him. 'All right?' she asked.

He picked up his coffee cup and ran a hand through his hair.

'They look to be. The changes I wanted have been made, the ones we talked about.' He looked over at her then, smiling as she collected her coffee and came over to join him.

She sat down in the Windsor chair next to his and gestured to Sebastian to join them. 'Come on. Sit down with us.'

'By the way, I talked to Matt,' Adam said over his coffee cup. She smiled alertly. 'And?'

'He's interested. He wants some time to think about it.'

Sebastian took a seat at the table. 'And what would he do?'

Adam slid down more comfortably in his chair and stretched his long legs out beneath the table. He set down the cup and clasped both hands behind his head. 'I want him as one of my instructors.'

'I thought you were going to do the teaching.'

'I intend to. But there'll be a lot of administration involved in this thing. Libby's school has given our idea their blessing, and we've already gotten a tremendous response from the students. Most of them and their parents will go for it. And I can't cope with the thought of dealing with all those kids by myself.' he added with a grin, tossing Libby a look.

She looked toward Sebastian, smiling. 'That's right, Sebastian. He's miserable with kids. You ought to see him with Jennie. It'd break your heart the way he's graduated her from riding with him to a pony of her own. And the way he handles her?' She sighed dramatically. 'It's just sad. Honestly, it's all he can do to stretch an hour's lesson out to two.'

Adam made no comment. Yes, it was something he'd never have envisioned a year ago, or even six months ago. Adam Bainbridge, engaged in some version of philanthropy. How laughable, how incongruous, how undeniably satisfying. He straightened after a moment, reaching over to flip on the overhead chandelier, and went back to the drawings with a light frown of concentration. Compulsive, he thought idly, and picked up his pencil as he studied again the drawings that had given such meaning to his life—almost as much as Libby Rutledge had. 'I'm putting in another ring,' he commented absently.

'Hmmm. Adam, have you gotten the final cost estimate?' Libby asked.

He didn't look up. 'Don't worry about it.'

She shook her head. 'Don't worry about it,' he said a thousand times over, for a thousand things. 'I'd just like to know,' she said mildly.

Laying aside his pencil, he gave her his full attention then.

'Bills aren't your province. Any of them. Which, by the way, reminds me. Where are the ones on this place?'

She shifted uncomfortably. 'Adam, I told you . . .'

'And I told you. I've been telling you for months. I want them.'

'Adam, I have more than enough money to cover what I need. You know that. Granted, teachers don't make a fortune, but my salary added to what I got from the sale of the farm is far more than adequate.'

'You're right. I do know that. And it's got nothing to do with it.'

She sighed. This matter of his supporting her before they were married had given them hours of disagreement. She knew, of course, that he could afford to, and that the whole issue stemmed from his desire to relieve her of any worries whatsoever; he'd said as much, and as always, she was touched by the sentiment. Yet the idea didn't set particularly well with her principles, and, even more important, it seemed like an encroachment on her self-sufficiency. She'd worked too hard for that independence to let it die so easily. But this was not a subject to discuss before an audience, not even Sebastian. 'If you don't look out, you're going to make me into a kept woman.' she hedged lightly, hoping he'd leave it alone.

He didn't. 'That's right. Kept in every respect. To have and to hold.'

'We haven't done that part yet.'

'All but.'

Libby flushed at the retort and averted her face from Sebastian. 'Adam, we'll discuss it another time,' she said pointedly.

As always, Adam was amused by her sudden discomfiture; she hadn't the slightest objection to their intimacies, but didn't want them to be acknowledged aloud. And though she'd leveled on him all her reasons for resisting his support, he had his own assessment of her motivation and had told her so. Hypocritical morality. He might've looked on it with more impatience had it not been one of the things that set her so apart from all the other women he'd ever known, had that tinge of unsophistication not been so appealing to him. He let her off the hook finally. 'All right. We'll discuss it another time. But we most assuredly will discuss it.'

It was Sebastian who put an end to her embarrassment. He stood up suddenly, asking. 'More coffee anyone? Lizbeth, your cup has runneth out.'

Gratefully, she slipped into their routine. 'Nope. As a matter of-fact, I'd like a glass of wine, *garçon*. You might inquire as to the needs of my gentleman friend here, also.'

Sebastian turned to Adam with a look of studied civility. 'Spirits, sir?'

Adam gave him a long-suffering grin and got up. 'Yes, but I'll make the drink. Sebastian, your talents are innumerable, but I'm afraid they don't run to bartending.' He began whistling to himself as he turned toward the kitchen, then stopped mid-stride as the doorbell rang.

Libby frowned over her shoulder in the direction of the door. 'Who could that be at this time of night?' She pushed back her chair, making ready to rise.

'Stay put,' Adam said shortly. 'I'll get it.'

Anyone he encountered on the other side of the paneled door would be unexpected, for they were anticipating no guests. But he was nothing short of stunned when he unlocked the door and opened it to confront the figure beyond.

It was Edwinna Rutledge, all silvery blonde and wrapped in mink, and she smiled exquisitely into his handsome face as she picked up her small overnight case and glided past him into the room.

# Chapter 13

'Adam, who is it?' Libby's light frown deepened. She rose and stood by the cherrywood table, the fingertips of one hand resting absently on its surface as she looked quizzically in his direction. There was a sudden air of conspiracy in the room, and she didn't like it; Adam wasn't given to leaving her at such a disadvantage, yet there'd been no sound of voices for her to identify, not even his, only the closing of the door and the faint rustle of movement by the small table just inside the doorway. She couldn't keep slight annoyance out of her voice as she repeated, 'Adam, who is it?'

Winna's blue eyes were dancing as she glanced up at him again, her finger still pressed against her lips in a gesture of silence. They were near the louvered doors of the coat closet, and Adam smiled his consent to let her answer. When she finally did, it was in a lilting voice. 'Well, who else do you think?'

Libby drew in a sharp breath and put a hand to her breast. 'Winna?' The whisper was not really a question; her sister's was a voice Libby could recognize as instantly as Adam's. It took a moment to register completely, but when it did, delight rushed into her face. 'Winna!'

Winna's silver mink flowed around her as she crossed the room in one fluid motion, her own face shining. They met halfway across the floor, near where the couches flanking the fireplace ended, hands outstretched; they fell immediately into a warm embrace. Libby was laughing openly by then, throwing her head back as she hugged her sister; of all the people in the world, Winna was the last she'd have expected to ring her doorbell late on this Sunday evening. There'd been her frequent telegrams over the past months, yes, but in none of them had she even hinted she might be planning a visit. They embraced a moment longer, then broke as Winna stepped back and took hold of Libby's hands again.

Adam remained near the closet, looking on at the breathless reunion in open pleasure, his arms comfortably crossed. She was so beautiful, Libby, when she was flushed with excitement, and he stole a glance at Sebastian, preparing to wink in shared satisfaction. He didn't however, but rather studied the other man briefly in surprise. Sebastian wasn't smiling; he stood rigidly where he'd risen in front of his dining room chair, his hands balled lightly into fists, his usual kindly expression replaced by a stiffness at his mouth and the bridge of his nose. Adam watched him for a moment, then shrugged and looked back at the two women; Winna was giving Libby a careful once-over as she kept hold of her hands, her head tilted in that same attitude of interest so particular to Libby. In the glow of the soft lighting, her hair was like spun silver, caressing the fur on her shoulders, and she dropped Libby's hands finally. She looked over at Sebastian. 'And Sebastian, you're here, too.' She moved between Libby and the sofas, crossing to give him a warm kiss on the cheek.

His expression didn't change; there was a brief flicker of some emotion Adam couldn't identify in his eyes, but it didn't soften them. 'That I am, as always. As always, Edwinna, I am here,' he said stonily.

Libby had turned to the sound of their voices and extended a hand in their direction. 'Winna, come over here. I want you to meet Adam. Formally, that is.'

Bypassing Libby, Winna swept toward Adam in a smooth, gazellelike motion and offered him her hand; it was as slender and elegant as Libby's. 'It's a pleasure to meet you, formally, that is. Thank you for catering to my penchant for surprises.' Her eyes danced again as she dropped his hand and studied him briefly. 'And are you the reason my sister looks so radiant?' Without waiting for his answer to her disconcerting remark, she looked back at Libby, a curious smile coming to her lips. 'Your glasses. I just noticed. You don't wear them any longer?'

'Adam doesn't like them,' Adam responded easily, taking a step toward Libby as she approached. He drew her to his side, slipping his arm around her shoulder. 'It's a pleasure to meet you, too, Edwinna, after all this time.'

He took that moment of brief introduction to study her in thoughtful objectivity. She was taller than Libby by some inches and extraordinarily beautiful, without question; her fine patrician face, set on the long column of her slender neck, had the photogenic bone structure that made fashion models, and her complexion the glow of meticulous care. Her eyes were the same wide-set almond shape as Libby's, and as long-lashed, but the color was distinctively blue. Aquamarine, he thought. Her right eyelid, he noticed after a moment, was set infinitesimally lower than the other; it was the only flaw in a perfect face. He might have decided she was the most beautiful woman he had ever seen as he looked at her smiling up at him, her thin, faintly colored lips perfectly sculpted, if he hadn't met Libby first. There was really no comparison between this fine, superficial comeliness and Libby's; hers was of a richer, warmer kind, unmatchable, springing from within and flowing outward to light up her expressive face. Or was that unfair? he wondered vaguely. For all their basis in experience, his weren't the most reliable of judgments any more; Libby had become so much a part of his life that she left no room for any other woman, not even in idle appreciation.

Libby had remained silent for as long as she could; a thousand enthusiastic questions were running through her mind, and she began on them. 'Winna, what are you doing here? Why didn't you write or call? How long are you staying? What . . . ?'

Adam laughed. 'Libby, take it easy. One at a time, when we get settled. Edwinna, here. Let me help you with your coat.' He saw Libby to the couch first, then went to Winna, stepping behind her to assist with the immense coat. And he knew exactly the quality of that fur as he laid his hands on it; he had been around many such coats in his lifetime. Perhaps, had he paid a bit more attention, he might even have been able to identify the designer. It was merely a casual observation, registering in his mind as he headed to the closet, that Edwinna Rutledge knew and wore expensive clothing. 'We were just about to have a drink,' he said over his shoulder. 'What would you like?'

Edwinna had joined Libby on the couch; the green ribboning through the chinoiserie pattern picked up the jade color of her silk shirtwaist, and she smoothed the fabric down over one attractive knee as she glanced back at him. 'Oh, gin, I guess. With tonic, if there is any.' She took a brief, visual tour around the familiar room, as if getting reacquainted, before transferring her gaze back to Libby.

She was facing Winna and had one leg drawn up under her comfortably. When Adam returned moments later with the drinks, she accepted one, feeling the touch of his fingers on hers as he guided them to the stem of the wine glass. She took one sip, then set it down. 'All right, Winna. Now tell me why you didn't write and let me know you were coming.'

'I wanted to surprise you.'

'You did that all right!' Libby laughed. 'How long can you stay?'

'How long do you want me?' Winna crossed her legs, sliding one arm along the back of the couch; at her wrist was a scarab bracelet, worn, like Libby's gold necklace, as a memento. It'd been a gift from her father on her sixteenth birthday.

'Winna, you know that doesn't matter. Don't tell me you're actually going to stay put somewhere for awhile. You sure you're not just between stops?'

'Of course not! I thought for once we ought to spend Christmas together. Suit you?'

'Suit me?' For a moment, Libby had no adequate response; her expression spoke for her, however, and Winna reached over, briefly squeezing her hand. Libby voiced her reaction then. 'Winna, yes. That suits me. I can't think of anything I'd like better. It'll be marvelous, with all of us together.' She relaxed back against the arm of the couch and ran her fingers up the back of her neck, absently lifting her mane of hair from her shoulders as she anticipated the holiday. She supposed the day would come, some year, when she'd have to relinquish this lingering enchantment with Christmas; it seemed somehow unbefitting a woman who, before too long, would be staring middle age right in the face. And yet, she hoped she wouldn't change, for all the same reasons she hoped she'd never stop trying to convince a classroom of small children that toeless goblins had charm. They did; they really did.

'Good.' Winna was looking at her, and the faintest trace of uncertainty had crept into her expression. After a moment, she reached out again, placing a hand tentatively on Libby's arm. 'Libby, you really shouldn't go without your glasses. I . . . shall I get them for you?'

'There's no need.' Sebastian objected crisply. He sat stiffly in one corner of the opposite couch, beside Adam, and his brow was creased in disapproval. 'Libby is fine as she is. I've been trying for years to remove them. Only Adam was able to.'

Winna flushed under his reprimand. 'Sebastian, I only meant . . .'

'Will you please stop going on about it?' Libby's expression was momentarily stern, then softened as she turned to Winna. She should've remembered, of course. 'If it bothers you, Winna, I'll put them on,' she said quietly and rose, disappearing into the hallway.

Adam watched her go, making no attempt to help her; though he objected strenuously, he made no comment. He'd recognized

174

the expression on Libby's face and understood it all too well; he'd seen it enough times when she'd talked of Winna. She felt the need to protect Winna from any reminders of what had happened so many years before, and if she believed her sightless eyes—beautiful and unblemished as they were—presented an even starker reminder than the glasses, then he'd respect that, even if he could not agree.

Libby returned in moments, glasses in place, but rather than join them all again, she continued on into the kitchen. 'Be out in a minute,' she called from the far side of the counter. Sebastian seemed needful of some activity and went to join her; he flipped off the light over the dining table as he went, throwing the small area into shadow.

Adam watched the two of them moving behind the dividing counter for a moment, then looked back at Winna. Picking up his cigarette case, he held it out to offer her one.

She waved a hand. 'No thanks. It's a vile habit.'

'You're right.' He grinned briefly and lit one for himself, relaxing against the cushions. And with their moment alone, he expressed the thought that had been very much on his mind. 'I'm glad you're here. You're very important to her. It'll cap what I was hoping anyway was going to be a very special Christmas.'

Winna tilted her head, brushing her silver hair back from her face. 'I wanted to come. I really did. Libby needs her family. I'm sorry I can't be around more often, since I'm all that's left. It bothers me a lot sometimes.'

Adam was about to remark further when Libby and Sebastian re-entered. She was holding a tray, and he reached up and took it from her, setting it down on the coffee table. Taking her hand, he guided her down next to him; Sebastian was forced to sit down beside Edwinna. When they were all settled once more, Libby clasped her hands in an attitude of expectancy and looked across toward Winna. 'Okay. Now. Tell us what you've been doing, where you've been.'

Winna was sipping her drink delicately and eyed the tray. 'Really, Libby. Carrot cake and cocktails?'

Libby had forgotten that Winna specialized in disjointed remarks; she felt the first stirrings of annoyance but checked them. 'We do things like that around here,' she said mildly. 'Had you come just a little earlier, you could've joined us in a little flat cake.'

Winna looked puzzled. 'Flatcake?'

'A private joke,' Adam supplied dryly.

'Oh.' She set down her glass, stretched her arms above her

head, then brought her hands down and languidly ran her fingers through her hair. 'What've I been doing? Well, let's see. Traveling, always traveling. The sights, Libby! You just couldn't believe them!' She looked over at Libby with excitement, letting one hand drop to the tufted arm of the couch. 'Paris, Rome, Amsterdam. My favorite of all, I think, if I had to pick one, would be Venice. I just adored Venice. Or maybe it's Monte Carlo.' She looked musingly toward the hearth; a small pyramid of logs rested on the brass horse-head andirons, ready for Adam to light them into a warm fire. She seemed lost there for a moment, then roused, looking back at Libby. 'Yes, actually, I think that's it. But it's all just spectacular.'

Libby smiled. 'It sounds divine. And you sound as though you're happy. I'm so glad. Winna, I'm really so glad.' And she meant it; Winna's happiness was as important as her own and perhaps more elusive. Somehow, for reasons lost now to the archives of childhood experience, Libby often felt a responsibility for helping Winna find that happiness.

Winna straightened, working off her shoes before tucking her legs up under her as she shifted position. She reached for her glass. 'And I wanted to remember to tell you about a little hamlet I discovered in England. Picture-postcard colors, with the dark country inns and all that atmosphere. Well, you'd just have to see it to believe it!' she said with a gay wave of her hand. 'But we can talk about all that later. I want to talk about you. How are you, Libby?'

'Fine.' Libby shrugged, smiling dismissively.

'She rides.' For the second time, Sebastian joined in the conversation curtly.

Winna's eyebrows went up. 'My goodness!'

Libby's expression then was a peculiar mixture of pride and quiet emotion; though she didn't reach out to touch him, she was acutely conscious of Adam sitting next to her, his arm resting along the back of the couch behind her. 'Yes, I do.'

Winna was shaking her head. 'And how . . . ?'

'Exquisitely,' Sebastian said stiffly.

Winna touched his arm, her smile warm. 'I'm sure. She always did.'

'Alone.'

Winna's smile remained intact, but her glance at Adam and Libby had gone decidedly uncomfortable; Adam had begun to frown lightly, and Libby was pursing her lips in open annoyance.

'It was Adam's doing,' Sebastian went on relentlessly, looking at Winna dispassionately.

'Sebastian!' Libby frowned sternly. 'Please. You're being rude.'

'Oh, he wasn't being rude,' Winna dismissed graciously. 'Just proud of you, I suspect. And I don't blame him. I think that's marvelous, Libby. I really do. And you'll have to tell me all about it, but right now, I wonder if you'd be terribly upset if I went off to bed? I'm exhausted. I hate those interminable flights.' She leaned over to collect her shoes.

'Of course no one minds. I wasn't thinking,' Libby said, accepting Winna's abrupt cut-off of the conversation. 'We can talk about everything tomorrow. Your things. Did you bring them all in?'

Winna was on her feet by then. 'I have a small overnight case. I carried it in with me.'

Libby laughed in genuine surprise. 'An overnight case? With clothes enough to last until Christmas?' She was genuinely nonplussed; Winna never traveled anywhere without her entire wardrobe, not even for a weekend, much less for a stay of several weeks. 'Winna, where are the rest of your clothes?'

Winna skirted Sebastian's knee as she passed between them and the coffee table. 'Oh, I was so tired of everything,' she said, leaning down to pick up her case at the back of the couch. 'I got rid of it all. I'm going out tomorrow to buy a fresh wardrobe. I only brought enough to get me here.' She gave Libby a gay smile then. 'Won't it be fun? We can go together. You can help me pick everything out. Oh, and I nearly forgot.' Her expression turned to chagrin. 'Would you mind if I borrow some night clothes? Just for tonight?'

Libby shook her head. 'Winna, from the time I can remember, you were always out of something. Of course I don't mind. Come on.' She touched Adam lightly on the hand, to say she'd be back, then rose, disappearing with Winna into the hallway leading off toward the bedrooms.

Adam watched them go, then transferred his gaze to Sebastian. He also had risen and was looking moodily after the two women. He glanced down at the floor for a time, seemingly uncertain about something, then finally looked at Adam. He started when he found Adam was watching him. 'You staying the night?' he inquired abruptly.

It was Adam's turn to be startled. He uncrossed his legs and sat forward, resting his elbows on his knees. 'That's a rather personal question, don't you think?'

Sebastian didn't return the smile. 'Of course. Are you?'

A frown crept into Adam's eyes. 'Why?'

'Do.'

'Thanks for the permission,' he said dryly.

'Do, Adam.'

Adam purposely said nothing and watched with a light frown as Sebastian crossed the room to retrieve his coat and sweaters from the closet. At the door, he shifted the clothes to the other arm as he put his hand on the brass knob, then turned back to Adam. 'Don't leave her alone,' he said darkly, then pulled open the door and was gone.

Adam stared after him, his face grim. He abruptly dismissed the man from mind, however, as Libby finally reappeared. He rose and met her halfway across the room, pulling her to him and arranging her arms around his neck. 'That's better, except for one thing.' He reached up and removed her glasses, tossing them onto the couch.

'Those damn glasses!' she said in exasperation, clasping her hands behind his neck.

'That's what I say.' He embraced her, then held her away, looking down into her face; he gently brushed a stray lock of hair from her eyes and kissed her. 'Happy?'

She was smiling up at him serenely, her auburn hair drifting down nearly to the middle of her back. 'Oh, Adam. I'm so thrilled she came. You just don't know!'

'Yes I do. I can see it in your face.' He looked at her a moment longer, then pulled her back to him. They remained that way for some time, merely embracing, speaking in a language that needed no voice. At the brief recollection of Sebastian, Adam's lips twisted in a slight smile. 'By the way, Sebastian's given me permission to stay the night.'

She leaned back at that, tilting her head. 'What do you mean?'

'Just what I said. As a matter of fact, he insisted. And it's a suggestion that has considerable merit.' His eyes darkened then, and he slipped his hands lower on her back.

'I hate it when he acts like that.' Libby said, frowning crossly up into his ardent expression; her look went a long way toward dissolving his passion. 'And he always does when she's here. It really infuriates me. Well, you saw him, how rude he is.'

'Sebastian's an oddball, hon. There's no figuring the man any time, any place. You ought to know that far better than I.'

'That's no real reason.'

'You're right. But forget it.' He cupped her chin in his hand, raising it up toward him. 'Just don't worry about it. Are you

178

going to be all right here alone?' He asked quietly then. It wasn't often he left her, or didn't take her home with him. There was no practical reason for it, only emotional ones; as far as he was concerned, she'd spent enough years coping by herself.

She arched an eyebrow, molding herself to him as she slid her arms more tightly around his neck. 'I thought you'd decided Sebastian's suggestion was worth consideration.'

His grin took on the same suggestiveness as hers. 'And here I'd thought you were ignoring me,' he remarked, then cocked his head. 'I do think his suggestion is worth considering. It's just that I doubt very seriously I could take you up on it without stepping all over that sometime morality of yours.'

She laughed a little as she pushed him away. 'Leave, Adam Bainbridge,' she directed good-naturedly.

He would, but caught her back to him first. 'In a minute.' He kissed her in earnest then, for some minutes, pressing her body to his with a hand low on her back. When he finally loosened his embrace, he ran his cheek along her silky hair. 'I meant what I said,' he murmured. 'Will you be all right alone?'

She leaned back from him, still smiling but stepping out of his embrace. 'Adam, I'm not alone. Winna's here. I'm in the very best of hands.'

'No, the second best hands,' he corrected, chucking her lightly under the chin. Then he strode briskly over to the closet to collect his coat.

# Chapter 14

Adam Bainbridge, dressed casually in twill slacks and dark-green plaid shirt, was reclining along the suede couch in his living room, reading the morning paper. He briefly scanned the financial page, then turned to sports. Absently he reached over to the glass-topped coffee table, searching for his mug. He found it, brought it to his lips, then set it back down abruptly with a grimace of distaste; the coffee was cold. The sun glared into the room through the sliding doors that led onto the balcony, giving the chrome and glass surfaces all around the spacious room a high sheen, and he swung himself upright on the edge of the cushion, laying aside the paper. Just as he made a movement to rise, the doorbell rang, and he frowned at it a moment. The housekeeper? No, this was Monday; she came on Tuesdays and Thursdays. He puzzled over his unexpected guest another instant, then rose, going over to open the door. He found Sebastian standing out in the hall, wrapped in his heavy wool topcoat, his neat worsted slacks and inevitable vest and blazer beginning to appear from beneath it as he unfastened the buttons. His thin silver hair stood straight up, as if he'd just raised his head from a pillow.

'Good morning.' Adam ushered him in and accepted his coat, following Sebastian's back with a pleasantly wary look as his guest continued into the living room.

'For some reason, I wouldn't have thought you'd be up so early.' Adam remarked with a half smile as he entered the room himself. Then he checked his watch, starting in surprise. It was nearly eleven thirty. 'Sorry. Time seems to have passed me by. I was reading the paper. How about some coffee? I was just on my way to make some more.'

Sebastian nodded. ' 'Twould be a welcome pleasure. It's cold outside.' He watched Adam disappear into the kitchen, then turned and wandered over to the glass doors, peering out. He

180

liked this view of the wide stone terrace and white-fenced, rolling Virginia hills beyond, especially with the ice-crusted snow encasing the distant trees and glittering along the terrace rail in the bright morning; he'd looked out on it many times over the past months when he'd been invited for dinner or a leisurely weekend luncheon. By Libby, of course, the incomparable Libby, who'd hear none of his polite protests, who always included him because she didn't know how to care less, no matter what. He sighed heavily and straightened his bifocals. Adam's feet made no noise on the carpet as he re-entered sometime later with the coffee, and he stood contemplating Sebastian's motionless back a moment before finally speaking.

'Quite a view in the snow, isn't it?' He set down the coffee. 'Have a seat.'

Adam lit a cigarette and followed his own friendly directive. He watched Sebastian do the same on an adjacent section of suede couch, then fiddle with the preparation of his coffee. Adam drank his own black and settled back with it, waiting with mild impatience for Sebastian to stop staring into his cup; the man wasn't in the habit of idle visits, and Adam only hoped it wouldn't take him too long to get to the point. He was due for a meeting with the architects in little more than an hour. 'Okay. What's up?' he ventured after a moment. Sebastian merely became more engrossed in his coffee, and finally Adam expelled a breath. 'Sebastian?'

He answered then, without looking up. 'It's Libby.'

Adam nearly doused the whey-colored rug with his coffee as he sat bolt upright; he'd talked to her no more than half an hour before and been pleased to discover she planned to spend the day with Winna. 'What's happened?' he demanded.

Sebastian did look up then, in surprise. He realized the impact of his words and gestured dismissively. 'Nothing, nothing! Sit back. Nothing's happened. Yet,' he added darkly.

Adam slowly relaxed again. But his face was set in a frown of irritation, and he picked up the cigarette burning down in the ash stand beside the couch. 'Sebastian, don't play games with me. What are you talking about?'

'Edwinna.'

Of course. The uncompromising sidewise glances, the rigid posture, the cryptic exchange before Sebastian had taken his leave the night before . . . Adam's broad shoulders loosened completely, and he tapped his heel restlessly against the thick pile of the carpet. 'What about Edwinna?' he inquired shortly. He'd come to like Sebastian, most of the time.

Sebastian was stirring his coffee again. 'I wish she hadn't come.'

'How can you say that?'

'Easily.'

'Look, Sebastian, it was pretty clear last night you don't like her. Well, that's your business. But do me a favor; don't step on Libby's happiness, all right? Let her enjoy Winna's visit without having to be all tied up in knots because you're acting . . .' Oh, what the hell. 'Odd. And she will be. Upset, I mean. She was last night. You've got no right to do that to her.'

Sebastian's chin came up. 'I've got a right to protect what I love.'

Adam had no immediate response and massaged his forehead. 'Meaning?' he relented finally, holding the man's steady gaze.

At that, Sebastian rose again, stuffing the gold watch chain further down into his vest pocket as he began to pace the room. He stopped abruptly. 'Adam, I know you think I'm a foolish old man.' He raised a hand. 'No, you're right. I am, much of the time. But not always. No, not always.' He paused. 'Adam, there are things you don't know about Libby and Edwinna.'

'I know that they're very close,' Adam countered without hesitation. 'I know that they're delighted to see each other. Or let me say, I know Libby is. I'd have to assume Winna feels the same way or she wouldn't have nearly knocked Libby over trying to hug her. Now, what's your problem?' he demanded shortly.

'There are things you don't know. I've tried to point these things out to Libby, but . . .'

'She won't listen, right?' I can understand that, Adam thought, and felt the need to rise. He did and walked in the direction of the door, away from Sebastian. He cared far too much for Libby to toss her friend out on his ear, but at the moment he was sorely tempted. He had no time for Sebastian Vickery's fantasies, whatever they might be; there were things he had to do. 'Oh, come on, Sebastian,' he began in some annoyance.

'You will listen to me!'

Adam wheeled, startled. Sebastian's shrill command had pierced the air, and the man was visibly gripped by some emotion. Adam crossed to him immediately, laying a placating hand on his shoulder; he looked as though he might be close to having a stroke. 'All right, Sebastian. Calm down. I'll listen. Now sit down.'

'I'll stand, thanks,' Sebastian said stiffly and hiked down his vest with both hands. He watched Adam return to the couch and paused only briefly before going on. 'Adam, these two girls, they're not close, not in reality. Oh, Libby thinks they are. She loves Edwinna. She always has, and she'd do nearly anything in the world for her; she has done, time and time again. She's of that nature. But it isn't good for her to love like that. Not with Edwinna. With you, me, yes. But not with Edwinna.'

'Sebastian, I don't understand what this is all about,' Adam said resignedly, 'but you seem to feel strongly about whatever it is you came to say, so I'll hear you out. That's not to say, however, that I'll give credence to it.'

'Adam!' Sebastian's voice was as near to cutting as it could ever be. 'You've been around only a short time. You've not seen what I've seen. You know Libby better in some ways than I, obviously, but I know better what's around her. I've seen it, so you must give me credence!'

Adam had no choice but to be impressed; Sebastian unquestionably believed what he was saying. 'All right. Go on.'

'Adam, there are people in this world who should never be thrown together, people with personalities that interplay wrongly, that set up atmospheres. Atmospheres for destruction.'

Adam eyed him skeptically. 'That sounds a bit melodramatic, don't you think?'

Sebastian nodded once in affirmation, his eyebrows knit together earnestly. 'Perhaps, but it's true. It exists. Libby and Winna are two such people. Adam, nothing good can ever come from that relationship, not for Libby, possibly not even for Winna, but my concern isn't for her. It's for Libby.'

'And just why is their relationship so bad?' Adam inquired, sliding down into the deep cushions of the sofa as he stretched his legs out in front of him on the table. 'What can be bad about two sisters who so openly care for one another?'

'Adam, Winna doesn't care.'

His only response was a raised eyebrow.

Sebastian agitatedly moved to the window, then turned. 'I've watched those girls for years. I see what goes on. Frankly, I was thankful when Winna chose to go away. When I saw her standing there last night . . .'

'Sebastian, get to the point.' Adam said testily, glancing at his watch.

Sebastian eyed him for a moment, then drew himself up to his full height. 'The point is, Libby isn't safe when Edwinna is around.'

'Oh? Why? Is Edwinna going to push her off a cliff?' Adam

watched Sebastian through the curl of his cigarette smoke; it was hard to contain his exasperation.

Sebastian was undaunted by Adam's tone. 'No. It isn't so simple or open as that. It's more subtle, more dangerous than such a blatant threat, against which one can arm oneself. Adam, Edwinna's personality is flawed, dangerously so.'

Adam was frowning again. He wished Sebastian had acknowledged his own facetious comment; it would've been far easier to dismiss him then. 'Go on.'

'Edwinna Rutledge is a user.'

Adam's expression was cynical. 'There are a lot of them around.'

'True,' Sebastian conceded immediately. 'But not so many, perhaps, with Edwinna's turn of personality, her ugly turn.' He ran a hand briefly through his thinning hair. 'Adam, she's completely without remorse, that woman—born without it. It allows her to demand things of people that are unthinkable. She cares nothing for consequences to other people. Remorse, you know, is what makes for judgment.'

Adam crossed his arms, throwing his head back so it rested against the papered wall. 'Obviously, I can't agree with you since I don't know her. But . . .'

'Exactly,' Sebastian said crisply. 'That's why I'm telling you all this. There's no time for you to get to know her, although it takes no time, really. But you must speak to Libby. Persuade her to listen to you.'

Adam was shaking his head. 'I'm afraid I'm still missing the point. I'm not making the connection somewhere, Sebastian. And just what exactly am I supposed to be telling Libby? That someone thinks her sister is not a nice person? We do all have our opinions, you know.'

'Adam, Edwinna uses Libby!' Sebastian repeated, as if perhaps Adam had misunderstood before. 'She uses her over and over again to get what she wants. And Libby is susceptible. Libby doesn't see Winna as she really is. Libby, who knows so much and sees so much despite her blindness, can't see this relationship clearly. And whether you think so or not, it *is* dangerous to her, perhaps not in so apparent or melodramatic a way as you suggested, but the potential is there. Winna hurts her! She takes things away. I don't know,' he went on, shaking his head. 'Perhaps Winna cares when she can, when things are going as she wants them to, but I doubt it. All I do know is that when she begins to need things, that need overshadows everything else, including Libby's welfare. She'll do whatever she has to to get what she wants, regardless of what it means to Libby. And that is the danger!'

Adam was massaging his forehead again and looked up almost tiredly. 'Sebastian, I think you're overreacting.'

'No, I'm not. But you won't understand that. Not now, not until you've seen them together awhile. And you're a perceptive man, you'll see it. But,' he added, 'even that may not matter, because even you may not be able to make Libby understand.'

'Sebastian, I don't intend to allow Libby to get hurt in any way, by anyone or anything, if that makes you feel better,' Adam offered.

Sebastian had turned to look out the window again, and his dejected prophecy drifted over his shoulder. 'You may not be able to stop it.'

'Dammit, Sebastian!' Adam stubbed out his cigarette and stood up again. 'You *are* being melodramatic, and frankly, I don't like it. Soap operas aren't my thing, in case you didn't know.'

Sebastian turned around. 'Did you ever wonder about Libby's accident?' he asked abruptly.

Adam's eyes narrowed slightly. 'Meaning? That it wasn't an accident?' he said slowly. Again Sebastian had his attention. Completely.

'No, it was an accident—I think. I wasn't there, of course. Only Libby and Winna were there, and frankly, I discount some of what Libby says about it. She's unaware of what's really going on. Winna has never allowed questioning of the incident, and believe me, I've tried. I wanted to see what she had to say about it, but I never got anywhere. Of course, she would hardly confide anything to me, anyway. As a matter of fact, she can barely tolerate my presence. It makes her uncomfortable,' he said with heavy sarcasm.

Adam's irritation surfaced again. 'So, if you think it was an accident, why bring it up? No one's ever said it was anything else.'

Sebastian looked at him keenly. 'Adam, do you know how it happened?'

'Yes.'

'You've never wondered about it?'

'Sebastian, what in the hell are you talking about?' The subject was too close to his heart to discuss it easily. He looked down at the floor for a moment, 'I've thought about it, yes,' he said, raising his head. 'I think about it every time I look into

Libby's face. But what good does that do? Nothing can be changed.'

'Only prevented. Something equally destructive to her can be prevented.'

Adam was on the verge of losing his patience entirely. 'Sebastian, I think we're about through,' he said shortly.

Sebastian ignored him. 'She was going after a bird's nest. For Winna,' he murmured, his eyes growing faraway, as if he'd drifted out of the elegant room and back in time, back to the big old farmhouse he'd visited so often before Trevor and Jocelyn had died. He'd come to know the family quite well by then, come to know Libby, his courageous young friend down the hall, and he knew the details of the accident, knew Edwinna —oh, so well!—as even Jocelyn and Trevor never had. And he'd looked at that porch, time and time again, standing below it on the drive, seeing the tree, almost visualizing the small body as it fell from the railing, the dark auburn hair spilling out over the treacherous extension of gray rock foundation as it hit.

'I know that,' Adam said clearly.

It broke Sebastian's reverie. 'Did you know that Libby didn't want to go up that railing?'

No, he hadn't known; he'd never pressed Libby for the details. 'No,' he conceded finally.

'But she went up anyway. Even though she was terrified and knew better.'

'She told you that? That she was so afraid?'

'Yes. Once, when we were talking, she told me all about it. Things she'd never said to anyone, I suspect. She couldn't really help herself because she'd gotten caught up in all the emotion again. Oh, her attitude was dismissive, of course. Ever protective of her Winna!' he said harshly. 'She's obscured much of what happened in her effort not to place blame, I feel. She never has blamed her, you know,' he said almost matter-of-factly. 'Not even once, in all the time since it happened. Jocelyn told me that. At any rate,' he said, getting back on track, 'That one time when we were talking a lot of things came out, and she couldn't help but tell me she'd been afraid. That Winna had insisted she go up on that railing.'

Almost without realizing it, Adam had gotten up and moved to a chair, closer to Sebastian. He perched on its arm, watching Sebastian alertly. 'Go on.'

'Of course I wasn't there,' Sebastian repeated, thrusting his hands in the pockets of his tweed blazer, 'but I can picture it. I know those girls, know what goes on between them. Winna

wanted the bird's nest, needed it for, who the hell knows why!'
he said, anger crinkling the corners of his eyes, and Adam
realized it was the first time he'd ever heard Sebastian curse; he
was glad to discover the man possessed at least a modicum of
normalcy. 'And it doesn't matter. What does matter is that she
wanted it, and that she was afraid to go on that railing, too.
Libby told me that.'

Adam waited, but Sebastian remained quiet for a time. Now it
was Adam's turn to want to continue the conversation, and he
prompted him finally. 'And, so what is your theory? You have
one, obviously.'

'Oh, it's no theory,' Sebastian said, beginning to move again.
He came to a standstill a short distance from Adam, looking at
him earnestly. 'It's fact. Winna was using her to get what she
wanted. Libby told me, though she didn't realize what she was
saying because she doesn't understand it herself.'

'What did she tell you?' Adam asked, his voice tense.

Sebastian pursed his lips, as if bringing it all to mind once
more. 'I'd asked her why she went up there if she was so afraid.
She was reliving it all as she talked, and even then I could feel
the little girl's fear radiating from her. She went up because
Winna'd maneuvered her into it, played on her emotions with
the ploy that if Libby really cared about her, she'd do it. And
Libby was all but begging me to understand as she recounted it,
to understand Winna's insecurity and that she hadn't wanted
Winna to doubt her love. "Winna's so afraid no one really
cares," I believe were her words.'

Adam was frowning heavily again. 'That's absurd. I can't
imagine Libby falling for something like that.'

'Stupid. And dangerous. And that's how it happened.'

'All right,' Adam said, getting up to walk over to the table and
light another cigarette. 'Maybe she felt that way, but she was
just a child then. Children don't understand things like that.'

'I've seen it since,' Sebastian whispered, his eyes trained on
Adam. They were both locked in the gaze, and Sebastian went
on rapidly. He had him now, really had him. 'Adam, I'm not
exaggerating! It happens still. Oh, it's more subtle than when
they were children, but nothing has changed. Adam, don't you
see? Libby cares too much; she can't understand. She's at the
psychological mercy of someone who uses her remorselessly!'

Adam blinked once. 'Sebastian, are you sure you're not
imagining all this?'

And he'd lost him again. In frustration, Sebastian balled up

187

his hands, letting out an audible breath. 'Did you listen to the conversation last night?'

Adam pointedly looked at his watch. 'Yes,' he said tiredly.

'Didn't you hear it?' Sebastian's eyes were wide, boring into him.

One more minute and the man was going to be on his way, either under his own steam or with a little assistance from Adam. 'And what was I supposed to have gotten from that conversation, that I obviously missed? All I heard were two sisters who've been separated for a long time say how glad they were to see each other again.'

Sebastian got the message; it was no longer any use. 'You only heard. You didn't listen. To Winna talking about the colors, the little hamlet in England. "Oh, Libby, you'd have to see it to believe it!" Cruelties! Her conversation is filled with cruelties! We tell her about colors, you and I. We make her see them. We don't just dangle the inference before her sightless eyes.' He turned as if to leave finally, then turned back abruptly. 'And the glasses! What about the glasses?'

Adam truly lost his temper then. 'Sebastian, did it ever occur to you that Winna might not want to be reminded any more than is necessary about what happened, that for her the sight of the glasses is easier to take? And Libby? Well I recognized her expression, and she understands. I might not agree with it, I might not like her wearing those damn glasses, but I respect whatever's between the two of them about it. Why don't you try doing the same?' he said hotly, venting his full anger in stubbing out the half smoked cigarette. He straightened, his face hard as he looked at Sebastian again.

The man was already on his way to the coat closet, his shoulders slumped in defeat. He collected his coat, shrugged into it, and at the door, turned to look at Adam for the last time. His voice when he spoke was toneless. 'Adam, Edwinna doesn't care about the accident, but I see I'm not going to make you understand. Only your own eyes and ears will do that. As for Libby, she never will understand, not until someone helps her, and that's why I came to you. You're the only one who can possibly do that, because you understand each other, you don't lie to each other. Maybe she'll believe you, but maybe even that won't be enough.' He paused. 'Maybe even you can't stop her from being hurt again, and I have no doubt it will happen. Somewhere, sometime. Edwinna hasn't come home for a visit. She needs something. She never does anything without some selfish motivation behind it. Mark my words.' He put his hand on the knob and turned it, pulling open the door. A last thought struck him.

'By the way, Winna doesn't like Libby to take off her glasses because she knows Libby is the more beautiful of the two, really. It doesn't please her. It has nothing to do with anything else.'

And then he was gone.

Adam stood staring at the closed door for a moment, then returned to the couch and sprawled down on it. He rubbed his eyes in an effort to erase the ache behind them. The last thing he'd planned on doing that morning was examining the delusions of one Sebastian Vickery, and after a moment he rose and paced over to the windows, where he stood looking out, his eyes shadowed. The bright morning helped to relieve the jaded atmosphere Sebastian had left in his wake and made him rethink his decision to pick up the phone and call Libby; he'd been longing just to hear her voice. And he almost laughed then. Let him overreact to Sebastian's overreaction; that should compound matters sufficiently. Yes, he loved Libby too, but he hoped not so unstably that he'd take what might conceivably be a minor imperfection in the relationship between the two sisters and blow it all out of proportion. It was nonsensical.

He checked his watch again, then strode briskly into the bedroom, beginning to unbutton his shirt as he went. In twenty minutes he was showered, shaved, and redressed in a three-piece herringbone suit, and as he thrust his wallet into his jacket pocket, he reached into the coat closet and grabbed up his overcoat, shrugging off the last vestiges of Sebastian's disquiet as he went out the door.

# Chapter 15

Libby was humming to herself as she stood at the counter in the kitchen, working the lid from a marmalade jar. The fluorescent lights were on overhead and in the inset beneath the oakgrain cabinets, illuminating the yellow fleur-de-lis tiling on the floor, the faintly gold brickwork at the back of the counter, the pots hanging neatly above the stove on their wrought-iron hooks. She was still in her blue chenille robe, the belt tied tightly around her waist, and as she worked at the balky lid, she tried to identify the familiar melody issuing automatically from her throat but couldn't immediately; after a moment, the lid popped loose and the tune ceased altogether as she felt the onset of a sneeze. Hurriedly, she fished in her pocket for a Kleenex, stifling the spasm just as it erupted. Lucky for her that Adam and Sebastian hadn't been around to witness that, she thought as she suppressed a slight smile; she'd never have heard the end of it. And the tune had been 'O Tannenbaum', she realized abruptly.

Breakfast was coming along, and she was experiencing that familiar stab of satisfaction she always did when she was being particularly self-sufficient. It was a universal experience, of course; she didn't imagine it belonged only to her and her circumstances, but the taste must certainly be sweeter. Adversity, the spice of life. Or something like that, she mused idly and moved to the right when she heard the toast pop up, extracting it from the small appliance. For some reason, it made her imagine the patter of small feet running into the kitchen behind her, small voices clamoring for the crusted bread that would be slathered with all kinds of jams and jellies to smear little faces Libby had probably just taken great pains to wipe clean of all dirt. That had come up in their many discussions, of course, the question of children; she didn't need to be told how important a Bainbridge heir was to Julian and Augustine, but she had needed to be told how important it might be to Adam. She'd withheld her own

190

opinions until he offered his; it was too crucial an issue to have him swayed by her own feelings. He'd been frankly indifferent, leaving the choice, as usual, to her. Confident that there was no eventuality she couldn't handle, he'd nevertheless tossed the ball into her court, and she smiled as she remembered his remarks. 'A born molder of little individuals. I don't particularly care one way or the other, but it'd be a crime against humanity if the world were deprived of your maternal talents. And it's not as if you wouldn't have the resources for employing help if you wanted it. However, do as you like, only don't get all tied up in imagined inadequacies.'

Damn that man, she loved him so much, and yes, she could get all tied up in inadequacies, imagined or not. It was a tall order, caring for children without benefit of every faculty, and she would want to do it herself; as she'd told him, she felt some innate rebellion at the prospect of others sharing the responsibility. Yet for all its dimensions and difficulties, it wasn't something she thought impossible. She simply hadn't resolved the whole issue in her mind. Let it rest, had been Adam's advice, and she'd taken it, adding the problem, she thought wryly as she stacked the toast on a plate, to that growing list of things she'd think about next week. Or whenever.

She heard Winna stirring by the hallway and put aside her private thoughts, hurrying to get everything in order; she wanted the meal all ready so she could spring it on Winna. She listened to Winna yawning and the rustle of her movement as she strolled across the living room, and when she'd reached the near counter, Libby turned and gave her a bright smile. 'Good morning.'

Winna's eyes were barely open, and her hair was still tousled from the pillow, drifting down her back and sensual in its disarray. Her elegant body was almost visible through the filmy lavender gown she'd borrowed from Libby, and she adjusted one of the lace straps, sliding it firmly back up on her shoulder. It'd surprised her, actually, when she'd slipped it on the night before. Such a revealing gown for what she remembered as her very conventional sister seemed out of character; Adam's influence, obviously. 'Good morning,' she returned finally and stretched her arms above her head before letting them flop back down at her sides. She peered along the spotlessly clean formica counter, at the cluster of brailled cookbooks at one far end and the vase of dried flowers at the other. 'Where's the coffee? Got to pry open my eyes.'

Libby's smile remained in place as she turned back to the interior counter and a percolator plugged into the wall by the refrigerator. 'Right here.' She poured out two cups, and Winna watched as Libby passed into the small dining area and carried them to the table. 'Come on, sit. Breakfast'll be ready in a minute.' She set one cup at Winna's placemat, one at her own, then rested her hands on the back of her chair. 'I've fixed you a feast.'

'Uh!' Winna groaned, padding over on bare feet to slide lithely into the chair. 'I never eat in the morning! It makes me feel wretched. You shouldn't either. Puts on weight.' Propping one elbow on the table, she rested her chin in one hand and lifted the cup.

Libby remained where she was for a moment, then sank down slowly into her chair. 'Oh.'

Winna glanced over, read the trace of deflation in Libby's expression and expelled a small sigh. 'Oh. I should've told you. I guess you went to a lot of trouble. But honestly, Lib!' she said defensively. 'You should've asked!'

Libby didn't bother to answer; after all, Winna was here. In the whole scheme of things, it didn't matter one whit whether she ate breakfast or not. It just simply wasn't worth getting all in a stew about. She picked up her own coffee, and when she smiled again, it was in genuine dismissal. 'Never mind. I was just showing off my talents, anyway. I'll feed it to the birds. Besides, we can get an earlier start this way. I've taken the day off.'

Winna had propped one foot on the saddle seat of her chair and held it there with one arm wrapped around her knee. She studied the effect of the morning sunlight filtering into the apartment through the pale blue curtains at the sliding glass doors, then transferred her gaze to her hand. She frowned in light concentration as she inspected a fresh chip in one finger-nail. 'From what?' she inquired absently.

'Work, of course!' Libby laughed.

Winna looked up, smiling ruefully. 'Oh, right. I forgot. I'm out of the habit, you know.' She uncurled herself, combing her fingers through her hair as she leaned back and crossed her long legs. 'Lib, hon. Want to put on your glasses?' she said abruptly.

Damn. She'd done it again. Flashing Winna a look of quiet apology, Libby rose and went to the bedroom. This on-again, off-again routine had to go, she thought as she pulled open her bureau drawer and withdrew the leather case. She couldn't forever be traipsing back and forth to the bedroom, now on for Winna, now off for Adam. She made the decision right then and there, as she put on the wire-rims, to wear them all the time until

192

Winna left. Adam wouldn't be happy about it, but it was important to Winna—of more immediate importance than Adam's annoyance. It was her habit to qualify things like that, set priorities in feelings. Winna's feelings came first for the moment, by reason of the past they shared, and if Adam voiced any objection, she'd simply make him understand. She returned to the dining room and took her place once more at the table. 'Winna, I'm sorry,' was all she said.

Winna went back to the inspection of her fingernail. She made a mental note to file the jagged edge when she got dressed later —in the one dress she owned at the moment. She glanced up at Libby again, toying with the thought of borrowing one of hers, but rejected the idea immediately. Their figures were similar, in hips as well as bust, but there'd be that unavoidable problem of length. She picked up her coffee, eyeing Libby over the rim. 'I want to go to Woody's. Shopping, I mean.'

'Wherever, Winna.'

Winna watched her an instant longer, then lowered her eyes as she took a studied sip. 'By the way, Lib. I was going to charge everything.'

Libby had risen and was on her way back to the kitchen; Winna might make it a practice to go without breakfast, but Libby didn't. She was hungry. 'So?' she tossed over her shoulder as she rounded the door into the kitchen.

Winna waited for her to return; that was some minutes later, and she watched Libby settle with a plate of bacon and eggs, pick up her fork, and balance a mouthful of eggs on the prongs. 'Charge everything to you, I mean,' she elaborated finally.

The fork remained briefly suspended a hair's breath from Libby's mouth, then came down slowly as Libby digested the statement. Her thoughtful expression grew concerned. 'Winna, don't you have money?'

Winna laughed lightly. 'Well, of course! Just not with me. It's got to be transferred back from Europe. That takes awhile, you know. And I'll pay you back, of course.'

Libby smiled and relaxed. She picked up the fork again, this time getting the eggs into her mouth. 'I didn't think about that,' she said between bites. She chuckled suddenly, laying down her fork. 'I'd better warn Adam.'

Winna arched an eyebrow. 'Oh?'

Libby laughed outright then; Winna's wardrobes were never modest, nor inexpensive. 'Yes. He's been pressuring me for all my bills. I think it's about time he got them.'

Winna seemed discomfited by Libby's private amusement and

shifted, drawing up one leg again. She pulled the lavender fabric of the gown down over it and secured it with her clasped hands. 'So. Tell me about Adam, Libby. Frankly, I hadn't expected to come home and find a man in your bed.'

Libby flushed. 'Well . . .'

'Oh, don't go all prim! I doubt very seriously it suits you any more. Adam whatever-his-name-is doesn't look to me like a man who'd leave one prim for very long,' she observed.

Libby pushed away her plate. 'Bainbridge,' she said, ignoring the remark. 'Adam Bainbridge.'

Winna began folding the napkin by her plate as she kept her eyes on Libby. 'And what does this Adam Bainbridge do?'

Libby's smile then was quiet and seemed to emanate from somewhere within. 'He's working at the moment on setting up a riding school for the blind.'

'Hmmm. Novel idea. Yours, obviously.'

'My suggestion. His project. Believe me, I'd never have gone about it the way he has. I wouldn't have known how.'

'Undoubtedly,' Winna murmured. 'But when he's not setting up a riding school for the blind, what does he do?' she pressed.

Libby clasped her hands on the table in front of her, tilting her head. 'Well, actually, it takes up most of his time right now. There's a lot that goes into the planning.' She paused, thoughtful for a moment, then shrugged lightly. 'He teaches Jennie, of course. She's one of my students. He's teaching her to ride. The same way he did me.'

Winna's narrow face lit in a dry smile. 'This man is either independently wealthy or doesn't eat very much if all he does is set up projects and teach little kids how to ride.'

'He has money, yes,' Libby acknowledged, then leaned forward with an eager smile. 'Winna, the school is tremendously important. To him and to me. And it's quite a project. We're going to set it up in conjunction with the school where I . . .'

'I'm sure,' Winna said shortly and rose. 'More coffee? I'm going to get some.'

'Sure.' Libby listened to her movements as Winna headed into the kitchen and heard the clink of cup on saucer, the faint rush of coffee being poured out into porcelain. So, she would tell Winna about it another time. If she was interested. And if she wasn't, well, most people had little real enthusiasm for things not directly connected with their own lives; it was a sad fact of human nature.

Winna returned, slid Libby's cup across the table, and sat

back down. 'What kind of family does he have? Sisters? Brothers?'

Libby smiled. 'One brother, that's all. Christian.'

'Hmmm.' She was watching Libby steadily, the way the light picked up the color of her hair; it was particularly striking against the lavender of the robe. She touched her own hair involuntarily and arched an eyebrow. 'And so, he's keeping you.'

'I wouldn't put it quite like that,' Libby said and frowned.

Winna emitted a worldly laugh. 'Hey, hon. It's a terrific deal! Take it if you can get it. And I hate for you to be alone. You need to have someone around every now and then.'

Libby wasn't about to let the inference go by and spoke with quiet emphasis. 'Winna, we're going to be married.'

At that, Winna eyed her thoughtfully, then glanced down at Libby's hand. 'How nice. How come you don't wear a ring?'

Libby sat back in her chair, unconsciously rubbing one hand with the other. 'I didn't want one. It upset Adam, a lot I think,' she added, almost as if to herself. 'But I just didn't want one. Well, it doesn't matter,' she dismissed, smiling. 'We're going to have matching gold bands. Of his choice.'

'And when is all this going to happen?'

'In time.'

Winna's expression grew wise. 'Oh. One of those.'

Libby gave her a puzzled look. 'One of what?'

Winna sat back with a sigh. 'Libby, please. Do me a favor? Don't count too much on it, okay?' she said. 'I don't want to burst your bubble or anything, but "in time" is bad news. When a man tells you "in time", don't go around holding your breath. You'll only get blue in the face.'

'You think?' A rueful smile crept into Libby's face. 'Winna, it's not him. It's me. He wanted to get married months ago. I'm the one who's putting it off.'

Winna's eyebrow arched in surprise. 'That's unique. How come?'

Libby remained resting against the back of her chair, her face pensive. Finally, she sat forward and began rearranging the amber glassware at the front of her mat. 'I just want him to be sure, that's all. There's a lot to consider, you know.' She looked toward her hand tracing the base of the heavy glass, and spoke down to it. 'Winna, you know as well as I that the difficulties of my life are inseparable from it. But they're not part of Adam's life. They'd be imposed on him, and I worry sometimes that it would be too much.' Abruptly she raised an openly troubled

195

face. 'Winna, if I marry him, what I'm asking is that, for love of me, he take on a life totally different from the one he's known. Can I do that? Should I? He'd be deprived of so many things he takes for granted, things he'd be able to do with another woman. That's not an easy thought to come to terms with, that perhaps I'd be more of a burden to him than anything else. I . . . there's a lot of guilt involved for me.' She shook her head. 'There are just so many things to consider.'

'Have you talked about this?'

'Of course. We've talked about it a lot. It's sort of a main issue around here, you know.' She raised her head, managing a faint smile.

'And what does he say?'

'That he's made his decision, and it's what he wants.' She traced the edge of the mat under her hand. 'That he's considered everything and wants to be with me for the rest of his life. Marriage is such a long haul under any circumstances, but with me? Even if I could find reassurance in the knowledge that he loves me now, can I expect that not to change? That's my biggest fear, really. That the things he feels for me now, and his own happiness, will be eaten away over the years by all the . . .' She broke off suddenly and frowned. 'Oh, I don't know, Winna. I just want to be fair to him, and I haven't worked it all out in my mind. I suppose because of my own feelings of . . .' Of what, Libby? she asked herself, yet she knew the answer. With love of this man had come new emotions and uncertainties. New vulnerabilities to the fact of who and what she was. 'Of inadequacy,' she finally admitted quietly.

Winna's eyes were brilliant as she kept them trained on Libby. 'Lib, don't blow your chances. You're not going to get very many. Sorry. That wasn't kind, but true. And if the guy's loaded . . .' Her words drifted off meaningfully.

'Winna, I don't want to discuss it any more, all right?' Libby said abruptly. The confidence had brought with it emotions she didn't want to deal with at the moment, and anyway, the whole conversation had had the wrong tenor all along; it wasn't appropriate to what existed between her and Adam, and she didn't intend to let it go on. 'Look,' she said and smiled brightly. 'We should hurry and finish. Since it's an entire wardrobe you're talking about, we'll probably be all day at it.'

'Okay.' Winna unwound from her knotted position on the chair. 'And Lib. Sorry about Adam. Didn't mean to put you in a froth.'

Libby smiled dismissively and began collecting her dishes.

'I'm not in a froth. Now, come on.' She made a movement to rise.

Winna forestalled it with a hand on her wrist. 'In a minute. Sit back down.' She waited for Libby to comply, then said, 'There's something else I want to talk to you about before we go.'

Libby smiled expectantly.

'Sebastian.' Winna's voice had suddenly gone cold.

Libby drew an inaudible breath; she had known the subject would come up eventually. It always did. 'Winna . . .'

'Libby, he's such a nuisance,' Winna complained, frowning crossly.

'Winna, he's just funny sometimes. You know that. Don't let him bother you.'

'Well, he does.'

'I'll speak to him.'

Winna's lips had drawn into a pencil-thin line with the searing tension that had begun to grip her somewhere behind the temples. It was happening so much more often now, that vicious ache that came upon her in an instant, when the world around her and everyone in it became impossible; the ache made her feel short of breath, trapped in a vacuum of suffocating agitation. She eyed a pin cushion near the wooden sewing box resting at the edge of the table. Unconsciously, she extracted a pin and began pricking the small red cushion repeatedly, after a moment running it all the way into the felt, as if the cushion were some living thing she was spearing. 'It won't help!' came sharply from her throat. 'It never has. I can't bear the way he watches me, as if I'm some kind of insect under a miscroscope!'

Libby listened to the odd sound she couldn't readily identify, the repeated whisper of something, on something. She dismissed the mental activity of trying to figure it out, however, and pressed her lips together. She hated this subject, whether it was Sebastian or Winna who raised it.

'Winna, please. You know how I feel about Sebastian, but if he bothers you so much, I'll see to it that the two of you aren't thrown together. Now, I don't want to hear any more about it, all right?' she said and raised her chin firmly.

All right. Winna began to smile again, brushing lightly at her forehead for the ache that even then was subsiding considerably; she discovered the pin in her hand and laid it aside, looking brightly at Libby as the dark tension left her completely. "Hmmm. Now come on, let's get going. We can't sit around here all day, you know!' she admonished and rose, reaching across the table to pick up Libby's dishes and carry them out.

197

Libby remained where she was for a moment, her half smile bemused as she listened to Winna head for the kitchen and move about in it, dumping dishes into the stainless steel sink, clattering plates along the counter. If she didn't know and love Winna so well, she might have started screaming in exasperation; as it was, she began to laugh.

The fashionable shopping mall on the outskirts of Alexandria was newly built, and enormous; four wings connected the chic department stores on two levels, sprawling out in a bevy of small shops numbering in the dozens from a central, circular arcade. Along them were fountains, center-aisle concessions, and tremendous pots of trailing vines ornamenting the niches where the escalators ran up to the second level. Libby had been there before on several occasions with Sebastian and Adam but hadn't, of course, gone into all the stores. She did that day. Winna hit every boutique, every shoe store, every lingerie and cosmetics emporium, remaining sometimes minutes, sometimes longer if her fancy was struck, sifting through rack after rack of dresses, trying on one pair of shoes after another while Libby sat or stood somewhere nearby, listening in patient pleasure. She didn't mind the wait, for Winna's high spirits were infectious, and their camaraderie revived happy recollections of childhood companionship, when the exigencies of life had been no more than a stack of homework papers waiting to be done or a list of simple chores to be divvied between them, stuck up on the refrigerator door.

They spent three hours in Woodward and Lothrop.

'Hope your credit's good!' Winna commented gaily as they made their way down the main aisle, laden with packages.

'Me too,' Libby returned dryly, hiking her shopping bag more securely up under one arm as she swept the floor in front of her with her cane.

Dresses, slacks, sweaters, lingerie, shoes, even perfume —Winna had purchased them all with the small cards from Libby's purse. Plastic, Libby thought as they stood at the hosiery counter; where would the modern world be without it? For her, it was more than a simple luxury. It was a way of paring down the number of situations in which she had to deal in cash; the bills were sent directly to her bank to be taken care of. At other times, when the purchase was too small or credit cards weren't acceptable, Libby carefully made payment in hard money. The coins were easily identifiable, as were, in fact, the bills. Each was folded into a different shape by Sebastian, who placed ones, fives, and tens into different compartments of her wallet. He had been particularly pleased with his inspiration when it had hit, proudly instructing her exactly how to fold each different denomination so she could accomplish it herself when a salesperson delivered change; she had been duly impressed, expressing amazement and kissing him warmly on the cheek. Adam had laughed all those years later when she'd fondly recounted the story.

After an hour in Lord & Taylor, they finally stopped for lunch.

'Winna, my feet are screaming!' Libby made the good-natured complaint as she settled herself gratefully into the comfortable restaurant chair and retracted her cane, slipping it into her purse. Her heeled leather dress boots were only barely meant for walking, but her loyal friend at the dress shop in Fairfax where she purchased all her clothing had insisted on them when she'd outfitted Libby with the dark plaid kilt, tan sweater vest, and corduroy blazer.

Winna didn't respond to the jesting remark but instead slid a box across the narrow table toward her. She smiled enigmatically when Libby started at the touch of the box on her fingertips. 'Open it.'

'Winna! What . . . ?' Libby laughed and pulled the box over, lightly running her hands across the flat surface before lifting the lid to separate the tissue paper inside.

Winna leaned forward eagerly. 'Go on, take it out and feel it.'

Oblivious to the murmurs of conversation from the luncheoners crowding the tables around them, Libby withdrew the long rectangle of cashmere fabric, her quizzical smile changing, after a moment of inspection, to one of comprehension. 'It's a neck scarf. Winna, I . . .' She began to laugh again. 'What color is it?'

Winna sat back abruptly, smiling in satisfaction. 'Camel, of course. So it'll go with your coat.' The heavy belted garment lay over the back of Libby's ladderback chair, its satin lining visible where it buckled slightly at the collar. 'Do you like it?'

'Of course. But what's it for?'

Winna shrugged merrily. 'Just because. I wanted to buy you a present, something nice, that's all.'

Libby smiled quietly, replacing the scarf in the box before moving it to a spot by the others down near her feet. A gift, from Winna to her. Or from her to her, depending upon how one wanted to view the immediate payment. She didn't voice her thoughts, however. It was Winna's thinking of her that counted, and she was enormously touched. 'Winna, it's lovely. Thank you.'

Revived after the leisurely luncheon, they spent the rest of the afternoon in more shopping, finally arriving at Libby's apartment near six o'clock. Winna immediately got down to the business of storing away her extensive purchases while Libby saw to the preparation of a light meal; when she'd finished, she went in search of Winna and stopped in the doorway of the spare bedroom. There, she could hear the sound of Winna opening and closing drawers, balling up bags, drawing hangers along the metal rod in the closet. She smiled as she leaned against the doorframe. Winna spied her after a moment and frowned crossly. 'Libby, how do you live in this place? The closets are minute!'

'So you keep telling me every time you come here,' Libby remarked dryly. 'You have to remember that some of us don't have a change of clothes for every hour of the day.' She gave Winna a sly look and pushed herself away from the doorway, crossing over to sit down on the bed.

Winna grinned. 'Not every hour, every two.'

Libby laughed, then stretched out full length along the double bed. 'Well, I hope somewhere in all of that you've got something suitable for a formal dinner. You're having one. Rather, we're having one. For you. Sunday night, I think.' The thought had come to her in the kitchen and stuck; an official welcome home.

Winna was interested. 'Oh. How nice. What'd I do to rate that?'

'Put in an appearance,' Libby answered drolly.

Winna laughed, hanging the last of the dresses in the closet; she held back the thick mass of clothing in one hand, closed the door on it, then joined Libby on the bed, perching near the pillow. 'I'd really like that. Who's coming? You, me, Adam? The three musketeers!' Her musical laughter floated into the air, then she abruptly grew serious. 'Lib, isn't there someone else we could invite? Perhaps . . . what about the brother, what was his name? Christian? I really couldn't bear to be a fifth wheel.'

No, Libby knew that; she couldn't, either. Sebastian had been neatly excluded from the roll call, but then Libby would've done so herself; it was simply the way it was going to have to be. And then she smiled to herself as she digested Winna's suggestion; it was a good one, actually, for the man was certainly suitable as a date. The only hitch was going to be getting around Adam's reaction. 'Good idea. I'll work on it,' she said.

Winna smiled and reached up to loosen the pins holding her hair in an elegant chignon; it fell all in one silver mass around her shoulders. She shook her head, then relaxed back against the wooden headboard. 'Tell me, what are the plans for Christmas?'

'As a matter of fact, it's up in the air right now. It was originally going to be here or at Adam's. But the Bainbridges have invited us down there. All of us,' she hastened to clarify, then bit her lip; she could just imagine Augustine's tone of voice when she discovered she'd invited four, not two.

Winna was picking at a thread in the nubby bedspread; it was the same neutral color as the carpet, given life by two chocolate-brown throw pillows matching the draperies at the window. It was a room of modest decor but comfortable. 'Where's "down there"?'

'At the estate.'

Winna glanced up. 'Oh, my. An estate no less. He does come from money, doesn't he?' she remarked.

Libby's mind was elsewhere. 'So, come on! It's time you filled me in on everything. What have you been doing in all those marvelous places? And is there a man in your life, too?'

Winna stretched out then and crossed her legs. 'And who would you like to know about?' she inquired mildly. 'Lib, dear, I'm not so quaint as you, although settling down with one man might have its advantages,' she mused aloud. 'But there's no one in particular.'

Libby accepted the dodge, if that's what it was. 'So, where've you spent most of your time?'

'Monte Carlo.'

'That sounds risqué. And expensive.'

Winna glanced over again and grinned. 'Only if you lose.'

'Do you gamble, Winna?' Libby asked outright.

'For fun, silly.' Winna's gesture in her direction was dismissive. 'Of course. Nickel and dime. They all laugh at me.'

'Do you have a place there?'

Distaste etched itself into Winna's expression. 'Good God, no! I'd hate that. It gets so dreary, seeing the same old scenery all the time. Hotels, Lib. I stay in hotels. It's far more convenient, and you can pick up and go when it gets boring.'

Libby tilted her head against her hand. 'Do you bore so easily?'

Winna shifted her legs, straightening one to look at it critically before flopping it over the other. 'Love, the whole world's a bore sometime or other.'

'Well, I'll try to see to it you don't get bored here,' Libby said almost absently; she'd been toying with a thought ever since the topic of Christmas had come up and had finally made a decision. She sat up abruptly. 'Winna, I want to show you something.' She disappeared into her bedroom and Winna could hear a drawer open, then close again. After a moment Libby reappeared, a small wad of tissue paper in her hand. She rejoined Winna on the bed and began to unwrap the thin white paper carefully.

Winna was watching with interest, and finally Libby had the object unwrapped completely and held it out. It was a wood carving, a three-dimensional horse and rider, stylized, with no details of face either on the animal or the figure of the man. The wood was all natural, beautifully finished except for the body of the horse, which was stained white. In the man's left hand was a shield, with no marking but unmistakable nonetheless. The workmanship was excellent. Winna eyed the object with a mild frown. 'Cute. Who's it for?'

'Adam,' Libby said quietly and took the object back, running her hands over it gently. 'I did it myself. With some help, obviously, but I really did most of it myself.'

'Cute,' Winna reiterated doubtfully. 'What's it supposed to be?'

'A man on a white steed,' Libby answered with a peculiar, introspective smile.

'So?'

Libby immediately began rewrapping the small object. Winna would never understand; no one would. It was something very private between her and Adam. 'It's a personal thing,' she said and stood up. She left the room then to replace the gift in her bureau, and when she returned, she didn't cross to the bed but remained instead in the doorway, 'Winna, the sandwiches are ready. I'm starved. Come on.'

Winna dragged herself upright. 'Okay. We can talk at the table. I have so much to tell you!'

'I want to hear all about it, Winna. I really do,' Libby said encouragingly and smiled as Winna approached.

Winna took her arm and moved them back through the doorway, reaching behind her to absently flip off the light. 'Oh, I've been to so many wonderful places—just wonderful,' she exclaimed, then let out a gay peal of laughter. 'I'm not sure I can even describe it all to you. You'd just have to be able to see it to believe it!'

202

# Chapter 16

Williston Harries strode briskly into the paneled library at the Bainbridge estate, nodding a brief 'thank you' to Manning in the doorway as he passed through. Briefcase in hand, he crossed the length of the room to Julian, who was moving out from behind the massive oak desk, his thin frame draped in a burgundy brocade morning jacket. Harries smiled broadly as he approached and extended his free hand. 'Sorry I'm late, Julian. I was in court longer than I'd anticipated.'

Julian accepted the dapper man's hearty handshake and returned an indulgent smile. 'That's all right. Understandable.' Glancing over his friend's shoulder at Manning, he nodded in dismissal. 'That will be all. If you would close the door on your way out, please.' He paused until the butler had left them alone, then moved away and gestured toward the leather wing chair facing the desk. 'Sit down. Would you like coffee? It's here.'

Harries glanced at the silver service on the edge of the desk and shook his head. 'No thanks. I've been drinking coffee all morning.' He sat down then, resting the calf-skin case up against the carved leg of the chair before settling himself comfortably. A man in his early sixties, his physique was still lean and fit, kept that way by his devotion to racquet sports. A thatch of gray edged his dark hair at each temple, and his face had a deep Florida tan, compliments of a second home on the Keys. He watched Julian move back around the desk and perch down alertly on the edge of the high-backed swivel chair. 'How is Augustine?' he inquired.

'Fine, as always.'

'And you?' Harries looked at him closely. 'You're looking well. I trust this latest session at the hospital was merely for tests. You didn't tell me you were going in,' he said, and his tone was faintly admonitory; it was something only a longtime family lawyer could affect and get away with.

'I didn't need to tell you,' Julian said shortly. 'It was merely on the whim of an over-zealous physician driven by his obligation to the Oath. Or to his pocketbook, perhaps.' He smiled cynically. 'And yes. It was merely for tests. I'm feeling as well as I look.'

'Good.'

Julian leaned forward then and clasped his veined hands out in front of him on the blotter. He studied the attorney wordlessly for a moment, pushing aside a sheaf of papers with his elbow, then finally spoke. 'Will, we are both busy men. Let us get straight to the point. What have you found out?'

At that, Harries leaned down and opened his briefcase, withdrawing several legal-size papers and a manila folder. Averting his face from the glare of a shaft of sunlight streaming through the tall window, he tossed the loose papers onto the front edge of the desk, relaxing back with the file folder in his lap 'When you have a few free moments, look over those contracts.' He motioned toward the white legal sheets, red-lined down the left side. 'I think you'll find they're in order. When you're ready to sign, I can come back out or we can do it sometime when you're in town. It doesn't matter.'

'Fine.' Impatiently, Julian picked them up and added them to the stack of papers near his elbow. He gestured toward the file in Harries' lap. 'So?'

'You know, it hasn't been easy getting the information.'

'I don't pay you to do easy things,' Julian said crisply, easing himself back against the stiff cushion of the leather chair. 'I pay you to see to my wishes.'

Williston Harries had been dealing with Julian Bainbridge for too many years to take offense at the terse response. He smiled the engaging smile that had won him a number of impressive courtroom victories and crossed one leg over the other, drawing back the jacket of his pin-striped suit as he rested a hand on his hip. 'Which I always have. Even when I don't know the reason behind them. I don't do that for just anyone, you know.' He met Julian's direct look without discomfort, but when no immediate explanation was forthcoming, he shrugged and opened the folder.

'All right, then. The girl comes from a good family. They had money at one time, several generations before she came along. Good stock. English. The parents were killed four years ago in a boating accident. One sister.' He rattled off the information on the paper without looking up. 'She's a teacher at a school for the blind. Lives alone.' Here, he looked up and smiled broadly

204

again. 'Well, mostly alone. So far, Adam has continued to maintain his own apartment in McLean and even goes there sometimes.'

Julian was watching him intently, his fingers unconsciously running along the blade of a silver letter opener lying nearby. 'I know most of that. Except the sister and the parents. And Adam's sexual habits are irrelevant, with her or anyone else,' he dismissed impatiently. 'What about the other?'

Harries shifted his hand from his hip and balanced his elbow on the arm of the chair. 'As I said before, it wasn't so easy getting the information. My man had some difficulty. There's confidentiality to contend with, you know.'

'Degree of confidentiality is directly proportional to the amount of money one is willing to offer,' Julian replied. 'You know that as well as I do. And you had more than enough.'

Harries eyed the implacable man; behind him on the wall was a large portrait of his father, and the two tall windows on opposite ends of one wall let in enough morning sun to brighten even the faded oils. 'Yes, of course. And I might add here that for a man I know to be usually cautious with his "investments", you were quite generous in your allotment for persuasion. I was surprised.'

Julian propped his elbows on the arm of his chair, resting the pyramid of his fingertips against his chin. 'I pay for what is important to me. You know that well enough, too. And this is of utmost importance. Now, kindly tell me what you have found out.'

The lawyer nodded; sparring with Julian Bainbridge had its own particular limitations. He thumbed through the papers and brought out a medical report, peering at the nearly incomprehensible notations for a moment before summarizing them. 'She has detached retinas. Received from a blow on the head—there was a fall of some sort. At the time it happened, every avenue for corrective surgery was pursued, to no avail. There were two times in the hospital, with no result.' He looked up from the sheet of paper. 'Quite simply, Julian, there's nothing to be done. The girl is permanently blind. I could give you a run-down on all the ins and outs of her condition, insofar as I understand them, if you like. Or I'll leave this with you.' He slid the paper across the desk toward Julian. 'But that's it in a nutshell. Which is what you wanted to know. Whether or not the girl could be made to see again.'

Julian rose from his chair and moved away from the desk. Without a word, he walked slowly to the window and stood looking out, his back to the room. 'Was it a matter of not having enough money for the proper kind of operation?' he asked finally, over his shoulder.

Harries uncrossed his legs and shifted forward to the edge of the chair. 'It's a matter of no amount of money in the world being enough to buy that girl her sight again. The physician made that quite clear. It wasn't possible then. It's not possible now.'

'I see.'

Julian's tone had been constrained, and Harries remained poised on the edge of the chair, waiting for him to say something more. When he didn't, the attorney rose and thrust both hands in the pockets of his trousers, strolling up behind the man he'd known and served for nearly thirty years. In some ways, there was a good deal of understanding between them, yet in others, none at all; Harries could not fathom Julian's motives in this situation as he stood looking at his motionless back. 'Julian, I don't know what this is all about, although I can make some deductions on my own, of course. Apparently, Adam is quite involved with this woman. Is it serious?'

There was no response.

Harries eyed the toe of his patent leather shoe for a moment. 'I see. In other words, it is.' He looked up again. 'From what I could see, despite her handicap, she gets along rather well. Remarkably well, I'd say. She seems to be quite a woman. Highly respected at the school.'

'Yes, in some respects I suppose that's true. That she's remarkable. Interesting in some ways.' Julian spoke without looking around and instead peered hard at the formation of an icicle hanging from the branch of a pine outside the window.

'Well, you've been anxious for a long time now for Adam to settle down,' Harries offered. 'And if he loves her . . .' He shrugged.

'Yes, if he loves her,' Julian repeated in a monotone; he might have been trying out the sentence, to see how it sounded spoken aloud.

Harries had gotten an inkling of inspiration. 'And because he loves her, you want to do this for her, I suppose. It's good of you, but unfortunately not possible.' He paused purposely and when Julian didn't answer, he went ahead and voiced his thoughts, cynical as they were. 'What's the matter, Julian? Afraid to admit that even your money can't buy her what she needs?'

Julian whipped around, his eyes like pinpoints. 'What I'm

afraid of is that because he loves her, my son is going to disgrace this family by bringing into it a woman who is permanently handicapped!' Harries was visibly taken aback by the vehemence of the response, and his look of shock made Julian put a hand to his forehead. After a moment, he went on, in partial conciliation. 'I had thoughts, perhaps, something could be done for her.'

He moved away from the window, and returned to the desk, sitting down heavily in the swivel chair. 'And I don't know how serious the relationship is, but I have my suspicions. Yes, the woman has certain qualities,' he allowed again, almost tiredly. 'I have only had minimal contact with her, but she is impressive in her way. Yet there are considerations for this family to think about, its good name, to be exact. There are some things that just aren't done. That I won't allow. If there had been some way to correct her circumstances, that might've put a different light on things. As it is, any permanent relationship between the two of them is unthinkable.'

Harries had been watching him intently, both hands still thrust in his pockets as he stood silhouetted against the bright window. Uncertain as to how to respond, he offered a bland palliative. 'If you feel so strongly about it, talk to him. Talk to Adam and get him to understand your position.'

Julian didn't respond immediately; he was lost to momentary recollections. Of Adam's brief visit home, the only one he'd made since July—he'd refused even to discuss Libby. Of that July visit itself, when his son had displayed attitudes Julian had long waited to see in him, but for all the wrong motivations. And of a certain look in Adam's eye. Julian shook his head, effectively dissolving what might have been empathy; it had no place in pragmatic decisions. 'Talk to him?' he repeated finally, looking up at the lawyer. 'Oh, yes. I intend to talk to him, just as soon as the opportunity presents itself. And to do whatever I have to to see that Libby Rutledge never becomes his wife.'

## Chapter 17

The caterers Adam had engaged for Sunday evening were a discreet pair, professional men with references from some of the finest society hostesses in Washington, a town renowned for the quality of its hospitality. They arrived at his apartment punctually at six o'clock with trays of hors d'oeuvres already prepared; elegant canapés, cheeses, quiches, and ingredients for an elaborate dinner for four. Adam himself saw to the wine list. Dom Perignon of an excellent year, and Libby's favorite white wine; to her laughing complaint that there'd been nothing left for her to do, he'd kissed her lightly. 'My pleasure,' he'd said that Saturday afternoon before as they were preparing to leave for their round of errands. He'd been standing behind her, holding her camel coat as she slipped her arms into the sleeves. 'The next one's on you. Besides, I want to be sure *some* things are going to be done my way.' He'd been referring of course to Christian; Libby had received the good-natured complaint with a faint smile of apology. It had been a concession underhandedly won, with a good deal of guile, she thought, and she'd promised herself she'd make it up to him. Not, however, that she didn't suspect he'd known all along what she was doing. And let it work.

They were engaged only through dinner, the tuxedoed pair, and dinner was going to be late, for Edwinna was late. The caterers stood out of the mainstream of things, hovering out of sight in Adam's kitchen or moving quietly about the spacious dining room, feigning lack of interest in the three people conversing affably in the living room: two uncommonly good-looking men and a remarkably adept blind woman. Libby was the perfect hostess, as comfortable at Adam's home as she was in her own, and that night she wore a chartreuse evening gown of elegant simplicity that softly hugged her contours and fell to a V at the bodice; her only adornment, as always, was the fine gold chain encircling her throat. She saw to it that Christian was engaged in steady conversation, keeping him entertained and revising to some degree his estimation of just exactly what kind of situation his brother had gotten himself into.

'. . . and so it's more a matter of readjusting than anything else,' Libby was saying to his tentative inquiries into her circumstances; he'd actually been rather interested in the conversation his father had initiated so many months before, not for the tone of it but for the information itself.

'I'm impressed.' His voice was as smooth as his smile, and he adjusted his silk tie; it was flecked with dashes of silver that matched his dark gray suit. 'No wonder Adam finds you so fascinating,' he added.

Adam was nearly immune to Christian, but not entirely. 'It's not Libby's blindness I find so fascinating.' He smiled pleasantly, though there was a faint warning light in his eyes.

Christian flashed him a conciliatory look. 'That's not what I said.'

'It's what you inferred. And there are a number of other topics that we could discuss besides Libby's circumstances.'

'Another drink?' Libby inserted the mediating remark lightly, looking toward one then the other. 'Christian? Adam? I'm bartending,' she said, and rose gracefully.

Adam glanced up at her. 'No thanks, hon. Not for me.'

She skirted the enormous glass table expertly, stopping by Christian's chair. 'Christian?'

'Thanks,' he murmured, holding up his glass. It amazed him how easily she had found him, and it. He watched speculatively as she disappeared through the dining room into the kitchen; there, she'd be going to a second bar set up strictly for her accommodation, with facsimiles of her own cut glass decanters at home. Christian knew that; he'd inquired into that, too. At length, he turned his attention back to Adam. Christian nodded toward the kitchen. 'My compliments.'

'Thanks.'

'Planning on marrying her?'

'Absolutely.'

A crooked grin came to Christian's thin lips, and he ran a hand through his dark hair. 'That ought to set Julian on his ear.'

Adam's return smile was dark. 'I don't give a damn.'

Christian made no remark and looked down at his leather shoe. He raised his eyes again after a minute to find Adam's still on him. 'I have to talk to you,' he said abruptly.

Adam shifted, removing his arm from the back of the couch to balance it on his raised knee. 'If it's about money, save your breath.'

'Hear me out . . .'

'I've heard you out about as far as I can stand.'

As always, Christian felt the faint stirrings of resentment at having to petition for money from his brother. 'It's important,' he pressed tightly.

'It always is,' Adam sighed. 'How much are you in for this time?'

Christian kept his eyes carefully trained on his hands: on the little finger of his right one was a diamond signet ring, monogrammed 'CLB' in Florentine script, its small, faceted gem flashing brilliantly in the light. 'A lot,' he said finally.

Adam contemplated him wordlessly: he'd seen him only once since his visit home in July, and the dissipation that had marked him even then had spread. He was struck by the sudden realization that he'd have the privilege of watching his only brother disintegrate before his very eyes, and he wondered vaguely how long that would take. Another year or two, five maybe? 'Christian, why don't you knock it off?' he said abruptly and frowned.

Christian looked up. 'Oh, come on, man. I just want a loan. I'll pay it back.'

'That's not what I meant.'

Christian studied him a minute, finally identifying the expression on Adam's face: it irritated him. 'Oh, Jesus. What's that? Compassion?'

'Some version of it, I imagine,' Adam said quietly. 'You're a sorry sight.'

Christian's passive expression didn't change. 'I didn't ask for that. Just give me the money.'

Libby reappeared on the heels of the remark and handed Christian his drink.

It was an awkward moment, but she gracefully made her way around the coffee table, and as she neared Adam, he reached to take her hand and guide her down beside him. He looked at Christian then and relented. 'Talk to me later. I'll see what I can do,' he said shortly.

Christian nodded, shifting more comfortably in the plush chair. He drummed his fingers lightly on the arm, after a moment remarking for conversation's sake, 'I understand you've been invited for Christmas. How nice.' He raised his glass in a toast, then upended it.

'Don't fall all over yourself yet,' Adam said. 'I'm not sure we're coming.'

Christian lifted his eyebrows in exaggerated surprise. 'What's the matter, the prospect of a Bainbridge Christmas have no appeal? Why, we could bring out the dirges and hum along. Who knows? They might even put up a tree if they thought they'd be having company.' He drained his glass.

Libby was setting her drink down on the coffee table, and at Christian's remark, looked up in astonishment. 'You don't have a tree?'

Christian picked up Adam's gaze, attempting to share his derisive smile; it didn't connect. He glanced back at Libby. 'Not usually.'

Libby had moved back and was sitting perfectly still beside Adam, directly in line with the Picasso original on the wall above the couch. 'How can you not have a tree?' she asked, nonplussed.

'Easily,' Adam offered then and leaned toward her slightly. 'I told you once not to try to remake things in my life the way they've been in yours. Not at my parents' house, at any rate. Here is a different matter.' At that, he reached over and brushed her softly under the chin.

In preoccupation, she pulled away from his caress. 'Adam, I think that's dreadful!' Her frown turned to a look of wonderment. 'What do you do at Christmas?'

It was Christian who obliged, expansively. 'Oh, well,' he said and flashed his empty glass at one of the caterers. 'It's a perfectly festive affair! We sit around listening to no Christmas music whatsoever echo around the room. Sometimes we talk. Sometimes we even look at one another. Then everyone trades perfectly useless and disgustingly expensive gifts, remarks indifferently upon them, and we go on about our business. It's fun. You oughta come,' he finished fliply.

Adam was watching him dispassionately; actually, it had been a fairly accurate description, if incomplete. He'd left out the part about shifting around uncomfortably in your chair as the thoughtless gifts were passed around. Once upon a time they'd made an effort, when he and Christian had been younger, but that had been years before, and Adam had long since foregone taking part in the lifeless affair. He changed legs, propping the right over the left as he began on an entirely different subject. 'Lib, listen. About . . .'

'I think that's awful,' Libby repeated quietly, disregarding Adam's opening. She moved forward to sit at the edge of the

211

couch, her hands resting lightly in her lap as she looked from one to the other of them. 'You mean to tell me there are no Christmas carols, no decorations?'

Christian shrugged; it was a boring topic once he'd gotten in his few thrusts. 'When we were younger . . .'

'We're going,' she said flatly.

Adam had been in the process of lighting a cigarette and abruptly looked up past his hands. 'Hon . . .'

'We're going, Adam,' she repeated firmly, laying a hand on his knee. 'And there's going to be an honest-to-goodness Christmas at the Bainbridges' this year.'

'Hold on a second,' Adam said sternly. She was on her way, he could tell; she was getting herself all primed to take that enormous compassion for humanity down to his parents' place, forgetful of the fact that she was going to run right straight into a brick wall. 'Just a minute.'

She was too caught up in her own feelings on the subject to defer to his comments at the moment. 'Adam, we're going. And we'll take all those things I have up in the storage room with us. We'll bring the decorations, the lights, we can buy wreaths on the way . . .' She paused thoughtfully as she mentally ticked off a list of everything they'd need.

'Libby!' Adam said sharply but nearly laughed. Actually, he was expanding upon a caricature in his mind: his incorrigible Libby, marching down to the Bainbridge estate in a huff of Christmas spirit, with Christmas tree, wreaths, lights and decorations spilling out in her wake, and he went on to imagine her reception, Julian's and Augustine's apprehension as they watched her flash on into the house and proceed to dump season's greetings all around. A deathlike pall would descend over their expressions as they realized that they just might have to cheer up and have a merry Christmas after all. It was too much for him, and he did laugh then, outright. 'Honey,' he said after a moment, doing his best to regain some measure of sobriety, 'Hold it!'

Christian was at a loss to know why Adam was so amused; there was nothing even remotely humorous about the Bainbridge holiday. The caterer returned with his drink, and he accepted it with a nod of thanks, turning his attention back to the two people on the couch.

They were facing each other, Libby turned catty-corner on the edge of the couch as she looked toward Adam encouragingly. 'Adam, it'll be fun, you'll see.'

'Libby, now stop it.' He took one of her hands in both of his and looked at her seriously. 'Listen to me for just a minute. Regardless of whether or not we could get away with being so demonstrably pleasant about the whole affair, arriving with twinkling lights and a song on our lips, there are a few other things to consider. We've got Sebastian and Edwinna to think about, for instance.' He was aware of the situation between them, of course, far more so than Libby might've suspected when she'd briefly explained Sebastian's uncharacteristic absence that evening; he'd made no remark at the time but now he said pointedly. 'Think about it.'

'That's got nothing to do with anything. It's not going to be a problem,' she insisted. 'I'll see to that. And I don't think your family would mind if they came along. Not really, would they?'

To her mind, that was the real rub: added guests and the presumption of bringing them along uninvited. In her holiday mood, it hadn't even occurred to her that the Bainbridges might view her mode of celebration as an intrusion. Yet, with the brief pause in conversation, she had the opportunity to give the matter some clear thought, and abruptly she conceded to what she really knew to be true: of course it was a consideration. That it was as much a presumption as the other, perhaps even more so. And she had enough knowledge, first- and second-hand, of the Bainbridges to understand that what she was proposing, however well-intended it was, might very well create problems. However, she couldn't easily let go of the idea. And she wasn't ready to give up on the Bainbridges just yet.

Adam was watching her steadily, slowly shaking his head; he really ought to put a stop to all this now, but as he watched her expression grow suddenly reflective, he found he couldn't, not so summarily, anyway. There were many things he knew and perceived about her that made him understand this near blind spot she seemed to have on the subject of families in general and bringing Christmas to the Bainbridges in particular: years of reviving fond memories of another life, a certain loneliness he suspected she'd had since her parents' deaths, and the plain and simple fact that Libby Rutledge cared about and wanted to give to other people. And, too, there was the strategic problem of presenting her gift. He continued to remain quietly studying her, turning it all over in his mind, and it was Christian who finally broke the silence. 'Oh, hell. Why not?' he said. 'Come on. Who cares if there are a couple more? Two, three, a hundred? Damn place could bed down an army.'

'Adam, please.' Libby spoke quietly, no longer unmindful of

his own feelings. She just felt it was the right thing to do. 'It'll be nice.'

He reached over and stroked the side of her face. 'And you'll make it that way, right?' he said softly. He studied her a moment longer, then abruptly released her hand and leaned forward to pick up his cigarette burning down in the ashtray. 'All right. We'll go,' he relented and even started to grin darkly at the idea, as some perversity he couldn't altogether contain began to take hold of him. 'Every damn one of us. And we'll bring the decorations, too. And presents. Real ones. And buy a tree.' He paused only long enough to sit back and draw Libby comfortably to his side before adding irreverently. 'And hang a wreath all over that obscenity of a door knocker.'

It was sometime later that the doorbell finally rang and Adam admitted a breathless and windswept Edwinna into the apartment. She allowed him to take her coat, then went directly toward Libby. 'Oh, Libby, I'm so sorry! When I told you earlier that I had a few things to pick up, I had no idea I'd totally lose track of time.' She skirted the coffee table and perched down next to Libby on the edge of the couch, pursing her lips in earnest chagrin. 'And then, when I realized, I had to stop at the apartment to change, call another taxi . . . thank goodness you gave me Adam's address!' She laughed ruefully, briefly touching Libby's hand in emphasis.

Wisdom born of experience, Libby wanted to say dryly, but didn't; Winna had been charmingly forgetful of the time all week, all her life, in fact. If she'd been faintly annoyed that Winna had chosen this particular afternoon for another excursion, shopping or whatever, she'd dismissed it in the knowledge that that was Winna: mercurial, always on the go. She'd spent the week breezing in and out, shopping, sightseeing, finding a night life for herself in the dozens of places in town that offered it. It seemed to Libby only to be increasing as she grew older, that need Winna had for constant entertainment, outside stimuli; Libby could wonder what she was searching for, but felt she knew the answer even as the speculations passed through her mind; some sense of self; Winna had never really had it, even, or perhaps especially, as a child. That distressed Libby now as it had then; it was only one more reason why she'd taken such heated exception to Sebastian's remarks over the past week about Winna's 'thoughtlessness in being out so much.' Even Adam had felt the need to comment along the same lines once or twice, though not so indignantly. Well, they simply didn't understand, either of them. 'Never mind,' she answered Winna, then smiled and gestured toward Christian. 'Winna, I want you to meet Christian Bainbridge.'

At that, Winna turned interested eyes toward the man and rose slowly. Christian was already on his feet in front of his chair, his half finished glass of bourbon suspended in mid-air. Winna went directly to him, cordially extending her hand. 'It's a pleasure to meet you.'

Christian didn't accept the hand immediately and was at a momentary loss for words. He'd known a lifetime of elegant women, but had never been so immediately struck by one. She wore a black cocktail dress, open halfway down her back and hooded behind her neck in a halter effect to leave her slim shoulders bare; the V down the bodice, unlike Libby's, was patently revealing. He might have decided it was that which caught the eye had she not had such perfection of chiseled features. Or such an extraordinary color of silver hair brushed away from her high forehead and falling in soft waves down her back. His perversity in accepting the invitation to dinner turned abruptly to gratitude, and he found his voice finally at the same time he took her hand. 'It's a pleasure to meet you, too, Edwinna.' After holding onto her hand for a moment longer than necessary, he dropped it when Adam's voice drifted into the expectant atmosphere that had sprung up between them.

Adam had interrupted with the offer of a cocktail; when he returned with Winna's usual gin and tonic, he found she'd settled herself in the chair opposite Christian. Adam rejoined Libby on the couch then, and the ensuing three quarters of an hour before dinner belonged to the new acquaintances. They monopolized the conversation, Winna laughing often in that particularly infectious way of hers, Christian equally as charming as he regaled her, and indeed all of them, with his brand of badinage. When dinner was announced, they strolled together to the linen-draped dining room table, Winna's blue eyes sparkling as she listened to yet one more of Christian's piquant anecdotes; he assisted her with her chair, she saw him to his, opposite her, with dancing eyes and a light remark. But where the newly introduced couple had held center stage out in the living room, it was Libby and Winna who took it during dinner. Across the candlelit table sparkling with crystal and bone china, the shadows of the flickering flames playing on the silk-papered walls around them, they enchanted their masculine listeners with fond memories and recollections, stories told on Winna by a laughing Libby, affectionate reprisals offered back by Edwinna.

215

Intriguing tales of haylofts, snipe hunts—growing up; they inspired indulgent smiles, raised eyebrows, created a mood as mellow as the wine Adam attended to. The dinner was a resounding success, and it was after the plates had been cleared and coffee served that Christian took the first opportunity he could to catch Adam's eye; it came on the heels of one of Libby's remarks. 'Can we talk?'

Adam frowned. 'Later,' he murmured.

'Adam, if the two of you have things to discuss, go on. We'll wait in the living room. It's no problem,' Libby said tactfully.

He glanced at her, then at Christian; they might as well be done with it, he decided. 'All right. Christian, go on into the den. I'll check with the caterers, see what else needs to be done . . .'

'Adam, go,' Libby insisted. 'I think I can take care of everything.'

'And better than I,' he agreed immediately and rose, going around the table to take her arm as she stood up. 'We won't be long.'

'Take your time.' She listened as he moved away, on into the living room and beyond, then turned to go into the kitchen, tossing over her shoulder at Winna, 'I won't be a minute. Go ahead and get comfortable. I'll join you.'

Winna watched her go, and rose after a moment to stroll into the living room. Rather than sitting down, however, she began a slow circuit of the handsome room; she hadn't had the opportunity before to give it her full attention and appraisal. It reflected a designer's choice of fabrics, texture, and color, yet she did not doubt Adam's taste was evident here. She lifted objects here and there: a primitive ashtray, a small porcelain vase, a piece of modern sculpture. She examined with curiosity the collection on one table of various hand-carved items and wondered at them; she lightly touched a woven basket that had the unmistakable touch of Libby's hand.

At the sliding glass doors she glanced out into the dark night, barely able to distinguish the stone terrace beyond, then drifted on to the bonnet-top secretary that stood against one wall. She admired the walnut grain, running her fingers caressingly along its patina, letting them drop after a moment to the surface of the desk itself. Idly, she leafed through the papers there, brushing aside a cleaner's receipt, glancing casually at an open bank statement beneath. After a moment, she continued on, humming almost inaudibly as she began a tour of the artwork on the walls, peering at each painting as she came to it, arriving finally at a large, bold canvas next to the den door, which stood slightly ajar. She stood directly in front of the painting and remained there for a very long time, tilting her head curiously first to one side, then the other as she studied the swirls of color; the muffled voices of the two men could just be heard in the room beyond. When she eventually heard Libby enter behind her, she turned immediately, smiling brightly. 'Everything all right?'

Libby moved to the couch and sat down. 'Fine.' She waved as the caterers took their leave by the front door, then turned to Winna, who'd come to sit down beside her.

'Dinner was lovely, wasn't it?' Winna relaxed against the cushions and brushed idly at the suede fabric under her hand.

'Yes.' Libby pursed her lips then in some chagrin. 'Thanks for repeating that little story about the attic.'

'Me?' Winna said indignantly. 'Tit for tat, you know!'

Libby conceded with her own laughter. 'I know.'

Winna glanced up and around again. 'Libby, this is a beautiful apartment. Your friend Adam has impeccable taste.'

'So he keeps telling me,' Libby remarked, then, very much woman-to-woman, she said, 'You and Christian seemed to hit it off particularly well.'

'He's interesting,' Winna admitted. 'I . . . tell me, is he . . . I assume he's unattached or he wouldn't have come tonight.'

Libby's look was faintly admonishing. 'You needn't be quite so tentative with me, you know.' She let her smile show then. 'Yes, he is. That interested?' she inquired shyly.

'Lib, it's a fair question, after all. I'm not as versed in this family as you, and I simply wanted to know. And I'm not interested in complicated relationships. Wives in the background and that sort of thing.'

Libby frowned with her mild laughter. 'Winna, I wouldn't do that to you!'

'No, I know,' Winna returned, patting her hand. 'They share equally in everything, I assume?'

'What does that have to do with anything?'

'Nothing.' Winna reached for a small carved elephant on the table and toyed with it as she sat back. 'It was just a nosy question. I told you, I'm not versed in this family. And it was a fair question, too. Listen, what are the plans for Christmas? Has anything been decided yet?' she went on without drawing a breath.

Libby smiled to herself; in retrospect, she guessed she'd been rather overbearing. 'As a matter of fact, yes. Seems I decided for us. We're going down to the Bainbridges.'

'Oh, good!' Winna was genuinely pleased and tossed the small elephant in the air, absently catching it, then repeating the idle motion once more. 'That'll be fun. Just the four of us. And the Bainbridges, of course,' she added in gay afterthought.

'And Sebastian.' Libby's hesitation was imperceptible but there.

Edwinna was eloquently silent.

'Winna, I know how you feel,' Libby began in a calm voice. She'd contemplated making no remark at all for the moment, yet that was foolish; dodging the issue wasn't going to resolve it. And it had to be resolved. 'But it's the way it must be.'

Winna's eyes strayed to something across the room; after a moment, she transferred them back to Libby. 'I thought we'd talked about this.' Her tone was chilly.

'We did, and I've already made the only concessions I can. I feel bad enough that he's not here tonight, that I've had to divide up all my time all week.' She moved to the edge of the couch then, facing Winna earnestly. 'Winna, you've got to understand. I simple can't exclude him. It's out of the question. He's part of my life. For the last four years, it's been just the two of us together at Christmas. It would hurt him beyond words if I told him not to come. And me, too.'

Winna's foot was tapping soundlessly on the carpet as she gave Libby an arch look. 'And what about me? Doesn't it matter how much you'll hurt me?'

'Winna!' Libby had said it more loudly than she'd meant and looked in the direction of the den door; she hoped it was closed.

'I see that it doesn't!' Winna countered, her own voice slightly raised.

'Don't be silly, Winna.'

'Libby, I can't bear to be around that man.'

'Winna, I simply can't and won't exclude him.' Libby's tone was quiet again but firm.

It propelled Winna up off the couch and across the room, her sylphlike body tense under the black dress as she paced to the window. 'It doesn't matter the way I feel then!' she flung bitterly over her shoulder.

'Of course it matters . . .' Libby began in a placating tone.

Winna's fingers were pressed to her temple, her eyes closed. 'Libby, if you really loved me, you'd tell him not to come! He makes me miserable. He's rude and ugly to me and says things I can't bear!' It came out all in one breath, in tempo to the ache

218

behind her ears. She spun around, as if to say something more but didn't; she saw Libby getting up off the couch, her expressive face set in a mixture of consternation and determination. Libby. Yes, of course. This was Libby; Winna's shoulders suddenly relaxed.

Libby skirted the furniture and approached with her hand outstretched. 'Winna,' she began again in a voice of quiet resolution.

'No, Libby. Never mind.' Winna's voice was its own quiet contralto again. She studied her sister for a moment, then touched Libby's hand briefly as she infused brightness into her tone. 'Listen, I found your present yesterday. I'm going to wrap it tomorrow, then tomorrow night we can exchange gifts. We'll have our own little Christmas together. It'll be nice.' It came out beautifully unconvincing. 'Really,' she added.

Libby hadn't made the switch and was frowning perplexedly. 'Winna, what are you talking about? We can't do that before Christmas.'

'I won't be here then.' The words were a despairing whisper. Quickly, she reached for Libby's hand and slipped into an attitude of entreaty. 'Libby, it's all right! Really. I . . . I didn't mean to get so upset before. I can't help it sometimes. I, well, never mind. And I'll be all right.' She continued to hold onto Libby's hand, tightly.

Libby was too stunned to speak for a moment. When she did, finally, it was to object strenuously. 'Winna, you can't leave!'

'I have to.' She paused, then let out a weary breath as she dropped Libby's hand. 'Lib, we've always been honest with each other. We've had to because of . . . everything. I should be able to refuse to let Sebastian bother me so, I know that, but I can't. I've never been able to do a lot of things.' She paused again, then moved to the upholstered chair nearby and sank down, resting her head in her hands and looking bleakly down toward the rug. Although Libby couldn't see her pose of defeat, Winna was caught up in the enthusiasm of her own performance. 'I lied to you just before,' Winna said abruptly. 'About being honest, I mean. I haven't been honest with you about the things I've been doing, about how happy I've been. The traveling, all of it—it was fun for awhile, but I . . .' She sounded as if she couldn't go on for a moment, then abruptly cried, 'I've been so lonely!' She put her face in both hands then, lowering her head, and let the muffled sounds of weeping filter out from them.

Libby was appalled. She could envision the unhappiness on Winna's face and went to her chair, kneeling down. She found

Winna's forearm, traced it up to her hands pressed against her face, then let her own shift backwards to clasp Winna's wrist tightly. 'Winna, Winna, it's all right,' she said several times, consternation etched on her own expression, and she rested her other hand soothingly on Winna's knee; in her mind's eye all she could see was a young Edwinna, afraid, and so unsure.

Winna's efforts at sobbing abated then. 'I didn't want you to know. I didn't want you to know how empty its been. There's so much else for you to worry about. I . . . I thought it would help, all the fun, the gaiety.' She elaborated on a sudden inspiration. 'I thought it would help ease the pain of Mom and Dad, of the farm being gone. But it didn't ease it, it only covered over everything. For awhile. And then I couldn't hide from it any more, and it hurt so much, and I was so alone.' She lifted her face suddenly and reached out to grip Libby's shoulders. 'Oh, Libby. I don't want to be alone!'

Libby rose on her knees and hugged Winna tightly. 'Winna, you're not alone. You won't ever be alone. I'll always be here.'

'And Christmas was coming.' Winna seemed unable to staunch the flow, and let Libby continue to embrace her as she went on haltingly. 'And all I could think of was coming here to see you, to have Christmas the way we used to at the farm. It was so important, it meant so much.' She finally extracted herself from Libby's embrace. 'I just wanted to have someone to share with again,' she said dully and sat back heavily.

Libby sank back down on her heels and searched again for Winna's hand. She found it dangling limply off the arm of the chair and took it in both of hers. 'You do, Winna,' she said, tilting her head as she smiled up. 'You always will, and I promise you that we'll have the Christmas you were looking forward to so much.'

'No, I can't. Not with Sebastian there.' She shot Libby a keen look, then slipped back into the role; her voice grew sorrowful. 'Time has passed on. I see that now. Things have changed between us, just like everything else, and you need him more than . . . oh, Libby, don't you see? Rightly or wrongly, it just won't be the same.' Her voice broke beautifully, and she drew a breath before adding evenly. 'I'll just go on my way, I . . .'

Decisions of the heart often require no more than a moment of caring; Libby's was from a lifetime of caring. 'Winna, he won't be there,' she interrupted quietly.

Winna's uncertain eyes searched her face, 'But . . .'

In reassurance, Libby's tone was authoritative. 'No, Winna. He won't be there.' She smiled again, warmly. 'It's all right. I didn't know it meant so much to you. And it'll be the way you'd hoped. We'll make it that way,' she said clearly.

'Libby, you're sure?' Her tone was plaintive.

'I'm sure.'

Libby could feel Winna's tension ease. Her own dissipated with it, and she remained kneeling by the chair in quiet reflection. So, she'd been right all along; if only Winna had acknowledged the truth sooner. The hurt of their parents' death, the sale of their home, the final goodbye of their childhood had been too much, and Winna, who could never handle things as well as she despite her greater years, had tried to run away from it all but couldn't. She continued to hold Winna's hand and rubbed it once, lightly. Some sense of self. No, Winna had just never had it; she took it from those around her, those who meant something to her, and she'd come home, then, in search of it. As she'd done all her life, Libby knew she would always be there to give it to her. And she knew, too, that the time had finally come to give Winna all those things in the box in the closet of the spare room; the time had come to give Winna back some small part of the past she'd lost. She smiled again, this time for her own thoughts, and didn't move immediately to get up.

Neither did Winna; she remained sitting quietly, her hand still clasped in Libby's on the arm of the chair, her body once more relaxed as she contemplated her sister with dispassionate eyes. She closed them after a moment, easing her head back against the cushion of the chair, and it was only then that she let herself smile, a very slow, impenitent smile of complete satisfaction.

Adam didn't move immediately either; he remained where he'd stood throughout most of the exchange, out of the line of vision, in the den doorway. Disbelief had passed from his handsome face and turned to disgusted anger. He watched the tableau of the two women for a moment longer, then abruptly wheeled and strode soundlessly back into the den.

# Chapter 18

'Your drink, Edwinna.' Christian smiled as he stopped briefly by her chair, then crossed to the one opposite her and settled down in it. He was feeling good, and when he caught her eye again, he raised his glass in salute. 'To you,' he said gallantly and watched as a flattered smile drifted to her lips.

They'd broken up their meeting finally, he and Adam, just several minutes before. He'd come directly out on Adam's heels, then gone to mix his and Edwinna's drink at the bar nestled in the secretary; Libby had declined his offer. And as he'd stood there stirring Winna's cocktail, he'd felt vastly relieved that the ordeal with Adam was over and done with. They'd have finished earlier, he thought caustically as he sat admiring Winna's svelte figure, if Adam hadn't felt the need to pontificate for the hundredth time on the subject of his excesses, or monitor the upraised voices filtering in from the other room for a matter of minutes. He, himself, hadn't been particularly fazed by either matter; he'd spent too many years honing his ability to tune out all Bainbridge rhetoric on the subject of his personal habits to do anything more than slouch uncomfortably in Adam's leather wing chair as he listened in boredom while Adam talked, and whatever had been going on in the other room between the two women was their own business. He'd merely wanted a check. And gotten it, at long last.

He shifted more comfortably, bringing the glass to his lips to drain half the contents; he was well acquainted with the faint lightheadedness it induced and ignored it. And it was as he opened his mouth to make some further conversation with Edwinna that Adam finally reappeared from the kitchen, forestalling Christian's remark; he'd gone directly there from the den without speaking a word to anyone in the living room as he passed through, and Christian noted that he still wore that ruminative look of ill humor that had come over him toward the end of their meeting. He smiled darkly to himself; there was some perverse pleasure to be taken in the fact that Adam found their financial discussions as unpleasant as he did. He watched Adam stride directly to the edge of the coffee table, toss down his whiskey, then set the glass sharply down. 'The evening's over,' he announced in a clipped voice. 'Libby's tired.'

Libby had been sitting quietly on the couch, her pensive face lowered. At his abrupt statement, her head snapped up. 'Adam!'

Adam's face was set, and he looked over at Christian, ignoring Libby's objection. 'I'm sure you won't mind taking Edwinna home. Libby's staying here tonight.' And he glanced then at Libby for the first time. 'Libby, give Edwinna your keys.'

Libby sat tensely now at the edge of the couch, both hands gripping the cushion; she was completely nonplussed. 'Adam!' she repeated indignantly.

'Where are they? In your purse?' he inquired tersely, then turned and strode over to where the purse had been left on the table by the door. He glanced through the contents, brought out the small keyring, then tossed it across the brightly lit room to Christian; it landed with a jingle at his feet. The younger man leaned forward slowly to collect it, keeping wary eyes on his brother the whole time.

Edwinna, too, was staring, her expression a replica of Christian's; this man was unnerving when angered, she thought, and wondered just exactly what had gone on in the den. Giving his rigid stance a last covert glance, she set down her glass and smiled. 'He's right,' she said and rose lithely. 'She's tired and so am I. I've been on my feet all day.' She stood briefly in front of her chair, smoothing her skirt, then threaded quickly through the furniture to Libby. There was still a kindred air between them, and she perpetuated it, murmuring as she touched Libby's arm, 'I'll see you tomorrow.' Turning then to Christian, she tilted her head prettily. 'Mind?'

He was already on his feet. 'Not at all.'

Libby's heated protestations were lost completely in the flurry of activity that ensued at the coat closet; hurried goodnights followed, and she was left, finally, where she'd gone to stand, in the middle of the room, seething in angry confusion and frustration. When she heard the last bolt on the door click into place, she turned on Adam. 'And just what was that all about!' she demanded hotly.

He strode directly to her, taking her by the arm. 'You and I are going to have a little talk,' he said shortly.

She jerked away, throwing up her chin. 'You're damn right we are!'

He should have tempered his tone, but he was too angry to realize that. Angry at Edwinna for the person he now knew her to be, angry at Libby for being a victim of her own emotional blindness, but most of all, angry at himself for so cavalierly dismissing Sebastian Vickery, who had every reason in the world to know better than he what went on around Libby. He stood looking down at her and abruptly vented his anger once more. 'And get rid of those damn things!' He reached up and pulled off her glasses, flinging them onto the carpet.

Libby was seething with indignant fury. 'I'll do with them whatever I please, and don't you ever do that again! Don't you ever treat Winna like that! I had no idea you had the capacity to be so incredibly rude!' she stormed.

Adam's eyes were snapping. 'No, don't ever be so rude to poor, sweet Edwinna. Insecure Edwinna, who can't stand Sebastian because he knows too much—Sebastian, who'll ruin her whole Christmas if he comes. The Christmas she's looked forward to because she's been so lonely, and please Libby, make him stay away even though it'll break your heart and Sebastian's, too!' His tone was disgustedly mocking. 'Oh, she got it all in, didn't she? The things between you, the wrenching suffering for so much that's been lost, the play on your affection —Jesus Christ, Libby! How can you fall for that crap she dishes out? Sebastian was right. Your dear, lovely Edwinna is a first-class bitch!'

She struck him right across the face, hard, not even a hair's breadth off target; unconsciously, he raised a hand to his cheek, feeling the heat of the angry mark rising up to his palm as he stood, momentarily stunned. And it did, finally, what nothing else up to then had been able to: it woke him up. This was no way to approach anyone on any subject, much less Libby and the problem of Edwinna. He began again, more reasonably. 'Libby . . .'

She, however, was completely unstrung. She began to tremble visibly with the rage that had found no release even in physical retaliation. It engulfed her entirely after a moment, and for want of any further way to vent it, she fled from it instead, turning spasmodically to rush in the direction of the bedroom. She got no further than several steps away, however, for in her agitation she hadn't gotten her bearings and ran headlong into a table along the wall, falling against it and knocking aside the objects on its surface as she flung out her arms in an effort to catch herself. 'Libby!' Adam exclaimed in horror and made a grab for her. He was too late, however, even to break her fall. After a brief clutching at the table's corners, she fell heavily to the floor. He reached her just at that moment. Instantly going down on one knee, he gathered her up into his arms. 'I'm sorry, Libby. I'm so sorry. Honey . . . honey . . .' he moaned over and over again as he cradled her, and he leaned down over her, caressing her hair, pressing his face to the side of her neck.

She lay perfectly still in his arms, the fabric of her dress flowing down over his knee and across his legs. She hadn't uttered another sound since the stunned exclamation when she felt the pain of the table in her ribs, and merely let him hold her while she remained silent. Stricken. After a time, she began to push at him, forcing him to loosen his embrace as she struggled to get up. He tried to resist her efforts to leave him, then finally gave in to her, taking her hands and helping her to her feet. When they were up, he looked with troubled eyes into her pale face. 'Are you hurt?'

'Leave me alone,' she said into the darkness that surrounded her. It was so complete; it always would be. Always, always would she be at the mercy of what she couldn't see, barred from escaping those things that would hurt her. She couldn't see the pain etched in Adam's face, nor even perceive it at the moment; hers was too great. She reached out a trembling hand and pushed at this man she loved. This man who had just made her do the unforgivable in front of him. 'Just leave me alone,' she repeated woodenly and hugged herself tightly, shutting out the world.

Adam reached out for her again, then abruptly dropped his hands. It was no use; there was no communication—nothing. Libby unclasped her arms finally and took a tentative step forward, reaching out her slender hand for the guidance of the wall. 'I want you to leave me completely alone,' she repeated carefully, not for him but for herself, because she was so close to shattering. She made her way along the edge of the room, her blindness a stark reality between them as she was forced to make so deliberate an exit. When she came to the bedroom, she disappeared into it gratefully, closing the door behind her, shutting out the agony of Adam's witnessing of the painful departure. She knew the number of steps to the bed and walked them carefully, falling onto the mattress when she reached it. And it was there that she finally began to cry, hopelessly, for all the confusion around her, for all the burdens that were hers to bear, but ultimately, for the indignity she'd just suffered in the eyes of the man she loved.

She lay there for a very long time, stretched out on her side, dry of tears after awhile, emotion spent. She dozed off finally, awakening sometime later when she heard the door open almost silently and felt Adam's presence enter the room. He hadn't turned on a light, she knew; there'd been no click of a switch.

'Libby, may I talk to you?' he said quietly.

She remained motionless, facing the opposite wall, her hair fanning out across the pillows. Her voice when she finally answered was tired. 'Yes.'

Adam, looked at her lying in the shadows on the king-size bed, the light of the moon shining in through the uncurtained window. He approached the bed slowly, standing alongside it for a time before sitting down on the edge. He'd removed his jacket and pushed back the sleeves of his turtleneck so his forearms were bare. 'Libby, I'm sorry.'

She made no move to turn. 'It doesn't matter.'

'It matters very much. Very, very much.'

She was silent.

'Libby, will you look at me?'

'I can't, remember?' she said, her voice momentarily tight.

He cursed his inaccuracy, and the episode that had made it matter. 'Will you turn toward me?'

She sighed quietly. 'Adam, leave me alone.'

He put one hand down on the russet-colored bedspread, resting his weight on it; in the darkness, the spare contemporary furnishings were only shadows around the edges of the large room, its terra cotta color scheme lost to the cloak of night. 'No, I won't. I won't ever leave you alone. I love you. I don't intend to let Edwinna come between us, too.'

His words fanned the flames again, and she rolled over onto her back in agitation. 'Edwinna, Edwinna!' she cried. 'Do you imagine I care what you think about Edwinna!' Her face was suffused with frustration. 'I don't! You can listen to whatever lies you want. Obviously, Sebastian has talked to you, but I don't care!' And as suddenly as it'd come the temper vanished. She rolled back over onto her side, away from him. 'It doesn't matter to me,' she said dully.

Adam was left with nothing to say; he'd spent the last two hours preparing himself, pacing the floor, whiskey glass in hand, working out in his mind how he'd try to undo what he'd done. And it had all been for naught, because she didn't care what he thought about Winna. But if she didn't care, why was she still locked away from him? His uneasiness grew. 'All right,' he said carefully and straightened. 'You don't care. I'll accept that and say no more,' he lied. 'Now look at me,' he said more sternly.

It made her burst abruptly into tears again, small ones, for that was all that remained. His uneasiness bloomed into heartache; she lay like a wounded doe before him, vulnerable to whatever it was he was doing to her. He reached out for the first time and laid a gentle hand on her arm. 'Libby, tell me what it is,' he implored. 'Tell me what I've done, if it's not about Edwinna.'

And suddenly she wanted to go at him, tooth and nail, to pound him in the chest for her helplessness. She rolled over and found him with her hands. 'I hate you!' she cried and began to swing at him, thrashing about in the darkness.

He fielded her wild blows uncomprehendingly, calling her name over and over again. At length, he gave up trying to deflect her attack, grabbed both her arms and rolled over all the way onto the big bed. He pinned her down then, every muscle in his body contracted as he rose up over her and watched her writhe in anger beneath him. He was consumed with dread and confusion as he listened to this woman he loved above all else spit back hate at him. Hate! 'Libby, for God's sake!'

'I hate you, I do, I do! I hate you!' she moaned as she struggled with him, tears once more streaming down her face. Suddenly, her strength gave out, and her body went limp under the hurtful grip of his hands. 'I hate you,' she said one last time in a small, too-young voice.

He let out a long breath as she stopped struggling, then released her wrists. He moved his hands so they straddled her on the mattress and relaxed beside her, looking down with pain-filled eyes. 'Hate me? I've wanted to make you feel a lot of things, but hate isn't one of them. Don't hate me, Libby. Just tell me what it is I've done.'

Oh, God, don't let me say it, she begged with silent urgency, closing her eyes against the feelings too private to share, but it was out before she could get it back. 'You made me fall,' she said in a high, unnatural voice and rolled away from him, cringing from the words that hung in the air.

They hit him right in the face. 'Libby . . . ' he groaned.

And then other words she despised and never wanted him to hear tumbled out, though she kept her face muffled in the pillow. 'Don't you know?' she said brokenly. 'Don't you know how much it matters what I look like to you? Don't you know that want to be like all those other women you've known and graceful, pretty, feminine? Not like I really am. Clumsy slow and . . . blind.' She bit into her lip, drawing blood.

227

could you have said those things to me, that would make me do that, make me have to run away . . . make me fall right in front of you?' Dear Father in Heaven, let her death come now, because she never wanted to face Adam again.

Adam caught her to him, rolling her over as he stretched out alongside her on the bed. He held her so hard he might have broken her ribs. 'Oh my God, Libby,' he breathed into the spill of her thick hair, 'you're embarrassed! I've embarrassed you!'

It was even worse when he said it. 'I hate you!' she yelled into his shoulder, closing her eyes tightly.

Adam put his hand behind her head, pressing it more tightly to him as he looked bleakly at the far wall. 'I don't blame you,' he murmured. How could he have been so insensitive as not to have realized! How could he not have understood right away? Because he wasn't blind, that's how. He laid his cheek against her hair, running his hand soothingly along her back. 'My sweet, beautiful Libby, I'm so very sorry. And you're not the least bit ungraceful. You're not anything even remotely close to that. Honey, I never thought . . .'

'How could you?' she demanded, shifting against him, so very much in need of his reassurance, yet so desperate for him never to know all the secret things she'd just told him. 'You don't live in darkness. You're not trapped by it, forced because of it to do things that are . . . humiliating in front of someone whose opinion of you is the only thing in the world that really matters.' She struggled to get a hand in between their bodies so she could touch her lip. It hurt.

He didn't know what to do first—tell her what she needed to hear, what he felt, or hold her, kiss her, make love to her; he intended doing all of them so he could remove this wretched feeling of inadequacy he'd so stupidly precipitated. In the moonlight, he watched her touching her lip again and again; he laid his own fingertip gently against it, feeling a wetness there. 'Honey, your lip . . .' he said, frowning briefly.

'Is bleeding. I know. I bit it.'

't made him ache for her all the more. 'Oh, Libby!' he said, ʼg her close again. 'You've never been more wrong in Never. I don't think any of those things about you.'

ʼu, Adam?' she asked quietly, turning her cheek ʼlder; the scent of his musky aftershave drifted to ʼaking her close her eyes. 'You should, because ʼ the woman you should have. There are so ʼny who could please you, who are whole,

228

who can give you the kind of life you should have. Women you wouldn't have to spend a lifetime picking up off the floor.'

It didn't occur to him at that moment to object in words; he had a better way, a more effective one, and he began to touch her then, in a way only they knew between them, in a way he'd never touched any of those other women. He'd never loved them as he did this woman, Libby; had never loved them at all. Quietly, he moved his hands along her body over the soft fabric of her dress, touching her intimately, everywhere, stopping nowhere, letting the sexuality that existed between them say what he could never have put into words. As always, it brought her close to him, physically, emotionally, and when he'd removed most of the barriers, he leaned down and kissed her tenderly on the mouth. 'I don't want all those other women. I want you.'

It had been too big a blow to her pride to be relieved by his lovemaking alone, although that was having its effect. 'You don't have to go on pretending I'm just as normal as the next woman.'

'Pretending? Is that what I'm doing?' He entwined his fingers in her hair, gently pulling her head back as he leaned up on his elbow and looked down into her face. 'You might've been pretending, but I wasn't. Nor will I ever. I don't have to pretend. I only need to look at you, to look at your beauty and grace, to see you to know the way you really are. To know how normal a woman you are. And I do, you know,' he murmured, leaning down to kiss the side of her throat.

She arched it toward him, closing her eyes again to the feel of him. 'Adam, it'll never work,' she whispered.

'What'll never work?' he asked as he ran a finger lightly under the line of her breast; it was like a whisper that said a thousand eloquent things.

She touched his hand. 'Us.'

'Why?'

'Because I love you too much.'

He raised his head at that and laughed quietly. 'Now, that doesn't make a lot of sense, but I'll take it. A moment ago all I was getting was hate. Well deserved, but unacceptable to me, coming from you.'

Libby looked up toward him beseechingly. 'Adam, plea Don't laugh at this.'

'I'm not really laughing,' he answered seriously. 'Not on And it isn't you who should be feeling embarrassed beca what happened. It's me, for acting like such a fool.'

She hid away from the reference again, putting her head against his shoulder as she was lost once more to her feelings of confusion and inadequacy. And as if he could read her mind, he began to talk, quietly, running his hand along her slender back as he rested his cheek against her head. 'Oh, my Libby, how much you could teach us all about courage, how much you do teach us. You're like no other woman I've ever known. And you have to suffer for our missteps, not your own, because without us, you wouldn't make them. I've watched you, watched you walk about this world confidently, elegantly, handing out those particular rays of sunshine only you know how to give, making your way with no difficulty until I, or Sebastian, or . . . others come along and trip you up. How can you let us make you feel so inadequate? How could you possibly lie here feeling uncertain and unattractive—of all things!—because you've had the misfortune to get yourself entangled with a man who can be so abysmally inept? Oh, my darling, you are only beautiful, more beautiful than any other woman that exists, and it's I who shouldn't encumber you, only I'm not so noble. I want you, and I need you. For my selfishness, I'm afraid you're going to have to suffer for the rest of your life.'

'Adam, I love you,' she whispered, wrapping her arms around his neck as she held onto him tightly.

'And I love you, too,' he murmured into her hair, feeling her breath warm on the side of his neck. 'And you wonder, don't you, why it is the world around you has suddenly gone lunatic?' he asked then. It had to be said; he had no intention of pursuing it then, but it needed to be spoken aloud so he could dismiss it for the time being. 'Don't you?' he pressed softly.

'What I wonder,' she said, her voice muffled against his broad chest, 'is how this damn day ever got put on the calendar in the first place. Just whose idea was it, anyway, to make me go to sleep last night and wake up this morning instead of tomorrow?' she demanded more loudly as she leaned away from him to look toward his face. 'And I also want to know just what exactly ~sed you to put a table in such a ridiculous place, there ~he wall where every idiot and his brother walking room will run right smack into it and fall all over 'l me that, will you, Adam Bainbridge?'

'e love to her then, catching this incredible ~hen he'd gently but urgently removed her ~ the night they lay together, her soft ~ding unreservedly to his demanding male one as he took her with a passion more overwhelming than any he'd ever known before.

The next morning Adam understood only too well the frustration Sebastian had been feeling that time a week before, when he'd come to him about Edwinna; in the light of the new day, across the breakfast table from Libby in the bay-windowed dining alcove of the kitchen, he was afforded painful, first-hand experience. Dressed in a navy wool pullover and camel slacks from her small supply of clothing kept in his closet, her auburn hair casually twisted up and clipped on top of her head, Libby was very much herself again. She sat calmly, her hands clasped together out on the table in front of her as she listened dutifully to Adam's reasonable repetition of Sebastian's observations and warnings.

'You're wrong,' she said simply when he drew a breath after nearly twenty minutes of talking.

Adam fell back against the chrome bentwood chair, massaging his forehead with his fingers. After a moment, he let out an audible breath and wearily dropped his hand. 'Libby, I can't understand how someone as perceptive as you are can be taken in so completely. But then, there's no accounting for human nature, is there? It isn't always reasonable.' He paused, half smiling. 'And the hardest thing in the world to do sometimes is to see those close to us clearly. People just can't believe that the ones they love the most would use them so selfishly, so remorselessly,' he added pointedly.

Libby was sitting perfectly straight in her chair, drumming her fingertips on the table. 'Adam, listen to me,' she said clearly. 'You've had your say and now it's time for me to have mine. You're wrong about Winna, dead wrong. Sebastian, too. You're seeing her from the wrong angle. You're too wrapped up in me, both of you, which seems to have your imaginations working overtime. She has faults, yes. We all do. But she doesn't use me. She needs me, she needs my affection. And I want her to. Can you understand that?' She frowned earnestly for a moment, then continued. 'I love her, Adam. I want her to know that. Because of one accident, Winna has to suffer in Sebastian's eyes, and yours too, for the rest of her life. The two of you would put some dark connotation on the whole thing—and everything else she does. Well, she's not "dangerous" to me as you both so absurdly seem to think. She's sweet and tries and sometimes has a hard time. I, for one, intend to try to make things a little easier for her.'

231

'And what about last night?' Adam asked passively.

Libby frowned again. 'Adam, you don't know Edwinna very well,' she said pointedly. 'She's easily upset. And last night she told me things I've suspected for a very long time, things that only she and I can understand. She's been lonely! For God's sake, you heard her! She's been trying to run away from all the hurt, the pain of things that were so hard to lose.' She shook her head, putting her forehead briefly in her hand before looking back up. 'I can understand exactly why Christmas is so important to her. A warm, comforting Christmas.'

Adam drew another exasperated breath and ran his finger along the collar of his white shirt. What had Sebastian said? 'It doesn't take any time to know her.' How right he'd been. About everything. He voiced another of Sebastian's statements then. 'Libby, I'm sorry, but I don't believe for one minute she's come home because she's lonely.' She started to interrupt, but he went on.

'Yes, I know that hurts you. But that's what we're talking about here, isn't it? How she hurts you. I don't know why she's come, but like Sebastian, I seriously doubt Edwinna does anything without some strong motive behind it. Some totally selfish motive. No!' he said sharply, silencing her again. 'Hear me out all the way, and then we're going to drop the subject. It's obviously one we're not going to agree on for the time being, and we both have to accept that. But hear me out. Edwinna uses you, Libby, whether you choose to believe that or not, and in the process hurts you over and over again. Frankly, the very best thing you could do for yourself is get her out of your life. I'd like to see that, today. But since it's not going to happen, then for God's sake, just understand her, understand how she works you!' He sat forward, looking at her with an earnest frown. 'Libby, the words. Listen for the words! It's the key. "If you really loved me . . ." Christ!' He fell back roughly again, his anger of the night before surfacing momentarily. 'How can you be taken in by that!'

Libby brushed a stray wisp of hair up off her neck, tucking it under the clip. 'As you said, Adam, we're not going to agree on the subject, and we're going to drop it,' she said coolly. 'There are things between Winna and me that make our way of dealing with each other different from other people's, but I don't intend to try to make you understand. Obviously it's impossible. I'm astounded and not just a little upset to find that you of all people suffer the same delusions about all of this that Sebastian always has, but that's your problem, not mine.'

Adam sat forward again. 'And so, you're really going to uninvite Sebastian for Christmas, huh?'

Libby drew a quiet breath and opened her mouth to speak; nothing, however, came out.

'It hurts, doesn't it?' Adam said sharply. 'It hurts you to do what Winna wants, doesn't it?'

'Adam, it's important to her!'

'Who are you dodging by not answering my question, me or yourself?' he inquired mildly, then sighed. 'Never mind. That's a question you can answer in your own mind.' He paused, studying her for a time; sitting across from him with her hair drawn up from her long, slender neck, away from the soft features of her face, she was a vision of one young, yet old; strong, yet vulnerable; wise, yet so humanly fallible. A study in contrasts; it was what had always made her so fascinating, played on every emotion he could feel. And at the moment, the primary feeling was protectiveness. 'At any rate,' he said finally, 'I've seen to it that you won't have to try to live with this particular hurt for the rest of your life.'

Libby frowned. 'What are you talking about?'

'I'm talking about the fact that I've invited Sebastian for Christmas myself.' He took a brief sip of his coffee, looking over at her matter-of-factly. 'I talked to him this morning, right after I called the school to tell them you wouldn't be in and before anything else could be said.' It'd been a brief conversation, one of apology and explanation.

Libby raised her chin indignantly. 'Adam, you have no right to do that!'

'On the contrary, Libby, I have every right. It's my home, remember? I may invite whomever I choose. And I chose to invite Sebastian. And he chose to accept.'

'Adam . . .' Her renewed objection didn't get very far and she wondered why. Because she knew Adam was unmovable in his decision, that was why. Pensively, she looked down toward her mug cupped in both hands on the table in front of her. She'd have to find some way of explaining to Winna that the whole matter had been taken out of her hands, and she didn't dwell on what might have been faint stirrings of relief in the back of her thoughts.

Adam seemed to read her mind. 'That's right. That's the way it is and will be in the future. I fully intend to put a stop to whatever else Winna might try to maneuver you into. I can, and I will until you finally see fit to understand for yourself. And

233

ultimately, you do have to do that yourself. Now, end of discussion.'

'End of discussion,' Libby repeated firmly, looking back up, and determined as always to have the last word where Winna was concerned, she added, 'nor will it be discussed again.'

Adam merely looked at her, at the renewed determination in her chin, at the set of her slim shoulders. He had no doubt she'd have gone ahead and done this thing about Sebastian, no matter how much it hurt, no matter what it took away from her. And a sharp pang of uneasiness shot through him suddenly as it occurred to him to wonder just how much more, if unwillingly, she'd have given up.

# Chapter 19

They walked into the downtown discotheque at nine thirty on Friday night. It was Washington's most popular nightlife spot, and the disco beat reverberated around the room and across the platform floor. Under a kaleidoscope of revolving colored strobe lights, a throng of satin-suited, glittering dancers moved in an undulating mass, and the swell of noise rose and fell, then rose again and again into a crescendo of syncopated, hand-clapping music and revelrous voices. Just inside the awninged doorway, Edwinna scanned the feverish scene eagerly, tossing Christian a brief smile as he slipped the coat from her shoulders. Her slender figure was revealed then, exquisitely sheathed from throat to ankles in a silver sequined gown that flashed under the roving overhead lights, reflecting alternately red, blue, green, then silver again. Throwing the luxurious mink across one arm, Christian linked his other with Winna's and guided her through the crush of milling humanity, his eyes searching for a vacant table. He spotted one in a corner of the darkened room and threaded them to it, draping her coat over the back of the chair while she settled herself. On the wall behind them, a jagged splash of silver foil zigzagged through the background of the black wallpaper, a pattern repeated all around the room, and Christian stood silhouetted against it as he remained briefly standing, his hand in the air to flag a waitress. When he had, he pulled another chair close to Edwinna and sat down. 'Gin?' He was nearly shouting as he raised his voice over the pandemonium.

She nodded, then transferred her attention to the excitement around her. There was a shallow ring of small tables peopled with chattering guests along the edges of the room, and from her vantage point, she could see directly through it to the dance floor beyond. As she watched it raptly, her shoulders under the shimmering gown began moving rhythmically with the beat of the music. The waitress finally came and went, then returned sometime later with their drinks. Relaxing back with hers, she leaned in close to Christian. 'Watch the couple in white,' she said directly in his ear.

He was settled with one arm across the back of her chair, and her shoulder rested against his chest. He didn't take his eyes from her. 'I'd rather watch you,' he said and let a slow smile drift to his face.

She drew her eyes away from the elegant dancers and looked up at him. Her return smile was as familiar. 'You've been watching me all week,' she murmured near his ear, then reached over with an air of intimacy and straightened his ascot pin. 'You're crooked, darling.'

He gave her an indulgent grin. 'No, not I. You. You're the one who so solicitously tied it for me.'

She laughed then, throwing her head back slightly; it made her hair snake down across one shoulder and brush against his arm. She sipped her drink, after a moment running a finger under the satin lapel of his velvet jacket. Yes, she'd clipped the small gold pin in place on the linen neckpiece earlier. And not only that but selected the jacket also, glancing through his extensive wardrobe at his ornate Louis XV hotel suite in the city until she'd found one she liked. She'd pulled it out and taken it to him as he stood assessing himself in the gilt mirror, fussing with the collar of his silk shirt. 'You're right,' she said at length. 'My fault. I'll see to it I do a better job next time.'

He grinned, then drained his glass. Raising his hand again, he nodded to the waitress's inquiring look and, while he waited for the refill, joined Winna in an interested survey of the room.

It was his milieu, this crowd of revelrous socialites. He frequented this and the other discotheques often and knew a number of the regulars, although he'd been here more often over the past week, with Edwinna, than was even his habit. He glanced at her face, inches below his, and studied her fine profile as she kept her eyes turned forward. All in all, a hell of a woman, he thought, elegant, interesting to be with. In every sense of the word. His eyes moved downward, and he looked openly at her shapely legs crossed at the knee, a stretch of smooth thigh revealed where the slit in her gown fell open. Yes, a hell of a woman, worldly, liberal. In the short space of one week, they'd done the town at break-neck pace, sightseeing, lunching, art-gallery hopping; she had an eye for 'things', expensive 'things'. The nights had belonged to the clubs, discotheques, and intimate time alone at his suite. She preferred

236

French cuisine, and they'd dined out every night in elegance. He didn't mind. In fact, he enjoyed it; it was precisely his own style. His thoughtful reflection was interrupted abruptly by the waitress as she set down two more glasses. Smilingly, he offered up several bills and accepted his change; it went, as always, into a monogrammed gold money clip, and he slipped it back into his trouser pocket, glancing once more at Winna. Yes, definitely a most entrancing woman. She'd have him out of circulation, undoubtedly, until she left again in a few weeks. Well, he could handle it; he was between women at the moment anyway. 'Care to dance, love?' He gave her his practiced smile, caressing her lightly under the chin.

'Of course.' She touched his fingers briefly with her own. 'But I need to find the ladies' room first.' She smiled gaily and picked up her small sequined purse as she rose. 'I won't be a minute.'

She threaded her way past his leg and the table, then began her travels across the room. It was thick with people and conversation, blasting music and cigarette smoke, and somewhere in the vicinity of the bar—she could see the Budweiser sign blinking overhead—she became sandwiched in among the crush. She stood looking for some avenue of passage through the crowd, swaying as bodies knocked against her; she began to frown, and after a moment, a hand touched her shoulder. She looked up crossly into the face of a smiling, tow-headed man. 'Care to dance?' he inquired.

The sour look turned to an absent smile. 'No, thank you. I'm just passing through.' She studied the wall of backs again, biting her lip in vexation.

'That could be an accomplishment,' he remarked; he was English, with a distinct Oxford accent. She'd heard enough of them in her travels to recognize the inflections. 'Let me buy you a drink, then.'

She looked back up at him, thoughtfully this time; he was rather attractive with sharp, thin features and blue eyes, and he wore an impeccable steel-gray suit. A man of affluence, she estimated, and by the look of him, right at home in this fast crowd. She glanced over her shoulder in the direction she'd come, unable to see Christian but aware of him nonetheless, somewhere at the far side of the room. A small, complacent smile came to her lips, and she gave the stranger a last look. 'No, thank you. I won't be needing it.' He raised his eyebrows quizzically, then watched her disappear through a sudden opening in the crowd.

The ladies' room, when she entered, was empty. It was overly bright, papered in rich, gold foil, with a wide dressing counter stretched all along one wall, and an enormous lighted mirror above it. She went to it, sat down in one of four delicate skirted chairs, and became engrossed almost immediately in her reflection across the way. She smiled at it, carefully assessing the effect; it was good. Well, excellent, actually. She opened the small purse, withdrew a folding hairbrush, and relaxed against the heart-shaped chairback. She began to brush her silver hair then, in long strokes, tilting her head.

The stranger's face drifted into her abstracted thoughts. His puzzled expression had been amusing, though she didn't blame him for being surprised at the cryptic remark. Actually, she had been herself; she hadn't meant to voice her thoughts that way. She frowned briefly in concentration, trying to bring to mind the word for such things. A slip of the tongue? Something like that, she decided, and gave up the small mental activity. And it hadn't been a completely accurate verbalization; had it been, she would've said, 'I won't be needing you.' She straightened suddenly, tossing her head so that her hair flipped back behind her shoulders, and refolding the small brush, she put it away before leaning back once again to contemplate her full-face image with a satisfied smile.

No, she wouldn't be needing him, the interesting stranger. She wouldn't be needing any of them any more, all the unknown men in the world; she had her own now. She arched one eyebrow in unconscious complacency, remembering the scene with Christian earlier in his bedroom. She'd handled it with just the right amount of finesse, she thought, that business about his jacket. A touch of anxious-to-please garnished around the edges with conjugal familiarity. She'd been practicing the wifely attitude on him all week, alone in his elaborate bedroom, and in public with small, feminine gestures and nuances of expression; she'd soon be needing to refine it, and more quickly than Christian Bainbridge might ever have anticipated. She roused for a moment, raising her hands to run them slowly through her hair, from temples to crown. Her attention settled on her slender hands; next to her tumble of extraordinary hair, they were the most pleasurable of her vanities. She held out the left one, stretching her arm as she tilted her head back and posed her graceful fingers. She had no intention, as Libby had done, of refusing a Bainbridge diamond. On the contrary, she'd help Christian select one, when the time came. When she'd orchestrated the time. Tiffany or Cartier, she hadn't decided which yet, but it'd be one or the other. Perhaps she'd let Christian make that choice. She smiled again, then dropped her hand abruptly, almost surreptitiously, as the door behind her swung open, admitting two young women, a blonde and a brunette, chatting breezily.

Winna smiled a greeting at their reflections in the mirror. The dark-haired woman continued on into the lavatory, while the other took the chair beside Winna, bringing out her own brush. Winna made one final inspection of her face in the mirror, leaning toward it as she studied her lipstick. After a moment, she caught the stranger looking at her out of the corner of her eyes and arched an eyebrow. 'Something I can do for you?' she inquired coolly. It had always irked her, catty appraisals. As if one were inspecting for flaws.

The blond-haired woman smiled warmly. 'Oh, sorry. I was just admiring your hair, the color of it. It's so unusual.'

Winna smiled graciously then. 'Thank you.'

'Tell me, where do you have it done?'

A tiny frown crept into Winna's brow. 'Done?'

'Colored.'

The chair legs grated across the tile floor as Winna pushed it back and stood up abruptly. She looked down at the woman coldly. 'I don't color it. It's natural,' she snapped.

The blonde turned away quickly; Winna looked at her archly a moment longer, then scooped up her purse, thrusting it up under her arm as she marched to the swinging door. It opened suddenly as several more women and a young girl came through, and they jostled her as they passed, knocking the purse from under her arm and to the floor, spilling the contents.

With a murmured oath, Winna knelt down; the sultry silver gown crumpled along the floor around her feet as she rapidly collected the lipstick, brush, and tapestried change purse she carried everywhere and slipped them back in her bag. Straightening again, she stood for a moment under the fluorescent lighting, brushing at the sequined fabric as vivid as the sea of gold foil around her and reflecting back in the mirror, then reached for the door handle; she felt the touch of a hand on her shoulder before she had a chance to pull it open.

It was the attractive blonde again; her smile was forced as she extended two small slips of paper toward Winna. 'You forgot these.'

Winna looked down at the woman's hands, her eyes widening slightly, then snatched them from her. 'Thanks,' she murmured. And pulling open the door, she walked out.

Only a muffled tattoo of sound in the ladies' room, the ear-pounding din now fell around her like a jangling, pulsating cloak as she stepped back into it. She stood for a moment, letting her eyes readjust to the dimness and the strobe lights that pierced into it, then moved forward finally into the milling crowd. Her progress back to the table was slow, and she was completely unaware of the colorful people through which she treaded her way; her mind was momentarily trapped back in the glitter-gold lounge, in vexation.

Not only had the blonde woman been insulting with her remark about her hair but she'd been intrusive on top of it, looking openly at those slips of paper before handing them back. Winna couldn't abide that. Her personal affairs, no matter what form they took, were strictly her own business, and she thought disjointedly that she'd have to be sure to make that perfectly clear to Christian at some point, for the years to come. As she pushed her way on through the crowd, smiling absently at several strangers who spoke in passing, she realized the papers were still in her hand, and she slipped them finally into her bag, this time stuffing them securely into the tapestried change purse. She didn't know why she'd saved them, really; prudence, her self-acknowledged strong point, would've dictated otherwise. Yet she had. Perhaps they were mementos of sorts, or more rightly reminders, as if she needed any. And as she glanced up at the sign over the bar—a landmark—an analogy struck her. Symbols. That's what they were; symbols of what her life had become, those two pieces of paper: an overdraft notice and a pawn ticket. Unendurable.

She waved at Christian when he came into view finally, tossing him a look of keen exasperation as she pushed past the last tangle of bodies. He sat back in the corner, his arm stretched along the back of her chair, and he returned her look with quizzical impatience, extending one hand toward her as she approached. She took it, maneuvering her way past him and the table and sank gratefully into her chair. 'My God!' she expelled, tossing her purse out in front of her.

He was frowning good-naturedly. 'I was about to come after you. What the hell were you doing?'

'Trying to get across the damn room.' Then she broke into a smile. 'I need another drink.'

He grinned and gestured toward her glass. 'I've already gotten you one.' He watched as she put her hand around the tall glass, then up-ended his own.

Winna eyed it sharply as it came down from his mouth. 'How many does that make?'

He gave her a slow, level look. 'Don't worry about it.' And as if in some further comment, he drained the contents. 'Miss!' One more time, he held up two fingers, smiling laconically as the young girl came forward.

Winna's annoyance was momentarily acute; his cavalier attitude was almost more irritating than his penchant for liquor. The ill humor passed as quickly as it'd come, however. The man's habits, in the final analysis, were his own business and had no affect on her or her plans, other than incidentally; he could be inordinately annoying, in a lot of ways, when he was drunk. Yet it was hardly an issue for argument, at this stage of the game anyway, and when another glass had been given him, she smiled up gaily. 'Have a drink, then dance with me.'

He looked at her lovely smile and forgot his brief belligerence; she could make a man forget a lot of things, he thought dryly and pulled her up. The drink could wait, and he was reminded of the sensual show he was about to be given when she began to move her shoulders in rhythm with the music as they pressed their way out toward the dance floor. Edwinna Rutledge was a seasoned disco dancer, as he was himself, and they quickly found a spot for themselves amid the crush of people, falling in with the beat.

Edwinna let herself go free; the strobe lights played against her slender body in patterns of colored dots, the reflection bouncing off the sequins as they undulated along the length of her. She stood out in the sea of rich colors around her—the silver woman—and threw her head back, feeling the music in every fiber of her body. It was energizing, liberating, and she wanted suddenly to burst into a frenzy of laughter. She might even have done so—she wasn't sure; the music and hand-clapping around her were deafening. But it didn't matter whether she had or hadn't; it merely mattered that she wanted to again, could again, and all for the handsome man so expertly following her movements.

A mere two weeks before, when she'd so reluctantly arrived on Libby's doorstep, she hadn't imagined that she'd be feeling such lightness of spirit so soon; an interminable, and in all honesty, desperate, several months had led up to that moment when circumstances had forced her to seek out her only refuge. There'd been no room for whimsical emotions such as this. She reveled in it, throwing her arms up toward the ceiling, her blue eyes glowing with release; it was the way she should be feeling, what she deserved.

She'd seen it all coming, of course, even as long as a year ago. Champagne taste, luxury hotels, flitting from country to country as part of a tribe of neo-Beautiful People; it'd all taken a toll on her reserves. That and certain other expensive appetites she'd acquired. And the real problem had been a mere miscalculation in timing, procrastination in beginning work on some alternate arrangement, not any unawareness of reality. Frankly, she'd hoped to set something up for herself on the continent, bypassing the necessity of coming back to the States, home to Libby's, where life was so relentlessly dull and filled with all that careful movement; it grated on her nerves. As did Sebastian, so annoyingly devoted to Libby, so intolerably unresponsive to her. And meddlesome. There had been suitable men in those last months, enormously affluent men she'd attached herself to —even a count, for a time—but they'd quickly found other interests, gone their ways without her, leaving in their wakes only some token apology. She remembered the most galling, that morning in Rome when she'd come down for breakfast in the elaborate hotel restaurant with its Florentine columns, fountains, tables set with starched linen tablecloths, and on each a bud vase with a single red rose. In hers had been stuck a note —'Had to move on. It's been fun. Hope to see you around sometime.' No man waiting at her table, as she'd been expecting, only a note, a goodbye note. And a hundred dollar bill. If she hadn't been in such dire financial straits, she'd have ripped it into shreds and thrown it on the floor; as it was, she'd put it in her purse and tossed the curious waiter an acid look. Another time there'd been a long letter in the mail, more palatable, but as succinct. Fickle creatures, men, and boring in a lot of ways, she thought caustically at the recollections, then smiled gorgeously at Christian as he caught her eye.

But it hadn't mattered, those men. She hadn't really wanted them anyway; they hadn't been good enough for her. Merely ships in the night until she could light upon the ideal arrangement. Unhappily, it hadn't materialized in time. Reduced finally to a boarding room existence, and at the crass suggestion of a friend that she find work, she'd finally made the only decision she could. Always conscious of her options, she'd had foresight enough to pave the way for an extended stay at Libby's, if it became necessary, with chatty telegrams and notes over the months, and she'd flown home finally, on the wings of unchar-acteristic depression and the money from her clothing pawned in

242

London. As it was, she needn't have succumbed to useless despondency over the injustice of her financial dilemma; Libby had had the inordinate good sense to get herself involved with an extraordinarily wealthy man who just happened to have a brother as rich as he was and available to boot. A useful commodity, Libby, every now and then.

Christian interrupted her thoughts abruptly as the tempo picked up and he took hold of her hand, swinging her around; she gave herself up again to the joy of the music, and in moments, they had the crowd of other dancers falling back, giving them center stage. Under the flashing lights that patterned the floor around them, they gave a stunning disco performance, turning, whirling, moving together, moving apart as if they'd been a team forever, captivating their audience for nearly a quarter of an hour before exhaustion finally took hold. They slowed, then stopped altogether, holding hands in breathless laughter as the clapping erupted into applause. Winna let Christian lead her from the floor, her breast under the silver gown heaving from exertion and excitement. Once more by their table, they merely stood, regaining their wind.

'You're a helluva dancer,' Christian complimented. He'd brought out his handkerchief and briefly mopped his brow, running his hand once through his blue-black hair before reaching for his glass. He tossed down the dregs.

Winna had a hand at her throat and could feel her racing pulse finally begin to subside. 'So are you.' She smiled up at him sincerely. 'Let's take a breather, then give it another go.'

At that, he checked his watch, then leaned over and pulled her coat up from the chair. 'Tomorrow night, maybe. It's time. Are you ready?'

Winna had just taken up her own glass, but replaced it quickly on the edge of the small table. Her face when she looked up was eager. 'I didn't realize.' She turned pertly then, holding her hair up from her neck as he settled the immense coat over her shoulders. 'And I'm always ready. You know that,' she tossed back at him.

He made no remark, but merely smiled. It took a moment for him to hand Winna her purse, pay the tab, then shrug into his own expensive tweed overcoat. Winna was oblivious by then to the rhythmic thumping of music and swell of voices around her as she waited for him with a small, complacent smile on her lips.

Arranging things; it was, really, what she did best. And this

243

time she'd managed to arrange for herself a man who not only could give her the kind of life to which she'd grown accustomed but who also knew where to find all the best poker games in town.

# Chapter 20

The following weekend was the last before Christmas, and the spirit of the season was at its peak. The Hunt Club lounge, when Christian and Edwinna arrived early Saturday night, was no different. It was thronged with guests, laughing, drinking, toasting the twinkling tree in the corner. Swags of silver garland were draped around the ceiling friezes, shimmering in the dim light of the Tiffany lamps over the private tables, and above the long cushioned bar was a string of large block letters, gilded, that spelled out 'Season's Greetings.' The masculine room, with its dark damask paper and leather furnishings, had been turned festive with the bright decorations, and the archway from the entrance foyer into the lounge itself was hung with a sprig of mistletoe. Edwinna and Christian entered arm in arm, joining a cluster of people in the anteroom.

'Slightly crowded,' Winna remarked dryly.

'Slightly,' Christian murmured and slipped out of his coat. He helped remove Winna's, and she watched as he crossed the narrow room and handed them across the small counter to the coat check girl; she offered him two claim checks. When he returned to her side, Winna held out her hand.

'The receipt?'

Christian arched an eyebrow as he looked down at her. She wore a red gown that night, long-sleeved, its collar standing up behind her neck like a queen's ruff and falling to a modest, open V in the front. Her hair was arranged in a chignon, flatteringly off the face that was turned up to him expectantly.

'You know, Edwinna, sometime you might trust me with your things,' he remarked and handed over the small piece of cardboard.

She smiled, slipping it into her purse. 'Habit,' she said. 'How long do you think it'll be?'

Christian frowned as he looked past the guests about the large room. All the tables had been taken. 'I don't know. Looks pretty hopeless.' He went over to have a brief word with the tuxedoed maitre d' and returned with a shrug. 'He'll let us know.'

Dressed in a tuxedo himself, with white shirt and a wine-red cummerbund, he presented the perfect image of the well-heeled man about town, and Winna smiled. 'Buy me a drink while we're waiting?' She watched his lips curve into an insouciant grin as she added to her request the familiar, caressing touch across his cheek.

'Of course, love.'

She watched him move into the crowded room, smiling, shaking hands with friends and acquaintances along his route to the bar. Brendan, in a red brocade jacket, exchanged pleasantries with him and finally handed two glasses across the counter. Christian took them, then wended his way back, handing one to Winna when he reached her side. 'He saw you waiting over here and told me to tell you he's never seen you look so stunning. A flattering sort, Brendan,' he added with a grin.

Winna smiled prettily at the compliment. Brendan had good basis for the camparison; he'd seen her in the lounge nearly every night for two weeks. 'An honest sort, you mean,' she countered lightly.

'Christian!' The pleasantly surprised female voice broke abruptly into their conversation, floating up from behind Christian's right shoulder. He turned abruptly to see Genevieve Barstok holding a drink in hand and smiling curiously at him as she cast brief sideward looks at Winna. 'How nice to see you. It's been awhile.'

'Genny.' He ran his eyes briefly down the length of her. She looked stunning as usual in a black gown, and her gold hair was swept in soft waves around her bare shoulders. He forced a smile with the murmured greeting and shifted uncomfortably; it was always decidedly difficult, fielding old girlfriends when he was in the company of a new one.

'Introduce us, Christian,' Winna was smiling sweetly, and as she turned to face the other woman squarely, she pointedly slipped her arm through Christian's.

He coughed involuntarily. 'Edwinna Rutledge, Genevieve Barstok.'

There were the obligatory gracious nods between the women and Genny motioned toward a tall man approaching as she looked back at Christian. 'Peter and I were just going to have a drink at the bar. Join us?'

'No, thank you. We're hoping to get a table.' Christian found he was feeling enormously relieved at the sight of the lanky stockbroker, and he shook hands with him as he came up. In the manner of casual acquaintances, their conversation was brief, and when the couple had finally taken their leave and drifted off into the crowded room, Christian relaxed completely.

'She's lovely. An old and dear friend?' Winna's eyebrow was arched as she kept her smile in place.

He glanced down at her. 'Actually, she's an old girlfriend of Adam's.' Well, it wasn't strictly a lie; she had been once upon a time, before Adam had lost interest and Christian had moved in. He felt the need to elaborate. 'They were pretty thick for awhile. Frankly, until Libby came along, we all thought it would be the two of them. Or at least, Mother and Father did.' Chose to, he might've added. He, himself, had been aware of Adam's strictly casual intentions. All the women had been casual, until Libby. 'She fills their bill to a tee,' he remarked. 'Good family, good looks. You know, good teeth.' He smiled rakishly at the comment and purposely caressed her under the chin; it seemed to mollify her, and he took a relieved sip of his whiskey.

In fact, she was mollified, and watched the attractive woman and her date disappear into the throng of elegant guests crowding the bar before turning her eyes to the large room in search of what really interested her. It was faceted with many corners, private niches with circular tables apart from the mainstream of smaller tables in the center, and it was to these that her attention went. 'I don't see the others. There will be a game tonight?' It was more a statement than a question.

Christian followed her gaze absently as he raised his glass to his lips again. 'They'll be here, if they're not already,' he said when the glass came down. 'There's always a game. You should know that by now.' Then the implication of her question registered, and he gave her a nervous smile. 'But there are hundreds of other things in the world to do. Why don't we just have a drink here and go on into town?'

Edwinna wasn't listening. Her high forehead creased in sudden realization as she rummaged in her change purse, counting the bills there. After a moment, the frown deepened, and she clicked the small tapestried bag shut. 'Damn!'

Christian raised inquiring eyebrows, and Edwinna looked up. At his expression, she removed her look of annoyance and replaced it with one of chagrin. 'You won't believe this, but I've done the stupidest thing. I forgot to go to the bank today. I haven't any money for the game tonight.'

Well, it was fairly close to the truth. Actually, it had been

247

Libby who hadn't gone to the bank that day, even though Winna had asked her to. And thanks to Libby's bent toward circumspection where other people's affairs were concerned, Winna had been obliged to offer only the most minimal of explanations as to where the money she'd been borrowing over the past two weeks was going, healthy sums that she'd told Libby were for 'investment purposes'. She'd elaborated only sketchily on a 'need to get in on certain excellent growth stocks while the time was right,' as advised by some nebulous stockbroker she'd supposedly met. It had been a matter she'd specifically wanted to see to while she was home, this protection of part of her capital, she'd added in canny afterthought. She'd effectively assuaged what she'd known was Libby's mild concern over the subject of her spending, and Libby had been content, then, to hand over her own carefully supervised money in an effort to aid Winna's financial prudence. And in the belief that it was all going to be returned eventually. 'When the transfer came through.' Winna might have laughed had she not been so aggravated.

Christian was still smiling, by then in genuine ease; his unthinking decision to stop at the club was going to be exonerated after all. 'Don't worry about it. There'll be plenty of other times. As a matter of fact, why don't we just forget the lounge,' he repeated. 'We'll probably be standing here forever. Let's go on over to the restaurant. We can have a nice, quiet dinner.'

'I don't come here to be wined and dined.' Winna looked up abruptly; she hadn't meant to speak so sharply. It had just slipped out at his absurd suggestion that they leave. She smiled brightly, tucking a stray lock of silver hair back in its pins. 'What I meant was that I'm not particularly hungry. We had a late lunch, remember? And you wouldn't mind, darling, if I took out a loan for tonight? I'll pay it back to you after the weekend.'

So short-lived, his reprieve. He shifted uncomfortably, fingering his tie. Adam's hold-over loan hadn't lasted as long as he'd anticipated, and at the thought, his expression went sour. It'd been the cards; the damn, lousy cards he'd been getting all week. He looked at Winna again, wishing he'd gotten them out of there sooner. 'We can forget the game tonight. Come on, let's . . .'

The sharpness had come back to the edges of her smile. 'Not play tonight? Don't be ridiculous.'

Christian couldn't help but grin at that. 'You know something? I think you're worse than I am, if that's possible,' he remarked with uncharacteristic honesty. 'Even I take a night off every now and then. My love, the cards will still be warm next week.'

Winna brushed a fingertip lightly across her temple for the mild ache that had begun to nag there. And had she been asked, she couldn't have told just exactly when the casual thrill for the roll of a die or the flip of a card had turned to compulsion, but it had, somewhere back on the continent, under the bright lights of the casino gaming tables, in the dim atmosphere of the back-room poker games. Or not compulsion; that was an odious word, befitting the glassy-eyed, desperate breed of gambler out to recoup losses for wagers poorly made, hands amateurishly played, not her. Avocation, keen avocation; that was more appropriate. Something she owed herself to pursue because she did it so well, and deserved the pleasure of it. And *worse* than he was? No, better. She could bluff him and all his cronies right under the table when she wanted to and had, on several satifying occasions; they'd taken it in stride, all those wealthy business-men, throwing in their cards to the beautiful woman at the head of the table who drew in the pot with slender, elegant hands. It was the code of the seasoned gambler, deferring graciously to superior skill. She looked back up at Christian then, forcing a sweet look of appeal. 'Well, if you're not in the mood, we don't have to stay long. You don't even have to play. If you could just give me enough for two hands?'

He studied her for a moment, then let out an abrupt laugh. There was no way out but to tell her; he'd already had occasion to sense that iron will simmering just below the surface of her. He liked that in a woman, as long as it wasn't excessive. Or disruptive. 'You leave me no choice, love, but to tell you. If you must know, I've got no cash either, so forget the loan. And the game. Fifty dollars isn't going to go very far, for you or me.'

Winna was staring at him blankly. 'No cash?' How could that be? A Bainbridge with no cash? She digested his statement, then shrugged, taking a sip of her drink. 'Well, then get a loan. Go see the manager,' she said blithely.

Christian frowned. 'Winna, they don't do that here. This isn't a casino, you know. Now come on, babe. Let's go.' He took her arm, moving them back through the couples still crowding the small waiting room. It had filled up even more since they had arrived, and there was barely room for them back near the door. He drained his glass, setting it down on a small table near the coat check.

Winna's headache had increased and vented itself when they'd stopped again in the staccato tapping of her heel against the bare wood floor; he was being so impossible. She looked at him, his handsome face drawn into an earnest frown, then let out a sigh of resignation. After all, there was really no reason to be so irritated with him; she'd done the same thing herself; come without money. 'Oh, all right, she relented, remembering to smile for him. 'It'll just have to wait until Monday night.'

Christian was rubbing the bridge of his nose, half his attention on the crowd chatting quietly around them, the other half warily on Winna. 'Well, babe, to be honest, Monday's no good either,' he admitted. 'We'll have to wait until the end of the month. I won't have money until then. A damned nuisance. Some tie-up or other with the bank,' he added in a lame attempt at blasé dismissal, then had a sudden, bright thought. He grinned. 'Why don't you give me a loan?'

Winna was staring at him again, then abruptly closed her eyes against the rush of searing head pain. Not only was her evening ruined, but he was proposing that the next several weeks be similarly demolished; she couldn't come here without him, money or no. And to suggest that she give him a loan! Her breast under the bodice of the red gown began to rise and fall visibly, and she opened her eyes as abruptly as she'd closed them to find Christian's eyes on her worriedly.

He was watching in some confusion; he had no idea why some of the color had drained out of her face. 'Are you all right? Look, babe, if . . .'

'Kindly tell me how in the hell a Bainbridge can have a tie-up at a bank! That's positively nonsensical!' erupted from Winna's throat. Heads turned in their direction, at her shrill tone. 'I can't believe that, but if it's true, then for God's sake, get a loan from them. Just go on in there and tell them who you are!' She put her fingers against her forehead, reaching around to clumsily set her half-finished gin and tonic on the nearby table.

Christian was glancing around self-consciously and took the glass from her hand before she dropped it. The gilded mirror above the small table reflected the consternation in his eyes as he set the glass down firmly and attempted to take her arm. 'Edwinna, we'll discuss this somewhere else,' he said, making a movement toward the coat check.

He didn't know her well enough. The situation was clearly beyond her control and so, consequently, was she. Jerking her arm away, she took a step back from him. 'You don't intend to do anything, do you?' she snapped. 'You have no intention of trying to work something out. You'll just stand there mealymouthing around about a tie-up at the bank, ruining everything for weeks at a time. Well, I can't stand it, do you understand? I won't stand it! Do something. You're a Bainbridge. Act like one. God damn it!'

Christian was appalled, not only for the public outburst but also for the visage she presented to him. Gone was the beautiful woman of moments before; in her place was a shrew, her patrician face contorted by seemingly uncontrollable fury into an ugly caricature of itself, her mouth petulantly turned downward, her eyes icy and pinched around the edges. He might have been more inclined to analyze the import of her disproportionate reaction had he not been so acutely embarrassed. 'Edwinna,' he said under his breath, at a loss.

In her mind, his conciliatory tone only added insult to injury. She threw up her head, propping her hands on her hips. 'Well? ' she demanded.

He spread his hands, opening his mouth to say something; nothing came out.

She sighed audibly. 'Never mind. Just never mind! Apparently you don't care enough to do anything at all for me. Well, fine. That's just fine!' she spat, then pushed her way through the crush of people. Their voices had gone up in a reproving buzz, and when she reached the coat check, she fished in her purse, then thrust the ticket at the wide-eyed girl. 'Get my coat!'

Chirstian had followed almost reluctantly and put a hand on her arm. 'Edwinna . . .' he murmured again, shaking his head.

'Leave me alone!' she snapped. 'Call me a taxi. I'm going home.' She took the coat from the young girl, thrusting her arms into it. Pushing back through the openly shocked guests, she stopped momentarily at the door, majesterially, her chin raised as she looked past the couples to Christian. 'Don't call me, I'll call you!' she announced, delivering the slight with pleasure, then pushed open the door and stormed out into the snowy night.

Christian remained near the coat check for a moment, painfully conscious of the eyes trained on him from all directions. After a sheepish shrug, he squared his shoulders and finally made his way first to the telephone for the required call, then to the bar in the other room. When a stool was vacated, he took it, nodding at Brendan, and accepting the usual glass of bourbon with a grateful smile when it was brought him. And he sat there then, trying to recuperate from the stunning humiliation Winna had dealt him; even after three quarters of an hour he was still shaking his head, staring down into his glass as if he could see there a relentless replaying of the scene and the unnervingly enigmatic woman. Finally he raised his head and looked at his reflection in the mirror above the bar. Unconsciously he lifted an eyebrow in conclusion to his thoughts.

Yes, Edwinna Rutledge was a hell of a woman, but hell on wheels when she wanted to be, and like so many men before him, he knew now, beyond a doubt, that she was one woman he wouldn't want to be hooked up to for life.

## Chapter 21

Libby was humming along to the strains of 'God Rest Ye Merry Gentlemen' issuing from the stereo as she stood at the fluted white mantlepiece in her apartment, carefully winding a strand of fresh holly around one of a pair of brass candlesticks there. Comfortably dressed in faded jeans and a cableknit sweater, she gently felt the placement of the bit of greenery, checking it before breaking off her accompaniment to the carol and stepping away with a satisfied smile. She moved back over to the couch and took up another handful from the cluster of holly and pine clippings spread out along the cushion and returned with them to the mantle.

It was a ritual, this laying of greens rich in the fragrance of the season, a ritual carried out every year and inspired not only by a particular appreciation of the vibrant scents but also by the recollection of a picture seen once long ago. It had been a faded photograph of an old-fashioned living room with an enormous fireplace. Among the other holiday decorations, pieces of pine and holly had been arranged about the mantle and draped along the window cornices, and the whole scene had inspired in her young, impressionable mind a vision of warmth and friendliness that she'd never forgotten. In a desire to effect it for herself, she had incorporated a trip to the wholesale nursery into her Christmas routine, and the proprietors who had come to know her well took the lengths of roping she selected and cut them as she wanted, sending her on her way again with a bag filled with pieces just long enough to arrange about her things. Sebastian —and Adam this year—had taken her, of course, then left shortly after bringing her home again. It was as she wanted, and Sebastian had understood from years of experience. Adam when it had been explained to him. There were some things that were strictly her own, that she took pride and pleasure in for her ability to give them to herself; this was one of them.

She laid the handful of clippings down on the Pembroke table nearest her and reached up again to the mantlepiece. Carefully bypassing the carved paperweight Adam had done for her, she located the mate to the candlestick and reached back behind her to bring up a clipping for it. She had just begun to wind it around the circular base when she heard sounds on the far side of the hallway door. She stopped what she was doing instantly, her hands poised at the mantle as she listened intently, her brow creased lightly in concentration. It couldn't be Adam or Sebastian, returning for something forgotten; either one of them would have called her name through the door. Adam insisted upon it, for her peace of mind. She listened another moment or so, finally identifying the sound of a key in the lock. It made her lay aside the clipping and head across the room to the door. When she neared it, she could hear the murmur of a voice, agitated and female.

She recognized Winna's voice and began to smile. Picking up her pace, she had almost reached the door when it flew open, and it went on to bang back against the wall, rattling the grouping of pictures there and sending them askew. 'Libby, why in the hell don't you do something about the locks in this place!' Winna snapped as she marched in past her. 'That key, it sticks every damn time. I just can't stand it!'

Libby was momentarily taken aback, then quickly readjusted. Purposely ignoring Winna's obvious agitation and the fact that the door had very nearly caught her right in the face, she said calmly, 'I didn't expect you so soon.' She found the edge of the door and moved with it as she pushed it closed. 'You don't usually get back until it's almost time to get back up again.' *If at all,* she might've added, but didn't; she wasn't quite that archaic in her attitude, no matter what Adam might half seriously comment to the contrary.

'Well, I'm here,' Winna muttered as she shrugged out of her mink and flung it across the room; it landed in a careless drape across the back of the near couch.

'Christian's loss, my gain,' Libby said, still determinedly unconcerned in the face of Winna's mood. She turned away from the door and smiled. 'And our paths have crossed at the most opportune moment. For once, I'm not mired in homework papers and a thousand nitty gritty details of Christmas at the schoolhouse, and for once you're home.' Immediately, she grimaced inwardly for the tactless remark. She'd meant only to clear away some of the tension, not chide Winna for her behavior; there were enough other people around to do that. And if nothing else, the fact of their having seen almost nothing of each other since Christian had come into Winna's life had spared her the effort of having to address the issue of Sebastian and Christmas, something she hadn't quite decided how to approach. But that was irrelevant, she thought in some annoyance at herself; Winna was free to do as she pleased. She smiled and sought to repair her comment. 'I didn't mean anything by that. I'm just glad we'll have a chance for some time alone, that's all. And I'm really pleased you've had Christian around. It's been just what you needed to revive your spirits, I'm happy to see.' Oh, good, Libby. And why not be patronizing while you're at it? She sighed and hoped Winna hadn't caught that.

She hadn't; she wasn't even listening. 'Oh, hell,' she cursed under her breath as she kicked off her red sandals and cracked her ankle against the couch. She reached down and rubbed it briefly, then in an even worse humor, straightened abruptly and marched into the kitchen.

Well, so much for bright conversation as a panacea, Libby thought as she listened to Winna bang around in the kitchen. She crossed the room to flip off the stereo. Then moving over to the couch, she sat down and tucked her legs up beneath her, settling in calmly to do the only thing she could at that point: wait for however long it was going to take for Winna to simmer down and tell her what had happened.

She didn't have long to wait. Winna reappeared moments later with a shallow glass of straight gin and leaned up against the kitchen doorway. Libby listened to her movements against the wall, then finally gave her a light smile. 'I assume it'd be rhetorical to ask if you and Christian have had an argument.'

Edwinna's narrow face was creased heavily in a frown, her gaze leveled somewhere in the direction of the cerulean carpet under her feet. 'It would be rhetorical, yes,' she answered shortly.

Libby tilted her head, smiling encouragement. 'Want to talk about it?'

The offer of a sympathetic ear for some reason sharpened Winna's razor-edged temper again. 'There isn't anything to talk about. The man's an incredible boor! For God's sake, he had no money!' she snapped. Renewed annoyance kept her garrulous despite herself. 'He had no money for the evening. As a matter of fact, he informed me that he'd have none until the end of the month!' She laughed then, harshly. 'Imagine that. A Bainbridge with no money until the end of the month. It kills me, it really does!'

She pushed herself away from the doorway then and paced over to the windows; there, she pulled back the draperies and peered out. When she spoke again, it was over her shoulder. 'He made some remark about a tie-up at the bank. How in the hell can a man with unlimited credit have a tie-up at the bank, I'd like to know!' she demanded and abruptly raised her glass, taking a good healthy swig before lowering it as she continued to stare into the dark night. She became aware all of a sudden of Libby's reflection in the glass. Libby sitting behind her quietly curled in the cleft of the couch arm, and the content of her outburst registered almost as immediately. She sought to recover. 'Never mind,' she said to the reflection. 'I . . . don't mind me. I guess I was in the mood for an argument. Full moon or something,' she murmured, wondering uncomfortably at Libby's thoughts.

In fact, they'd have surprised her, for they weren't centered on Winna's ill humor; tirades over nothing weren't entirely out of character for Winna. But rather, she was contemplating the lead-in Winna had just afforded to a matter that had been bothering her for weeks, and wondering if she ought to take it. 'Well, Winna,' she said slowly, 'actually his credit's rather poor.'

Winna wasn't listening; she was staring past both their reflections again as she absently fingered the soft blue curtain under one hand, her thoughts riveted on the episode in the Hunt Club lounge. It had been imprudent flying off at Christian that way. With rationality abruptly restored, she could see that now. It was just that it had come upon her so suddenly, that viselike tension. She touched her forehead absently, in remembrance; it brought back even the cloying feeling of being almost unable to breathe. She shook it off, as she shook her head with a frown at the blackness beyond the window and let her thoughts get back on track.

Yes, it had been definitely unwise, but really, he'd started the whole thing, being so impossible. Yes, when one looked at it in true objectivity, she concluded at length, it had really been his own damn fault, not hers. Not at all. She smiled faintly for the vindication and remembered the slight she'd delivered to him with such satisfaction at the time. That had been deserved, too, not only for his complete unconcern for her happiness, but also for the whole uncomfortable issue of the money. Her pensive expression faded altogether as her thoughts pressed on. Actually, her response had probably been the right one, an effective tactic. Let him worry a little; it would do him good. He'd be that much more relieved to hear her voice in the morning when she called him. And she would. Another time, she'd go ahead and let him stew about her awhile longer, but not this time. There was rather a lot riding on Christian; she wasn't about to let her future hang in the balance of the not-always-intelligible male psyche. She raised her glass again, her expression completely serene at that point as she contemplated what would undoubtedly make for a very poignant scene of reconciliation.

Behind her, Libby was preoccupied with her own thoughts. Her own lead-in had just fallen flat on its face, and she was debating whether or not to voice it again. After all, there was that problem with lead-ins; they lost their impact when they had to be repeated. Like the punch line of a joke. She bit her lip mildly in indecision, then finally sighed. 'Winna, actually his credit's rather poor,' she said again loudly.

Winna turned absently. 'Hmmm?'

Well, one could never tell. Libby smiled briefly at herself, then grew serious. 'Winna, I'm really sorry your evening got ruined, but I suppose it's just as well you found out a few things right off the bat.' She paused momentarily, then said as gently as she could, 'Winna, Christian's a compulsive gambler.'

Winna gave her an arch look and downed the rest of her gin. 'Libby, don't be such a prude,' she remarked on her way to the kitchen. From there her voice filtered out. 'There's nothing wrong with gambling.'

Libby waited for her to return. When she heard Winna's movement back in the room, over near the window again, she went on clearly. 'Winna, I'm not a prude. I never said there was anything wrong with it, as an occasional pastime. But that's not the case with Christian. It's a compulsion with him, the kind of thing that ruins lives, not just a game every now and then. I . . . he hasn't mentioned anything to you?'

'No,' Winna said flatly.

Libby nodded. No, of course he wouldn't. It wasn't the sort of thing one goes around admitting to new acquaintances. 'Well, it is. A compulsion, I mean, and he loses enormous sums of money. Winna, Christian's gambling is a sickness.'

Winna had switched to wine and held the delicate glass gracefully as she peered out the window again and pursed her lips in annoyance. The last thing she needed at the moment was a lecture from Libby. 'What he does is his own business,' she said over her shoulder.

'True,' Libby conceded immediately. 'But you ought to know about it, for your own good. You seem to care a lot about him,' she said outright. She uncurled herself then and got up, crossing over to Winna. When she stood next to her near the folds of the dark draperies, she touched Winna's arm briefly before continuing. 'He runs through his allowance in the space of a week or two. Winna, it's not my business how or with whom you spend your time, and if you really care for Christian, that's fine. But I don't want you to get hurt. And it's not that I think Christian will hurt you, but I . . . it's just that he's got a few shortcomings, that's all,' she finished somewhat lamely.

Winna had turned now and was frowning at Libby. 'Allowance? What do you mean allowance?'

It took Libby a few moments to backtrack. When she had, she absently fingered the ribbing around the collar of her sweater and smiled. 'Oh, well. He's given a certain amount each month, sizable obviously. Unfortunately, he can't seem to live within his budget,' she added dryly. 'He hounds Adam constantly to up it, but Adam just can't see doing that. Nor could I if I were in his position. Every now and then he'll give him a loan, but he's pretty much put his foot down on that, too. Christian's a grown man. He's got to learn to get along on his own sometime.' She sensed Winna's sudden tension and reached out to place a hand on her arm, her expression a mixture of apology and commiseration. 'Winna, I'm sorry you had to find out this way. About Christian's gambling. I . . .'

Winna was standing perfectly still, staring. 'Libby, what do you mean he's always hounding Adam to up it? What does Adam have to do with it in the first place?'

What had Winna said? 'I'm not as versed in this family as you are?' 'Sorry,' she said. 'I don't mean to keep dropping these cryptic remarks. Winna, it's Adam who controls the Bainbridge money. Everything involved in the family finances, including Christian's allowance, has to go through him. He's not crazy about the arrangement, but that's the way his father wants it.'

'. . . won't have money until the end of the month . . . ,' '. . . a damned nuisance . . . ,' '. . . why don't you give me a loan . . .' Christian's voice rang through an echo chamber in Winna's mind. Christian. Who apparently couldn't subsidize his own habits on his allowance, much less those of anyone else. Her blue eyes narrowed as she looked at Libby, but she kept her voice casual. 'In other words, unlike Adam, he has access to nothing more than this allowance?'

'That's right.' Libby shifted, slipping one hand in the back pocket of her jeans. She felt rather uncomfortable, even with Winna, discussing the Bainbridges' finances. Yet it would help to make her point if Winna knew that even his parents realized the extent of Christian's problem. 'Winna, frankly, it would be disastrous to give him a free rein. It's, Winna . . . well, it's that bad. His father simply would never let him get his hands on anything except his own allowance. And Adam agrees.'

Winna wasn't listening any more; she had turned back to the window and stood there for a long time, saying nothing as her thoughts spun around and around. Libby endured her strange silence as long as she could, then sighed. Well, it had needed to be said; it had been for Winna's own good, she told herself yet again. But there were so damn few men around, good, interesting men; she knew that as well as Winna and regretted that she'd just put a black mark on one Winna had thought was promising. Suddenly she had to say something, anything. 'Look, what about getting something to eat? Have you had anything?'

Winna turned just at that moment, not in response to Libby's suggestion but to her own preoccupied thoughts. She started to move forward and in the process nearly walked right into Libby; she hadn't even seen her. Winna shook her head, trying to dissolve the fog. 'What did you say?'

'I said, what about something to eat?' Libby smiled.

'Whatever,' Winna murmured. And as she continued to look at Libby, her calculating thoughts took another turn. She was once more fully alert, and studying Libby sharply. Inspirations were coming quickly now. She moved finally, skirting Libby as she headed off across the room. 'By the way, Lib. We ran into Genevieve Barstok tonight, Christian and I.' As she set her untouched wine glass down on the drop-leaf table, she turned to watch Libby keenly; there was no reaction from her other than a curious smile as she stood listening to Winna's direction, her hands clasped loosely in front of her.

'Who's Genevieve?'

Winna collected her sandals from where they'd landed—one in front of the couch, one under the table—when she'd kicked them off; she straightened and looked squarely at Libby, a shoe dangling from each hand. 'Oh, I thought you knew,' she said. 'She's Adam's old girlfriend. She's really a knockout, I must say!' she added conspiratorially. 'The kind of woman you'd expect to find him with: beautiful, sophisticated. And apparently some rider. I understand from Christian that they used to tear up the hunt course. And what a dancer! We were all entranced watching her and her partner. I heard it remarked that the two of them were even better than she and Adam used to be. You know, you ought to let him go on over to the club sometimes, Lib. His friends were asking after him, said he's been a virtual stranger from all his old haunts in the last six months or so.' She smiled at her fluent improvisation, another of her strong points, then went to pick up her coat and drape it across her arm. She looked over at Libby finally, to assess her reaction.

It was exactly as anticipated. Libby was standing perfectly still in front of the window, her smile still in place, but with how much conscious effort, even Winna couldn't know. Winna could see the flatness at the edges of her mouth quite clearly, however, and the faint crease of demoralization in her brow. Satisfied, she laughed sweetly. 'Oh, Lib! Did that ever come out poorly! All I meant was that you ought to be awfully proud of yourself, whisking him right out from under the nose of a woman like that. I know I would be. There aren't too many men in this world who'd change their style as completely as Adam has since he met you.' She moved off toward the hallway, saying over her shoulder. 'Take it from one who knows. It's a real feather in your cap.'

In the bedroom Winna dumped the coat and shoes and picked up her hairbrush. Standing before the mirror, she reviewed the brief exchange with Libby. Granted, it'd been short, but just long enough, and most effective in playing to Libby's doubts, she concluded as she visualized her sister's expression. And those doubts were going to be necessary later on, when it was time for all the loose ends to be tied up. She smiled suddenly for the maxim she'd always sought to follow in everything she said and did. Proper preparation: it was an essential ingredient to any well-planned arrangement.

Or rearrangement, as the case might have to be.

# Chapter 22

Adam stood in Morgan's stall, tightening the girth on his English saddle. The Monday afternoon sun filtered in through the iron grate high up on the cement wall, catching one shoulder of his black riding coat, and the faint aroma of citronella drifted up from the bay's head, mingling with the scent of saddle-soaped leather and fresh hay in the manger. Leaning in to the horse, he shifted the woolly sheepskin pad under the girth, and after a moment, Morgan craned his head around and sniffed curiously at Adam's sleeve. Adam watched him briefly, then reached out and stroked the velvety muzzle. 'Yes, I know. It's the very last thing you want to do, amble around that indoor ring. Well, I don't blame you, and you're not alone in your misery. Libby feels the same way.'

He grinned sympathetically, then went back to his activity, testing the tautness of the girth with a hand between it and Morgan's belly. It was too loose, and he unfastened the buckles again, pulling up hard on the leather strap as he worked at readjusting it.

Jennie's lesson had ended half an hour before, and she'd gone home in a taxi; Adam smiled unconsciously at the recollection of the young girl, highly pleased with herself, giving directions to the driver. Four months ago, she wouldn't have even contemplated traveling alone in a taxi. But then, four months ago, Libby Rutledge's and Adam Bainbridge's medicine for intractable dejection hadn't been administered. He marveled again at Libby's intuition; the riding lessons had done the trick.

Of course, he and Libby still supervised Jennie's getting home most days, and Libby was never far away during the riding lessons themselves. Usually she perched in the bleachers lining three sides of the enormous indoor facility while Adam put his young student through her paces in the ring below. He liked to look up and see her there, knowing she was an integral part of it

261

all, and she always looked every bit the professional woman, in her smart suits and with her auburn hair pulled back with tortoise-shell clips. Had it been anyone but Libby, the immaculate clothes might have seemed out of place in the dusty enclosure. But they didn't, for Libby Rutledge was a woman to whom a little dirt on her clothing or mud on her shoes was of no consequence, not when there was work to be done. Her kind of work: the giving of new hope and life, along with the will to get back up on the horse one more time.

That day, however, Libby wasn't dressed so elegantly. She had arrived in a full riding habit of buff-colored jodhpurs, black coat, and boots, and she was waiting for him even then to bring out their horses. They'd done almost no riding since the snows had come; with such weather, they had to confine their riding to repetitive circuits of the indoor ring, and Libby had denounced them as boring, telling him that they 'stifled her imagination.' He supposed they did, and had laughed at the facetious explanation; nevertheless, he forced her on up into the saddle every now and then. 'Just to keep your relearned skills fresh,' he'd explained reasonably. 'More likely so you can preserve your role as master and mine as slave,' she'd countered good-naturedly. She might be right, he conceded as he finished adjusting the girth; it was the one area in which he had full control of her destiny and knew it was secure. Too much time had elapsed since their last exercise, and that day he'd made a detour by her apartment, with firm instructions that she change her clothes. She'd voiced the required complaints, of course, only to be admonished by the young, over-confident Jennie. 'But Miss Rutledge, it's good for you!'

He chuckled to himself at the recollection of her remark and ducked under Morgan's head, leaning down to pick up the animal's right foreleg. He had come up lame the week before, from a rock imbedded in the sensitive frog of his hoof. He'd seemed all right that day, but Adam checked the hoof anyway, a frown coming to his face as his errant thoughts switched abruptly to Edwinna.

Odd that she'd come along with them this afternoon when they'd left Libby's apartment for the club. Odd, in fact, that she'd even been at the apartment. Up until now, she'd expressed no real interest in the things that made up Libby's life. He was tempted to laugh scornfully at the sudden show of sisterly concern, but didn't; in view of everything, he hardly found Edwinna's actions humorous. And of course her propensity for spending night and day away from home suited him in some ways. It was thoughtless toward Libby, but it had spared him the effort of maintaining a civility toward her that he no longer felt, and it provided that much less opportunity for Libby to be exposed to her influence. He contemplated the fact that she and Christian had apparently fallen head over heels and smiled darkly at the thought. They ought to; they were two of a kind. Well, that might be a little harsh on Christian, actually.

He straightened finally, and went back around Morgan, making a last, brief inspection of the tack. As he reached over to take up the reins and sling them back over Morgan's head, he felt the light touch of a hand on the back of his shoulder. It had Libby's softness, and he turned with a smile of surprised welcome. It faded instantly, however, when his eyes met the aquamarine of Edwinna's.

Her eyes were dancing with interest as she stood behind him, her hands thrust in the pockets of a pair of fashionable pleated trousers drawn in at the ankles. Her soft white shirt was opened one extra button, and a maroon cashmere sweater was casually thrown over her shoulders, its sleeves falling over the bodice of her blouse and knotted loosely at midchest; her hair was drawn back severely into a ponytail and braided, completing the fashion-plate look. She didn't flush in the least under his brooding appraisal, and smiled lightly.

'Libby's been regaling me with all sorts of praise about your horse. I thought I'd come see for myself.' She smiled more engagingly, then turned her eyes curiously to Morgan. She moved away to survey him critically from a distance, then stepped forward again to run her hand admiringly along his flank. 'Yes, he's a real beauty.'

Adam's expression was inscrutable as he watched her slow progress along the side of his horse. 'Thank you,' he said.

'Thoroughbred?' Her eyes met his briefly in inquiry, then dropped immediately back to Morgan.

'Yes.'

'Do you hunt him?'

'On occasion.'

At the brief, noncommittal responses, she gave him a direct look, faintly quizzical. He was still standing by the saddle, one hand unconsciously on it, the other at his side. When his unreadable expression still didn't change, she resumed her admiring examination of the horse, continuing on up Morgan's side as she talked. 'We used to ride all the time, Libby and I, when we were kids. We had horses, though not like this.' And as if registering a realization of what she'd just said, she gave him a pretty look of chagrin. 'Of course, you know all that. God, it's been years since I've ridden myself. I really miss it sometimes.'

Adam moved finally. He threw one arm across the saddle and leaned there casually, drawing back one flap of his black riding coat as he propped a hand on his hip. At her remark, an enigmatic half smile came to his lips. 'Do you?' he inquired with studied interest.

At his tone, Winna glanced up. 'Yes, I really do,' she said, laughing slightly. 'This seems to be your business, teaching people how to ride, or reteaching them, as the case may be. I ought to get you to do the same for me.'

'Should you?'

There was that same polite tone, with an undercurrent to it that she couldn't quite identify. He was still smiling, however, and it prompted her to retrace her steps along Morgan's side until they stood directly across from each other, the span of the saddle between them. A single shaft of light spread in a long triangle across the dirt floor from the half door standing slightly ajar, deepening the shadows in the far reaches of the corners of the enclosure, and the silence that had suddenly fallen down between them was palpable. As she listened to the heavy breathing of the bay horse and the other faint equine noises filtering in from down the corridor, she realized the moment was upon her, and took it. She remained standing in line with the saddle and spoke finally into the quiet. 'Yes, I should.' She began toying then with the leather saddle flap in front of her, tilting her head slightly as she kept her eyes trained on her hands. 'I'd like that,' she continued. 'It's one of the things I've been meaning to do, begin to ride again. And you seem to be such a skillful instructor.' She moistened her lips with the tip of her tongue, then very slowly let her eyes drift upward; they met his and locked. 'Besides,' she said softly, 'it would give the two of us a chance to get to know each other better.'

Adam didn't move. His black coat was still drawn back slightly from his chest by the languid hand at his hip, and his wavy hair whispered softly against the collar at the nape of his neck. The half smile on his face was the only thing that shifted; it widened slightly. 'You'd like that, would you, for us to get to know each other better?' he returned just as softly.

Edwinna let her eyes drop demurely. She remained silent for an eloquent length of time, seemingly engrossed with the strip of leather, then finally looked back up at him. Her lips parted slightly, revealing a gleam of perfect teeth. 'Yes, I would. Wouldn't you?'

He ran his eyes over her face, then downward to the cleavage visible where her blouse was unbuttoned; it was an open appraisal, and after a moment, he abruptly pushed himself upright and moved up to Morgan's head. He stood there then, his brow slightly furrowed as he busied himself with the throat latch of the horse's bridle. After a fruitless moment of waiting for the verbal acknowledgment of what his eyes had told her, Winna joined him at the horse's head, coming to stand inches away; in such close proximity, she could smell the scent of his appealing aftershave, all but feel the scratchy wool texture of his riding coat rubbing against her face—as it would when he took her into his powerful embrace. She almost smiled right then for the success of her 'rearrangement'. And it was going to be far more suitable in many ways, for Adam as well as for her, she thought as she stood looking from under half closed eyes at his broad shoulders fitted exquisitely into the well-tailored jacket. She assessed his continued silence and concluded finally that it was in deference to the rules of the game; he would know them, of course, as well as she did. All right; she'd do her part. She smiled up at him coyly, murmuring. 'Adam . . .'

'Edwinna, I wonder if anyone's told you that Libby and I are going to be married.' He'd spoken without looking at her. Now he paused a moment to let the remark settle, then abruptly dropped his pretense of interest in the bridle. He turned to her with narrowed eyes. 'I'm in love with her and only her. Period, paragraph.'

There was no mistaking him this time. As for her reaction, it was impossible to divine, for, chameleonlike, her sculpted face had immediately taken on an indignant frown. She stepped away. 'Well, I would hope so! Knowing how she feels about you, I'd certainly hope so,' she repeated emphatically.

'A moment ago, I'd have thought you didn't feel quite that way.'

It was time to leave; she didn't look at him again as she moved down the length of the horse. 'Adam, you misunderstood me,' she said lightly over her shoulder. At the horse's flank, she stopped momentarily, pointedly checking her watch. It made her frown again in dismay. 'My God, I've left Libby sitting in the bleachers all alone for nearly half an hour! I'd better be getting back. How long shall I tell her you'll be? Another five or ten minutes?' she inquired, still without looking back.

She should have; she'd have seen his look then and not been so jarringly startled when his deep voice rang out sharply behind her, just as she was putting her hand on the bottom half of the Dutch door. 'Edwinna!'

She spun. He was still standing by Morgan's head, but now there was something almost menacing in his stance. He was planted squarely on both booted feet, his legs slightly apart, and Morgan's reins held unconsciously in one hand. Yet, his voice when he spoke again had gone as soft as silk. 'I don't misunderstand you at all. And as a matter of fact, I'm glad we've had these few moments alone so you don't misunderstand me.' He paused only briefly. 'Libby's welfare is of primary importance to me. Above and beyond everything else in the world.'

'Well, of course,' she allowed breezily and turned to leave.

'Edwinna!'

She spun around again, unconsciously biting her lip.

'Hear me and hear me well. Libby may not see you for what you are, even though I've tried to tell her, but I do. Oh so very well.'

An insistent tapping had begun at her temple; she could no longer maintain her pleasant manner and slipped into an attitude of bored annoyance. 'Adam, I'm afraid I don't follow . . .'

'Then let me clarify things.' His voice was still ominously low. 'Sebastian is coming for Christmas. I have seen to that. And I don't want to hear that you've brought the subject up to Libby again in any way, shape, or form.'

Such a brief statement, yet so eloquently damning—just as he'd meant it to be. Comprehension was so fleeting in her eyes that it might not even have been there, but Adam caught it. He smiled grimly. 'That's right, Edwinna. I was there. I heard it all. I know all about you.'

She opened her mouth to speak, then closed it abruptly. It took a moment, but finally she was able to smile and did, slowly, in complete unconcern as she casually adjusted the sleeves of her sweater draping her breast; it was sufficient evidence that she wasn't in the least bothered by him and his remarks, she thought. But just to emphasize it, she lingered nonchalantly in the doorway a moment longer before finally turning away without another word.

The corridors in the large barn were wide and lined with boxstalls opening out along both sides. Various pieces of tack, grooming tools, buckets, and pitchforks were lying about, and Winna's heels clacked sharply against the cement floor as she walked away from Morgan's stall. She began humming halfway along, looking from this side to that in open interest as she studied the horses stabled behind each door, and she smiled prettily at a workman in khaki approaching from the opposite direction. When she'd finally reached the corner of the long passageway, she rounded it nonchalantly. Once on the other side, however, and effectively out of sight of Morgan's stall, she stopped abruptly and flattened herself back against the wall. And it was then and only then that the expression of blasé unconcern left her, to be replaced by one that was almost hunted.

It wasn't supposed to have gone that way. He was supposed to have responded, willingly, as susceptible as every other man in the world to the charms she hadn't up until then seen fit to turn on him. For God's sake, she could certainly offer the man far more than Libby ever could. She raised her head, closing her eyes against the nagging throb behind them, then rested her head back against the wall. Yet, he hadn't responded, and on top of that had revealed the fact that he'd witnessed the little scene with Libby. It was unnerving, she had to admit—not merely vexing as it was with Sebastian—to know he had a certain awareness; after all, this was an entirely different kind of man, much more formidable. Options, options; they were beginning to disappear like clay pigeons being shot out of the sky. And yet her concern could by allayed in the knowledge that there was a certain invincibility to her relationship with Libby—provided by Libby herself. Libby might yet prove useful. It was that thought that held her captive for a very long time as she remained resting against the wall and kept one ear out warily for the sound of Adam's bootheels or the clatter of Morgan's hooves, which never came. Finally the vicious tension began to subside and a clear thought emerged. She deliberated for another instant, then straightened and brushed the dust from her clothing. And it was with a renewed attitude of resolution and confidence that she finally began walking once more in the direction of the riding ring and Libby.

Christian; it was going to have to be Christian, for there was no other way. She didn't know how or when, or even where, but time would undoubtedly tell.

She'd make it.

## Chapter 23

They went down to the Bainbridges' in the late afternoon on Christmas Eve. Twilight was descending, and as they left the suburbs, a light snow began to fall, dusting the busy highway with a thin layer of white that made the roadways slick and swirled up around the headlights of Adam's car. The snow grew more insistent and the traffic thinner as they reached the open countryside, and some distance down the two-lane road, Adam pulled into a curbside nursery twinkling with a string of colored bulbs stretched across the parking lot. Libby and Winna remained in the car while Adam and Sebastian braved the weather, fastening their coats more securely against the rising wind and gathering snowfall as they made several circuits through four rows of firs and pines stacked in pairs against rickety wooden sawhorses. Settling finally on a Balsam pine and three wreaths of holly, Adam paid the nurseryman and got them on their way again, the trunk of his Jaguar coupe loaded with greens and tied down with rope. It was slow going now in the storm, and the narrow, winding drive leading to the Bainbridges' was treacherous and barely passable by the time they reached it. Adam navigated it handily, however, finally pulling the car up directly in front of the door of the house, to an audible sigh of relief from the back seat.

Sebastian reached forward and patted Adam's shoulder. 'Well done.'

The collar of Adam's heavy sheepskin parka was still pulled up and brushed the back of his neck as he grinned into the rear-view mirror. 'Thanks. And you're driving home.'

Beside Adam, Libby turned slightly toward the back seat; she didn't need to see Sebastian's expression to read his reaction, and laughed. 'I think he's kidding, Sebastian. But there'd be no problem if we had your little four-wheel sled, right? Or perhaps Winna might let you off the hook.' She'd dropped the remark lightheartedly into the strained silence between Sebastian and Winna; it had been painfully acute all through the drive. Winna had said virtually nothing, even back at the apartment, when Libby had done her best to try and explain the circumstances of Sebastian's being included. She'd given up finally in the face of Winna's rigid silence. Well, it would be a matter of showing Winna then, that she still took her feelings very much to heart. Still, Libby was undeniably glad that Sebastian had come along.

Winna made no response to the remark, and Sebastian answered doubtfully. They all stepped from the car into the snowy drive and the men began to unload the luggage and decorations under the bright outside spotlight.

As Libby and Winna made their way to the front door, it opened suddenly to reveal Augustine, her thin figure silhouetted against the enormous chandelier-lit hall and winding staircase at the rear. Introductions were made as Libby and Winna stepped into the house, and Manning took their coats, but Augustine continued to watch Adam and Sebastian lift the roped pine out of the trunk. 'Adam has brought a tree,' she observed, and it sounded like an accusation.

Libby stood at her elbow in a lemon wool dress, contrasting vividly with Augustine's lavender dress. She smiled immediately. She wasn't about to let Adam be indicted for this thing she'd done.

'Mrs. Bainbridge, it was my idea.'

'We don't do that,' Augustine said disapprovingly. 'Christmas here is a quiet time, and what decorations we have had in the past have been stored away.' As she'd done when confronted with Libby before, she shifted her gaze uncomfortably off to the left of her as she talked. 'There'll be nothing to put on it.'

'We've brought the decorations and everything with us.' In the face of Augustine's undisguised displeasure, it came out sounding flat and unpersuasive. She was obliged at that point, however, to go on. 'They're really quite nice. They're all the old things from Winna's and my home.'

'Mother, there's no harm in it.' Christian was standing in the center of the hall and interjected the pacifier. He had a drink in one hand, and the other was thrust in the pocket of his burgundy smoking jacket. He glanced down as Edwinna, by his side, moved away. She was dressed in a sporty silk shirtwaist, and was giving the exchange only intermittent attention between interested appraisals of the imposing room. She crossed to an ormolu commode against the wall and ran her hand admiringly across its surface, and Christian let his thoughts momentarily center on her. Although he'd had reservations, he'd succumbed to her efforts at reconciliation nearly a week before. After all, they were going to be thrown together for Christmas anyway. And she did know so well how to go about things. He'd taken her to dinner afterward, to Pierre's, and they'd been enjoying a good facsimile of their old relationship ever since. He smiled briefly at the recollections, then focused back on his mother and the issue at hand. 'We can put the thing in the living room. God knows it'll be out of the way in there. The room could handle a football stadium.'

Augustine didn't reply, and her lips were a thin line as she looked back at Libby, who was standing with a quiet smile on her face, her chin slightly raised in the manner of those who cannot see and who must rely on their hearing to understand what is going on around them.

'Do as you like,' Augustine said abruptly, her tone unmistakably begrudging. 'But tell your brother to see to it that the furniture is left intact.' With the indirect rebuke, she gave Christian a last look, then briskly left the room.

The tree was brought in and set up in front of one of two tall mullioned windows along the far wall of the living room. Edwinna and Christian took no part in the activity, but disappeared instead up the banistered staircase on a tour of the lavish house. They spoke briefly to Julian as he passed them on his way down. He joined Sebastian, who'd brought Libby to stand in the archway separating the living room from the hall, and with the three of them as his audience, Adam slit the ropes from the tree. Critically surveying the spreading branches for a moment, he nodded in satisfaction, then shrugged out of his coat and tossed it onto a nearby chair. He came over to where Libby stood; then took her hand and led her to the tree. 'What do you think?'

She'd reached out and was running one hand lightly over the branches. 'It's so fragrant.'

'I know. That's why we got it.' He cocked his head at her mildly pensive expression. 'Anything wrong?'

'Oh, no. Nothing really.' She gave him a brief smile, and absently continued to finger the tree's branches. 'I suppose I was just wondering whether we should have brought it after all.'

He arched an eyebrow briefly in surprise, then let it relax as comprehension came; he remembered she'd been standing with his mother in the doorway as he'd removed the tree from the car. He dropped his voice slightly. 'I see. Mother has already had something to say about it.'

'More or less.' Libby smiled dryly at the understatement.

Adam let out a breath. 'Libby, I warned you.'

'I know.' She dropped her voice; this wasn't a discussion for anyone else's ears. 'And I was the one who insisted.' I just didn't think that it would be quite so painful, she thought, and might have added that it appeared the mantle of good intentions wasn't nearly so invincible in the heat of battle as it was when one was still standing apart, observing the fray. But she didn't voice any of those thoughts, nor did she go on to divulge something else she'd discovered when standing face to face with Augustine's displeasure; that suddenly it was no longer so easy to field the Bainbridges' attitude toward her. Before, the pressures on her had been different; in some ways, she too had been different. And she realized right then just how much she and the exigencies of her life had changed, how much more open she'd become to certain vulnerabilities, with love of this man. Very simply, she desired at least some measure of acceptance by these people who were his family.

She put away the private revelations and did her best to smile up at him resolutely. 'Next time, remind me to listen to what other people have to say.'

Adam had felt obliged to voice the uncomfortable reminder, but he had no intention of continuing to feed her discouragement. 'Well, forget it. And it'll be fine. Whether or not anyone else wants to participate, we can do it for ourselves, can't we?' He chucked her lightly under the chin.

She smiled at that. 'Yes, of course.' And once it was all done, perhaps the rest of them would have some appreciation. After all, that had been her original hope. And for Winna to have the Christmas she wanted. She looked up toward Adam inquiringly. 'By the way, where's Winna?'

'She and Christian were disappearing up the steps when we came in.'

Libby turned back to the tree. 'Well, let's get started. I'm sure she'll be along shortly.'

Adam kept his voice even. 'I'm sure.' He turned to Sebastian, still standing over by the doorway. 'Come on. Let's bring the boxes over.'

Soon they had transferred most of the cardboard containers to a spot near the tree. It was Adam who picked up the last of them, and as he hiked it up to chest height, he felt his father's hand on the back of his shoulder.

Julian's black smoking jacket hung loosely on his gaunt frame, and he was looking at Adam keenly; up until then, he'd

271

remained in the doorway, removed from the activity in which he had no interest. 'I want to talk to you.'

Adam eyed him, then glanced across the room at the tree. It seemed out of place, framed in the latticed window, a barren thing against the rich colors of the room surrounding it. Off to one side, Libby was already kneeling, the skirt of her yellow dress flowing around her on the floor as she worked at the flaps of a cardboard box. He watched Sebastian join her there, impeccable in his usual vest and blazer ensemble. He knelt beside her and murmured something that made her laugh; it only increased the impatience Adam had felt at his father's interruption, and he looked back at Julian over the top of the box. 'Later,' he said.

Julian's determined look didn't waver. 'Now, Adam.'

Obviously, it was either go along or argue, and Adam felt like doing neither; the latter, however, had the least appeal, and so he capitulated reluctantly. 'All right. Let me take this over.'

'I'll be in the library,' Julian said and moved off in the direction of a door at the far side of the room.

When Adam joined him some minutes later, Julian was idling near the bookshelves along one side of the room, studying the faded leather bindings there. Adam tossed him a look and crossed to the carved oak desk diagonally set in one corner; behind it, the tall leather swivel chair was swathed in shadows from the light illuminating the portrait above. He sat down on a corner of the desk, watching as Julian moved over to the door and closed it firmly. Adam arched an eyebrow. 'Father, this is Christmas Eve. I'm in no mood for business.'

'This isn't business.' Julian returned to his post at the bookshelves and became engrossed there again. He looked as if he were reading the titles, but Adam knew he wasn't; he'd read every book in the paneled room at least once, probably twice.

'Father, what do you want?' This time Adam couldn't keep the impatience out of his voice or his expression.

Julian turned then. 'Christian tells me that you intend to marry Libby.'

Ah. He should have been prepared for this. 'I thought I'd already made that clear. I didn't know it would take Christian to get the point across.'

'Don't be flip.'

Adam didn't react, other than to draw an inaudible breath. 'Father, what do you want?' he repeated calmly.

Julian studied the rug under his feet, then looked back up at Adam, across the room. He was perched on the edge of the desk, one leg dangling, the dim portrait of his grandfather above him on the wall in the background; with their dark hair, just touched with gray, and their strong features, they could have been twins. Julian slipped his hands into his jacket pockets and said flatly, 'It's out of the question that you marry her.'

Adam's smile was deceptively casual. 'Oh really?'

'Adam, I'd hoped that you didn't actually intend to go through with this thing. I'd hoped that perhaps it was merely an infatuation, that you'd get over it and all this other nonsense about riding schools and the like. You are aware that she is permanently blind, that there is nothing to be done for her?'

At that, Adam raised his eyebrows. 'Yes, of course I'm aware of that.' He frowned then, studying Julian in dark speculation. 'Why would you make that remark? As if you'd been researching the issue.'

'I have,' Julian said simply.

Adam raised his chin. 'For what purpose?'

'To see if perhaps her circumstances could be altered,' he said, then went on before Adam could remark again. 'There are a few things that have to be considered here, Adam. Oh, I realize the woman is interesting in her way. I've always granted you that, but you've got to think about appearances. She simply isn't suitable, not for this family. Frankly, I won't have it.'

Adam was studying the toe of his leather shoe. The hollows in his cheeks had deepened, and when he looked up again, his expression was set.

'I don't give a damn about appearances. That's number one,' he said tightly. 'Number two is that I resent your snooping into things that don't concern you. Number three is you've got nothing to say about any of it. And as to your comment, the appearance Libby Rutledge presents is far above that made by anyone in this family, except for my own maybe. Frankly, I've come to like the fact that when I look in a mirror, my face doesn't have Bainbridge stamped all over it.'

Julian's eyebrow twitched. 'I take that as an insult.'

'You should. It was.' Adam stood up abruptly and turned to stand with his back to Julian. He rubbed his forehead briefly, then dropped his hand and turned. 'You're going to listen now to what I have to say, and then this conversation is never, ever going to be repeated.' He paused, studying his father. The elderly man was standing framed by the shelves of richly bound volumes, his hands once more thrust into the pockets of his jacket, and Adam went on.

'We came down here because Libby wanted to come, because

273

Libby wanted to bring some version of Christmas to you people, even though I told her it wasn't worth the effort. But she thought it was, because, whether you can understand it or not, she happens to care about people, she wants to try to get along. Well, apparently that simply isn't going to happen, no matter what we do, and frankly, it suits me just fine.' He strode out from behind the desk then, walking directly up to Julian. When he stood face to face with him, he thrust his own hands in his trouser pockets. 'I intend to marry Libby, and there's nothing you can say or do about it. It's simply the way it is. And while we're here, I expect everyone in this house to be pleasant to her. See to it that Mother gets the message. She's already annoyed me once,' he said coldly. Giving Julian a last level look, he moved past him and headed toward the door.

Julian was watching him stonily. 'And what about children?'

Adam had his hand on the brass knob and turned. 'What about them?'

'Do you intend to have any?'

'I don't see that that's any of your business.'

'It's entirely my business. Everything to do with this family is my business. Everything,' he repeated pointedly. He moved across the room in the direction of the desk. When he reached it, he turned, his expression suddenly mild. 'Adam, you've lived a very comfortable life up to now, very comfortable. With no effort whatsoever on your part, I might add. If you persist in this attitude toward Libby, well, perhaps you just might find that comfortable life style whisked right out from under you.' It was his trump card, of course, but though he flashed it, he had no real intention of following through. His backups weren't that great.

If Adam suspected that, he had no way of being certain. His stance went suddenly languid, and he rested his weight on the doorknob. His expression was light with curiosity. 'Oh, I see. In other words, if I marry Libby, you intend to disinherit me?'

Julian picked up the silver letter opener on the desk behind him and studied it, turning it over and over in his hand. He answered without looking up. 'You might consider the import of that.'

'I asked you a direct question.'

Julian raised his head then, regarding Adam from across the length of the room. 'Perhaps I might,' he hedged with a thin smile. 'And what would you do then?'

Adam's smile went all the way up to his eyes. 'Get a job,' he said pleasantly and walked out of the room.

When Adam returned to the living room, Libby and Sebastian were well into the process of trimming the tree. The dapper little man was on his feet beside her, glowering at a snarl of Christmas lights in his hand, working at two opposite ends to separate them. Below him, Libby was sitting on her knees, her hands clasped in her lap, and she seemed recovered from her earlier dismay; her face was raised toward him, a genuine smile of amusement trying to displace her composed expression. Adam watched the tableau wordlessly for a moment, then went over. 'What's the problem?' He addressed Sebastian but was looking at Libby; he crouched down, and before she could answer, kissed her.

She laughed self-consciously. 'What was that for?'

He touched her hair softly. 'Everything,' he murmured. At her quizzical expression, he kissed her lightly again, then turned his attention to Sebastian. 'Need some assistance?'

Libby laughed and felt for Adam's arm, resting her hand on it when she found it. 'Every year I carefully wind up those lights when I pack them, so that all you have to do is stretch them out again, and every year Sebastian somehow manages to ball them up.' Her laugh turned to a fond smile, and she tilted her head. 'I think you do it on purpose, Sebastian.'

His eyebrows were knit furiously as he eyed first the lights, then Libby and Adam below him; they were a handsome couple, he thought, and both doing an exceptionally poor job of containing their amusement at his expense. It made him smile despite himself, however, and abruptly, he extended the coil of wire down to Adam. 'Takes an engineer, not a scholar,' he muttered. 'You'll have to do.'

Adam laughed and straightened. In a moment, he had the knot of bulbs and wire untangled, and enlisting Sebastian's aid then, set about stringing them around the tree. Libby kept her post on the floor amid the boxes, carefully lifting out ornament after ornament, listening to the two men as they worked to the accompaniment of their own companionable repartee. After a time, Winna's lilting voice filtered to her from across the room, and she turned immediately; it'd been very much on her mind, seeing to it that Winna was drawn into the activity when she returned. It was what she'd been so anxiously anticipating. 'Winna?' She smiled a warm invitation, extending her hand.

Augustine had joined the small tour group of two somewhere in the ornate upper hall, and had blossomed in uncharacteristic cordiality at Winna's lovely manners and undisguised interest in her home. They were strolling in the direction of the hearthplace grouping of furniture, and at Libby's call, Winna broke off the conversation with her hostess, glancing over impatiently. 'You go on. I'll help with the tinsel or something,' she said vaguely and turned a luminous face back to Augustine. They settled then as a threesome, the two women and Christian; their conversation resumed without missing a beat.

There's no accounting for human nature. Where had she heard those words before? Libby wondered as she turned slowly back to the ornaments in the box. A thousand places in a thousand contexts, of course. She didn't realize she was frowning lightly until Adam called her name and she caught herself at it. His good-natured 'What next?' effectively jostled her out of her momentary pensiveness, however, and it didn't even occur to her to wonder if he'd done it by design.

He had. The brief exchange hadn't escaped him, or surprised him. And if Winna's cold indifference didn't speak eloquently enough for itself at the moment, it would someday. As if Sebastian had read his mind, he caught Adam's eye, and a look passed between them. It prompted Adam to glance across to the far side of the room, where his mother, Christian, and Edwinna were engaged in low, animated conversation, the mantled hearth with its brass-handled tools in the background empty of the glow of a fire but set with a stack of logs ready to be lit anytime. Julian had reappeared, he noted, and sat in his wing chair nearby, his fingertips pressed into a pyramid against his chin as he silently took in the activity around him. The eternal, patriarch, Adam thought darkly, and found himself wondering at the man's thoughts, realizing after a moment that he didn't really give a damn. Turning back to Libby, he watched her lift several more ornaments from the box before going over to crouch down beside her again. 'What's next?' he repeated.

She gestured collectively to the sea of objects around her. 'Need you ask? I'll hand, you and Sebastian hang.'

And it was in that way that the tree came to life. Libby extended ornament after ornament alternately to Sebastian and Adam, who transferred them to the tree, one here, one there; remember, fellas, to spread them out and don't leave holes at the back or you'll have to do it all over again. Adam laughed at the mock—dictatorial instructions, and she laughed back, picking up whatever ornament was next in line, feeling it briefly before raising it up to a waiting hand. Red, silver, blue, and gold glass balls, tiny sleds, a pair of elephants, Santas, angels, reindeer, snowmen. They were all there in miniature, bright and colorful as they dangled from the ends of the branches. The tinsel came next, then the star at the top, and finally it was time to illuminate the lights. It was done, and both men simultaneously took two paces back. Adam surveyed the finished product and discovered after a moment that he was smiling with a great deal of satisfaction. 'All done and a work of art, if I do say so myself.' He shot a look around the shimmering tree to Sebastian, who was preening at his own handiwork, then looked at Libby.

She was smiling indulgently, and somewhat mysteriously. She'd shifted position slightly and tucked her skirt around her knees as she worked at the flaps of a last carton. 'A work of art, I've no doubt, but not quite done.' She gave Adam her school teacher look then. 'Sit down, Mr. Bainbridge, because this is my part, with a little help from my friend Sebastian, that is.'

Sebastian seemed to know what was going on, and he moved to help her, hiking up his trousers at the knees as he crouched down with some difficulty. Adam took several steps backwards and perched on the arm of a chair. He crossed his arms then and watched in open curiosity as they rummaged in the cardboard box. They began bringing items out of it, one by one, and as they carefully arranged everything under the tree, Libby supervising the entire process, a slow smile of comprehension came over Adam's face. They worked for some minutes, and when they'd finally finished and switched on the electricity, he laughed aloud in outright enchantment. Leave it to Libby, he thought.

Beneath the tree glittering with its lights and fanciful ornaments, and around the very edge of the red felt skirt it sat on, ran a miniature locomotive, complete with an entire landscape of tiny green bushes, a red, white and blue depot, two trainmen, a striped railroad gate, and even a Pepsi Cola billboard. The train of four cars and an engine was complete except for a caboose, and at every pass through the junction of the little gate it emitted a very small, but very authentic whistle. Adam was captivated, watching it for two circuits around the track before finally standing up to go to Libby. She felt him come near and reached up for his hand, clasping it as he lowered himself to the floor beside her. 'It's Sebastian's and my special "thing",' she said. 'We picked the idea up from a display window once, and so we started our own, the first year it was just the two of us.' It had been a panacea, in some ways, the little project of collecting the cars. For losses that had left a ringing emptiness. She didn't express the thought, but instead smiled up at him inquiringly. 'What do you think?'

He slipped an arm across her shoulders, extracting his hand so he could arrange her hair down across her shoulder; it lay against the side of her throat in a silky mass. 'I think it's marvelous. Like you.'

Libby didn't answer, but merely shifted and sat listening to the whir of the small wheels against the tracks. She was aware of Sebastian standing close by, and aware also of the murmur of voices across the length of the room behind them. She made no attempt to call to any of them, however, not even Winna. She'd done what she wanted, set up for them what had so much meaning for her; it was going to be up to them now to take pleasure in it or not, as they chose. And as for Winna's lack of involvement, she felt certain that was a defense against emotions Winna couldn't handle; she sighed inwardly for all those things about Winna that made her have to retreat into gay, superficial conversation.

Across the room, Edwinna was laughing once again at her own remark, and sipping from a small brandy snifter. She'd entwined her arm through Christian's, as she'd done rather pointedly all evening, and had her eyes fixed on Augustine, who was smiling thinly at her engaging anecdote. At the sound of the small whistle, the smile was jarringly dissolved, and she looked disapprovingly across the room.

Winna reacted immediately; she hadn't forgotten Christian's casual remark about Adam's former girlfriend: 'Good family, good looks. You know, good teeth.' She hadn't calculated just where that attitude might take her, but it couldn't hurt to play to it, as she'd played to every other attitude of Augustine's all evening. Unhooking her arm from Christian's, she shifted forward to the edge of the love seat and set her glass down on the tea table before saying in a low voice, 'I tried to tell her we should leave everything at home, but . . .' Her tone implied there'd been little she could do, and she let her gaze follow Augustine's to the threesome across the room. Adam had gotten to his feet and was murmuring something to Sebastian; he nodded, and they left together after a moment. Winna looked back at Augustine, crossing her shapely legs. 'Libby's pleasures are, well, rather uncomplicated. They have to be, you know,' she went on softly.

Augustine was still looking across the room and spoke abruptly. 'Julian and I were both so fond of Genevieve.'

Winna was momentarily disconcerted, then cast a sidelong look at Libby. What she saw was Libby kneeling near the tree, seeming to be perfectly relaxed except for one hand poised inches above her knee, as if she'd been about to rest it there, then halted alertly in mid-motion. To listen. Winna deliberated quickly, deciding finally it wouldn't hurt to nudge that one along some more. After all, one never knew. She raised her own voice to Augustine's conversational level. 'I can understand why. Christian introduced us once. She's lovely.'

'Yes, we all thought so.'

Christian eyed Winna warily for the turn the conversation had taken, but relaxed as she slid back beside him and gave him a luminous smile. Augustine fell silent then, and at the lull in conversation, Winna let her eyes drift around the room. They appreciatively swept the heavy furnishings upholstered in velvets and satins, the Oriental carpets laid end to end across the room, the portraits scattered along the walls, framed ornately in carved rococo gilt. She admired the one over the fireplace for some time, letting her eyes drop at length to the objects on the mantlepiece below it. She was taken with one in particular and rose after a moment to give it a closer inspection.

It sat directly beneath the portrait, among several impressive examples of Sèvres porcelain—a black leopard some ten inches long, his fine head raised proudly and turned to one side, as if he were overseeing the room in front of him. She went to it, running her finger lightly over the porcelain surface. 'What an exquisite animal,' she murmured to no one in particular.

It was Julian who responded. He'd barely participated in the conversation going on around him, but instead had remained silent for the most part as he sat by in his chair. Observing. At Winna's comment, his hawkish face took on a light expression, and he looked over. 'It is, indeed. It's been in Augustine's family now for several generations, as have many of the things in this house.'

Winna's head was tilted to one side as she studied the object from another angle. After a moment, she gave him an inquiring look over her shoulder. 'Meissen, isn't it?'

'Yes.' He smiled, propping his elbows on the arms of his chair as he clasped his hands in his lap. 'And it's quite rare. It was crafted in the mid-eighteenth century.'

Winna couldn't seem to draw her eyes away from it. 'Hmmm. It's priceless, I imagine.'

Julian's sharp eyes had taken on a keen light as he looked at the lovely woman standing, entranced, at the mantle. 'I see you know a good deal about antiques.'

'Yes,' Winna said without turning, then smiled unconsciously at the leopard. 'I just love them.'

Julian smiled, too, as if the last pieces of some puzzle had just abruptly fallen into place. He eased his head back against the chair, the comfortable smile remaining in place. 'Yes, my dear, I believe you do,' he said, then repeated softly to himself, 'I believe you honestly do.'

# Chapter 24

The library at eleven thirty was filled with the shadows of night. Only two lamps were lit: a tall table lamp in the corner near the door, and a small brass lamp on the desk. Even the lights above the portraits around the room had been switched off, and Edwinna was having a hard time making out the figures in the dimness, even when she leaned up close to inspect them. Somewhere behind her, Christian was sitting tensely on the arm of a leather chair near the fireplace, his whiskey glass resting on his thigh as he kept his eyes trained warily on his father. Julian had just re-entered the room and closed the door firmly behind him.

'Father, it's late. What do you want?' It was an echo of Adam's earlier impatient inquiry and made for much the same reason: Christian was in no mood for one of his father's lectures, not anytime and certainly not now, in the presence of a witness. He ran his hand briefly through his dark hair and suppressed a sigh. They should have taken the back staircase, he and Winna. That way, Julian wouldn't have had a chance to waylay them as they followed everyone else up for the night.

His father did not reply. Apparently he was reluctant to get to the point—or was pressing some unknown advantage to the hilt, Christian thought acidly. He appeared to be content to watch Edwinna's back as she moved on to another Bainbridge relative dimly rendered in now faded oils. He let her study it interestedly for some time before finally speaking. 'Sit down, my dear. Would you like another brandy?'

She turned, giving Julian a mildly curious look. After a moment, she took the chair opposite Christian and held up her glass. 'No, thank you. I'm not quite finished, as you can see.' Arranging her skirt around her knees, she settled in then, waiting expectantly.

Julian merely smiled and began to pace the room. Christian stood it for a few minutes, then let out an exasperated breath. 'If you've asked me in here merely to watch you walk the room, then I'm going on up. Besides, Santa's coming. I wouldn't want to cramp his style.' He grinned at the remark and lifted his glass to his lips.

Julian eyed his son narrowly. His expression cleared after a moment, however. 'The two of you make a handsome couple. Have you considered marriage?' he inquired mildly.

It had the desired effect; both heads snapped around in astonishment. The similarity of reaction ended there, however, for Winna's eyes went clearly speculative and Christian's clearly skeptical; his brief glance in Winna's direction was eloquent. Julian caught both and let a slow smile drift into his face. He walked calmly across the room then, coming to a standstill directly in front of Edwinna. He thrust one veined hand in the pocket of his smoking jacket and smiled down at her pleasantly. 'You will pardon my abruptness, my dear, but as you will learn, I believe in confrontation. It saves time. And money.' He paused only momentarily before going on.

'I've been watching you all evening. You seem quite enamored of my son. Indeed, he's one of a kind.' He shot Christian a look, satisfied to note that the remark had connected; the art of dissembling wasn't something Christian had ever mastered. He turned his attention back to Edwinna, his continued smile at odds with the sudden sharp light in his eye. 'And aside from your patent interest in Christian's finer points, I believe I can safely comment that you would find a marriage into this family, by whatever route it might come, enormously pleasing.'

Edwinna said nothing; she didn't make admissions until the terrain was completely explored. She didn't, however, look away, and Julian read the look in her eyes. 'So I thought. And perhaps I might afford you the opportunity to show that you're worthy of it,' he murmured, but the words drifted away as he turned and moved across the room. Christian's voice finally halted him.

'And what, might I ask, brought all of this up?'

Julian spread his hands as he turned. 'Merely that the two of you make a handsome couple, as I said. Your children, I have no doubt, would be just as attractive. As you well know, heirs are of immediate importance to me. Time is passing for both you and Adam. Something must be done by one of you, and soon.'

Christian broke into a cynical smile, eyeing Julian over the rim of his glass. 'Heirs? My, my. And here all this time I thought that was Adam's province. Heirs and responsibilities, that is.'

It didn't elicit the reaction he'd anticipated. Julian turned away again, and a frown settled on his forehead as he looked toward the faded rug. 'I can't count on Adam for that any more,' he murmured. 'No, I can no longer count on Adam.'

Christian wasn't interested in Julian's difficulties with Adam, not at any time but particularly not at the moment; what was of immediate concern was the tenor of this conversation and Edwinna's patent interest in it. Reconciliations for the passing moment were one thing; anything else was quite another with this woman of the strange undercurrents. He recalled the scene at the Hunt Club lounge and sought to end the discussion. 'Father . . .'

Julian ignored his tone of dismissal and went on. 'We would bless a marriage between the two of you, your mother and I. I think I can speak for both of us in saying that. She hasn't known you long . . .' He turned to Edwinna. 'But she seems to find you most captivating, Edwinna. Believe me, that is a rarity, though you have seen to that matter admirably,' he added sharply, then turned gracious again. 'However, I quite agree.' And with disconcerting abruptness, he turned on Christian then. 'You, apparently, don't. I gather marriage to Edwinna has no appeal to you.'

Christian averted his face from Winna, studying a spot on the rug. 'Father . . .' he began again, at a loss.

'Not even if it were worth your while?'

Christian looked back up, eyeing Julian carefully. His father stood swathed in shadows. 'And how is it worth my while?'

The answer came with no hesitation whatsoever. 'A substantially larger allowance. Out from under Adam's control.'

Christian's eyebrows shot up; it was totally unexpected. And even on split-second consideration, enormously appealing. He contemplated the suggestion, unconsciously rolling his glass around so the ice clinked against the sides. After a moment, however, his thoughtful expression dissolved into one of suspicion, and with his own brand of insight, he said doubtfully, 'And so for the promise of a passel of beautiful grandchildren you'd do that?' His eyes went even more skeptical. 'Come on, even I can't buy that one. You've never been that generous with me. There's got to be more to this. What is it?'

The trace of a smile crossed Julian's mouth; he hadn't expected Christian to see through him so quickly. 'You know, you do surprise me sometimes,' he said cuttingly. 'I never gave you credit for being so astute. And don't misunderstand me.' He looked at Christian narrowly. 'I have no more love for you now than I ever have. You've been an abysmal failure all around. Frankly, I don't really expect that to change, though I'd hope you might have some better success at reproducing yourself,' he added irreverently. 'But no, you're right. That's not all.' He moved behind his desk then and stood looking up at the picture of his father. He remained there for a long time, staring at that face so unlike his own, and some emotion played across his eyes. A version of regret, perhaps. It was gone, however, when he turned back. 'Your mother and I would be happy to see the two of you married, but there's one other condition. We want you to prevent a marriage between Adam and Libby. That is the other aspect of my offer, and any additional money depends on your success.' He raised his voice slightly now. 'I will see to it that you are given a larger allowance—a substantially larger allowance, not under Adam's control—only if you see to it that Adam ends this relationship with Libby.'

There wasn't a sound in the room, and after a moment Julian leaned on the desk with both hands, his gaze boring into Christian. 'It is simply unthinkable that he marry her. She is unsuitable, she is . . .' He straightened and stood sternly behind his desk. 'Deficient.' At that, he turned to Edwinna. 'I apologize, my dear, although I don't think it's really necessary.' He gave her a keen look, then smiled darkly. 'As I said to you before, I've been watching you all evening. The devotion lies, I think, with the other party.' When she didn't answer, he nodded once. 'I thought so.' Turning back to Christian still perching on the arm of the chair, he went on. 'I've tried to talk to Adam about this, but I have no influence on him any more. He won't hear a word I say. And I'm telling you it can't be, it mustn't be. I will not stand for any son of mine being married to a blind woman!'

Christian was watching his father thoughtfully. Yes, it most definitely had appeal, a substantial increase in his funds. He calculated the effect it would have on his life style and liked what he saw. And then there was the bit with Adam; he'd be out from under his control. He couldn't keep the sardonic smile from his face. Oh, yes, it was all very definitely appealing. And completely out of reach. 'You left one consideration out of all your conniving,' he said, giving Julian a direct look. 'Adam is immovable. In case you haven't noticed, he's really in love with the woman.' He stood up at that, downing the rest of his drink. 'There's nothing I can do about it.'

Julian watched Christian move off to the far side of the room, his lips pressed together. As always, Christian's immediate defeatism was irritating, and though it had no place in the scheme of things, Julian reacted. 'And so that's it? You tell me it can't be done, and that's it?'

Christian wheeled, the frustration he'd tried to disguise erupting. 'What the hell do you want me to do? I have no influence over Adam. Christ, we don't even speak unless we have to. If he won't listen to you, what in the hell makes you think he'd listen to me?' He scowled abruptly down at his empty glass, thrusting one hand savagely into the pocket of his burgundy jacket.

Julian took the cue Christian had supplied. 'As always, I can see that it is I who will have to take care of this,' he said with a show of heavy resignation. 'You've disappointed me one more time, and although we'd still be pleased to have Winna in the family, you must understand that there isn't going to be any additional money for you.' He began heading for the door.

He'd nearly reached it when Edwinna's voice rang out clearly. 'We accept your offer. And on your terms.'

Julian stopped without turning, smiling in satisfaction to himself; Winna had taken the marriage bait, as he'd calculated she would, and the rest would follow. He turned back to face her finally, his expression by then fashioned into startled surprise. 'Oh?'

Edwinna was standing in front of her chair, smiling. It was Christian who spoke, however. And quickly. 'Edwinna, first of all, the terms are impossible, as I said. And second, there is no "we".'

Edwinna set her glass down on a small table and began to move slowly about the room. Idly, she fingered objects as she passed by them, tilting her head in exaggerated interest as she paid the two men no immediate attention. What had Julian said? 'Time was running out?' It was apropos to far more than just the issue of his two sons producing heirs. She had to do something, and fairly quickly, if for no other reason than the fact that she didn't know how much longer she could continue to convince Libby to keep lending her money. She bit her lip absently, marshaling her thoughts. Julian's offer, of course, was precisely the kind of thing she'd been hoping to arrange, somehow; how convenient that it was being handed to her on a silver platter. Of sorts. After a short consultation with her better judgment, she decided to lay some of her cards on the table with Christian, and nearly laughed aloud for the apt analogy. Another time, it might have been imprudent to be so open, leaving room for slip-ups, but not now. After all, it was she who held the key to the success of Julian's goal; that was the best insurance she could have. She looked over at Christian finally. He was watching her as warily as he had watched his father before. She smiled. 'The terms aren't impossible, as for the "we"?' She shrugged lightly. 'Your father is quite right, you know. We do make a lovely couple.'

In those moments of her circling the room, Christian had made a few decisions of his own. He intended to speak as openly as she, even though he wasn't one, normally, for the direct approach. Unless he was cornered. He set his empty glass down on a table and crossed his arms. 'Edwinna, even if I were in the market for a wife, which I'm not sure I am, it wouldn't be you.' It came out with more difficulty than he'd expected, and uncrossing his arms abruptly, he picked up the glass and crossed to a small butler's bar, drawing out the decanter of whiskey from the tantalus. He poured out a shot, downed it, then poured another. Sufficiently braced, he finally turned back to Edwinna. 'Your waters run a little deeper than I like to tread.'

Winna threw up her chin, sending her silvery hair snaking softly down her back. It was on the tip of her tongue to snap at him, but she realized this was no time for her to take umbrage; he'd already made her do that once before. With some difficulty, she ignored the comment. 'Your father was quite right about another thing,' she said evenly. 'I would find a marriage into this family most appealing. I admit that.' Her composure returned completely as she watched him down the second shot and pour a third; he was such a poor opponent when he was drunk. She went on almost gaily then, brushing a hand up under her silky hair, from nape to crown. 'Christian, I would be very good for you in many ways. I could give you, for one thing, the sort of children who would make your father proud of you.'

It was a depressing thought, being saddled with the chore of bearing children, yet it was a small price to pay, really, to get what she deserved. She smiled more widely. 'And I suspect you wouldn't mind being one up on Adam. Not merely for being out from under his iron financial hand, but because of the far superior appearance you and I would present to the world. That's rather important in the circles in which you like to travel.' She let that register for a moment, then went on. 'We would make a good partnership, you and I, all the way around. And my dear man, it need be nothing more than that.' It was all going to be just as she'd planned, although, of course, she hadn't expected to be so blunt about it. Or, more accurately, so blunt so soon.

Christian had moved over to the desk and perched on it in exactly the same spot his brother had taken hours before. He was watching her detachedly, sipping at his scotch. 'A hoard of adorable brats doesn't happen to be my aspiration. It's my father's, remember?'

'Of course.' She took several steps forward to a leather wingback and sat down on the arm, arranging the fabric of her skirt. She looked back up at him, undaunted. 'However, I doubt you'd object to the superior position that having an heir would put you in. I can give you that.'

'So can a lot of women,' he countered immediately.

'Perhaps.' She smiled complacently. 'But no other woman can give you access to the money you want so badly,' she said softly. It was her real trading point, of course, and she offered it coolly. 'I can. A partnership, Christian. You give me what I want, I'll give you what you want. Marry me, and I'll see to it that you can have your money.' It was out then, the bare bones of it all. Whatever further explanations he might want, he wasn't going to get; the 'whys' and 'hows' were none of his business. The phrase 'take it or leave it' came abruptly to mind, and her smile widened; she hadn't known him long, but she knew him well.

Very well. As he sat there looking at her reflectively, he was already arranging the qualifications of his acceptance in his mind. And his doubtful objections. And all the other padding necessary to his final acquiescence to her; it justified his allowing himself to be maneuvered for the sake of grabbing at a chance that probably wouldn't come along again. He sipped at his scotch, then rested the glass on his thigh.

'You sound very sure of yourself,' he remarked. 'And if that's the case, then I'm afraid you're operating under a few misapprehensions. I said it to Father, and I'll say it to you. Adam is immovable. You don't know him at all. He's got Libby under his skin, whether or not anyone cares to believe that, and when he feels that strongly about something, that's it. It's one of his virtues,' he added sarcastically. 'I just wanted to make that point again before I finish what I have to say.' He paused. 'I don't love you, Edwinna. I'm not sure I even like you, other than . . .' He let the words drift away meaningfully; he was suddenly enjoying his brief shift at the helm. 'As I told you, your waters run a little too deep for me. However, I will marry you. On this one condition. I'd strike up this "partnership" with you if you are able to find some way to meet the terms of Father's offer.'

Julian had remained near the door, listening to the exchange he'd as much as orchestrated. He'd been aware all along, of

287

course, that it was going to be she, not Christian, who might have some way of accomplishing his objective. Christian's doubts, as irritating as they'd been, were no more than Julian himself admitted. And the bait had been aimed as much at her as at Christian, perhaps more accurately, at both of them; one was no good without the other. He considered for a moment the fact of the additional money he was proposing to hand over to Christian's extravagances and grimaced inwardly. But he would do it; he was a man who made good on his contracts. And everything had its price.

When it appeared that Christian had finished and that Edwinna had nothing further to say, he moved back into the depths of the room. They sat some distance apart, like opponents squaring off for the next round, and Julian stepped into a point equidistant between them. 'It seems you've settled things between you,' he remarked blandly, looking from one to the other. 'Marriages of convenience often work out far better than those made for more passionate reasons,' he felt inclined to comment. 'However, that's neither here nor there.' He turned to Winna then and took a step toward her. 'Now, to several matters. First, you do understand that ending this relationship is the only trading point?'

Her silvery smile didn't waver. 'Perfectly.'

He nodded once in affirmation, then gave her a brief, enigmatic smile. 'It gives you no qualms.' He didn't wait for her answer to his remark, but went on. 'And now I would like to know just how you propose to do this. You have heard what Christian has said about Adam, and he knows him far better than you do. So do I, and I happen to agree with him. You will obviously be working in another direction, and I'm interested in exactly how.'

Edwinna stood up then and brushed at the wrinkles in her dress. Crossing wordlessly to the small table, she collected her empty brandy snifter, walked quietly to the door, and laid her hand on the brass knob. There, she finally looked at the two of them, her face radiant with the high flush of confidence. 'Don't worry, I know exactly what to do,' she said.

And then she was gone.

# Chapter 25

The Georgian dining room the next morning was bright and not as formidable as usual, with the sunshine of Christmas Day streaming through the tall windows banked all along one side. Libby and Winna were the first ones down, and they entered through the arched doorway to the aroma of fresh coffee and piping hot food; all across the surface of a long mahogany sideboard, under the hunting mural, were set out chafing dishes of eggs, bacon, ham, and sausage, steaming and as yet untouched.

With Libby's arm in hers, Edwinna took her to the table and waited while she settled herself in a high-backed chair. 'Coffee?' she inquired brightly after a moment.

'Please.' Libby smiled briefly and took up her napkin, arranging it in her lap as she listened to Winna cross the parquet floor to the far side of the room and clink cup on saucer, twice. She'd chosen for the day a simple navy blue dress, with a small round collar of white lace at her throat; her hair was drawn back as she often wore it, clipped away from the temples with two barrettes of gold. She checked one briefly, then smiled again as she heard Winna return and set a cup on the porcelain plate in front of her. 'Thanks.'

Winna slid lightly into the adjacent chair. 'What a feast! Do you suppose they always eat like this?' She described the contents of the sideboard, and as she talked, she reached for the pitcher out in front of her and poured a dollop of cream into her cup. Taking up her spoon, she stirred for a moment before looking back over at Libby. When she still didn't answer, Winna prompted, 'Lib?'

Libby roused herself with a start and smiled immediately. 'I'm sorry, I wasn't listening. What did you say?'

Winna studied her lightly. 'I said, do you suppose they always eat like this? There must be eight trays of food over there.'

Involuntarily, Libby turned back toward her coffee cup and absently traced the rim with one fingertip. 'I suppose.'

At Libby's subdued response, Winna laid down her spoon. Her hair was drawn back in a flattering chignon, and her own dress was as simple as Libby's, apricot in color, a warm hue that flattered her complexion. She reached over and touched Libby's arm with a feigned worry. 'Are you okay?' Pausing appropriately, she went on in a concerned tone. 'You're not dwelling on what I said this morning by any chance, are you? I was just making idle conversation while we dressed. I didn't mean anything by it.' She studied her again, then seemed to grow defensive. 'If I'd thought I was going to get you all upset by popping in to join you like that, I wouldn't have done it. You didn't take anything I said out of context, did you?'

Libby smiled in reassuring admonishment. 'Winna, you know I didn't mind your coming in. And no. I didn't take anything out of context.' It was, of course, exactly what she'd done, but that wasn't Winna's problem. It was her own, that she had felt inclined to take Winna's offhand observations about families like the Bainbridges and fit them into the shape and size of her own anxieties. Such a universal perversity, that need to find things to worry about even when none was readily at hand, or exaggerate those that were, she thought and repressed a sigh. Looking back toward Winna, she forced another smile. 'Winna, I'm fine. Really. Just suffering anticipated exhaustion.' Well, it was a little lame, but it would have to do.

A covert look of satisfaction passed across Winna's face at Libby's unconvincing tone. She removed it instantly, however, and squeezed Libby's arm lightly. 'Well, don't. Save it for later.' She eyed the glasses near Libby's plate then. They were blue crystal like everything else on the table, and there was an eye-pleasing consistency to the entire, extensive collection. All were heavy, with the same ornate, cut-glass pattern covering the surface of each piece. Shapes were purposely identical, straight and cylindrical, and even heights had been duplicated where they could be: the cream pitcher with only the most inconspicuous of spouts and no handle, for instance, was the same height as the juice glasses in front of every place; they could easily be mistaken for one another, if one didn't look closely enough. Winna remained studying it a moment longer, then shifted forward as if in solicitude. 'Lib, water's on the right, juice on the left.' She reached out, rearranging two of the shorter pieces, then relaxed back.

'God! I wonder when all these things were set out? I haven't seen hide nor hair of the kitchen help. Crack of dawn, I suppose.' She nudged Libby lightly with her elbow. 'Don't forget to drink your juice.'

Libby shot her a look of mild annoyance. 'Winna, you needn't sound quite so maternal, you know. And I'll get to it when I'm ready.'

Winna laughed. 'Sorry. It just slipped out. I'm going to get a plate. Want one?'

Though she wasn't really hungry, Libby nodded anyway and put away the mild aggrievance at Winna's remark; she was only trying to be helpful. She sipped her coffee as she listened to Winna's activities across the room at the sideboard, then heard another sound: the firm, brisk thud of heel on stone in the hall, then on parquet as Adam entered the dining room. And against all reason or want, it sent a flood of adrenalin through her, then a rush of cold brought on by formless anxiety. Or not so formless, perhaps. She silently commanded her racing pulse to subside, but it persisted as she turned toward the sound of his approach.

He came directly over, and as he often did, studied her for a moment; her blue dress was belted at the waist and did wonderful things for her figure, he remarked to himself. The sun caught the tones of her hair, making it glow, and he leaned down finally and kissed the top of her head. 'You look terrific. And I thought I'd beat you down. Never let it be said that woman's vanity is greater than man's.' He grinned at that, then left her, crossing over to the sideboard to pour out a cup of coffee.

Edwinna was still there and gave him a stiff smile. He murmured a greeting, but was spared the effort of further civility as the others began to filter in and take their places at the long table. It was all he could muster toward her at this point, the restrained politeness, and even that was only for Libby's benefit. He wondered for the hundredth time, as he lifted the silver coffee urn and tipped it toward his cup, how adamant Libby's defense might be if she were aware of her devoted sister's unexplainable maneuvers toward the man Libby planned to marry, then dismissed the speculation entirely; he'd never know, since he never intended telling Libby. Even for the sake of making a point, there were some things better left unsaid. He nodded to his parents and Christian as he rounded the table again and sat down next to Libby. 'Ready for something to eat?' he asked, glancing at her plate.

It took Libby a moment to come out of the preoccupation that wouldn't leave her alone, and she smiled. 'No, thanks. Winna's getting it, I mean.'

Adam studied her wordlessly for a moment, his cup suspended in mid-air. Despite the brightness of the smile, she wasn't herself. No one knew her expressions better than he, and the one she wore now had a distinctly flat edge to it. It surprised him; she'd seemed all right when she'd left him earlier to go to her own room to dress. He'd lain in his big tester bed, his hands clasped beneath his head as he'd watched her slip on her blue robe and belt it at the waist, and he'd felt the necessity to caution her again before she'd left to temper her expectations of how his family might react to the opening of presents; it wasn't exactly their strong point, gift-giving, he'd reminded. She had no longer been unreceptive to his observations, but in her particular way, had still been optimistic, saying determinedly as she opened the door. 'I hear you, but never make predeterminations. They get you in trouble sometimes. Someone very wise once told me that.' And she'd gone out smiling then, as if in response to some private memory. He wondered as he sat studying her pensive expression if she'd taken his skepticism more to heart when she'd had some time to think about it, but decided not after a moment; Libby wasn't so easily moved from her convictions. Finally, he set down his cup and leaned close to her. 'Honey, do you feel all right? Tell me.'

What, Adam? That it's come back to live with me again, as if it had ever gone away? All the anxiety, the doubts, the worries about the two of us? That no matter how often you reassure me, even in one eloquent, beautiful night, it can still be resurrected by the reminder of who you are and who I'm not, by a mere idle conversation off-handedly given on 'the importance of the right kind of wife to men of such background?' She nearly voiced the thoughts, but caught herself in time. It wasn't the time or the place, but even if it had been, she still wouldn't have. He'd fought out this battle with her as far as he could. She couldn't continue to hound him for assurances but would have to look for them in her own heart.

Well aware of the extent of his ability to read her, she summoned up her best smile and gave it to him. 'Adam, I feel perfectly fine. Really I do. And considering the fact that I'm starved, you might inquire as to what happened to my waitress.' She tilted her head.

It was Winna herself who answered into the murmur of conversation around them. 'Right here.' She set the plate down in front of Libby, then slid into her own chair. 'Sorry, there was a line,' she ad-libbed with a grin and reached over, turning Libby's plate. 'The eggs are in front of you, bacon at eleven o'clock, toast at one. Oh, and I didn't get you any sausage. Didn't think you wanted any.'

Adam watched the small exchange, studying Winna briefly before looking back at Libby. Her smile was more genuine, and he allowed himself to be convinced, finally, that she was all right. He saw to his own plate then, and when he returned, everyone was in place, including Sebastian, who'd been the last to come down. He'd traded blazer and vest for a white shirt and blue cardigan sweater buttoned all the way down the front, with his gold watch chain dangling from one pocket. He was joking with Libby from across the table, and Adam sat down, striking up a friendly conversation with his father. That was for Libby's benefit, too. He'd issued a directive to his father that they all do their best to be pleasant; he intended to abide by it as well.

It was an excellent effort, all around; the conversation flowed steadily and in a light vein. It grew mildly political for a time, engaging everyone, then splintered into separate discussions at opposite ends of the table. As she ate, Libby listened to the clink of glass on glass, silver flatware on china, remarking now and then into each conversation. For the most part, however, she simply sat quietly over her meal, listening in genuine interest to what was going on around her. Across the table, Sebastian, telling anecdotes, was at his best, or possibly his worst; Libby had never been able to decide quite which it was. She smiled for the thought and finished her light breakfast, laughing right along with everyone else at Sebastian's tale despite the fact she'd already heard it at least three times. It didn't matter to her; what did was that there seemed to be a genuine congeniality to the group that morning, a certain thread of togetherness that might have been merely a function of the fact that it was Christmas day. She couldn't help but hope it was that something more: the beginnings of a basis on which they could share, be part of one another. She heard Adam's deep voice beside her, affable, relaxed as he talked with his family. It was that, more than anything else, that went a long way toward restoring her good spirits altogether, and she smiled down toward her hands as she folded her napkin and laid it beside her plate.

'And I must tell you about the trip Libby and I took to Monticello one winter's day. Years ago. It was, well . . .'

It was Sebastian, on another story. Libby reached for her juice glass, found it, then eased back against the chair to settle in for what was already promising to be a mildly embarrassing recital; Sebastian tended to deliver these stories with all the archness of an overindulgent parent. With good-natured resignation, she went ahead and put the vaguely chagrined smile in place—it would be required anyway—and lifted the glass, absently taking a sip.

It happened all in one mortifying split second: the narrow glass came away from her mouth with a spasmodic jerk as she choked audibly on tepid heavy table cream that should have been juice; the thick liquid sloshed down the front of her dress; the pitcher, when she finally got it back to the table and felt for the first, agonizing time the narrow spout at the very lip of the receptacle, clattered against her china plate then fell over, oozing the remainder of the thick liquid onto the linen table-cloth.

Stunned silence fell down around her like a stifling cloak. In that one moment, when she knew every eye was trained on her, she felt larger than life, separated from all the rest of them by her capacity for making such a humiliating mistake. As abruptly as it had fallen, the silence was finally broken as Winna and Adam both came to life simultaneously, grabbing napkins as they leaned toward her, patting her lap, righting the glass, rubbing her back when she let out one last cough.

A buzz of dismissive voices went up in the background as Libby said twice, almost unconsciously. 'I'm sorry.' Augustine at the far end of the table murmured insincerely, her expression going more pinched than usual as she eyed the white stain spreading across the bodice of Libby's dress. Julian grimaced, catching Christian's brief look in his direction. Sebastian was busily at work, his brow creased in a frown of high consternation as he stood up and leaned across the table to mop the cloth with his napkin, moving glassware around, setting aside a silver candelabra directly in the path of the spreading spill.

For Libby, the flurry of helpful activity around her was almost more dreadful than the incident itself. The two people flanking her were still at it, and she could feel someone, Sebastian she was certain, bumping the table as he, too, tried to be of assistance. In the confusion of voices, movements, and her own turmoil of emotions, Adam's voice finally penetrated. 'Libby. Are you all right?' He'd put aside his napkin and was leaning close, holding onto her arm; he didn't like her color, or rather the absence of it, at all.

'I'm fine.' It came out stridently, and she took her own napkin, pressing it against her damp breast. 'I don't know how I managed to do that . . .'

As her normal color began to return, Adam relaxed somewhat and picked up his own napkin again to dab at his trouser leg. The

294

trousers were a light wool, contrasting with his dark sports jacket and white shirt, and he brushed at the wetness unconcernedly, keeping his eye on her. 'You picked up the wrong glass, that's all,' he said calmly. 'It was the cream for the coffee. The glassware is identical.' He balled up the napkin, tossing it back on the table as he shot a look at his mother at the far end of the table. 'Change it,' he said sharply, then looked back to Libby. 'No harm done.'

Change it. For Libby, who might very well do it again. And no harm done because she can't help herself. Out of nowhere the unnatural self-censure came to her, and she pushed it away; it could have no place in her life. The intractable cold in the pit of her stomach had returned, but began to subside as she got herself in hand finally. It was nearly gone altogether, until Julian spoke.

He was eyeing Adam disapprovingly from his chair at the head of the table. 'Adam, I think the two of you can go up now and change.'

Libby's hand flew back to her breast, this time in consternation. 'Oh, Adam! Did I get you, too?' The cold came back in a wave, tensing her shoulders as a vision came to her of the two of them sitting drenched and disheveled against a backdrop of elegance and refinery. Any other time it would have made her laugh; she didn't then, however. She couldn't.

Adam did, intentionally. His handsome face took on a light grin. 'Of course, love. I've always told you your aim is superb. And frankly, I've never liked these trousers anyway. I only wore them because plaids and stripes go so well together.' He saw that the attempt at humor was going nowhere with her and gave it up, taking her arm as he rose. 'Come on. I'll take you up.'

She stood up immediately, and they left the room. When they'd reached the foot of the staircase, Libby stopped, putting her head in her hands. 'Oh, Adam.' The words came out muffled.

Without speaking, he removed her glasses and slipped them into his side pocket, arranging her arms around his neck as he pulled her into an embrace. 'Libby, don't be so undone. For God's sake, it was only an accident.' She was resting with her head against his chest, and he eased a hand between them, raising her face up so he could look into it; it was etched with uncharacteristic unhappiness. 'Honey, it doesn't matter,' he said, then cocked his head. 'And anyway, where'd you leave your sense of humor? You and I ought to be laughing uproariously right about now.'

Libby let her arms slide down away from his shoulders then

and stepped back, sighing quietly to herself. Her sense of humor? It was lying back there under the table somewhere, knocked out cold when she'd made them both look so—what? She didn't finish the thought and merely shook her head, feeling for the banister with her hand. She found it and began quietly mounting the stairs.

Adam remained at the foot, pensively studying her slender back as it moved slowly upward toward the galleried landing. Concluding that any further efforts at dismissive reassurance would merely compound the problem, he stood deliberating over some effective way to revive her equanimity. After a moment, his expression began to clear and a small light of inspiration came into his eyes. He went up after her then, taking the carpeted steps two at a time, catching her just at the landing. He was grinning by then and without a word, swept her up in his arms, looking down into her face with laughing eyes as he held her easily. 'I think, my love, we could do an excellent rendition of Scarlet and Rhett if we tried. That's providing, of course, I don't drop you on the way up.'

She'd been completely startled at the abrupt action and was looking up toward him speechlessly, her arms clasped loosely around his neck, her long hair flowing down past his arm. Another vision of the two of them came to her suddenly, making her close her mouth on what she'd finally been about to say: that of a handsome, broad-shouldered man on a staircase landing, holding in his arms a stupefied damsel in wringing-wet distress. It was too much, even for her disheartened spirits, and, abruptly, she threw back her head and gave him a very good display of her most uproarious laughter.

The tree in the niche of the living room window was lit. Behind it, the mullioned window rose nearly to the ceiling, and folds of royal blue velvet lapped down over the edges in generous swags. The snow-covered countryside with its pine trees and shrubbery beyond filtered in through the leaded glass like a montage of small, diamond-shaped pictures, and with its twinkling lights and tinsel dancing silver in the crystal clear day, the tree was like a fanciful jewel in a setting of colorful, beribboned packages. The small electric locomotive beneath whirred its way around like a miniature bearer of good will.

That was how Adam described it to Libby as they stood arm in arm in the arch of the living room doorway. She had changed into a tartan plaid skirt and white blouse that tied at the throat, he into an epauleted checked shirt and dark trousers. Winna and the family were dispersed about the long room, waiting for the couple's reappearance, and when Adam finished speaking, Winna came directly over.

She put her hand on Libby's arm, gazing worriedly into her face. 'Everything okay?'

Libby had thought and heard enough about the whole thing. 'I'm fine,' she said clearly, then looked out toward Sebastian somewhere in the room. 'I hear you've got the train running, Sebastian.'

He was threading his way through the scattered furniture toward them, and as he approached, he gave Adam a quizzical look; an imperceptible nod reassured him, and he kissed Libby then on the cheek. 'Of course. What's the Holiday Express without a reliable engineer?'

She smiled. 'Right. Now come on, I think we've held things up for long enough. Shall we get started?' In taking the initiative, she effectively put the episode behind them. It was more for everyone else's benefit than her own, which wasn't unusual; she'd been doing it all her life.

'Yes, let's.' Edwinna stepped away, motioning toward Christian to begin rearranging chairs. He did, with help from everyone else, and they were arranged into a semi-circle facing the tree. Julian's at the center. The group gathered then, and Libby directed Adam to make their post on the floor near the packages.

The whole thing might have had a poor start had it not been for Libby, once again. Determined to see the whole thing through, and in an effort to lighten the formality in the air, she drew out an oblong package immediately and handed it over to Adam. 'Read the tag.' She was on her knees, her hands clasped lightly in the folds of her pleated skirt as she waited expectantly. He called off his mother's name, then extended the gift from Christian. It was a Dior silk scarf in appropriate mauve, and she'd barely murmured her appreciation when Libby had another gift ready, handing it again to Adam. 'Don't be so slow!' she chided in a stage whisper. It elicited tentative laughter all around, and they were on their way.

Sweaters, perfume, jewelry, leather wallets, gold watchbands; they were exchanged with moderate congeniality as crumpled foil wrappings and lengths of ribbon began to litter the floor around the chairs. Winna's gift to Libby was a sterling silver stickpin, which she delivered herself after rooting around in the pile of packages. Libby's gift to her was a round gold locket, fitted inside with tiny photos of their parents and engraved on the back. 'To Winna, Love Libby and Adam, 1980.' The box of old mementos had been left in its place at home, in Libby's mind too personal a thing to be given so openly. She'd do that later, when they were alone and the time was right. The locket, she'd thought, was a suitable substitute, expressing the same sentiment. And another. Libby and Adam, 1980; it might have been the most meaningful of all.

Immediately after Winna had finished exclaiming warmly over her gift and set the small box aside with the others around her feet, Libby brought out another, handing it to Adam. He glanced at the tag, then grinned, handing it back. 'You can read this one yourself.'

It was one of her own, wrapped in a textured foil, the red tag struck in braille, then lettered out below in Adam's casual script. She ran her fingers lightly over the raised impressions, a small, mysterious smile coming to her lips. 'Merry Christmas to Sebastian. Love, Libby. To Happy Endings,' she read lightly, then held out the box in the direction of his hearty exclamation.

From their chairs in the crescent around him, the others watched curiously as he unwrapped the gift. When he had the paper off and the box open, he fell back against his chair in laughter, bringing out the object. It was a caboose, painted red on the sides and green on the top. 'To happy endings,' he harrumphed and rose, crossing first to plant a kiss on the top of Libby's head, then to the tree; he knelt down, rummaging in the packages before finally bringing one out. 'Out of order, I know, but appropriate, nonetheless. Read the card, pet, then open it.' He handed her the box, then eased himself back into his chair, perching on the edge as he waited in open anticipation.

Not one of her own, the tag was nevertheless struck in braille. 'To Lizbeth, Love Sebastian,' she read from her spot on the floor, then began tearing off the paper, opening the box to run her fingers lightly over the object inside. She burst into laughter, and at Adam's impatient inquiry, finally brought out the small object, holding it up with both hands. It was another caboose, this one green on the sides and black on the top. 'Well, Sebastian,' she said when her laughter had subsided, 'never let it be said there's no such thing as telepathy. And it's just what the Holiday Express needed. A pair of cabooses.'

'Cabeese,' Sebastian said loftily and settled back comfortably in his chair.

The ceremony went on; Manning in his impeccable uniform carried in a tray of coffee and cinnamon toast midway through, setting the ornate silver service down on a tea table near

Augustine's elbow. Winna called a break and played the role of hostess, graciously serving first Julian, then Augustine before going on down the line. When it was done, Libby resumed the distribution of the gifts, until finally there were only two gifts left to exchange: Libby's to Adam, and his to her. Unobtrusively, she'd found, then drawn out the small box and kept it under the fold of her pleated skirt on the floor beside her. When it was time, she brought it out. Its tag had no printing, only the tiny raised impressions. 'Here, Adam. Read the tag,' she said quietly.

He accepted the gift, looking briefly at Libby's lightly flushed face before turning his attention to the tag. He ran his fingers across the paper, a mild frown of concentration creasing his brow. It took him a moment or two, but finally he had it and repeated the inscription. 'To Adam, for what you are to me. Libby.'

Libby lowered her head, pressing her lips together as she clasped her hands tightly in her lap. Adam opened the box and unfolded the tissue paper inside, and after a moment, he brought out the small carving. He studied it wordlessly, turning it over and over, finally letting it lie in the palm of one hand while he simply looked at it.

'What is it?' Christian's voice broke into the stillness, and he shifted in his chair off to Adam's left, mildly uncomfortable for the palpable tension that had descended upon the room.

'A man on a horse. You wouldn't understand,' Adam murmured. He looked away from the carving finally and slowly over at Libby. 'You did this yourself, didn't you?' he asked.

Libby's lips were still pressed together tensely, and she nodded. He looked back at the object in his hand, completely at a loss for words. For all the expensive gifts he'd been given there that day, there was nothing that meant more to him than this; probably nothing ever would again. He searched his mind for something to say to her, something that might convey the depths of his emotion; there was nothing.

Libby was still kneeling beside him and finally could bear his silence no longer. Though acutely conscious of the others around them, she couldn't ignore her need to know his reaction, and, finding his shoulders, she lifted both hands to his face. Her fingers were almost tremulous as she softly touched his cheeks, his lips, trying to read his expression. Her own was visibly uncertain as she leaned toward him, willing him to say something to her. 'Adam, do you like it?' she whispered.

He looked at her, then slowly put down the carving and

reached over to remove her glasses and lay them aside. He took her face then in his own hands, as she still held his, and for a moment, all time seemed suspended as they remained that way, two people touching hand to face and joined together by a love so profound it could have no expression in the spoken word. It radiated from them, leaving their onlookers involuntarily spellbound in silence. Suddenly, Adam dropped his hands, pulling her into his arms. And he kissed her then, as deeply and passionately as if there was no one else in the room. As he cradled her in his arms, his heart was in his embrace.

She wanted to respond, but couldn't, not under such watchful eyes; she could never feel the same obliviousness he did. Acutely uncomfortable despite his eloquent reaction, she pushed at him, trying to make him release her.

He did finally and with it, the tension disappeared. Sebastian was the first to speak. 'Pet, I think it's safe to say he likes it.'

The remark brought a rustle of relieved movement. Adam watched Libby as she tried to regain her composure; her blush was high as she shifted to her knees beside him again and smoothed her skirt self-consciously with both hands. He ignored the disapproving murmur of his mother's voice and reached out to run the back of one finger softly along the contour of Libby's cheek. 'Yes, Libby. I think it's safe to say he likes it.'

Libby could merely shake her head and continue to look down toward her hands. Adam got to his feet then as the others began milling around, and went to a telephone at the far side of the room. He dialed, spoke briefly into it, then returned. Libby was still kneeling in her place on the floor, and he reached down to take her hand, pulling her up, 'Come on.'

'Adam, what are you doing?' She was laughing as she came to her feet and briefly brushed at the back of her skirt.

His smile was enigmatic. 'I have something for you. Come on.'

He took her then completely out of the room, into the hall and to the front door. She was smiling in anticipation and some confusion as he helped her slip on her camel coat, then shrugged into his own. A shaft of light from the circular window set high above the front door flooded across the cavernous room and illuminated the small band of people filtering out from the living room to follow. Adam took Libby's arm again. 'Where are we going?' she demanded.

He pulled open the door, smiling briefly at the wreath perched behind the ears of the gargoyle, all but obscuring it; he'd taken the utmost pleasure in hooking it there the night before. 'For a walk, that's all.'

And he took her all the way out of the house, out into the snowy drive; as they approached the appointed spot near the ornate bird bath in the middle of the circle, jeweled now and crusted over with snow, he glanced ahead of them and smiled at the stable hand approaching. He was leading a silver-gray Arabian mare, one hand on the bridle up near the mare's chin, the other holding the drape of the reins. Adam let the man get almost to them before gesturing for him to stop. He did, and the mare raised her fine head alertly, pricking her ears forward as she watched the two strangers approach. In the background, the ivy-covered house rose majestically toward the cerulean sky, its scattering of narrow leaded windows like eyes watching the scene below; in its doorway was a cluster of people, as silent, as watchful.

A brief gust of wind picked up strands of Libby's hair, blowing them about her face as she moved carefully forward with Adam. When they had reached the horse, Adam lifted her hand from the sleeve of his thick sheepskin parka and placed it on the mare's neck; Libby started visibly.

He smiled down quietly. 'For you, my love. The finest horseflesh I could find. It's a mare, the silver-gray Arabian you told me you always wanted. Now you have her.'

It was Libby's turn to be speechless. She raised one hand to her lips in disbelief, keeping the other tentatively on the horse's neck, running her fingertips along the delicate flesh. What she'd always wanted? Yes. A dream that to a young girl had been a confident anticipation, as certain as the next's day's coming, if only one had the patience to wait so long, and that as a woman had become just another wistful daydream, until a man named Adam had come into her life. She swallowed once, then suddenly stepped forward and threw her arms around the horse's neck, hugging it as she laid her head against the warm body. Curiously, the mare looked around and reached out with her nose, sniffing at Libby's motionless shoulder. At that, Libby raised her head and found, then softly petted the velvet muzzle, an unconscious smile lighting up her face. After a few moments, she turned abruptly back to Adam, holding out her hand to him; her green eyes were shimmering.

He took it, then slipped his arms around her as she stepped back to him. She rested her forehead against his shoulder briefly. 'Adam . . .' she began, at a loss.

His smile was deeply satisfied. 'Do you think it's safe to say she likes it?' he inquired at her pause.

She began to laugh then, reaching up to lay a hand once again against his cheek. 'I think it's safe to say.' She kissed him lightly, then turned her attention back to the horse. 'What's her name?'

'She hasn't got one. That's up to you.'

He watched her look down toward the deep snow underfoot pensively for a time, then saw the inspiration when it hit; it was etched in her smile when she looked back up at him. 'Then I'll call her Christmas,' she said softly, 'so that for as long as I live, I'll never, ever forget this day.'

# Chapter 26

Lunch at midday was light, for Christmas dinner later was to be elaborate: a dressed turkey, yams, vegetables, plum pudding with hard sauce. A servant saw to the disposal of the discarded wrapping paper and ribbons in the living room while the family was at the dining table; after the buffet luncheon, the group split up. In the hall, Winna saw Libby making her way alone to the living room and caught up with her, slipping her arm through hers. 'What a lovely day it's been so far. And I can't thank you enough for the locket. It's beautiful.'

Libby smiled. 'I'm glad you like it. I thought perhaps you'd want the pictures. There were some other things I wanted to give you, but I left them at home.' She paused, tempted to tell Winna just exactly what they were, but resisted; it would ruin the surprise. 'They're just some personal things, and I thought it had best be done when we have some time alone.' It brought to mind what else she needed to say to Winna, and she stopped. 'Winna, I have to talk to you for a moment. About Sebastian. I tried to explain before we left Fairfax . . .'

'Never mind, Libby. It's not important.' Which it wasn't, in the face of other things. 'I overreacted, that's all,' she dismissed vaguely.

Libby abruptly began moving again, putting the subject away for the last time. Perhaps Winna really felt that way now, but if she didn't, her hurt might be assuaged by time; Libby wasn't going to press any more. 'All right,' she said, and went on to another subject that worried her far more at the moment. 'I think everyone enjoyed the day, don't you? Adam was so very skeptical, but I think the Bainbridges were receptive, don't you?' Or at least not totally unreceptive, she qualified to herself. She flushed again at the recollection of Adam's reaction to her gift, in some renewed self-consciousness, but now that she was out from under scrutiny, in pleasure also. That and the enormity of his gift to her had actually dimmed her perception of everything else, which was why she'd put the question to Winna.

Winna heard but didn't respond immediately. They had reached the living room archway, coming to a standstill in it, and she glanced briefly into the room. Adam was there, lighting a cigarette; Julian was in his chair, his head resting back against the cushion, his eyes closed; Christian as always was mixing a drink at the bar, and Sebastian was idly leafing through one of the Bainbridges' beautifully bound books. He looked up just as their footsteps sounded on the bare floor and caught Winna's eye; the look held until she broke it. She turned back to Libby and took the opening the inquiry had offered. 'Well,' she said gravely and paused for the inference to sink in. 'I wanted to talk to you about that. And a few other things.' She turned them around abruptly. 'Let's go somewhere quiet. I . . . well, I'll tell you when we get there.'

Libby quelled the immediate stab of anxiety she'd felt at Winna's response. 'All right,' she said with a smile of conscious composure, not for Winna's benefit, but for her own. 'But let me tell Adam first. He'll wonder where I am.'

'No.' Then Winna softened her imperative tone as she began moving them toward the staircase. 'We won't be gone that long. Just a few minutes. Really.' She patted Libby's hand in reassurance.

'All right. But do me a favor? If I should nod off while you're talking, don't take it personally. I'm beginning to feel that exhaustion I talked about earlier.' Libby was taking the offensive against the still nagging disquiet.

Winna laughed at that and took them to the staircase, where they mounted slowly toward the upstairs hall. Below, Sebastian had come to stand in the archway of the living room, the book still open in one hand as he watched their ascent with a deep frown; they disappeared finally around the landing. He glanced back over his shoulder into the living room and, seeing Adam, thought of going to him. He didn't, however; he had nothing to tell him, really, except that Winna's show of devotion throughout the day disturbed him greatly, as did the incident at breakfast; neither was natural. He looked back slowly to the empty staircase, to the galleried landing with its full-length portrait of some long-forgotten female relative at the back, then sighed, discovering abruptly that the open book was dangling from his hand. 'Devotion,' he murmured darkly to the faded woman in the distant picture, then turned to walk pensively back into the living room.

Christian turned away from the bar and looked over at Adam, silhouetted against the tall window. Christian eyed him a moment, then strolled over. 'Black jack?'

Adam gave him a passive look, then let his eyes drift over Christian's shoulder to the room beyond. 'No, thanks. I want to see about Libby.'

At that, Christian stared into the depths of his scotch for a moment, something unrecognizable passing fleetingly across his eyes. The recollection of this morning, and two people caught up in an emotion he couldn't possibly fathom. Or perhaps he'd already had too much to drink. He looked up again and waved his glass dismissively. 'She's all right. She and Edwinna went off somewhere, up to change. Or woman talk, maybe. Come on. Two hands?'

Adam looked around the room once more; Julian was dozing, Sebastian shifting about restively on a camel-back couch, his gaze leveled into the pages of a book. Something struck Adam, and he focused his eyes more sharply on the volume, after a moment letting out an involuntary laugh; it was upside down. He wondered vaguely at the man's preoccupation, then returned to his own thoughts of Libby. She had looked a little worn around the edges and had probably gone up to lie down. He decided it would do her good, and for lack of anything better to do, turned to Christian and capitulated. 'All right. Stud.'

Christian nodded and strode briskly to a tall Georgian secretary, locating a deck of cards in the third drawer down. They were settled in a matter of minutes at a small inlaid card table near the Christmas tree, and Christian dealt; settling himself back in the uncomfortable straight chair, one leg propped over the other, Adam opened. 'Five,' he said, eyeing his cards, then laid them down. He picked up his cigarette and looked blandly at Christian through the curl of gray smoke.

'Hundred?' Christian inquired offhandedly.

'Dollars.'

'Jesus, don't break yourself.'

Adam merely gave him a look. And lost the hand. Another was dealt, they played it, and afterwards another and another, until finally they switched to blackjack; Christian was in his element by then and dealt rapidly, flipping one down, one up to each of them. The time drifted by; Augustine came and went in intermittent trips to the kitchen, overseeing the preparation of dinner. Julian continued to doze in his chair by the fireplace, opening his eyes every now and then to glance across the way to Sebastian, engrossed in his book, or at his two sons lost to their card game. At length, Adam tossed in his cards and checked his watch, surprised to discover nearly an hour and a half had gone by since they'd begun. He straightened, running a hand briefly through his hair. 'I've had it.'

Christian leaned back in his chair, tilting the legs off the floor. 'Pay up.'

Although he'd heard him, Adam didn't answer immediately. His attention had strayed to the hall doorway and been caught by Libby and Winna, who'd just appeared arm in arm. He was absorbed in studying Libby's expression as she spoke smilingly to Sebastian, and he frowned unconsciously; her expression was the same one she'd been wearing earlier at the breakfast table, when he'd first come down. He roused himself finally when Christian repeated his demand.

'That was a friendly game,' Adam said casually.

Christian eyed him for a moment, then smiled. 'Yes. Yes, I suppose it was. A friendly game. Between brothers. Between one who holds all the cards and one who doesn't.' At Adam's faintly quizzical expression, he looked away abruptly; he'd expected to get a bit more satisfaction out of the remark, and the win at cards. He couldn't imagine why he hadn't.

Adam rose and headed in the direction of Libby and Winna over at the satin-striped love seat by the hearth, only to halt three paces later when Sebastian called to him.

'Relatives?' The elderly man had left Libby's side and was peering interestedly at a row of photographs grouped together on the wall, daguerreotypes of men in tails and top hats, women in petticoats and parasols, all of them with the sepia tint of age.

Adam glanced once at Libby, who was smiling at Winna, then back to Sebastian several feet away; the man was clearly interested, and Adam let himself be sidetracked. 'Unfortunately,' he remarked. 'I've been dragged through these things a hundred times, but I still couldn't tell you who they are. You should ask Father.'

'What?' Julian was already strolling up behind them.

'The family skeletons. Sebastian was inquiring about them,' Adam offered and fielded his father's dark look with a mild grin. It was a remark promising an exchange just to Christian's taste, and in moments he'd joined them too.

On the far side of the room, Winna had left Libby alone for a moment while she went over to the small bar. She returned with two cordial glasses in hand, and set one down on the coffee table in front of Libby's knees. 'Sherry. I thought you might like some.'

Libby looked up briefly. 'No thanks.'

Winna stood looking at her for a moment, then sank down on the edge of the couch, facing her. 'Drink it. It'll do you good.'

Libby pressed her lips together. 'Winna, I don't need anything.' Except another life, to be another person. She closed her eyes briefly at the thought, then opened them again, giving Winna a tired smile. 'I'm sorry. I didn't mean to be so short.'

Winna was biting her bottom lip, doing her best to look guilty as she perched on the edge of the couch in an earnest attitude, her hands clasped in a tight ball on her knees. 'Libby, I had to say those things. It was . . . I . . .'

Libby laid a quieting hand on her arm. 'It's all right. I know, Winna.' And I would have done the same for you, she added silently—would have had to. Because they were honest with each other, and without honesty a relationship could have no meaning, couldn't maintain its integrity. Honesty. She hated that word suddenly, a word she'd tried to live by all her life. It took away illusions and left only the stark realities of life. 'It's all right,' she said again.

'No, Libby, it's not all right, because I've hurt you. But I needed to tell you what I feel about you and Adam, what I see now that I've spent some time around the two of you. I can't bear for you to be hurt, and I'm just afraid . . .' She paused, then went on resolutely. 'Libby, I wouldn't feel this way if Adam weren't the kind of man he is, so . . . well, so different from you. You can't get away from the fact that appearances will always constitute a problem for a Bainbridge. With his family's apparent hostility toward you and after the embarrassing incident this morning, I . . .' She let up on the hammering repetition, then finished heavily. 'Well, I just had to talk to you, that's all.'

'I know,' Libby said again. They'd talked for a long time that afternoon, she and Winna. After a halting start, Winna had done what she felt she had to, expressed thoughts about her future with Adam that were no more than Libby, herself, had known all along. It had hurt, that outside acknowledgment of her inadequacies, drawn out in painstaking detail. She'd found herself making some effort at objection, but only a token one; irrefutable truths couldn't be denied, and now, with benefit of the vision of someone who had the objectivity of emotional distance, and with the disheartening evidence of the past day and a half, those truths weighed more heavily than ever before.

Winna was appraising her steadily. Satisfied finally with the effect, she went on. 'Libby, I said what I felt had to be said. But after all, that doesn't mean that's *all* there is to be said on the subject. Maybe in our efforts to be so painfully objective, we're both being too pessimistic.' Her tone grew decidedly cheerful, as if she'd just thought of the rationalization and was trying to believe it herself. 'Maybe we're making too much of all the problems. We've talked them out, we know they're there, but that doesn't mean things can't work out,' she said, touching Libby's arm. 'There are always ways to do that, and you ought to know that better than anyone. This situation's just going to take a little more effort, that's all. Just try a little harder, Libby.'

Libby gave her another tired smile, grateful that the subject was finally being dropped. She couldn't think about it any more, not now, and found herself after a moment clinging to the hope that, in the light of a new day, there might even be a way of believing what Winna had just said. The frail hope grew tenuously stronger in her need for it to. And leave it to Winna to try to make up for something hurtful she'd done or said, and with wording that left a good bit to be desired. Try a little harder? Winna would never in a thousand years understand just exactly what that meant, but Libby had long ago forgiven her and the rest of the world for their inexactitudes. There wasn't anyone who tried harder than she did, every waking moment of her life. Sometimes she tried so hard she wanted to start screaming, and go on and on until its echoes had made a ring around the earth. She was abruptly conscious of the self-pity and put it away; like so many other things, it had no place in her life either.

After a moment, she felt Winna rise and move past her legs. She could hear movements close by at the mantle, and at length, Winna returned, sitting down beside her again.

'On to lighter subjects,' Winna remarked brightly. 'I want to show you something. Here.' She placed an object in Libby's hands, then relaxed back against the taut cushion of the couch with a bright smile, pleased at her sudden inspiration. 'Remember the game we used to play when we were kids? "Touch and see" you always called it. Well, tell me what it is.' She crossed her arms, motioning with one hand toward the object. 'Come on. What do you think it is?'

Libby consciously kept her smile bland. She recognized Winna's tone only too well; she used it nearly every day herself, with the children. It said, 'Cheer up. We're doing something fun.' She wondered vaguely if she sounded so patronizingly smug, and determined she'd listen carefully the next time, so she could change her tone if that were the case. And yet, for all her mild irritation at Winna's murmur, she knew she was only trying to help. Well, all right; she'd play along. It was either that or sit here, a despondent lump of humanity propped against the arm of the couch. She felt better for the absurd mental picture that popped into her head and offered Winna a resolute sigh.

'Okay.' She settled more comfortably in the cleft of the sofa arm, and ran her fingers lightly over the longish object, touching its underside, its top, the details of its face. After a moment, she tilted her head and gave the required answer. 'It's a cat.'

'A leopard, Libby.' Winna's voice had taken on a trace of awe as she looked down at the exquisite antique in Libby's hands. 'It's just beautiful, and I wanted you to see it, to have a chance to feel it. It's Meissen, Lib. Priceless. It's been in Augustine's family for generations and probably really ought to be in a museum somewhere . . .'

'Take it!' Libby didn't mean for the words to come out as a strident whisper, but they did. She drew a breath against the unreasonable anxiety that had once again flooded over her and went on in a facsimile of her more normal voice. 'Winna, please. Just take it away and put it back where it belongs.'

Winna's eyes were wide, shimmering with a blue light. 'Libby, for God's sake. Don't be so worried about it,' she admonished and reached over to remove the object from her hands.

In her nervousness, Libby had transferred the leopard to both hands, and it lay on the flat of her palms, her fingers curled protectively around it. Winna lifted it from her hands, but just as she did so, she purposely jostled Libby's untouched glass of sherry out on the table in front of them with her knee, knocking it over and spilling it. She jolted as if in surprise and let go of the leopard abruptly.

And gave it back to Libby.

She was totally unprepared. At the removal of the pressure of the object, Libby'd relaxed and begun to lower her hands. Suddenly—unbelievably!—the leopard was there again, and in the small confusion of Winna's muttered oath and spasmodic movements toward the glass, Libby scrambled to get hold of the thing again, fumbling with it, juggling almost, knowing in those moments of desperation the taste of true fear. It washed over her entirely after a moment in a cresting wave, for she was unable to get any real purchase on the leopard and it finally fell out of her hands altogether.

The shattering came moments later as it hit the brickwork that extended in a wide border around the hearth, as terrible a sound as Augustine's simultaneous cry from the doorway.

'My God, she's broken the leopard!'

Across the length of the room, Adam spun, his startled eyes lighting first on his mother in the doorway, her face contorted in stricken horror, then on the two sisters, both on their feet by then. Winna's hand was clapped across her mouth as she stared down at the bricks, Libby's was clutched at the base of her throat, as if she were pinning inside some anguished cry. He crossed the room at a near run, the others on his heels, and they descended in a group on the two women. Augustine was still too stunned to move.

'Oh my God,' Adam breathed in consternation when he'd reached the scene. He was looking not at the fragments of the leopard scattered across the red bricks as he spoke, but at Libby. Her face was ashen, stark against the dark color of her hair, and he was afraid she was going to collapse any moment. He reached out toward her and took a step to move around the coffee table. It was in that instant that Augustine exploded.

'You are an impossibility!' Through the confusion of voices that had gone up in the room, Augustine's carried like a viper's hiss above them all.

Adam's motion halted just short of Libby, and he wheeled, his eyes wide in disbelief. 'Mother!'

She stood framed in the wide archway, a thin figure in gray, the veins standing out in her neck clearly visible even from that distance. She finally moved and began to approach slowly, her eyes like two pools of venom as she kept them riveted on Libby. 'You've done nothing but disrupt this household ever since you got here, you have done nothing but impossible things, and now this!' Her chin flew up as she gestured spasmodically toward the leopard.

Adam's eyes were snapping. 'Shut up!'

Augustine was not to be stilled, and she turned on him then as she stopped near the coffee table with its unnoticed puddle of sherry and the scene of destruction beyond. She was a diminutive figure of a woman beside Adam, yet towering in her violent fury. 'She is an embarrassment! A complete embarrassment! To us, to you, even to herself!'

Adam could barely find his voice in the face of this outrage. 'I'm warning you, Mother. If you don't end this immediately . . .'

'Don't you dare tell me what to do!' she snapped shrilly and threw her head up in a frenzy of uncontrollable wrath. 'This is my home, do you hear me? You will not tell me what to do or say in my own home!' She stamped a narrow foot against the thin carpet, beside herself with a lifetime's accumulation of repressed emotion. 'All your life, Adam, all your life you've been difficult, nothing but a trial, doing only the opposite of what your father and I would want or expect. He's put up with your incurable irresponsibility, and I've put up with your insults. Is that what this is then? The ultimate insult? Bringing this deficient creature into my home so she can offend us all by acting like an onerous child at the table, then go on to destroy the things that have been in my family for nearly a century? And you propose to marry her, so that she can continue to come here and bump her way around until there is nothing left and we are all writhing in humiliation?' Her eyes were glassy now. 'Well, I simply won't stand for it!'

'Then go straight to hell, where you belong!' Adam roared.

'How dare you curse at me!'

'How dare I curse at you? Oh, dear Christ!' He closed his eyes in impotent rage. When he opened them again, they were flashing a hatred he had never so openly acknowledged, even inwardly. 'It's not Libby who is the impossibility, but you!'

All around them, the small assemblage of people were stunned and rendered mute by the violent exchange, even Julian, who might have understood not to push so far. Edwinna was staring, her lips unconsciously parted, Libby still by her side. Augustine and Adam were oblivious to all of them, so furiously was the storm of their emotions raging around them. Augustine's lips were pressed into a colorless line. 'What do you intend to do about this?'

'Do?' he snapped in a deadly, low voice. 'There is nothing to be done. You're hopelessly poisoned with your own venomous prejudices, a spider forever caught up in your own web, in this mean, trivial little existence you lead. Here among your precious heirlooms!' His hand swept the room in one motion.

'For which you apparently have no regard!' Augustine took a step nearer, her chin raised disdainfully. 'You have no regard for anything of grace and elegance. You never really have. And now you'd prefer a life of constant disaster and embarrassment with this woman instead of the one you were born to! I should've expected no more from you. I should've known someday I'd be ashamed to call you a son of mine!'

'As ashamed as I am to admit to being one!'

In front of the narrow love seat, Libby was standing perfectly still, her lips pressed together, her fingernails digging into the flesh of both arms that were wrapped tightly across her body. Every word flung at and around her was like a white-hot iron being thrust into her, searing her heart, her mind. But she said nothing, did nothing: she couldn't. The world and all of life itself might have stopped for her, so motionlessly still did she stand in the face of the tirade, visibly flinching only once—she closed her eyes—at Augustine's relentless voice and the brutal cruelties it was delivering. Finally, she felt the warmth of a hand on her arm, Sebastian's hand. Protectively, he slid an arm across her shoulders, speaking near her ear. 'Come on, pet,' he said, his voice breaking slightly. 'You will not stand here and listen to this. Come on. Come with me.'

She wondered if her legs had turned to stone as she let him turn her; they would barely move. She took his arm then and quietly went with him from the room, the vitriolic exchange continuing unabated behind her as their departure went completely unnoticed. The last thing she heard as she passed through the archway into the cavernous hall was Adam's deep voice raised once again in recrimination. 'You've been as unfit a mother as you seem to think I've been a son!' and she closed her eyes to the vision of them, digging her nails into Sebastian's arm.

At the foot of the wide staircase, Sebastian stopped, removed her hand from his arm and placed it on the polished banister. His eyes were filled with pain as he looked down at her frozen expression, but he spoke calmly. 'Take the banister and hold my arm with the other hand.' She did as he told her, and they began their ascent. He watched her, the slender body held with such dignity, the chin raised as she moved up the stairs, carefully but with such sureness. Such graceful sureness. His own anger, held in check below only by the greatest of effort, nearly erupted then. What did they know of her, any of them, except Adam? He spoke in a voice quivering with repressed emotion. 'Don't listen, pet. You mustn't listen to these people. It isn't you. It's them!'

No, Sebastian, it isn't me, she answered silently as she moved on up the staircase, her hand sliding up the banister with each step. But it's because of me. Because of me, that mother and son are tearing at each other like enraged lions. Because of me, something irreplaceable has been forever lost. And even though he loves me, it's because of who I am that Adam would breathe in horror, 'Oh my God.'

They reached the landing finally and turned, taking the final five carpeted steps to the upper hall. And it was there, at the last step, that Winna's silvery voice came to Libby, as if it were tolling prophetically around the high, wide passageway. 'This one's going to take a little more effort, that's all. Libby, just try a little harder.'

Libby paused for the briefest moment by the fern at the top of the steps, almost as if she were listening to the last echoes of the lilting voice as they faded away. And then she lifted her chin and, on Sebastian's arm, moved with conviction down the length of the hallway.

There was no more trying to be done.

# Chapter 27

In the living room below, Adam was still confronting Augustine. The others had dispersed from the tight knot nearby, but seemed unable to leave.

Running a hand through his hair in sudden weariness, Adam lowered his head. There were only the embers of anger left in him, for it had been spent in the furious blaze of emotion that had engulfed them both. After a moment, he raised his eyes back up to his mother. 'Grace and elegance,' he said in a flat voice. 'You don't know the meaning of those words. Libby is grace and elegance, and I'm truly sorry for you that you'll never understand that.'

She still stood, unbending. 'What I understand are the things I have seen here today. What she had . . .'

'They were only accidents. Accidents!' He flared momentarily, then calmed abruptly. What was the use? And suddenly, he wanted only to get out of there, to get Libby and himself away from all of them as fast as he could. It was such an overpowering feeling, it turned him spasmodically toward Libby. He stared blankly for a moment at the spot in front of the satin couch where she'd been standing; it was empty.

'She left with Sebastian. I imagine they've gone upstairs.' It was Julian, speaking unemotionally from across the room. His eyes strayed almost involuntarily to the hearth and the remains of the leopard scattered there, and he frowned.

Adam hadn't the least inclination to analyze his father's look. He could think only of getting to Libby, and he turned toward the wide archway into the hall. Edwinna was there, one slender hand resting on the frame, her lithe body silhouetted against the dimness of the hall beyond. She was calm, collected, a vision of loveliness in apricot and silver.

And in her eyes was an unmistakable look of triumph.

It hit Adam right in the face. He stared at her blankly for a moment, then with all the knowledge he had of her, and all the glimmers of suspicion, playing across his eyes. His deep voice carried across the room. 'Accidents, accidents. They were only accidents.' Understanding, when it finally came, was so swift and incontrovertible it nearly knocked him over. His intention to go to Libby was completely overridden. And anyway, the damage to her had already been done; another few minutes—a lifetime, perhaps—no longer really mattered. His voice rang out finally in clear conviction. 'It was you.'

She should have left; she'd told herself that as soon as Libby had made her quiet exit with Sebastian. Yet this man's anger was transfixing; it had come over him again, though with a different quality than before. Darker. More menacing. She didn't, or couldn't, bother to answer him.

It didn't matter. Adam's thoughts were whirring, like the wheels of the little train under the tree, piecing, fitting, turning the vague picture into a crystal-clear image. He stood in the middle of the room, a tall, handsome man among the handsome trappings of his birthright, oblivious to them, fixated only on what had been done to a gentle woman more valuable than all the money represented in the lavish surroundings.

'It was you,' he said again, his eyes trained to Winna in the doorway. 'I should've known. I should've realized. Libby doesn't do these things on her own. It takes someone to help her along, some one of us who has every faculty intact, and it was you!' He closed his eyes briefly, visualizing the table at breakast, then opened them again. 'The glasses this morning. You switched them. How convenient for you that Mother is so fanatical about consistency at the dining table.' He turned to give Augustine another eloquent look, but she was gone. He looked back to Edwinna. 'The two of you were alone when I came down—another delightful convenience—and you had switched the goddamn glasses!' He cooled with unnerving rapidity from the momentary flare-up. 'And you were alone, the two of you, over here on the couch this afternoon. I saw you come in, but instead of coming over as I should have, I let Sebastian sidetrack me. None of us was paying attention. And you did it again. You dropped it, didn't you? Or no! You did it more cleverly than that. You gave it to Libby, then saw to it she dropped it. That's right, isn't it. Edwinna?'

She blinked once.

Her silence as she remained posed aloofly in the doorway was merely irritating, nothing more. Adam had secure hold of the drawstring and was unraveling it himself, nodding in acknowledgment of his own suppositions. 'Yes, that's exactly what you did. You set her up, both times, and it only remains now to understand why.'

Still she said nothing. But finally she let her eyebrows move upward, very slowly, into an expression of patent boredom.

Adam's lip curled. 'Oh, you are a bitch, aren't you?' he said softly. He moved a pace forward then and voiced his thoughts. 'You were setting her up. That's obvious. Setting her up to look bad. In eyes that are truly blind, that is,' he added for the benefit of everyone else in the room. 'But why? What would it get you?' He frowned again, unconsciously rubbing the bridge of his nose. It took a long moment for inspiration to come, but it did finally, in the recollection of her attempted seduction that day in the stable. 'Me? Was it somehow to get hold of me?' He looked at her in disbelief. 'I thought I'd made it clear to you once that I wanted no part of you.'

At that, Edwinna relaxed her stance in the doorway. 'Don't be so conceited, Adam,' she said crisply. This had gone on long enough. She really ought to be going up to finish the job with Libby. Granted, there was precious little left to do, thanks to Augustine's timely—and totally unexpected—assistance, but she would leave nothing to chance. Yet, with success all but in hand, she was feeling garrulous. And, too, she wanted to be certain Julian understood just how perfectly it was all going to work, just how clever she'd been. Though she regretted the leopard, it had been needed and had served its purpose admirably. And she knew Julian would understand, if he were to be given some insight into the actual circumstances of its demise. Like her, he would be one who appreciated 'ends', having an innate understanding of the irrelevance of 'means'; it was a mark of the truly bright. And now they were all about to get what they wanted. She looked finally at Adam, who was still watching her narrowly, and smiled sweetly. 'Adam, I'm not the least bit interested in you. I think what you're seeing is Libby's realization that she's too much of a burden to you, that's all. It's one of her greatest worries, you know. And completely valid,' she added offhandedly.

Adam was genuinely puzzled. 'What the hell are you talking about?'

Edwinna let her head go back as her laughter echoed around the room. She loved it, she really did; he was at such a loss. She moved out of the doorway then, going on into the room to perch on the arm of a chair.

'Appearances, Adam, among other things,' she said conversationally. Briefly she caught the eye of Christian, sitting beyond Adam, his expression unreadable. She studied his darkly handsome figure for a moment, then focused back on Adam. 'She's simply death to appearances. Didn't you listen to your mother? She's an embarrassment to your family. To you. Though I think Augustine went a little far in saying she was an embarrassment to herself,' she added. 'Libby has always had that marvelous capacity to be fair. She's quite fair to herself. She knows just the way things are. And Adam, she wants to be fair to you, too,' she added silkily.

Flashes of scenes were running through Adam's head. Libby at the breakfast table with Winna, subdued when she shouldn't have been. Libby coming into the living room that afternoon, arm in arm with Winna, and again looking decidedly subdued. His anger nearly erupted again, but he held on to it with the greatest of effort.

'You've been playing on her fears, haven't you? Whispering things in her ear, dredging up all her doubts again. Oh, Christ!' He put a hand briefly to his forehead as he imagined it all, digested it all. 'How did you know about that? Ah, I know! Libby told you, didn't she? In one of your sisterly chats. Libby, opening herself up to you, telling you her darkest secrets, knowing you'd understand, you'd sympathize!'

Oh, Libby, Libby. Your misplaced love. It's done it again, he thought. And who has been hurt? You. Always you. He almost went to her then, but he wasn't finished with Edwinna yet. Not by a long shot. 'So, it's to convince Libby that she's a burden to me that you contrived all these things. You've been talking to her about appearances, "fairness". Dredging up all her worries so that when you arranged for these little accidents to happen, they merely cemented it for her.'

He turned away, closing his eyes briefly as he ran everything back through his mind. It was truly unbelievable what she'd put Libby through. Again he felt bewildered. 'But why? To what purpose?' It took a moment as he stood staring at her, but it came finally. 'So she'll give me up?' He was mute for an instant as it registered completely. 'Why, goddamn it, Edwinna? What does it get you?'

She made the mistake of flashing a look at Julian.

Adam caught it. Understanding came again in a split second, more crushing this time than before. He turned very slowly toward his father, and his eyes were as cold as steel. 'You set this up.'

317

Julian seemed unable to meet Adam's eyes directly and kept his own lowered toward the rug underfoot.

Adam wouldn't be denied. 'Answer me, goddamn you! Did you set this up?' His breathing had gone shallow as he stood waiting, yet he already knew the answer.

There was a faint trace of some emotion in Julian's eyes when they finally met Adam's, but he spoke evenly. 'I didn't set this up . . . these things with Libby. No. I . . .' He paused, then raised his chin; he'd never run from a confrontation in his life and wouldn't from this one; he'd probably lost his son anyway. 'But it is as I wish. That you and Libby end your relationship. You know that.'

'No, you didn't set it up. But you set it all in motion,' Adam said disgustedly. He continued to stare at his father, and, suddenly, his anger disappeared in the face of a greater realization—that somehow they were all involved, his whole family. They were each one part and parcel of the cruelties that had been perpetrated over the course of the day. And he was stunned, truly stunned. He looked at his father again, then at Christian sitting uncomfortably nearby, and thought of his mother, somewhere in the house, and his eyes, which moments before had held only enmity, now filled with a kind of painful wonderment.

'I can't believe it,' he said. 'You're all in this together, aren't you? Every last one of you. I don't know exactly why, but you are. And for the accomplishment of your own ends and designs, whatever they may be, you would attempt to sever the relationship between two people who love each other more than anything else in the world. Who want nothing else in the world but to be together.' He took a step forward as he looked at them searchingly, throwing out a hand in unconscious supplication. 'Doesn't that hurt you, any of you? Somewhere?' He waited, but there was no response, not from Julian, not from Christian. Adam's disgust was complete, and he dropped his hand, running the other one wearily through his hair. And then the anger rekindled, and he turned again on Edwinna.

She was still watching him coldly. Adam eyed her for a moment in real hatred, then took two deliberate paces forward. 'So, my father set you in motion. I wonder if he knew just exactly what he was unleashing?' He raised his voice slightly to be sure his father would hear. 'But I still don't see what you're getting in return for doing this, Edwinna. Money?' He cocked his head. 'Yes, that must be it. That's all in the world he's got to offer. And I think yours is all gone. That's why you really came home, isn't it? I paid the bills for your clothes, you know.'

He remembered Libby's face when she'd finally relented and handed him the stack of papers, the mysterious smile she'd given him. He'd understood when he'd leafed through the statements, coming to three from stores Libby didn't frequent in amounts she didn't spend. Winna was waiting for a transfer of her funds, she'd told him. She'd pay them back. At the recollection, he laughed mirthlessly. 'Libby thinks you're going to pay it all back. That's funny, isn't it, Edwinna? And you must have expensive habits to have run through your money so quickly. What are they? Shall we contemplate those for a moment?' When she didn't answer, he shrugged. 'You're right. I couldn't care less what you are. But just as a point of interest, if you're in such dire need of funds, why didn't you take up hooking? I'm sure you'd be quite good at it. Or have you tried?' he added in a satin voice.

'Go to hell,' she said tartly and turned on her heel to walk out.

It ignited Adam completely. Only the merest thread of self-control had been holding him back. Now he strode across the room to her, spinning her around, and she found herself confronting a quality of wrath she'd never encountered before.

'Oh, no!' he said angrily. 'You're not leaving. Not until we talk about Libby. She's the real issue here. You'd take anything away from her to get what you want, wouldn't you? Anything. Even her whole life. It simply doesn't matter how much you hurt her, as long as you get what you want. You took her eyesight. Wasn't that enough?' A muscle was working tensely in his jaw. 'Come on, Edwinna. Let's lay it all out—just exactly how you feel about Libby. What was it like? I want to know. What was it like to watch her go over that railing twenty years ago? Did it feel good?'

Julian and Christian, who had been listening and watching in some astonishment, now saw a trace of fear pass across Winna's eyes as Adam continued to grip her shoulders. Christian wondered at the satisfaction it gave him.

Edwinna wrenched herself free, then brushed at her dress in an effort to smooth out the creases from Adam's hands. All traces of fear were gone from her eyes, and she leveled on him a glare as malevolent as his own before turning primly to leave again.

Adam was about to lose all control. He knew that, but they were past the point of returning to any semblance of civility. He gripped her shoulders again and whirled her around. 'Tell me, Edwinna! I want to know!' he shouted. 'How did it feel?'

This time, she jerked herself free immediately. She stared at

319

him, raising a hand to the ache that had picked up behind her eyes, then abruptly threw her chin up. All right. If he wanted to know so much, she'd tell him. She'd tell the whole world, because it no longer mattered. She'd already won.

'How did it feel?' she repeated coldly. 'It didn't. I didn't. I didn't care, do you understand that? I don't care now.' Suddenly, years of pent-up jealousy of Libby broke loose, and her eyes grew darkly bitter. 'Libby, Libby! So popular was little Libby, so popular is she now, except here, in this room. Well, that's fine. It's about time things stopped being so wonderful for her all the time!'

Adam struck her right across the face, sending her reeling against the doorframe. If the violence of his reaction shocked even him, he didn't show it. 'You will pay for that, Edwinna,' he said in a deadly voice. 'You will pay in hell for that and all the other things you've done to Libby. And there will be no more. I promise you that.'

Edwinna had recovered, even from the stunning physical reprisal. She was the one in control, after all, and at that thought, the dull throb at her temples faded. She faced him squarely, dropping her hand from her stinging cheek. 'No, it's not I who will pay, but you. The two of you, living out your lives in your own private hell. The hell of loneliness. I will see to that, and I can.' She regarded him steadily, a faint smile drifting to her lips—'You've already told me once you can't make her understand, and believe me, I know that better than you ever will.'

Adam had himself in hand again. 'You've forgotten one thing, Edwinna. In your efforts to accomplish this thing for my *father*,' he said, all but spitting the word, 'you've forgotten one thing. Libby knows very well that I don't give a damn about appearances and all those other things. Libby knows that I love her and want her as she is.'

'Well then, you have nothing to worry about, do you?' Winna said softly. She turned and walked out of the room.

Adam remained with one hand gripping the edge of the frame, his eyes following Edwinna's slow ascent up the banistered staircase, and just as she disappeared around the landing, he felt a hand on his shoulder. He didn't turn.

It was Julian, the mask on his face lifted to reveal a clearly troubled man. 'Adam, I had no idea. I didn't realize about her . . .' He paused, looking involuntarily back at the shattered leopard. After a moment, he turned back to his son. 'I didn't

320

understand what I would be setting in motion, what I would be doing by . . .'

'You'll never understand what you've done,' Adam said tonelessly and continued to stare at the empty staircase.

'Adam . . .'

'Leave me alone!' he said roughly and abruptly turned away from what he could no longer look at, moving back into the living room. His eyes swept it, making a full circuit until they arrived at the Christmas tree and came to rest finally on the small object propped up against one of the two cabooses: a tiny carved man with a shield in his hand astride a handsome white horse.

And for the first time in his life, he knew a fear that went all the way to his soul.

## Chapter 28

'Pet, we will go home tonight.'

Sebastian was sitting beside Libby on the four-poster bed in the bedroom she'd occupied before, the one other time she'd come to this house. At the moment, it was shadowed, for the damask draperies were drawn across the windows, and the small brass lamp on the night table threw only a sliver of light across the thick down comforter. Libby sat directly in its path, near the pillow, and at his statement, Sebastian took one of her hands resting in her lap and pressed it between both of his.

Libby raised her head. Her wire-rimmed glasses lay beside the lamp on the nightstand, and when she spoke finally—for the very first time—her face was composed. 'Yes, Sebastian, I imagine we will.'

It cut him, that tone of quiet resolution. No cry, no release of the pain inside. Just a simple acknowledgment of what would inevitably be. They'd been sitting there for nearly a quarter of an hour, he judged, like two statuettes. He'd said nothing more after his heated objection on the staircase, waiting for her to take the lead, but she hadn't. She hadn't said anything, and he could no longer stand it. 'You mustn't accept the cruelties of that woman. She knows nothing of you, she knows nothing of anything!' he said harshly.

At that, Libby seemed compelled to act; she rose and crossed to the window. Feeling for the panes, she touched the thick folds of fabric covering them. 'Sebastian, open the draperies, would you?' She heard him rise, the squeak of the floorboards under his weight, then heard the soft whisper of the draw cords and the heavy material as it separated beneath her hands. When she felt him come to stand directly beside her, she looked over briefly, then out toward the landscape beyond the tall, mullioned window. 'How deep is the snow?'

Pain was etched deeply into the furrows of his brow as he watched her. 'Pet . . .'

She might not have heard the entreaty in his voice; she didn't respond to it, as she normally would, but continued to look straight ahead, her face going suddenly soft with a smile of wrenching recollection. 'Adam told me about it once, about how it looked from this window—the trees, the hills in the distance. When we were here before.' She dwelled on it for a moment, the memory of the feel of his arms as he stood behind her, painting the picture for her mind, then let her smile return to its whisper of desperation. As if the memory weren't hurtful but somehow warming. 'If you tell me how deep the snow is, I can see it.'

Sebastian could barely stand this inconsequential talk of the snow, but knew it was to deaden her pain. He drew back the curtain a little farther with one hand, and peered out the window. 'It is some inches. Eight, perhaps.'

Libby's smile grew painfully wider. 'It's a good Christmas snow then, don't you think? Eight inches? There should never be Christmas without snow.'

'Libby, stop it!' Sebastian closed his eyes, then opened them abruptly, taking hold of her hand pressed lightly to the cold glass, and squeezing it so hard it hurt. 'You mustn't do this! You must let it out! You can't take it all to heart, the words of that woman!'

To heart, Sebastian? The vision of the snow-covered ground left her; it had never really been there, except for the fleeting, agonizing recollection of Adam. What do you know of this heart, Sebastian? she asked him silently. What can even you really know? It doesn't 'take' the unbearable cruelties of the world; it hears them, feels them, wears their scars, but it doesn't take them. It can't; it wouldn't still be alive if it did. No, Sebastian, it isn't the cruelty of Augustine and all those like her that this heart is taking, but the death of love. And I can't even tell you that because it is beyond bearing.

Sebastian was watching the shadows of pain flicker across her face; it was the only thing that looked any different about her, those brief flutterings of harsh emotion. The tartan skirt, the white blouse tied in a bow at her throat, the copper hair lying against her shoulders, they were all part of the Libby he knew so well, the courageous young woman from down the hall, whom he'd always loved. Yes, he had; it was an admission he'd made to himself years before. There were so many kinds of love that a man with no other family or ties could feel, could want to feel. His for Libby was strong, enduring, and yet not of the same kind as that of Adam Bainbridge. That came along only now and then, and not to every man. He looked down at Libby quietly; she so deserved to be the object of such a once-in-a-lifetime love, to possess it herself. He sighed slightly and slid a fatherly arm about her shoulders. It would help see her through this, that strong love of Adam's; he would be up any moment to help erase those lines of strain about her mouth. He was about to say something more when he heard the door opening behind them. He looked back over his shoulder, expecting Adam, but saw instead Edwinna. She remained framed in the doorway for a brief moment, then stepped inside, closing the door softly behind her. 'Oh, Libby!' she breathed in a tone of heartfelt devastation and came directly over.

Sebastian's chin came up, and he looked at her hostilely. If he hadn't the benefit of Adam's knowledge to understand Edwinna's complicity in the events of the day, he had enough of his own to suspect it. He'd made too many observations, over the years, of the depthlessness of those sympathetic blue eyes to feel otherwise. He spoke coldly. 'She doesn't need your commiseration, if that's what it's supposed to be.'

Winna gave him a calculating look, meanwhile leaving her hand on the back of Libby's shoulder, in consolation. Keeping her voice even, she said, 'I want to be alone with Libby.'

Sebastian squared his shoulders. 'I will not leave her with you, Edwinna . . .'

'Please!' Libby's voice came in a brief cascade of entreaty and she reached out a hand to the leaded window, to balance against the momentary surge of emotion. She needed Winna right then—her comfort, her understanding of what was really happening, where the pain really lay. And she couldn't cope with Sebastian's disaffections, not now. She turned toward him but didn't reach out. 'Please, leave us, Sebastian, I cannot bear your enmities, too.' She paused. 'And Sebastian, will you tell Adam I'm not ready to talk to him yet? Tell him I . . . . I need some rest. I don't care what you say, but please—I don't want to talk to him now.'

Sebastian gave Edwinna a long, level look over Libby's head, then laid a gentle hand on Libby's shoulder. 'If that's what you want, then that's the way it will have to be. I'll be downstairs if you need me.'

Edwinna watched his reluctant departure with a faint air of satisfaction, then turned her full attention back to Libby. She was still facing the window, her expressive face quiescent, her body still as she rested her hands on the sill out in front of her. Winna appraised her a moment longer, then lifted her hand from Libby's shoulder and crossed to the bed. She sank down near the post at the foot. 'Oh, Libby, it was dreadful!'

Libby didn't turn: her only movement was at her throat, as she swallowed. 'Yes. Yes, Winna, it was dreadful. Have they finished?'

Winna frowned perplexedly. 'Finished?'

'Tearing each other to shreds.'

Of course. It seemed almost a lifetime away, that particular skirmish, Winna thought, and eyed Libby's motionless back before answering. It wasn't what she'd expected, this deadly calm. She didn't know quite how to play it, and so followed her lead. 'Yes, Augustine finally left the room.'

'And Adam?' Libby made a small, involuntary movement.

Winna said from the bed, 'He was still there . . . talking to his family when I came up.'

Talking to his family? No, Winna, he isn't talking to them. He is dueling with them, to the death. 'And the leopard, of course, is unsalvageable.' She put a hand briefly to her head, in aggravation for the useless statement.

'I'm afraid so.' Winna sighed and rose lithely from the bed, crossing back to Libby at the window. There, she put both hands on the backs of her shoulders. 'It's over and done with, Lib. There's no use going on about it.'

'Yes, it's over and done with,' Libby repeated mechanically. 'There's no need to talk about it.'

Winna murmured inaudibly and looked at her very closely then, moving slightly past her right shoulder so she could have a better view of her face. 'But Libby, there are other things that must be talked about. Things about . . .'

'Adam?' Libby's voice was even, and she went on before Winna could say anything more; it might possibly hurt less that way. 'Yes, I know. It's painfully clear, isn't it? There isn't any way to work it out, not for all the amount of trying in the world.'

Winna smiled faintly. 'I had hoped, for your sake, that there was. But now, I just don't know. There are so very many things . . .'

'Yes, so many things.' Libby's tone was almost cutting. 'Shall we talk of them again? Shall we go over all of them again, or have we hounded enough all the ways I'm inadequate, all the ways I'm nothing but a disaster?'

'Libby . . .'

At Winna's seeming entreaty, Libby shook her head. 'No, Winna. There's no need for you to object, not any more. It's all true. And there are no more "maybes" to cling to.' A sad smile drifted into her face. 'Oh, how easy it is to see, now that the picture's been drawn for me.'

'I know.' Winna let herself concede heavily then. 'And the

picture has indeed been drawn. You've had a taste now of just exactly what the two of you would have to face when you move out of your own environment into others, and how hard it'll be for both of you. The people around you aren't always going to be so accepting. Appearances will blossom into monumental stumbling blocks.'

'Yes, appearances.' Libby's chin came up slightly. She'd taken exception to that issue all her life; it had nothing to do with who you were as a person. Yet she couldn't deny that it was an issue that mattered to many people. And as much as she might want to revile these people, the Bainbridges, for the way they felt, she couldn't altogether. Not when she knew in her heart that they really weren't so unusual in their attitudes. More avid, perhaps, and less inclined to hide their prejudice beneath the thin veneer of civility, but not so unusual, really, in their distress that their normal son just might marry someone who was irrevocably handicapped. At the bald thought, she pressed her lips together tightly. 'Yes, Winna,' she said after a moment. 'Appearances will be an issue for some people, though they aren't for Adam. He doesn't care.'

At the imminent digression from the proper track, Winna went on rapidly. 'No, but to his family they are.' Abruptly she sighed wistfully. 'If only love could exist in a vacuum. Then none of this would matter, other people's reactions wouldn't make any difference. But it can't. And Adam's family and their feelings can't be dismissed.'

'Perhaps.' Libby brushed a hand across her forehead. 'I didn't realize their feelings were so strong, that Augustine . . .' She had to stop momentarily, to summon up the strength to forge on through the recollection of the painful vilification she had been subjected to. 'I didn't know how violently opposed to me they really were. If I had, I might not have come.' Might not? Oh, Libby. Would not. She lowered her head toward her hands and spoke down to them. 'And I certainly wouldn't have insisted upon all this fuss about Christmas.'

'Yes, they hated that, Libby.' It came crisply from across the room. Winna had moved away and gone to lean up against the bureau, her arms crossed. She went on relentlessly. 'I watched them all along, when you were putting up the tree, and today, with the gifts. It was just, well . . .' She paused deliberately. 'They hate you, Libby.'

'I know,' Libby whispered. 'And I only meant to give to them, to bring them something that had always had so much meaning and warmth for me. I thought I could, but I was wrong.

It can't even exist, where there is no caring.' Brief recollections of all those other Christmases came to her, the memories they'd left. So many memories. Sometimes they seemed to be the only thing she had. Just one more reminder of who she was. And what she wasn't.

'No, and as long as the two of you are together, Adam will be forced to endure these violent scenes with them.'

Libby merely nodded in response and didn't go on to express the hope she'd always held out, that the breach between them could somehow be mended; that hope had died its final death in the room downstairs.

Winna waited for a moment, then went on. 'Libby, it hurts me as much as it does you to have to acknowledge all these things so irrevocably, but they're realities. And in the face of all of them, even though Adam loves you now and can take everything in stride now . . .'

'How long could it go on?' Libby finished for her, as Winna had known she would.

'Exactly, Libby. That, as we both know, is the real problem.'

'Yes,' Libby said and went on, as she had to. 'How long before his love would begin to erode after too many years of difficulty, too many falls, and unexplainable accidents that disrupt the world around him? How long before he tires of the friction with all those people who care about appearances and would make an issue of it?' She swallowed once, then continued leadenly. 'If he were another man, from another kind of life . . . But Winna, he's had every opportunity open to him. He's known so many other women— *whole* women, and when the glow has worn off our relationship, he's going to remember what they were like.'

She paused only briefly as her expression drifted into bittersweet conviction. 'And I can see it now more clearly than ever before, the ultimate scenario. When he's come no longer to love me but to resent me, when all the deliberate movement and slower pace of life—things he now accepts—have begun to chafe. When, because of everything, I've become nothing but a burden to him. The first hints of that might've begun already, I don't know,' she said almost to herself, but rushed on past the recollection of his heartfelt *Oh my God* at the sight of what she'd done. 'And imagine the sense of failure he'd have if that happened—the guilt! No, Winna, I can't do that to him, or to myself, and it's time now to do what I must. It's time now to let him go.' With the final vocalization of what they'd really been talking about all along, Libby made no movement at all but simply remained looking toward the window.

Winna was still leaning up against the bureau where she'd been all the way through the soliloquy, watching her sister stand, an almost inconsequential figure, against the stately window and recount the ending of her dreams. She was smiling lightly; Libby was thinking, feeling, saying all that she'd intended to orchestrate, and with practically no effort on her own part. It was very gratifying. It occurred to her to wonder how Libby would react when she discovered Winna was going to marry into this family she'd just so painfully relinquished, then dismissed the thought; she'd deal with that when the time came, explaining it away somehow. She always could.

Pushing herself away from the bureau, she crossed to Libby's side, taking her hand. 'Oh, Libby, I know how much all of this hurts you,' she repeated, 'but you're right. I'm afraid that's all you can do. For you, it's out of fairness to Adam, but for me, it's for the fairness to you. I couldn't bear for you to be hurt the way you inevitably would be, when he could no longer love you.' She paused for the proper amount of time, then let her tone grow authoritative. 'Libby, I'm going to take you home, get you away from here.' She dropped Libby's hand and stepped away a little, watching in some detachment as tiny flutters of emotion began to pass across Libby's face like ripples across a still pond; she paid them no attention.

'It's what you need, to be removed from this whole untenable situation, to get away from these people who hate you. And with Adam, you need to make a clean break. It hurts worst at first, but it's easier in the long run.' She began to talk more rapidly as she elaborated on what she'd already envisioned. 'You should tell him tonight. Yes, that's the best thing. Then we'll leave. He doesn't even have to drive you home. I'll make some other arrangement. Libby, the best thing for you to do is to go down right now, while I pack your things, and tell him . . .'

She broke off suddenly, rather startled. Libby had turned abruptly from the window to face her, and the whispers of emotion had bloomed into a recognizable expression on her face. Beseeching desperation. 'Winna, I can't!' The words were wrenched from her in a whispered cry.

Edwinna caught her breath at the sheer force of emotion in those three breathless words. 'What are you talking about?'

And it all burst forth then, all those things in Libby's heart that couldn't be denied, not for all the reason in the world. Her soul opened up and spilled out to Winna in an honesty so private it would have been unspeakable anywhere else, except there in that room, between them, where blood ties could listen and hear and 'know'. They stood silhouetted against that vast window, sisters, Libby's face turned up toward Winna's in naked anguish as she gripped both of Winna's arms.

'In all my life, Winna,' she said, 'in all my life I never thought I'd have something like this. Not with any man, but especially not with a man like Adam. Winna, women like me, we don't have many chances for these things. We wish and we hope and we dream. We live on those dreams, and Winna, we die with them!' She bowed her head at the bald admission, and when she raised it again, her face was begging for understanding. 'Winna, I love him. I love him more than my own life. He thrills me in ways I didn't think I'd ever know, he touches every part of my being. I know all the reasons to let him go, I know what could possibly happen to his life, but I can't. I'm just not that noble.'

Winna was working roughly to loosen Libby's grip on her arms. When she'd extricated herself from Libby's hold, she stepped back jerkily. 'Libby, we've talked it all out. You've seen what can happen. It's better for everyone!' she insisted hotly.

Libby had calmed the brief surge of emotion and stood looking toward Winna, an unconscious frown lightly settled on her face at the sharp reply. Who was everyone? They were talking now about her, only her, and what she had to do for her own happiness, rightly or wrongly. Winna, of all people, should want that for her and should accept this final decision, not argue against it. She was puzzled, and wondered if Winna hadn't understood. 'Winna, I'm talking now about what's better for me, not everyone else.' She stood for a moment longer at the window, then made her way back to the bed, where she sat down near the ruffled pillow cover. 'And what's better for me is to be with him. I just can't let go.'

Winna was staring at her, stunned. 'But Libby, you must! I've already told you, I can't stand for you to be hurt!' she snapped, then immediately amended her tone. She clutched the thick folds of drapery near her hand and said more gently, 'Libby, there's so much that can happen to you.'

Libby's brief smile was quizzical at Winna's continued vehemence. 'I know you don't want me to be hurt, but don't you see? This hurt is more than I can bear. It's more than all of the others put together, even what may come in the future. Surely you can understand that, can't you?' She paused briefly, trying to gain some insight into Winna's disconcerting attitude. 'Winna, he's my life,' she said finally.

Winna spun away from the window and paced back across the narrow room to the bureau, her body rigid at the shoulders. In the mirror above was her reflection and Libby's in the background as she sat near the post of the bed, but she didn't see them. Instead, she was scowling down at Libby's things spread out on the top of the chest, and her fingertip found its way to the side of her forehead. It had been hers; success had been hers until Libby had had to start bleeding all over the room for her lost love; that was so like her, to be purposely obstinate, to have her head in some romantic cloud. She turned back to Libby, gripping the edge of the bureau behind her with both hands. She forced herself to speak in an even voice. 'Libby, you're not being realistic. There is so much involved. So much at stake!' She heard herself and qualified the objection, bringing one hand back up to her head as she brushed away two stray wisps of hair. 'Your peace of mind. Adam's. You've said it all yourself. Yes, he loves you now. But will it continue? Can it continue in the face of all the difficulties?'

'I don't know, but I have to take that chance. He loves me now, and I want that.'

'Take the chance!' Unconsciously, Winna had begun tapping her foot, the sole of the expensive leather pump striking up a light staccato beat on the bare floor in front of the bureau. 'Oh, Libby!' She paused in agitated thought, then had a blinding inspiration. 'Libby, you're being selfish,' she accused sharply.

At that, Libby's intent listening to the adamance of Winna's foot-tapping was interrupted by a flash of insight. 'Maybe I am,' she said quietly, then looked back up. 'But I can't help it. For once I can't, Winna. Not this time.' She began to frown again as the rhythm of Winna's foot once more took hold of her attention. It was so—what? She found herself searching for a descriptive word and abruptly came up with one that was jarring: demanding.

It ceased as Winna's tension swung violently upward, and she looked at Libby, sitting pensively on the blue coverlet, and hardly saw her. 'Libby, if you really loved Adam, you'd let him go! You know that! You've just got to be fair to him!' She looked down at the pale rug beneath the bed, barely aware of it as she tried to remember all the things Libby had said, what she herself had pointed out so effectively earlier in the day. She scowled as she bit at her lip. It hadn't been enough, that was all; she shouldn't have stood by and let Libby carry on alone. She should have directed the scene herself. Quickly, she marshaled her thoughts, and raised her eyes again to Libby's face.

And what she saw there made the searing head pain behind her temple subside almost instantaneously. It was the dawning of some shattering realization—capitulation, of course!—etched all over the stillness of her sister's expression.

Hurriedly, Winna replayed through her mind what she'd just said. Fairness to Adam. Well, of course, that was the key; she'd known that all along. She was smiling again as she crossed to Libby in one fluid motion and perched on the bed beside her. She took Libby's hands in her own.

'I know how difficult a time this is for you. I know this isn't an easy decision to make, but you must make it and make the right one. One that's fair to both of you, but to Adam especially. Do you honestly want to burden him with an existence he shouldn't have to have? With an existence a man like him couldn't continue to lead happily?'

Libby hardly heard what she said, for other words were still ringing through her mind, *'If you really loved him . . . If you really love him . . .'* With difficulty, she focused on Winna's question and answered the only way she could. 'No.'

Winna pressed Libby's hands tightly between her own. 'And you saw what it was like today, what it can't help but be like in the future. That you'll do the wrong thing when it matters that you do the right one. That things will get destroyed, causing nothing but distress to everyone. How long do you suppose Adam could continue to take that kind of thing in stride? It's probably beginning already, that he can't.' She paused, wracking her brain for what Libby had meant so she could elaborate on it. It would have to have been the leopard incident. What had he done, said? She couldn't remember and went on. 'Libby, he'll come to resent you, even possibly come to hate you for it all. No, Libby, even in your selfish need to have what you want, you can't do that to him.'

Libby was looking toward her, her lips pressed tightly together to calm some inner turmoil. Finally, she said in a quiet clear voice, 'Am I really being so selfish? Do you really think I've never given anything back to him, made him happy in any way? Winna, is it that you think I never could?'

'I . . .' Winna had no immediate answer, and a deafening silence fell down between them. Finally she spoke into it, switching hastily back to her own track. 'Libby, all that really matters is that you can't do this to Adam. I can't let you do it. You've said it all yourself. You must be fair and let him go.'

This time Libby was unable to make any response at all. So, it was really true then; it had to be believed, all of it. But was that possible? She had listened to every one of Winna's arguments, as if she were being physically struck by them, arguments that, yes, she'd made herself. Yes, she'd been the one to say that about the portents of the future. Adam's voice came into her thoughts then, his deep voice. Calm, reasonable, always so reasonable and honest. Why hadn't she trusted him more? She closed her eyes briefly at the painful question, then finally looked back toward Winna. Again, her expression held that quiet desperation, of wanting not to believe.

'Do you really feel, then, that that's the only way it can be?' she said finally. She had to ask; it was the last chance for it all to be undone, for everything to be taken back, and she waited tensely, willing Winna to give anything but that one unequivocable, damning answer.

'Yes.' The verdict came with the sweeping finality of a guillotine blade, and as Winna looked at Libby sitting beside her, she knew the moment of her sister's resistance had passed. She could see it in Libby's face, in the sadness suddenly etched there, in the slackness of her shoulders. She released Libby's hand, slipping her arm around her shoulders.

'It's all right, Libby. Someday the hurt will go away. And you must end it now. End it quickly, so that it is only this pain and no more that you have to live with,' she said gently. 'Libby, I think you should go down right now and get it over with. Tell him now, while I pack your things.'

'Yes, you're right. I should tell him now,' Libby said tonelessly. She rose and stood for a moment with one hand on the bedpost; she felt as she had once before today—as if the life had been drained out of her.

Winna rose immediately and put her hand on Libby's arm. 'Are you all right? Do you want me to go down with you?'

'No. I'll go down alone. This is something I have to do myself.' She looked as if she were about to say something more, but didn't, and started for the door. Winna's eyes were luminous as they watched Libby's slight figure cross the short distance to the door, and they strayed downward to the bedside table very near her hand, and what was lying on top of it. She picked it up, then crossed immediately to Libby, catching her just as she was about to pass out of the room. 'Hon,' she said softly and put the object in Libby's hand, 'you forgot your glasses.'

Libby looked up toward her and tried to smile. 'Oh, yes, of course.' She put them on, and as Winna triumphantly watched Libby disappear out into the hallway, those words she'd heard for a lifetime filtered back in to her through the open door: Libby's almost inaudible and never more heartfelt, 'I'm sorry.'

# Chapter 29

Libby made her way along the hallway toward the staircase, the backs of her fingers running lightly along the wall. Her footsteps on the faded Oriental runner were muffled, and in the stillness around her, she could hear her thoughts as clearly as if they were ringing out and ricocheting around the hall.

Why must things always be so hard? Why was it that what must be done meant giving up what you loved so much? She closed her eyes briefly, then opened them again as she passed by the fourth door. Only one more to go and she'd be at the head of the stairs. At that realization, a small panic rushed through her. She could turn back; she could stop right where she was and not go by that final door, or perhaps disappear into it, into the unknown room where she could hide, alone. And yet there was no going back; she knew that, as surely as if Winna hadn't told her. 'I think you should do it now.' It had to be done, somewhere, sometime, and the best was now. Winna had given the reason for that, too: 'So that it is only this pain and no more that you have to live with.'

She reached the head of the staircase and stood near the potted fern for a moment as she searched for the newel post. She found it and began her descent. The shimmering glass chandelier above the galleried landing had already been lit, and as Libby passed under it on her way down, its warm light picked up the burnished copper tones in her hair, illuminated her figure as it moved inexorably on down the handsome mahogany staircase. She reached the foot finally, and it was there that she faltered appreciably in her resolution. She stopped, gripping the polished banister at the point where it curled back on itself, her face turned in the direction of the living room.

She had to go in there, into that room where, perhaps they would all still be. All of them. She bowed her head, resting it briefly in her hand. It was a room that held no place for her, where she was the odd one out, and only misunderstanding, prejudice, and yes, hatred, waited for her there. It would envelope her again like a miasma, pierce her again, if only by the echo of Augustine's vicious cruelties that would forever reverberate from those stately walls. And one could try to be the epitome of understanding, could wear the medal of forgiveness like an open badge upon a compassionate breast, yet it was still not so easily done. Just to walk right on in there. But she would, because she had to.

She moved away from the foot of the stairs finally after placing something on the banister. She crossed the stone floor of the vaulted hall in the number of steps Adam had taught her, and at length reached the arched doorway into the living room. There she stopped and put one hand on the doorframe.

They were all gathered there as a group, but each one alone, so emptily alone. Julian was in his chair by the hearth, where the broken leopard still remained, his head resting back against the cushion, his eyes unseeingly leveled at the ceiling. Christian was at the small inlaid card table, his empty whiskey glass resting forlornly on the edge, and he was playing solitaire, in brooding silence. Augustine had reappeared, forever the hostess if only in form, and she stood by the tea table near Julian's chair, pouring coffee from the ornate silver service, though no one wanted any. Adam was at the window by the Christmas tree, his hands thrust deeply into the pockets of his trousers as he stood with his back to the room and stared out across the snow-covered lawn. But it was Sebastian, seated near Adam, who saw Libby first. He happened to glance up from the pages of his book as he heard the light footstep and exclaimed. 'Libby!'

Adam spun, nearly knocking into the Christmas tree. There was movement all around him as everyone else started at the sharp call, but he was oblivious to all of it. He had eyes only for Libby, framed in the wide doorway, and they searched her: the so-familiar oval face, completely devoid of expression, the slender body held determinedly erect. The tension that had never left him since that moment he'd turned at his mother's cry and seen Libby with a hand at her throat grew even tighter across the back of his shoulders.

Libby didn't respond to Sebastian's call. She was here for one purpose only, to speak only to one person. 'Adam?'

'I'm here, Libby,' he said immediately, though his voice, to his own ears, sounded far away, surreal.

She moved into the room then, in quiet dignity. Adam threaded his way from the far side and met her halfway across

334

the room. Reaching out, he took her hand, stopping them just inches away from each other. And they stood then in the middle of the room, two players who had been brought to that spot by a script written by those all around them. Libby held onto his hand, feeling the warmth of it as it covered hers almost completely. Finally, she dropped it. 'Adam, I have to talk to you.'

He stood perfectly still, looking down at her. Her expression was wooden, dead. 'I'm here,' he repeated quietly, his eyes dark with pain. He wanted to touch her hair—that silky hair he loved so much—to trace the fine, delicate bones beneath her green eyes, no longer hidden by glasses as she turned them up to him, but he didn't.

'Adam, I love you,' Libby whispered abruptly.

What did it mean, the despair on her face? That Winna had already done it, had succeeded after all, had made her believe all those things? Were her words a means of easing the pain of saying goodbye? He closed his eyes to the vision of lonely years before him, then opened them to look at her again. And in that moment of seeing traces of harsh emotion begin to play across her face, he knew that he'd never accept those years, never accept what was happening to them, no matter if it meant a lifetime of fighting them all. 'I love you, too,' he said clearly.

Libby opened her mouth to speak again and found that she could barely say the words. Love doesn't die that fast, she thought. You can't just cut it out of your life without pain. Even though it's what must be done. Christmas, she thought brokenly. The time of year when all things are given, not taken away. And she'd named her lovely horse for it so she'd never forget this day.

The lights overhead in the long room came up abruptly, as the late afternoon sun faded finally. The two of them were spot-lighted beneath a curving brass chandelier, the flood of light leaving everyone else to stand in the background, in shadowy witness of what they had wrought. Libby bowed her head for a moment, then raised it again.

And tears came finally, in that moment when she reached up to touch Adam's cheek with trembling fingers, and felt his hand move over hers and press it there.

'Then help me. Help me do what I must. Send her away.'

'Libby, what's happened? What did she . . .'

'You were right, Adam, about it all. She doesn't care about me. She wanted to make me give you up. Somehow she needed me to do that, for herself. All day she's been talking . . . all those things have happened . . . oh, Adam!' Her hand slipped from his face and she felt him catch it tightly to his chest. 'I don't understand it, I don't know if I understand much of anything any more, but if you help me, maybe I can.

'If you just hold me forever—be with me forever and give me your strength—maybe I can finally put everything to rest. And someday find a way to tell her why it is I can never see her again.'

Adam's eyes were shimmering with relief as he looked at her for a moment, then quietly dropped her hand. And he took her into his strong embrace then, holding her tightly for a very long time before finally releasing her and walking her arm in arm from the room.

THE END